PORTHELLIS

PORTHELLIS

Gloria Cook

HEADLINE

First published in 1996
by HEADLINE BOOK PUBLISHING

10 9 8 7 6 5 4 3 2 1

British Library Cataloguing in Publication Data

Cook, Gloria
Porthellis
1. English fiction – 20th century
I. Title
823.9'14 [F]

ISBN 0-7472-1739-4

Typeset by
CBS, Felixstowe, Suffolk

Printed and bound in Great Britain by
Mackays of Chatham PLC, Chatham, Kent

HEADLINE BOOK PUBLISHING
A division of Hodder Headline PLC
338 Euston Road
London NW1 3BH

This book is dedicated to the memory of
my very dear mum, Betty Eley,
whose love and constant encouragement
in my writing I shall sadly miss.

Chapter 1

'For goodness sake, Matt, don't look so miserable,' Hannah Penney chided her husband. They had just arrived at the large, mid-eighteenth-century clifftop house of Roscarrock. 'It's a wedding reception we're going to, not a funeral.'

'But we went to the reception your parents held for Leah at their cottage, Hannah,' Matt sighed, as wearily as if he'd come home after a hard night's fishing. He leaned over the pram of their sleeping ten-month-old son and fussed with his covers. 'I don't see why we have to be dragged along here as well just because the high and mighty Opies are insisting they have drinks and cake too. And I don't see why—'

'Oh, stop complaining,' Hannah said, vexed. Matt's dark features had scowled all the way along the two miles of narrow, twisting lanes from Porthellis, the fishing village where they lived and where the wedding of Hannah's younger sister and Greg Opie had been held. She pulled the covers from his hands. 'Nathan's warm and comfortable. Stop trying to delay us going in. We're late as it is with him demanding a feed.'

Stuffing his hands into the trouser pockets of his smart navy-blue suit, Matt gazed wistfully back down the long winding drive. 'I was going to put in an hour on the allotment and then I wanted to be alone with you and Nathan. I don't get much free time and I'm not happy to be spending it at this sort of thing.'

Hannah ignored him. She loved Roscarrock; it exuded warmth and friendliness. Its tall windows overlooked the mild south Cornish coast, its wisteria-clad walls were framed at the back and sides by cedar, sycamore, ash and oak trees, and a small wood sheltered it from the elements near the cliff edge. Spring flowers and white ribbon adorned the railings of the six wide stone steps that led up to the imposing house.

Putting a hand on her waist, Matt looked into her deep blue eyes. 'We

1

don't have to stay long, do we, darling? I've never felt comfortable under this roof.' A grand building in magnificent grounds it might be, but Matt couldn't forget that if its owner had got her way, he and Hannah would never have married. 'Our mothers are in there with your Aunty Janet. There'll be the usual rush with Feena Opie to cluck over Nathan. It's not good for him and it drives me mad.'

Hannah looked down at her son's peaceful face and frowned; she, too, didn't like Nathan being fawned over by the four women who vied to give him the most attention and win his delighted chuckles. She stroked Matt's arm. 'We'll take him inside in the pram and hope he'll stay asleep. I expect Patrick will be eager to get away as soon as the speeches are over. He'll probably suggest you take a look around the gardens with him. I'll come and get you when I'm ready to leave.'

Matt put his other hand on her waist and gently pulled her close to him, his wide, sensuous mouth easing into a smile. Hannah responded warmly as he kissed her.

At the drawing room window, Adela Skewes, the Methodist minister's wife, was admiring the wonderful sweep of daffodils round the giant oak tree on the lawn when she spotted the embracing couple. She turned to Feena Opie, the dignified lady who owned Roscarrock, and fluted sentimentally, 'Anyone would think they were the newlyweds.'

'Well, Hannah and Matt are very much in love,' Prim Spargo cut in, to Feena Opie's annoyance; the two women despised each other. Prim darted off to the door to ensure she was the first to greet Nathan.

'Hannah is an exceptionally lovely young woman,' Feena said loftily to Mrs Skewes, her eyes on the blonde, shapely young mother who bore a slight resemblance to herself in her younger days. 'She's gifted and intelligent, and she proved to be an excellent housekeeper.' Hannah was helping Matt carry the pram up the steps and Feena signalled to Patrick Opie, her penniless, rather eccentric great-nephew, to go to their aid.

'You must regret losing her to Matt,' Mrs Skewes commented thoughtfully, giving an ingratiating smile. She was eager to get on convivial terms with Mrs Opie, even though Mrs Opie attended church and had scathingly voiced her disapproval of her grandson's wedding taking place in the Wesleyan chapel of the fishing village below her property. Roscarrock was the biggest house in the locality and the Opies were well-connected. They had had little contact with Porthellis over the years and only Hannah, Matt and a few of her family had set foot inside it in recent times. Mrs

Skewes hoped this event would encourage the Opies to widen their circle of friends.

'Love and romance must have its way,' Feena said with a forced smile. She excused herself from the minister's wife, hoping the woman had missed the sour note in the statement. Matt had taken Hannah away from her and he made no secret of the fact that he did not welcome her interest in his wife.

Feena bitterly resented Matt's interference. Hannah was her natural daughter, born out of an affair she had had with Jeff Spargo many years ago. The affair had turned bitter and Feena had tried to destroy Jeff's marriage by informing his wife Prim of Hannah's birth. She did not succeed. Instead, Prim had offered to bring up the unwanted child herself. Her marriage to the womanising Jeff had never been easy, and deteriorated further when she began to use Hannah to remind him of his sins until Jeff could no longer bear the sight of his illegitimate daughter. He blamed Hannah for a tragic boating accident in which her little brother had drowned and threw her out of the house. Hannah was ten years old at the time, and Prim's older sister Janet Rouse had taken her in. Two years ago Feena Opie had belatedly decided to take an interest in Hannah, primarily because her legitimate daughter had died, and she had employed Hannah as her housekeeper. The two women had grown very close, until Hannah had fallen in love with Matt and had subsequently learned the circumstances of her birth.

Feena slowly made her way to the hallway, walking with the aid of a gold-topped cane. She suffered from arthritis in her left hip which had been broken during a burglary at the house eighteen months ago, and she often used a wheelchair to get about. As she entered the hall, she saw that Prim Spargo, Janet Rouse and Matt's mother Mrs Penney were already stationed around Nathan's pram.

'Is he warm enough?' Janet put her handbag down on a marble-topped side table and felt the baby's forehead. 'I know 'tis spring but there's a cold wind today.'

Before a discussion could begin, in which the four 'grandmothers' were apt to compete with each other over who knew more about babies and childhood than her rivals, Matt spoke up briskly. 'I'll wheel him into the dining room where he can sleep in peace. Perhaps Mr Patrick would like to keep me company.'

Patrick Opie was grateful for the suggestion, he was totally at a loss in crowds. 'Splendid, splendid,' he said, rubbing his earth-stained hands together in anticipation of a talk about the gardens, his favourite subject. Next moment he tugged self-consciously at his straggly wide moustache as five sets of female eyes were turned on his rather peculiar face: Aged forty-seven, his softly formed mouth seemed too small for the full, rounded cheeks; his skin was the colour and texture of sand and his receding fuzzy hair stuck out over pixie-shaped ears.

Only Hannah's expression was warm as she smiled at him. Patrick Opie was the first of the three Opies living at Roscarrock she had met. A close bond had formed between her and the shy widower who had turned out to be her cousin. 'Thank you, Mr Patrick,' she said, using the term she retained when they were in company, for her relationship with the Opies was still a secret to all but a few people.

As the men withdrew with the pram, Mrs Penney politely excused herself and returned to the drawing room to mingle with the small number of guests. Hannah was immediately set upon by the three remaining women. When Nathan wasn't there she was next in line for their suffocating attention. It sometimes made life difficult but because of the circumstances of her birth and upbringing Hannah understood their motives.

The shock of discovering that Feena Opie was her real mother had turned her world upside down. Pampered more as a companion to the reclusive lady of Roscarrock than as a servant, Hannah had grown to love her new life as a housekeeper here, believing that Mrs Opie valued her company and services for their own sake. She had found it hard to forgive the web of lies and deceit that for so long had blighted her childhood and early adulthood, but the unlikely intervention of her father had finally brought her round. Jeff, Prim and Feena had all lived to regret their actions and Hannah had not wanted anything to spoil her future with Matt and their son, with whom she was already pregnant. She sometimes reflected on the irony that after such an unsettled childhood she now had three 'mothers'.

Hannah accepted the women's compliments on how lovely she looked in her new wide-brimmed hat and coral-pink and white linen dress. Her leather clutch bag, neat white gloves, almond-toed high heels and the jewelled stick-pin brooch Matt had given her enhanced her tall figure and proud bearing, giving her the air of a woman born and bred in these surroundings. Indeed, during her time at Roscarrock she had acquired a confidence that occasionally bordered on superiority, an addition to her open, honest character that Matt did not much like.

'I made the dress and I know what suits her best.' Janet pursed her lips and rubbed her horn-rimmed glasses on a handkerchief in her no-nonsense fashion. Hannah braced herself; Aunty Janet could be bluntly outspoken and was more inclined to upset Prim than Feena Opie whom the two fishermen's wives rarely saw.

Prim had at first refused to attend this second wedding reception; the only other time she had stepped over Roscarrock's threshold was the day she had carried Hannah out of it. But at the moment the fact that her decision to come after all obviously did not suit Feena Opie pleased her too much for her to take offence at her sister's continuing claims on Hannah.

'You look like a bride yourself, Hannah, my dear, but then you do have natural style,' Feena slid in triumphantly, looking disdainfully at Prim's plump figure which was stuffed into a two-piece rayon suit. The suit was new, made by Janet who was an expert seamstress, but its beige colour dulled Prim's sallow complexion and made her pale blue eyes look watery. Her small-crowned hat was like a saucer on her flat greying hair. Feena acknowledged that she herself was no glowing beauty; she was tall, slender and poised, and wore her chic London fashions with sophisticated flair – 'dressed to death and killed with fashion' was Prim's comment to Janet in the chapel – but her face had given way to gravity, wrinkles and puffiness. Jeff Spargo's good looks may have encouraged him to be a callous womaniser, she reflected, but it was no wonder he sought his pleasures elsewhere when he had such a frumpy wife at home.

Prim asked where the toilet was. Feena stopped a maid carrying a tray of hors d'oeuvres and ordered her to show the bride's mother where she could freshen up. Suspicious of her sister's intentions, Janet said she must powder her nose too. Feena invited Hannah into the drawing room.

'You are coming to visit me on Wednesday afternoon as usual, aren't you, dear? And bring Nathan with you,' Feena said smoothly while beaming a cultivated smile round the room.

The question was something of a demand; Feena liked to have her own way. 'Yes, of course,' Hannah replied, taking a glass of champagne offered by a bright-faced maid; despite her Methodism, she was allowing herself one drink today.

Hannah allowed Feena to monopolize her for a full quarter of an hour then extricated herself to make her way to Leah; it was the bride who should be receiving all the attention today.

While Hannah had worked at Roscarrock, Leah, scarred on the face in the boating tragedy, had painfully emerged from the shell she'd crept into and had taken a job here too. Childlike and innocent, she had met Feena's grandson, the playwright and novelist Greg Opie, and the two had formed an unlikely match. The relationship was generally disapproved of owing to the difference in their ages and class but now, fifteen months later, Jeff and Prim had reluctantly signed the consent form so the couple could marry. There had been many arguments over the arrangements for the wedding; it was the peace-loving Patrick Opie who had suggested they hold a reception in both houses.

Leah and Greg were standing in front of the marble fireplace, Leah looking happy but nervous, and breathtakingly lovely in her wedding gown. She was eighteen years old and looked disturbingly like a child. She wore her long, black hair down about her slight shoulders, in the hope that the glossy tresses and her veil would help conceal the scar on her right cheek. Greg was nearly ten years older, an academic who was as reclusive as the other two Opies. A fair-haired man with sharp grey eyes, he was inclined to be pompous and rude to all outside the family. He had adored Leah from the moment he'd set eyes on her and he clung to her possessively.

Hannah kissed and hugged Leah. She had a good relationship with the bridegroom who, strangely to her, was her nephew, but her secret forbade any show of affection to him. 'Congratulations,' she said warmly to them both.

Hannah had helped Leah into her wedding dress in their parents' cottage and it had taken a lot of encouragement to reassure her she was the traditional beautiful bride, reminding her that her scar was now no more than a thin white line.

'At least you've got the right to get married in white,' Hannah had joked while fastening the row of tiny buttons on the white crepe de Chine couture creation Greg had insisted Leah should have. 'As Matt and I jumped the gun I wore pale blue, remember?'

'I wish I wasn't a virgin,' Leah had wailed. 'I wish I had given myself already like you did then I wouldn't be terrified of what is going to happen tonight.'

'Leah!' Hannah was slightly shocked. 'It's never a good idea to do what Matt and I did. It nearly brought disaster on us.'

Another man in her life, one she had trusted from childhood but who had turned out to be as calculating as Feena Opie in keeping her and Matt apart, had insisted she marry him. Daniel Kittow had lost his reason when he'd realised she was expecting Matt's baby and had very nearly raped her. The memories of the happiness she could have lost made her shudder.

She held Leah's hands and smiled into her pale, worried face. 'You'll be fine, just leave it all to Greg. He loves you, I'm sure he'll be understanding. It's a wonderful experience every time with the man you love, I promise you.'

'I wouldn't mind so much if we were spending the night somewhere else and not at Roscarrock,' Leah whispered nervously, and Hannah wondered again if her sister was mature enough to get married. Leah was fascinated with Roscarrock but she did not want to live in it while Feena Opie, who could be very forceful, was its mistress. Greg's chosen lifestyle meant she would meet few of his friends and acquaintances.

Hannah surveyed the plushly furnished drawing room. 'Well, Sarah, Naomi and Lizzie seem to be enjoying themselves,' she remarked gaily. Sarah and Naomi were their older sisters and Lizzie was their cousin, all taking a well-deserved break from husbands, motherhood and household duties for the afternoon and enjoying a look inside the big house. They were sitting on a sofa, sipping champagne and nibbling tiny smoked salmon sandwiches. With them was another cousin, Jowan Rouse, Janet's fisherman son, another individual who had been keen to see inside the house but was now trailing his youthful eyes over Lily, the chirpy, freckle-faced under-housemaid who had taken Leah's place when she and Greg became engaged.

'Your sisters and cousins must come here any time they like, darling,' Greg said. He was anxious that Leah should feel totally at home at Roscarrock; he was only too well aware how shy she was of strangers.

Hannah glanced across the room and was surprised to see Mrs Opie talking to her father. It was obviously out of social politeness as they were not paying the courtesy of looking one another in the eye. Their loathing of each other was apparent and Hannah felt a queer lurch in her heart to think that if not for the union of these two people, who were worlds apart, she would not be standing here now.

Mrs Skewes approached the bridal couple with a smartly dressed woman Hannah had not seen before. Leah stiffened nervously; she did not know the woman either.

'Allow me to introduce you to my niece, Miss Grace Treloar,' Adela Skewes resonated first at Greg. 'She's staying at the Manse for a few weeks. She sat in the chapel to watch the wedding and when I introduced her to Mrs Opie in the forecourt, she graciously invited Grace to attend the reception here.'

'Pleased to meet you, Miss Treloar,' Greg replied gallantly. He didn't seek new friends and was not the slightest bit interested in the newcomer. His best man was signalling to him and he excused himself and Leah, leaving Hannah with the two women.

'It's the prettiest wedding I've ever seen,' Grace Treloar smiled at Hannah. She had a mellow, cultured voice. 'You must be very proud of your sister, Mrs Penney.'

Before Hannah could reply, Mrs Skewes said rather loudly, 'Leah has this gorgeous house to live in from now on. Grace lives in similar circumstances, Hannah. She has a large house in Kent with servants and a stable holding half a dozen horses.'

Hannah gazed at Grace. She had a longish face with clear tawny eyes, a slightly crooked nose and pronounced mouth and chin. A brimless Juliet hat sat on the crown of straight, chin-length, ash-blonde hair. Her clothes were plain but tailored and set well on her angular frame. She wore no jewellery or strong perfume, unlike her loquacious aunt. Hannah judged her to be in her early thirties.

Grace was embarrassed by her aunt's boastful comments and changed the subject. 'I'm very grateful to Mrs Opie for her invitation. This has been the ideal opportunity for me to meet some of the villagers. I only arrived in Porthellis yesterday morning.' She smiled. 'I enjoy walking and I intend to explore the cliff paths and beaches and swim in the sea.'

'There are many beautiful places known only to us locals,' Hannah said, responding to the natural warmth and ease in Grace's manner. 'I would be happy to show you some of them when I have some free time.' She still liked to roam unencumbered and there was no need for her to be tied to the house with so many willing hands to mind Nathan for a while.

'That's very kind of you. I've already strolled round the village. It's just as I imagined it would be. Pretty stone cottages straggling down the steep hill, fishing boats in the little harbour, the sea lapping up the shore, gulls perched on seaweed-covered rocks. I could sense the feeling of history and tradition all about me and I was intrigued as I stood on the pier to see the roof and the top of the wood of Roscarrock.'

'Grace has quite fallen in love with the place,' Mrs Skewes prattled on. 'I'm hoping to persuade her to stay with us for good. She could teach in the Sunday School, although she's not very fond of children.'

'My mother died recently and I've come down to Cornwall to stay with my aunt for a while before I decide what to do with my future,' Grace replied to the question in Hannah's crystal-blue eyes. 'I noticed the new house that has just been built below the Manse in Cobble Street.'

'It's close to Hannah's cottage, where the better properties of the village are,' Mrs Skewes put in loftily. 'I've told Grace all about it, Hannah, that it's for the pub landlady, although goodness knows where Maggie Curnow could have got that sort of money from. She was in there this morning putting up curtains, good quality ones by the look of them.'

'It's a fine house,' Grace said, jumping in quickly to prevent her aunt dominating the conversation. 'I wouldn't mind living in something similar myself.'

The house in question was much larger than all the other cottages in the village; it had indoor plumbing and was provoking a lot of envy.

'I saw one little cottage across the harbour,' Grace continued, 'which looks as if it's about to fall down. Has it been completely abandoned?'

As Hannah seemed reluctant to talk about it, Mrs Skewes explained. 'Oh, you're talking about the place next to Cliffside Cottage which is where Hannah's parents live. An old rascal called Rufus Kittow lived there. He never looked after it. He was a dirty little man, a scoundrel and a thief. I hate to think what it was like inside. He died last year, got drunk and fell into the sea and developed pneumonia. His grandson owns it now and he's another man who's rotten to the core, isn't he, Hannah?'

Hannah lost some of her colour and put her glass to her lips.

'It's not at all surprising that Daniel Kittow's in prison at the moment. He was convicted, Grace, of receiving stolen goods, resisting arrest and striking a police officer. It's a good thing he's got several months left to serve of his sentence. I hope with all my heart he doesn't come back to Porthellis when he's released.'

Hannah's graceful body gave a noticeable tremble.

'We could do without his sort amongst us,' Adela Skewes' tongue marched on oblivious of Hannah's disquiet. 'He tried to kill your husband, didn't he, Hannah? Well, as good as, anyway. He tried to push Matt into the water just after he'd been rescued and brought home by the lifeboat. And you'll have to go a long way to find a more dependable and hard-working man than Matt Penney. It's a pity you can't find a young man rather like him, Grace.' Grace fidgeted in embarrassment again. 'He's

9

quite well off for a fisherman and good-looking into the bargain.'

Grace adroitly changed the subject for the second time by admiring the plaster decoration of grapes, tassels and garlands above the magnificent fireplace which ended in a cornice near the ceiling. Hannah told her some of the house's history and was mightily relieved when the Reverend Skewes claimed his gossiping wife to talk to other guests, but she knew that Grace Treloar had been aware of her discomfiture over Daniel Kittow.

'I hope Leah will be all right tonight,' Hannah said. Already in her nightdress, she climbed on the bed where Matt sat undressing and kissed his bare back. Nathan was fast asleep in his cot in the room next door to the large, second-floor bedroom she shared with Matt. 'I think it would have been more thoughtful of Greg to have taken her away tonight to begin their honeymoon.'

Matt tossed the last of his clothes on the floor. 'She's got a massive four-poster bed to spend her wedding night in, but I don't expect she'll go to Greg like you came to me the first time. I'll never forget you seducing me on my little single bed in my old room.' He held up his big, calloused right hand. The top of the forefinger was missing. 'It was worth losing this to have you visit me as I recovered from the infection and having you throw yourself all over me.' Taking her into his arms he kissed her deeply. 'It's your fault Nathan's here.'

'So you keep reminding me.' She pressed her lips on the pulse at the base of his neck, knowing with delicious anticipation that she had him in her power, as she had the afternoon their baby was conceived. 'And I still say it's your fault for being irresistible to me.'

'Only God knows how much I love you, Hannah Penney,' he said huskily. 'Thank goodness I've got the rest of the night to show you.'

Much later, as Matt slept soundly with his arms round her, Hannah lay awake. Grace Treloar and Adela Skewes had brought something to the forefront of her mind, something which for over a year she had pushed firmly to the back of it. When Daniel Kittow came out of prison, would he come back to Porthellis? The other partners on the Kittow lugger had pulled out and the *Sunrise* floated abandoned in the harbour. Rufus was dead, the cottage uninhabitable. There was nothing for Daniel to come back to. And no one. Everyone in the village despised him, including Hannah, even though he had once declared he loved her. But she knew Daniel well. He was selfish and arrogant and unforgiving, traits that for a long time she had overlooked until she had so horrendously seen his real character. She closed her eyes and prayed long and hard. If Daniel came home to Porthellis, she would never again feel safe for herself or for her family.

Chapter 2

Hannah carried Nathan along the cliff path to Hidden Beach, a small stretch of fine sand a little way upcoast from Porthellis. The village children had played here for generations, its location hidden by gorse and bramble from the cliff path. Few adults came here but Hannah made the short journey at least once a week in good weather.

The sky was hazy, the sun pleasantly hot, a caressing breeze blew in off the blue-green sea. Hannah sat on the sand with her back against a rock, cradling Nathan as he slept in her arms. She was thinking about Matt, who had joined her father and the *Misty*'s other crew yesterday evening for a thirty-six-hour stint of hunting for flatfish. Matt had said he was looking forward to the day when he could take Nathan on board the lugger to learn the craft of a fisherman.

Hannah loved Matt with all her being but she felt a little envious that the child she had carried in her body and for whom she had endured a pain-ridden, forty-eight-hour labour to bring into the world would one day belong more to Matt than to her. She gazed in wonder at her baby. His body was strong and sturdy; he was going to be tall like her and Matt. Under his white cotton sunhat was hair as fair and silky as hers; beneath his closed lids were the wonderful dark eyes he had inherited from Matt and which often held the same intense gaze. The lines and angles of his chubby little face hinted he was mostly going to resemble Matt.

When Nathan awoke, as always with a long stretch and immediate smile, she carried him down to the shore where, despite the still air, restless foam-topped waves crashed on to the sand. She walked into the water, enjoying the delicious bite on her bare feet and ankles. Nathan blinked at her, slightly bewildered by the stronger smell of salt and hardier breeze hurrying over them, then recognizing the happy, fearless smile on his mother's face he chuckled contentedly and looked towards the sea, puckering his tiny features. Hannah paddled up and down the shore then dipped Nathan's feet in the warm pools of water left by the receding tide. He loved this and she lowered herself down so he could splash his fat legs.

Hannah had been restless all weekend over the mention of Daniel Kittow but she had made an effort not to convey her worries to Matt. Wives of fishermen did not like to send their men to sea with something on their minds and Matt would have hated the subject of his one-time workmate and partner being brought up. Hannah resolved to push her cares aside; it was months before Daniel Kittow was due to be released.

She suddenly got the eerie feeling someone was watching her and a second later a waft of cigarette smoke hit her senses. She looked up sharply. Her body convulsed and, clutching Nathan to her, she shot to her feet.

'Daniel!'

Daniel Kittow was only inches away from her. He stared at her for some moments, his expression stony and cold.

'Mrs Penney,' he said drily, his deep-set blue eyes turning into slits.

Hannah wanted to turn and run away from him but she couldn't. Frozen on the sand, she took in his appearance. His rugged face with its broad cheekbones and firm chin had an unhealthy pallor, his thick red hair was severely cropped, and his muscular body had lost weight. The clothes, smart but casual, were the ones he had been arrested in. Daniel had always been a hard man, easily provoked to outbursts of temper, but he had owned a sense of humour and a joy for living. Now, however, he seemed aloof and brooding; the energy that had led Hannah and others into many childhood pranks, including the boating accident that had led to her brother and another girl's deaths, had been replaced by a quiet deadliness. What Hannah had learned about Daniel told her she wasn't being fanciful.

She stepped backwards. 'I–I thought . . . I didn't expect . . .'

'That I'd be let out of prison yet? There's such a thing as remission for good behaviour. I was very careful to behave, Hannah.'

He spoke slowly and carefully but each word seemed to rush at her with a threat on its tail. She felt he was scoffing at her. He shifted his gaze to Nathan, the corner of his wide mouth curling up, but he made no remark. Hannah held Nathan tighter. It was hard to face this man alone. Only her desperate reminder to him that they were supposed to be friends had stopped him raping her. Now they were anything but friends. She had never felt so helpless and vulnerable.

He drew in on his cigarette and took his time exhaling the smoke. 'You're the first person I've spoken to since I arrived home. I don't suppose I can expect a warmer welcome from anyone else,' he said coldly.

Hannah took a deep breath. 'You can't expect people to be pleased to see you.'

His eyes bore into her. 'I don't care about that. I'm sure none of you want to see me back, but I am back and for good. I guess you all hoped I'd be found guilty of stealing those pathetic little village knick-knacks as well as for receiving them. I bet you all thought it a pity it was proved I was not in the village when some of the things went missing.' His voice dropped to an icier level and he moved closer to her. 'The strange thing is, Hannah, I'd received plenty of stolen goods in my time and passed them on to a fence and was well rewarded for it. But I had nothing to do with the things I was sent to prison for. They were planted in my cottage and I've a good idea who did it. It's him who won't be staying in Porthellis.'

Hannah shivered at the menace in his words. She could think of nothing to say in reply.

'Are you going now?' he muttered disdainfully. 'I came here to be alone.'

It was several moments before Hannah could make her legs move then she turned on her heel and ran to the rock where she had left her sandals. Sensing her disquiet, Nathan began to whimper as she pulled on her sandals. Before she pushed through the gorse bushes, almost against her will she turned to see what Daniel was doing. He had his back to her, facing the sea. She hurried back along the cliff path and through the village until she was home.

'Hannah, dear,' Mrs Penney exclaimed as she plunged through the back door into the kitchen. 'You're out of breath. Have you been running?' Mrs Penney held out her arms for Nathan and Hannah gratefully handed him over; he had grown heavy in her arms and, unusually for him, was fretting.

'I've just seen Daniel Kittow,' Hannah panted. She sank down shakily into the chair at the hearth that Matt most often used, and for a moment she had the comforting feeling that she was in his arms. 'I was alone on Hidden Beach with Nathan and I felt so frightened.'

'He didn't threaten you or do anything to you, did he?' Mrs Penney asked anxiously.

'No, but he was very hostile. Oh, Mother, I wish he hadn't come back.'

'I'm sure the men in the village will keep an eye on him,' Mrs Penney said soothingly but she couldn't disguise her nervousness; Hannah looked so fearful. 'Perhaps prison life has softened him up.'

'I don't think so.' Hannah did not believe that Daniel had had anything to do with the items that had gone missing from various houses and the general store in the village. It had been common knowledge that he had been involved in shady dealings but the village thefts did not bear his mark. A few minutes ago he had as good as announced revenge on the man he thought responsible for deliberately sending him to prison.

'Goodness me,' Mrs Penney exclaimed, handing Nathan back to Hannah. 'I forgot that we have a visitor. Miss Grace Treloar is in the parlour. She called to see you, Hannah. You go along and speak to her while I make some tea.'

Daniel entered the Ship Inn at the back and made his way through the short dark passage to the tiny parlour. He found Maggie Curnow relaxing on her sofa painting her toenails.

'Danny! she exclaimed, putting the bottle of bright red polish aside and standing up. 'It's good to see you again. So they let you out like you said in your last letter then? Been back in the village long?'

'A short while. This is the first house I've entered. I've been trying to get the prison smell out of my head with sea air.'

Maggie smoothed her tight skirt over her hips and pouted her thick shiny lips. 'You'll soon do that, Danny.' She rested her tongue on her lower lip. 'What you need is something to take your mind off it. You must be—'

'I've come for the keys,' he said tersely. He was in no mood for small talk or any other kind of conversation.

'They're in my handbag, but first,' she moved close to him and slid her fingers up under the lapels of his jacket, 'why don't we—'

He turned his face from her brassy features. 'Get them.'

Reluctantly letting her hands fall away, Maggie did as he ordered. Daniel exchanged the bunch of keys for a wad of money which she tucked down her generous cleavage. 'Now we've got the business out of the way,' she purred, 'why don't we go upstairs?'

Daniel stood back and ran his eyes over the curves he had often been on intimate terms with. 'You still giving yourself to Jeff Spargo?'

'Yes, but he doesn't measure up to your performance, Danny.' Maggie couldn't wait to get her hands on him. It had been a long time for a man with his appetite to go without a woman. She was eager to experience what would be unleashed.

'I don't want to follow a Spargo anywhere,' Daniel said harshly, adding on a kinder but brisk note when he got to the door, 'Thanks for your help. I won't be coming here again.'

Grace found Nathan's whining annoying and she stayed in Seaview Cottage only long enough to drink a cup of tea and arrange to take a long walk with Hannah along the cliff path at the end of the week.

She carried on along Cobble Street until she reached the new house, which like the Penneys' home was blessed with an unobstructed view all the way down to the harbour. She wasn't a nosy woman but Grace was drawn to the building which was as engaging as the two-storeyed four-bedroomed cottage she had just left. Aunt Adela had excitedly informed her that a furniture van, not an unmarked van so its contents must have been paid for and was not on the never-never, had pulled up outside it this morning and only new items of good quality had been carried inside. How could a village landlady who could not have made much money out of the hard-pressed fishermen's drinking habits afford to build the biggest house in Porthellis and furnish it so well? Perhaps, as Aunt Adela had put it, Maggie Curnow had been paid for other services.

Grace lifted the brass, anchor-shaped door knocker, hoping the pub landlady was at home and would invite her inside. It would be interesting to compare it to the Penneys' home which exuded a close family atmosphere and was charmingly old-fashioned in Grace's view. According to her aunt, it was better furnished than any other in Porthellis owing to Mrs Penney's origin as a sea captain's daughter. Seaview Cottage was tiled nearly to the ground in grey slate but this house was thatched and whitewashed, its walls at perfect right angles while most of the village houses bulged here and there due to uneven stones or because the cob was giving way. The paintwork on the door and window frames here was fresh royal blue. Everything about this new house was pristine, crisp and modern, more in keeping with what an outsider, an 'emmet' such as herself, might build in this quiet Cornish village.

There were no sounds coming from within and Grace glanced around to see if anyone was about. No one was and she did something she would not have dreamed of doing before, she peeped through one of the large bay windows. The abstract print curtains were pulled close together over thick white net curtains and she could make nothing out.

Shrugging her shoulders, Grace carried on to the next street, River Street, and she smiled in amusement that these narrow thoroughfares had been given the title of street. Here, she met the village eccentric. Sitting on a low wooden stool beside her granite doorstep was a tiny old lady with a pure white bun of thin hair on top of her head and whiskers sprouting from her sharp chin. She wore a mulish expression, one eye squinting because of the sun, as Grace approached her.

'Good afternoon,' Grace said cheerily. 'Are you Miss Peters?'

'What makes you think that?' the octogenarian snapped indignantly.

Grace had heard about Miss Peters' chariness and about her quick mind and natural mean streak. The evidence of who she was lay at her child-sized feet – the horsewhip she was infamous for, which she kept handy to crack at people's feet if they ignored or affronted her.

Miss Peters' darting eyes followed Grace's to the horsewhip. 'So Mrs Skewes has chattered about me, has she? I suppose I was easy to miss in chapel yesterday as my head doesn't reach much above the top of the pews.'

'It wasn't gossip, Miss Peters,' Grace said diplomatically. 'As I'm staying here for a few weeks my aunt thought I'd like to hear about the important people of the village.'

Miss Peters was mollified. She pointed to her uneven doorstep. 'Sit down if you've a mind to, Miss Grace Treloar.'

Grace sat down on the well-scrubbed step and stretched out her trousered legs.

Most people disapproved of women wearing trousers but Miss Peters gave a grunt of approval. ''Tis a mighty good thing t'be practical. Folk should wake up their ideas. After all, 'tis nineteen thirty-eight. You one of them sporty types?'

'Yes, I suppose I am. I enjoyed hockey and netball at school and I've ridden, taken part in shoots and hiked all my adult life.'

'You'll have to look further afield than Roscarrock to find the sort of shooting you're used to. You might get a farmer to let you ride one of his nags and of course there's plenty of places a fit young woman like you can walk to.'

'I'm taking my first long walk across the cliffs on Friday. With Hannah Penney.'

'Aw, aye, she'm a good little maid. You'll find most of us round here are good sorts. Do 'ee like the village?'

'I think it's beautiful,' Grace enthused, gazing down Porthkilt Hill to the water. 'Aunt Adela kept urging my mother and me to come down here for a holiday. I regret that Mother never did, she would have liked the sea air and views.'

'I'm sorry to hear your mother died. What was it?'

'Simply old age. She died peacefully in her chair.'

'That's a blessing. We'd all like to go that way. How long since your father went?'

'He died eleven years ago.'

'And you got no brothers or sisters?'

'No. I've got no one really in Kent. Mother didn't like to socialize and she wasn't keen on me going out and leaving her alone.'

'Well, you've got your freedom now.'

'Yes.'

'What're you going to do with it?'

'I might go abroad to live. I spent a few weeks in America once and thoroughly enjoyed it.'

Grace stayed chatting to Miss Peters for over an hour and met other villagers who stopped to pass the time of day. Then, fortified with a glass of Miss Peters' homemade, exceedingly strong, elderberry wine, she strode down the hill to look over the workshops.

Men were busy in the carpenter's shop and she stepped among the fragrant heaps of sawdust and thin, curling wood shavings to talk a few minutes with them. At the hot, steamy barkhouse she watched, from a distance so as not to get in the way, as men with brawny arms and clad in yellow oilskins and sea boots loaded a handcart with nets that had been 'cured' to withstand prolonged immersion in salt water. A fierce, unhealthy heat from the three furnaces that heated the cutch water and a pungent smell spilled out through the barkhouse doors and Grace marvelled that the men could work in such conditions. The handcart was trundled along the quay and the nets were painstakingly spread out to dry along the curve of the harbour wall.

Further on, Grace heard girls and women busy on net-making machines up in a loft singing in time with their work, but she didn't like to climb up and observe them without an invitation. Their voices rose and dipped in perfect union, the same sopranos, altos and contraltos she had heard in the chapel on Sunday. She loved the clarity and rhythm of the Celtic voices.

On the quay, on a long wooden bench, some gnarled old men were holding their daily 'parliament' and were happy to answer her questions about bygone days when the world was 'a much better 'n' safer place t'live in, certain, sure'. One pensioner muttered that he was convinced that with Hitler herding his army at will all over Europe there would be another world war, and Grace left the old gents to argue the point with passion.

The more Grace learned about Porthellis, the more of an affinity she felt with it. She lingered on the cobbled slipway, the pretty shades of copper, grey and cream stones polished by centuries of use. She watched the clear water of the swiftly-moving stream that emerged from an underground passage and ran alongside the slipway to join the larger regions of the sea. She breathed in the smells of salt and fish and crab pots, looked over the small craft temporarily abandoned as their owners sought to make their living on bigger boats. She glanced across at the solitary lugger owned by the fisherman in prison. Leaning forlornly to the side in a few inches of water, painted blue and white, the boat had a neglected appearance but looked in good repair. A gull strutted along the gunwale as if it had sole ownership.

About three-quarters of the village was situated on this side of the stream, and it was known as the sunny side of Porthellis. Across the flat slab of granite that formed the bridge over the stream was the dark side, so named because the few dwellings there stood in the shade of the cliff. Up above it, Roscarrock could be seen. Grace's eyes moved from Cliffside Cottage to the ramshackle building next to it. There were no Kittows about to forbid investigation and she decided to take a closer look at their home.

Outside the Spargo cottage, which was in serious need of fresh whitewash and a visit from the thatcher, a young man sat playing marbles with some small children. Grace bid him good afternoon but he did not respond. The five children, aged between about eighteen months and four years, gazed at her.

'Our Uncle Josh don't speak,' one child, who bore the typical Spargo black hair and good looks, told her.

The young man raised his scrunched-up shoulders and Grace got a glimpse of his twisted, nervous face. An imbecile, she thought. Poor man.

She could see her presence made him acutely uncomfortable and she moved on. She watched Josh Spargo and the children for some moments and was gladdened by how naturally they interacted. A perpetual child, he no doubt gave the young mothers attached to this house, and probably Hannah Penney too, a welcome break from their duties.

Grace couldn't stand and stare at the Kittow cottage unobserved so she walked round to the back. The small bit of land behind the building was wildly overgrown and choked with brambles yet made pretty here and there by hardy wild flowers and flowering weeds which favoured the shade. The wooden sides and roof of a tiny closet lay in a heap. In one spot lay the ashes of a bonfire. In the Spargos' garden and the garden on the other side were well-stocked chicken coops but no sign of there ever being one here.

Grace ploughed through the growth, four feet high in some places, to reach the back door. She looked through the smeared glass of the small, curtainless window beside it into what she believed the working class called the back kitchen. She frowned. Shelves hung off the walls, shrivelled vegetables lay scattered on the floor with pieces of broken crockery and battered saucepans. The disarray was more than just the result of neglect; the place looked as if it had been ransacked.

She touched the door and it swung inwards with a rasp on its rusty hinges. Without hesitation she stepped across the threshold and picked her way over the debris into the kitchen. A scene of such destruction met her eyes that she felt a strong sense of moral indignation. The room, dank and musty-smelling, festooned with cobwebs, had obviously been vandalised. The table was hacked to pieces, as were the chairs and other pieces of furniture, and there was evidence that the floor had been urinated on. The Kittows' possessions had been tossed about and broken as if the heel of a boot had been ruthlessly applied.

Grace moved on to the parlour. It told the same story. The brown horsehair couch had been slashed and its straw stuffing pulled out in handfuls. Everything on the mantelpiece had been swept off, the ashes in the fireplace strewn around the room. Grace knew the villagers hated the Kittows but this seemed the work of a madman. It was an outrage.

She picked up a screwed-up photograph and smoothed it out. In the limited light from the grimy window she could just make out a small, heavily-whiskered old man on the sepia coloured paper.

'Who the hell are you?'

21

Grace started. She turned round and, unabashed, steadily returned the hostile gaze of a tall, red-haired man. 'Who are you?'

'Never mind who I am. What are you doing in my house?'

Grace was surprised to be caught trespassing by Daniel Kittow and not someone who had no more right to be here than she had. But she was not easily intimidated.

'My name's Grace Treloar,' she said calmly. 'You must be Daniel Kittow. I apologize for intruding on your home. I'm appalled at its condition. I assume your late grandfather did not leave it this way. I'd like to offer my assistance in making the cottage habitable again.'

'My grandfather most certainly did not leave our home like this,' Daniel snapped, snatching the photograph out of her hand. He was furious at the double outrage to his home – the vandalism and an intruder. 'I don't need your bloody help. I've no time for do-gooders. Get out!'

Grace did not move. 'I can assure you, Mr Kittow, I am not a do-gooder. Usually I am happy to let people find their own way out of their problems but what I've seen here is a different matter. The damage was done deliberately and is unforgivable.'

'Even to a drunk and his criminal grandson?' Daniel loomed over her. He was getting angrier by the moment and wanted to terrorize this stranger, see her run from him.

'Even more so in the circumstances,' Grace replied evenly.

Daniel regarded her with suspicion. So she was a strong-minded woman. While he hated her presence here, as much as he hated Hannah Penney, the only woman who had rejected him, he could not stop himself comparing the two women. Hannah had turned into a haughty bitch just like the one with him now, but Grace Treloar did not have Hannah's beauty, poise or youthfulness. 'Who are you?' he demanded again.

'I'm the niece of Mrs Skewes, the minister's wife, and I'm staying at the Manse for a few weeks.'

'I'm not interested in religion either,' he snarled.

'I have a strong faith but I am not religious. My reason for being here is just plain nosiness.' He raised an eyebrow slightly at her honesty. 'I apologize again and repeat my offer of help.' Grace couldn't take her eyes off him. Few men of Daniel Kittow's colouring were traditionally considered good-looking but he was the most handsome man she had ever seen. And while she had not cared about looks in the few romantic encounters she had had, she found this man's broad, totally masculine build very appealing. There was a raw energy about him, derived, she felt, from a hunger to satisfy a multitude of needs.

Daniel sighed heavily, his breath hitting her face but she did not flinch. Short of throwing this damned woman out of the cottage he could see he wouldn't get rid of her. Perhaps if he propositioned her, crudely suggested they go upstairs to see the condition of the bedrooms, it would frighten her off. Looking at her resolute features, he thought that would not work either; she seemed quite capable of sidestepping the issue. Then he had another idea. He took two one pound notes out of his wallet.

'You can get me some food,' he said gruffly. 'The shopkeeper refused to serve me.' He smirked as he pictured the villagers' horror when they realized that this young lady had got herself involved with him. He could almost hear the urgent warnings she would receive.

'Has he indeed?' Grace said, indignant on his behalf and pleased to have obtained a little of his trust. 'Have you a shopping bag?' She glanced about the room to see if there was something she could use. 'When I come back I'll help you clean and tidy up the place.'

Daniel led the way to the kitchen and picked up a crib bag from the floor. He thrust it at Grace, and looked smug. From the gleam in her eyes he reckoned that perhaps the shopkeeper was going to get the rough edge of her tongue. 'Don't bring it back here. Take it to my other house, the new building in Cobble Street.'

'You own that beautiful house?' Her eyes lit up.

'Yes, and I'll see these damned villagers don't dare lay a finger on my property again,' he said venomously. 'By the ashes outside it looks like they've burned some of my possessions. I'll make the bastards who did it suffer.' He looked at Grace challengingly but did not receive the pious remonstration he was expecting. Maybe she would be a useful ally for his purposes. He gave her the keys to the new house and dropped his aggressive tone. 'You go on, let yourself in. The range is going. If you can cook and your charity stretches that far, you can make me a meal. I want to spend some time here alone then look over my lugger lying idle at the quay.'

He accompanied Grace to the door. In the back garden of the next cottage they saw a young man coming out of the outdoor closet. He was half bent over and clutching his stomach while trying to pull up his braces.

'Fred Jose!' Daniel boomed at him, startling Grace.

Fred Jose visibly quailed. 'D-Daniel . . . I . . .'

Grace could see the man, of weedy build and pale stricken face, was terrified of Daniel.

'Not out working today?' Daniel shouted jovially but there was a taunt in the words.

'N-no, g-got the runs. Good to, um, see you.' Fred Jose took to his heels and ran back inside the closet.

Daniel let out a laugh, a shallow grating sound, and Grace noticed that his face was as tight as the fists clenched at his sides. 'He and his father Curly used to fish on my boat. I have business with him,' he told her in a hard voice.

He went back inside and Grace strode up the village hill to the shop which doubled as the sub-post office and was run by a middle-aged man whose source of pride in the community was the fact that his family could be traced back in Porthellis for seven generations. She was pleased there were other customers in the shop to hear her give the shopkeeper short shrift for his unchristian treatment of Daniel Kittow.

'He's served his prison sentence and everyone deserves a second chance,' she fumed. 'Will you refuse to take his money off me?'

'Not as it's you, Miss Treloar,' Hamlyn Innis replied, red-faced from his public chastening but also livid with the young lady. She had only been in Porthellis four days and had no idea what a terrible man Daniel Kittow was. If she hadn't been related to the minister's wife he'd have refused her custom too – and he would tell his shocked, waiting customers so the moment she left. He produced the items she asked for and slammed the change down on the counter.

Grace thanked him tartly then paid a call to the butcher next door. Phineas Brown, short, fat, his broad smile a permanent fixture on his cherry-red bulging face, was a good Bible man and Grace was pleased he was not of the same mind as Hamlyn Innis. ''Fraid you won't find many like me hereabouts, m'dear,' he chuckled, sharpening a long-bladed knife on the steel. 'Daniel Kittow's a bad lot and I don't expect prison will've changed un. But he's not likely t'be saved unless shown some good Christian love, though 'twill be hard t'show it t'un.'

Grace's knowledge of cooking consisted of grilling sausages over a Girl Guides' camp fire and she asked the butcher for four pork sausages. She had never shopped for food and hoped she had all the basic requirements when she left the bakehouse a short time later with a large crusty loaf. She didn't bother to challenge Mrs Trudgeon and left the busybody to bemoan her failure at extracting the reason why the rest of her shopping, although well wrapped, was in a dirty old bag.

When Grace arrived at the new house she was watched by three women, including Mrs Penney, who were chatting, arms folded, on their doorsteps. Grace nodded to them and grinned at their amazed faces as she produced the keys out of her trouser pocket; no doubt they would soon be asking each other whether the new house belonged to Maggie Curnow or to her. For a moment she pondered how Daniel Kittow could afford the house; he could hardly have got a bank loan while he was in prison. Maybe he had borrowed the money from another source. However it had come about, she was sure he was in command of the situation.

Grace opened the front door with a sense of triumph that, except for the pub landlady, she had beaten the villagers in finding out who the true owner of the house was. There would be many shocked souls in the village when the news broke. Full of anticipation, she stepped inside.

Chapter 3

The *Misty* sailed into harbour just after midnight, breaking the silence which, except for the surge of the waves and battering wind, had fallen over the village. Most of the Porthellis fleet was already home. Matt, at the wheel, expertly brought the forty-foot lugger into its usual berthing place, alongside the abandoned *Sunrise*.

'There you are, boy,' he grinned at Alan Weekley, teasing the school-leaver the *Misty* had just taken on. The boy was almost sleeping on his feet from exhaustion. 'We'll land the fish tomorrow at eight o'clock. You'll soon be home in bed and no doubt your proud mother will bring you a cup of tea first thing.' Matt called softly to his father-in-law who was straightening his tired muscles after tying up the mooring rope on the quay. 'He did well his first time out, eh, Jeff?'

'Aye,' Jeff agreed, rubbing his prickly growth of black beard and looking with carnal intent at the pub; who could blame him for thinking of Maggie Curnow, he asked himself, with Prim sharing Josh's room instead of his bed? 'We'll make a fisherman of un, put biceps on un like a bull's. He's earned his uffy, be on a proper wage soon.'

Rolling along with their sea-leg gait, the other two partners in the boat, Graham and Malcolm Chellew, Alan's uncles, escorted their nephew home, aiding his occasional faltering step in his cumbersome sea boots. His widowed mother would be told how well the boy had done. Alan had proudly memorized every encouragement he had been given, only mild praise, the fishermen too busy and not of a mind to bestow any sort of indulgence on him, but compliments just the same. Alan had done better than he'd hoped, his one big worry removed in the face of his natural ability to bait the long line and haul it back in, heavy with fish: Fred Jose would still retain his reputation as the worst fisherman who'd ever lived in Porthellis.

Matt said goodnight to Jeff at the bridge, knowing the older man would cross over but only stay on the dark side of the village for as long as it took him to disappear from sight. Matt kept his thoughts on the matter to himself. He was concerned about Jeff's womanizing for Hannah's sake, yet grateful the habit had brought Hannah into being.

Here and there, a light glowed in a window of the homes of men not yet safely ashore. No such light burned in the Spargo cottage but Matt knew the bedside lamp would be on in his bedroom. He had a comfortable picture inside his head of Nathan snuggled down in his cot and Hannah fully awake eagerly waiting for him. The fatigue from the long hours lifted from his broad shoulders.

His pleasant dream was crudely shattered.

'Have a good catch, Penney?'

The voice from behind him came from the last man he wanted to see. Keeping control of the violent emotions that surged through him, Matt turned slowly and under the moonlit sky squarely faced his old adversary. 'I was hoping they'd keep you locked up for good,' he said icily.

'You and most of the village,' Daniel smirked, 'including your dear wife.' He was standing casually at the corner of Seaview Cottage, feet apart in the steadying stance of a fisherman, but there was a tension in his upper body which spread down to the large hands resting on the thick leather belt at his waist.

Matt let his allowance bag fall to the cobbled ground and strode to a breath away from the cocky young man with whom he had partnered one-fourth on the Kittow lugger until they had fought over Hannah. 'Have you spoken to Hannah?' he demanded.

'Not by choice,' Daniel replied as if he was spitting something bitter out of his mouth.

'Stay away from her, Kittow, or I'll rip your guts out.' Matt's voice was low and dangerous.

Hannah had heard Matt's familiar tread turning into the street. Puzzled that it had stopped at the front doorstep and not carried round to the back where he always entered the cottage to pull off his sea boots, she got out of bed and looked out of the window. Her heart stopped. It wouldn't be necessary to tell Matt the unsavoury news that had been buzzing round the village all day. He was fronting up to Daniel and they looked as if at any moment they'd have their hands round each other's throats. She struggled into her dressing gown as she ran barefoot down the stairs and threw open the front door.

Daniel was about to respond in kind to Matt's threat when he saw her over Matt's shoulder. 'Ah, here comes the little missus now,' he mocked. 'Come to join hubby in wishing your new neighbour well, Hannah?'

Hannah gripped Matt's arm; he was an even-tempered man but could be easily provoked on his family's behalf and wasn't the least bit afraid of Daniel. At first Hannah didn't understand Daniel, then she gasped. 'You own the new house?'

Daniel produced a bunch of keys from his jacket pocket, tossed them in the air and caught them in his fist. 'That's right. I designed the place myself,' he said at her astonished face, 'during the long lonely nights I spent cooped up in my cell breathing in other men's stench. I'm very happy with the outcome, it's exactly what I've always wanted. I won't be keeping it locked, there won't be the need with me being around to see it doesn't get smashed up like my old place. So, any time you want to borrow a cup of sugar . . .' He laughed gloatingly, thrust his hands in his trouser pockets and swaggered home.

Matt put his arm round Hannah and for once did not bother to go round to the back. They went to the kitchen. Hannah hugged him, hiding her pale face against his strong body. It was as if a nightmare had come true.

'The swine,' Matt muttered under his breath, kissing her hair.

She pulled his head down to kiss his cold, salty lips. He responded tenderly then held her shoulders. 'What's he said to you?'

Determined to keep the extent of her fears about Daniel's return to herself to avoid trouble between the two men, Hannah recounted the meeting on Hidden Beach, making it sound less alarming than when she had told Mrs Penney. 'We knew he would come back one day, darling. It was too much to hope he'd live elsewhere. We must ignore him and get on with our lives.'

Matt sighed wearily. 'You know it's not going to be that simple, Hannah, with him just down the street. When I worked the *Sunrise* with him he often boasted about building a big house. He must have been stashing away his ill-gotten gains for years and he probably had a large insurance out on old Rufus. Damn him, he could have built that house anywhere, there's plenty of empty spaces in and about the village. He couldn't wait to tell me he's not going to be far from us.'

Hannah couldn't deny what Matt was saying; she, too, had known about

Daniel's ambitions but he'd always said he'd have his house built down on the waterfront. She took Matt's face between her hands. 'You won't let him goad you, will you, Matt?' she implored him. 'Promise me that whatever he does, you won't let there be any unpleasantness between you.'

He gently took her hands away. 'I can't promise that. I'm sorry, but I won't let that evil swine ride roughshod over me and mine.'

'Oh, dear God.' Hannah raised her eyes to the ceiling and said a quick prayer. The set of Matt's jaw and the hard glint in his dark eyes told her there was no point in continuing to plead with him.

Moving to the cream-coloured Cornish range, its embers giving off a welcome heat, she kept the frustration she felt out of her voice. 'Do you want something to eat and drink? I won't be able to sleep now.'

'Yes, please,' Matt said, his voice still grim as he sat down to pull off his sea boots. Stripping to the waist, he washed thoroughly and scrubbed his salt-encrusted hands, though the beguiling smell of the sea never wholly left him.

'How much have you got to unload in the morning?' Hannah asked as she made cocoa and toast.

'About five hundred stone. We didn't do bad,' he answered in understatement so as not to tempt fate to bring bad luck to the boat on its next outing. 'We went out further than most of the others.' He gave her his warm and gentle smile, his eyes consuming every inch of her lovely face and soft feminine form.

Hannah's inner being became awash with the deep-rooted, exquisite emotion she experienced when he looked at her that way. She scanned every minute detail of his features, the wide brow, sensuous mouth, perfectly set nose and cheekbones. She knew him better than anyone else on earth, this man with thick, earth-brown hair that curled about his neck, and eyes so deep and dark they seemed to reflect the secret chasms under the sea. He was her husband, her mate, the father of her beloved child. She vowed then with all her heart that she wouldn't allow Daniel Kittow to hurt them or tarnish her life. She was strong and powerful now, no longer the frightened girl of a few hours ago on Hidden Beach.

Taking Matt's hand, she kissed it, pressing each finger to her searching lips then crushing her lips over his mouth. She led him upstairs to warm him by another fire, the flames of her love.

* * *

30

Next morning as the men unloaded their catch, Hannah popped into number seven Quayside Street where she'd lived with the Rouses. Her Aunt Janet was pleased to see her but disappointed she hadn't brought Nathan with her.

'He's sleeping. Mrs Penney's keeping an eye on him,' Hannah explained cheerfully, putting a parcel on the table. It contained a flannel nightdress she had made and two girls' liberty bodices. Hannah and Janet worked in partnership as seamstresses; Janet received the orders and passed the finished items on to the customers.

Janet tapped the parcel. 'Is this for Mrs Treseder and Lizzie's stepdaughter?'

'Yes. I'll start on Mr Nunn's mending later today. I don't know how the old boy wears his vests out so quickly.'

'I'll pass on the money for the things you've brought when I get it.' Janet studied her niece. Her face was aglow. 'Glad to see you haven't let him upset you. A hundred Daniel Kittows shouldn't be enough to ruin your happiness with Matt.'

'I won't let him hurt us, Aunty Janet,' Hannah said, reliving the wonderful moments with Matt last night. She added in a very serious voice, 'I'm glad you understand how things could be for us with Daniel out of prison. I'm waiting for him to cause trouble for me and Matt. I know him better than anyone, he's got a vindictive streak in him. Yesterday I recognized a certain look in his eye. What worries me is what Matt will do if he taunts him. He can be every bit as stubborn.'

'Well, you can't expect Matt just to ignore un if he does cause trouble but Matt's too sensible to let him really upset him.'

'I hope so, Aunty.' Hannah kept her concern for her own personal safety to herself; only Matt knew about Daniel's assault on her. Until things hopefully settled down, she'd make sure she was never alone where Daniel was likely to be.

'I don't know how that Miss Treloar could do his shopping and take it to Maggie Curnow's new house for un. I warrant Maggie entertained him in there all night. Bit too close to your doorstep, eh? Never mind, no doubt he'll be spending time in his own cottage after he's got some silly female admirer to clean it up for un. You'd think Grace Treloar wouldn't have nothing t'do with the likes of he.'

'She did his shopping out of Christian charity, Aunty,' Hannah said, having heard the tale of Grace's indignation in the shop. 'Misguided, of course, but then she doesn't know him. You haven't heard the worst yet. Maggie Curnow doesn't own the new house, Daniel does. He made a point of telling me and Matt last night.'

'Good heavens! That's a blow. Well, they say the Devil looks after his own. Never a more rotten heart beat in a man's breast than in Daniel Kittow's,' Janet ruminated like an ancient soothsayer. 'Well, never mind him, that's what your Uncle Roy would say. Daniel's got his lugger and the cottage to sort out. I feel bad about his cottage. Someone should have reported what happened to the police and it should have been tidied up. One of us might have got round to it if Daniel hadn't come home so suddenly.'

'I pity the person who smashed up his home if he finds out who it was,' Hannah said with feeling. She glanced at the kitchen clock. 'I'd better go across the stream and tell Mum all about it before I go home.' She made for the door before Janet started on something to detain her. Prim would be hurt if she spent more time here than with her.

'You going up to Roscarrock this afternoon?' Janet caught her arm before her foot got through the doorway.

'Yes, I always go there on Wednesday afternoons. You know that, Aunty,' she said, aware of what was coming.

'Right, you can leave Nathan with me. Mrs Penney has him now and Prim had him the last time you went.'

'I promised Mrs Opie I'd take him with me this time,' Hannah said, raising her hands to still Janet's protests that the lady of the big house had monopolized Nathan for much of Leah's wedding reception. 'I'm going for a long walk across the cliff with Grace Treloar on Friday. You can have him then.'

Janet was satisfied. 'You stay out as long as you like. A break will do you good.'

Hannah smiled ruefully to herself. If she took all the breaks she was encouraged to take since she'd weaned her baby she'd spend very little time with him.

Immediately after breakfast, ignoring Mrs Skewes' repeated warnings to keep away from Daniel Kittow, Grace let herself into the new house in Cobble Street. She found Daniel sleeping in his clothes on the settee, his head on the plump cushions, his hand hanging loosely to the carpeted floor, his long legs and bare feet stretched out under the low table. A half-filled unstoppered bottle of whisky and empty glass stood on the table. Grace didn't wake him. She ran her eyes up and down his body, taking her time, thoroughly enjoying the masculine spectacle. She liked best his bulging sinewy arms, large rough hands and the ruggedly handsome face that ensured he didn't have to work hard to ensnare all the hapless females her aunt had gone on about.

Through the misty hazes of his subconscious, Daniel recognized her musky perfume and thought he was back among the wreck of his old home and ordering her out. Beset again with the hurt and anger at finding his home violated and with an intruder inside it, he was suddenly wide awake.

'You're a forward bitch,' he snarled, seeing Grace was present in the flesh and not part of a dream. He sat up quickly, clutching his reeling head. Although he could have bribed a prison warder to smuggle him in some alcohol he had been determined not to risk losing a single day of his remission, so it had been well over a year since a drop of anything stronger than insipid tea had passed his lips. 'Do they just walk into people's houses where you come from? Thought your sort had more manners,' he went on sarcastically, wetting his dry lips and coughing to clear his arid throat. Lifting his cigarettes and lighter up off the floor, he lit up, and still the woman hadn't explained or defended her intrusion. He growled impatiently, 'Well, what the hell do you want?'

'I thought you might need some more help,' Grace said lightly, unperturbed by his ill humour.

'What sort of help?' he grunted, minding his language; the woman had been useful to him yesterday. He got to his feet, shaking his head to clear it.

Grace looked about the room in the critical way she had on entry the day before. Maggie Curnow had shown good taste in her choice of curtains and carpets and in the colour of the paintwork. The chunky modern lines of the three-piece suite, dresser, china display cabinet and sideboard suited the large square interior, but there was a hopeless higgledy-piggledy effect about where she had put the things; it offended Grace's perfectionist eye. 'Your furniture has been put in the wrong places. I suggest—'

'You cheeky cow!' The nerve of the bloody woman. He rubbed a hand over his stubbly jaw. Desperate for a drink of water to soothe his parched throat, he stalked groggily to the kitchen. Grace followed him. Splashing cold water over his face, he gulped down two cupfuls of water then turned to face her. Taking a deep draw on the cigarette, he said, 'If you can move the furniture by yourself, put it where you like.' He tapped his foot on the heap of clothes he had brought from the cottage and tossed on the floor. 'And you can wash that lot. They weren't ripped up and they're not dirty but they smell musty. There's a line in the garden and I expect Maggie has stowed some pegs away in here somewhere.'

'I'm not a washerwoman, Daniel,' Grace said demurely. She wouldn't know where to start.

'Well, Grace,' he scowled, 'you are if you stay here. If you want to help then you'll do as I say or you can bugger off right now.' He stared at her. He couldn't work out what she was doing here. Was it out of genuine Christian concern? Was she trying to prove something to the village? Was she after his body? He'd met women of her class before who liked 'a bit of rough'. He considered making a pass at her. She wasn't the sort of woman he usually lusted after. He preferred them young, fresh and innocent, with the energy they exuded when they felt the world was at their feet, qualities that had made him see Hannah as much more than his childhood friend. This woman was older than he was but he sensed she was untried, and she was attractive in a ripened kind of way. Goodness knew he'd gone without sex for a very long time.

He banished the thought before his loins burned and he got carried away against his better judgement; Grace Treloar was better kept on side and he didn't want to complicate things with her. Oh, yes, the good people of Porthellis would be expecting him to resume his old vices; he fully intended to, but not under their noses and certainly not in a way they'd easily notice – at first. Whatever this woman was up to, she wasn't easily rattled. She didn't take issue with his ingratitude, bad language or coarse behaviour.

'All right, I'll try to do it,' Grace said, careful to hide her abhorrence of undertaking such a menial task. The mustiness of the clothes was overriding the pleasanter smells of the new things in the house and the attractive scent of Daniel's masculine body. 'Have you a washing machine?'

'No, but there's a boiler beside the sink. Just put the clothes in the water, turn on the gas and it will heat up.' He patted an odd-looking contraption on the draining board. 'This is the wringer.'

Grace made a dismissive face at it. 'Did you enjoy the meal I cooked for you yesterday?' She was fishing for compliments.

'That dried-up mess you left in the oven?' he retorted. 'It was marginally

34

better than prison food, I suppose. I'm going upstairs to the bathroom.'
He ran his eyes over her clothes; a red and white spotted silk dress with
padded shoulders and high round collar, silk stockings and high heels
were hardly appropriate for housework. Shaking his head, he left her to it.

In the bathroom he stripped naked, scrubbed his skin, shaved, then not
satisfied with his first wash scrubbed himself again. He brushed his teeth
once, twice, three times, making his gums bleed, glad his sentence hadn't
been long enough to ruin his teeth which were white and even. He inspected
the length of his body in the mirror tiles; his muscles had not lost their
bulk but needed toughening up.

He put on new underpants and shirt. As he gazed at his pallid reflection
in the cabinet mirror, he was heavy-handed with the aftershave. His
grandfather had cared nothing for personal hygiene, Daniel had lived with
the stink of fish scales and guts all his working life, he'd breathed in the
putrefying odours of victims of drowning who had long floated in the
water, but nothing had been as vile as the overpowering stench of the
prison. On the way home from Exeter Prison he had stopped at a hotel
where he'd immersed himself in a bath of burning hot water, scrubbing
himself over and over with a bar of richly lathering soap with a non-
chemical smell and dried himself on thick clean towels. His next stop had
been a brothel, where he'd got a prostitute to check him for vermin, resisting
her usual services; he'd never resorted to a woman of her ilk before and
had seen enough sickness and disease in the last year and a quarter not to
take the risk.

Now he had things to do, things he would enjoy. First he must get the
Sunrise totally seaworthy. Fishing was a part of his life he craved and it
would give him cover while he acted as go-between for thieves and fences.
He had spent nearly all his savings on the house and he was eager to get
back to both his means of livelihood. Once he was settled in the old routines,
he would get on with his main reason for coming home to Porthellis:
revenge on some of its inhabitants, particularly Fred Jose, Hannah Penney
and her wretched husband.

Grace struggled with the washing while listening to Daniel moving
about upstairs. Several times she filled the large blue-rimmed bowl in the
sink with water heated from the range's back boiler and carried it across
to the small grey clothes boiler. Gingerly picking up the garments, she
threw them into the boiler then screamed in fright and indignation. She
had put too much water into the boiler and it overflowed and splashed her

feet, rudely breaking into her thoughts about what Daniel might like for breakfast.

'Damn,' she hissed under her breath, looking about for something to wipe up the spillage. She found a mop in a cupboard and wiped it over the green and yellow linoleum. She went back to the sitting room, mentally positioning the furniture in the best places. She would busy herself with something she would enjoy, knowing the reason she was really here was the excitement of putting herself into a position that was ill-advised and, if the more colourful rumours about Daniel were true, potentially dangerous. After years of being stifled of every freedom by her dour, uncompromising father and boring, old-fashioned mother, doing her duty as an unmarried daughter, she intended to indulge herself in anything that took her fancy, no matter what anyone else thought. And, she admitted shamelessly, she very much fancied the so-called villain who owned this house.

'You'll have to take the coloureds out of the boiler,' Daniel said sternly, striding into the room and putting his cigarettes and lighter into his trouser pocket.

'Why?'

'Because the colours will run and ruin the whites, and water that's too hot will shrivel up my silk shirt,' he said disdainfully. 'And,' he stressed unkindly, 'you've forgotten the soap flakes.'

It was her unsuccessful attempt at his laundry that finally made Grace redden. 'I'll see to it at once.'

As she moved past him, he shot out a hand and grabbed her shoulder. He had one or two things to straighten out before their relationship went any further. 'Haven't you heard about me? Whatever people are saying, I'll have you know it's all true. Apart from being a convicted criminal I've always lived on the wrong side of the law. I get involved in fights and I've had affairs with dozens of women – married women, girls just over the age of consent, they're all the same to me. I don't like anyone and I don't trust anyone. So what's your bloody game?'

'I don't play games, Daniel,' she said, unabashed that he was touching her, that she was looking straight into his blue eyes.

'Your uncle and aunt would be horrified to find you're here again and alone with me.'

'Why don't you let me worry about that?'

He let her go. 'All right, I will.'

'I was wondering,' she began, attempting to gain his confidence, 'what do you intend to do with the old cottage?'

'The building's sound. I'll fit it up and rent it. I need a new crew for my boat and they'll need somewhere to live. Get this straight, Grace, I don't need help in rehabilitation, if that's what you think. I know exactly what I'm going to do with my future.'

'I don't doubt anything you've said to me.' She smiled with warmth.

'Fine, as long as you know where you stand with me.'

'Can I make you something for breakfast?'

'No,' he disappointed her. 'I'll get something from the bakehouse. No one will dare to refuse me after the scene you pulled in Hamlyn Innis's shop. I'm off to take a long hard look at my boat then I'm going to arrange a memorial stone for my granddad. You get to the kitchen and rescue my washing.'

Hannah was chuckling as she left Janet's house. Jowan, Janet's son, had stopped her leaving sooner to question her about Lily, the under-housemaid at Roscarrock, and to ask her to try to find out if she might be interested in him. Jowan had recently dropped his hobby of astronomy for girls. Hannah liked Lily. Jowan could do no better than look in that quarter for a girlfriend.

She waved to Matt and Jeff as they unloaded their enviable catch of ray, ling, turbot, conger eel and skate for the merchant's men, and then turned towards Cliffside Cottage.

She caught her breath when she saw Daniel striding, head up, shoulders back, down the hill. He was eating a huge saffron bun and drinking from a bottle of Coca-Cola, looking intently at his lugger moored beside the *Misty*. He was obviously heading for the boat and even if she quickened her steps she couldn't avoid passing him.

As they got within a few feet of each other, she lifted her chin and looked straight at him. He eyed her coldly, said nothing, walked straight past her.

Hannah sighed heavily as she carried on her way. Outside her mother's cottage she watched as Daniel reached the busy scene on the quay. The fishermen, including Matt, stopped working for a moment and looked in his direction, as if they were frozen in time. From what she could see, none of them spoke to Daniel and he spoke to none of them. He leapt aboard the *Sunrise*, disappeared inside the cabin and the men returned to their work. If Daniel's return meant life in the village would always be as non-eventful, Hannah's heart would rest easy, but she knew as certainly as the tide went in and out twice a day that it wasn't going to be like that.

Chapter 4

Hannah preferred to stay at home when Matt was not at sea, but if she missed one of her weekly visits to Roscarrock, Feena Opie would get Greg or Patrick Opie to drive her to Seaview Cottage. Mrs Penney would give her a polite but cool reception, Prim or Janet would invariably turn up, and it usually led to sarcasm and back-biting. Hannah was in no mood for such behaviour today, but nor was she looking forward to fending off her real mother's continual interference in the way she was bringing up Nathan. Nevertheless, as the house came into view, she felt the same delight as on her first excursion here for the interview as housekeeper.

A light shower of rain in the early hours had given the earth a fresh healthy smell. White, yellow and pink rhododendrons and azaleas in deeper hues lined the drive, and the gentle scent of magnolia wafted over her. The flowering trees and shrubs had been planted by Patrick to give pleasure to all the senses. Somewhere in the woods a pigeon cooed and a blackbird sang up high in the giant oak tree in the middle of the lawn. Roscarrock never failed to weave its magic in Hannah's heart and although she loved her life in the fishing village, a small part of her wished she could live here, too.

Inside, the house had recently been given a fresh coat of paint throughout. The vestibule and hall and the high archway which separated them, and the intricately carved doors of the drawing room, dining room and the study-cum-library were pristine white. It gave the perfect backdrop to the Georgian and Victorian furniture and the grandfather clock. The plaster picture bays, which displayed many portraits in richly carved frames, were now a warm pink, contrasting tastefully with the thick, plum-coloured carpeting. Hannah carried Nathan up the first short flight of wide stairs to the exquisite Queen Anne window on the large square landing. She looked down on the back courtyard of the house and saw

39

Patrick Opie by the stable, pushing a wheelbarrow piled high with manure. She turned and climbed the next flight of eight steps.

She made her way along the corridor to Feena Opie's suite, hurrying past the room with a sea view that the lady had insisted she have when she worked here. It held bad memories for her. It was in there that she had read Feena Opie's journal, left on her bed by a spiteful nurse, and had learned that her employer was her mother. And it was on that bed that Daniel had thrown her and nearly raped her.

Feena had watched Hannah arrive from her balcony but was now seated in her wheelchair. Pogo, her little Pomeranian dog, was napping on a chair and jumped down to yap excitedly about Hannah's feet when she entered. Feena greeted Hannah warmly. She had got Lily to lay out some toys on a blanket near her feet and held out her arms for Nathan.

'Hello, my sweet darling.' She kissed his pink chubby cheeks. 'Have you come to see me?' She tickled his nose. 'Hannah, sit down, dear. I want to have a serious discussion with you.'

'Oh, yes?' Hannah sat with Pogo on her lap, absentmindedly caressing his silky ears. She hoped she wasn't about to be pressed with another of Feena's aspirations for Nathan's future. Last week she had been forced to stress that she and Matt had no intention of sending Nathan away to boarding school when he was seven years old. It was difficult arguing with a lady who gave orders rather than suggestions. 'Is something the matter?' she asked cautiously.

'It's about what Nathan will call me when he's learned to talk,' Feena said, happily allowing the baby to tug on the big yellow beads around her neck. 'We can't allow the truth to slip out, there would be a dreadful scandal, but I am his grandmother. I don't want him to call me Mrs Opie, it would create a barrier between us. Come to that, there's the question of what you call me, Hannah. You refer to me as Mrs Opie in company, which is the proper thing to do, but when we're alone you don't call me anything.'

'I hadn't noticed,' Hannah fibbed. After she'd recovered from the shock of finding out Feena was her real mother, she hadn't had a clue what to call her. 'Have you any suggestions?'

Feena smiled as if she was pleased with herself. 'My grandmother was also called Feena and was known affectionately by all the family as Bubsie. We can train Nathan to call me that. I don't suppose you can call me Mother, even in private. Someone might overhear. And you think of Prim as that,' she added rather sourly. 'People take it for granted that I grew fond of you when you worked here so when Nathan has got used to my name, you can call me Bubsie too. I think it's a splendid idea.'

Hannah agreed to the suggestion but privately thought the chosen name of Bubsie was ridiculous.

'That's settled then.' Feena gently squeezed Nathan who was now prodding the tiny buttons that ran from below her elbow to her wrist on her wool-jersey sleeve. She turned her inscrutable blue eyes on Hannah. Hannah was gazing vacantly at a porcelain shepherdess on the mantelpiece. 'You seem preoccupied today, my dear. Did Matt do poorly at sea?' Feena already knew the answer. She kept abreast of all Matt's work movements and, unknown to Hannah, got Patrick Opie to check that all of Porthellis's boats were safely home at the end of each work period.

'The *Misty* did very well, actually,' Hannah replied, returning to the present. 'Do you remember Daniel Kittow?'

'Of course. The man who was sent to prison. What about him?'

'He's been released and he returned home yesterday. As if that wasn't bad enough, it appears that the new house built just along the street from us belongs to him.'

'I don't like that,' Feena frowned. She knew Daniel had been furious after Hannah had spurned him. 'I've heard more about that young man from the Chief Constable. He would have been sent to prison years ago and for a much longer sentence if the police had managed to get the evidence against him. Don't worry, Hannah. I'm sure the police will keep an eye on him.'

'Daniel's too clever to be caught out easily. He told me he didn't steal from the village and I believe that's the truth. I pity the person responsible when Daniel gets hold of him.'

Feena looked at Hannah in surprise; she had not mentioned this before. 'Who do you think stole from the villagers?'

'A fisherman called Fred Jose. I think he hid the goods in the Kittow cottage and informed the police to get even with Daniel for mocking him. Soon after Daniel went to prison, Fred and his father persuaded my uncle Terence Spargo and his son Morley to ask old Rufus Kittow to sell them his and Daniel's share of the *Sunrise*. Rufus refused and bought them out instead. Only Daniel could have had that sort of money. I think Fred was too scared to fish with Daniel again.'

Nathan was getting restless and Feena bent over to put him on the blanket with the toys. 'Who would guess all that was going on in what seems like a sleepy little village?' she said lightly although her comment did not match what was running through her mind. 'Would you like to ring for tea, dear?'

'I'll pop down to the kitchen and order it,' Hannah said, knowing Feena would like some time alone with her grandson and it would give her the opportunity to speak to Lily. She put Pogo on his chair and then stopped at the door. 'Thinking about Daniel, I've forgotten to ask about Leah and Greg. Have you heard from them since they went on honeymoon?'

'Greg telephoned from Paris this morning,' Feena smiled up from giving Nathan a wooden soldier which he promptly put in his mouth. 'He said they're having a wonderful time. After Paris they're going on to Scotland. I think I'll arrange a small dinner party to welcome them home. I shall invite Grace Treloar, I found her an interesting woman, but not her insufferable aunt. Matt's got a passable suit. It won't put him to too much trouble to escort you.' She looked at Hannah closely. 'Your parents are welcome too, to see their daughter settle into her new home.'

'I doubt if Mother will come.' Hannah frowned, realizing that Leah was going to have to divide her life in future.

'Do ask your father. I don't want to be accused of excluding them. This will be Leah's home as much as Greg's.'

Hannah loved dining at Roscarrock. She didn't have an evening gown but she would wear the dress she'd worn at Leah's wedding.

Feena seemed to read her thoughts. 'I've ordered an evening dress for you from my local dressmaker,' she said. 'It's on my bed. You can try it on before you leave. If it needs slight alteration it won't take a minute for an accomplished needlewoman like yourself.'

'Thank you.' Hannah smiled, knowing it was useless to argue, and she did rather like being spoiled by Feena who had always been good to her.

In the kitchen she found Lily with Patrick Opie and Angie Miller, the middle-aged, thickly built housemaid, drinking tea at the long table.

'Ah, here she is,' Patrick said, springing to his feet. 'We've kept the kettle simmering for you, Hannah. We all want to see our little poppit before you leave.' Having returned from Africa, widowed, homeless and penniless many years ago, he lived at Roscarrock as part gentleman, part servant, and often took tea with the staff in the kitchen. He often did the cooking, something he excelled at. Hannah wasn't surprised to see him still in his baggy gardening clothes. He had a passion for gardening and produced the best vegetables and flowerbeds for miles around, spending more time outside than inside the grand old house.

'Thank you, Mr Patrick,' Hannah said.

Lily prepared the tea tray. Angie, who was painfully shy, blushed as she inquired, 'How is young Nathan, Mrs Penney?'

'He's very well, thank you, Angie. Eats like a horse and is very active. I'll make sure you get to hold him before I go,' she said, knowing Angie would never pluck up the courage to ask.

'Put plenty of my shortbread on the tray, Lily,' Patrick beamed. 'I'm sure the little man would like to nibble on one.'

'He'll love that.' Hannah smiled affectionately at him. 'You'll all be a bit busier when Mr Greg and Leah come back.'

'We're looking forward to it,' Lily said brightly as she bustled about energetically. 'Be some changes round here then. Miss Benson says she's going to give us new instructions. Me and Angie have started getting the big double bedroom ready. It'll be nice having someone round here my own age but Miss Benson says I must remember that Miss Leah will be Mrs Opie Junior and I mustn't be familiar with her no more.' Lily was a chatterbox but closed her mouth the moment the door leading to the servants' hall was opened.

A woman appeared, small in stature with short straight greying hair pulled back at the brow with a hair grip, dressed in a severely styled bottle-green dress and flat lace-up shoes. This was Miss Benson. She had been Roscarrock's housekeeper before Hannah, and had left to nurse her elderly father. He had died at the same time Hannah had married and Mrs Opie had been delighted to have the efficient Miss Benson back in her employ. Aged about fifty, she had a nondescript, forgettable face and tended to be dour and uncommunicative unless there was a staff or household concern to be dealt with.

'Good afternoon, Mrs Penney,' she said politely. 'Can I help you?'

Hannah knew that as Mrs Opie's visitor, and an important one by the way Mrs Opie treated her, as well as sister to Mr Greg's bride, Miss Benson did not approve of her being in the kitchen. 'Lily is making tea for me and Mrs Opie,' she explained humbly, then grinned mischievously at Patrick who reciprocated under the cover of pretending to scratch his nose.

'Lily will carry it upstairs for you,' Miss Benson stressed. She wouldn't countenance anyone not being kept to their rightful duties.

'Of course,' Hannah replied, thinking proudly that the house had been run just as well under her more relaxed supervision. She led the way up the narrow stone servants' stairs.

'Mrs Penney,' Lily said under her breath, glancing round first to make sure Miss Benson had not followed them, 'do you see much of your cousin?'

'Would that be my cousin Jowan?' Hannah said knowingly as they mounted the main staircase together.

'Yes, that's the one,' Lily said, unable to keep her eagerness out of her broad accent. Her young, slightly chubby face turned scarlet, accentuating the sprinkling of dark freckles across the bridge of her nose. She concentrated on not rattling the things on the tray. 'Well, I was wond'ring if he's got a girlfriend.'

'I don't think he has,' Hannah teased.

Lily swallowed hard. ''Tis an awful liberty I know but do you think you could find out? I mean—'

'Let me put you out of your agony, Lily,' Hannah laughed kindly. 'Jowan hasn't got a girlfriend and he was asking me questions about you only this morning. You're a Methodist, aren't you? Why don't you come to chapel on Sunday and I'll make sure you get the chance to talk to each other.'

'You'd really do that, Mrs Penney? You don't mind?'

'Of course not. I'm very fond of Jowan, he's more like a brother to me than a cousin and I think you'd be well suited. No need to get dressed up or anything. Jowan doesn't like people who put on airs and graces.'

'Oh, thank you, Mrs Penney, and thank you for the advice. I'll be down in the village on Sunday bright and early.'

Hannah opened the door to Feena's suite and Lily bounced in with the tea tray and out again in the same fashion. Feena was winding up a jack-in-a-box for Nathan but she watched Hannah pour the tea. 'Lily looked animated. Were you discussing anything interesting?'

'She met my cousin Jowan at the wedding reception and they hit it off straightaway,' Hannah answered; she didn't mind Feena's prying most of the time. She put Feena's cup and saucer on a table where Nathan couldn't reach it. 'I've been doing a bit of matchmaking. You don't mind if they walk out together, do you?'

'Well, I don't want you robbing me of my staff.' Feena tapped Hannah's wrist in mock chiding.

'You'll never lose Patrick, Angie or Miss Benson,' Hannah pointed out laughing.

Feena suddenly gripped her hand tightly. 'I don't care about anyone as long as I never lose you or Nathan, Hannah.'

Chapter 5

Hannah and Grace had been walking over the cliff for nearly two hours. They were not moving at a fast pace and Grace stopped often to look through her field glasses at small boats and white-sailed yachts in the dark blue waters of Veryan Bay, at Dodman Point rearing out in the sea behind them, over the land to where Caerhays church and a plantation of trees stood out on the horizon. It was hot under the blazing sun; the south-westerly breeze was bringing humidity with it.

They were now scaling the steep winding climb up from the tiny hamlet of Portholland. Hannah glanced behind her to see if Grace was tiring but she was clambering up the narrow rocky path with the loose, easy movements of a man.

'Shall we find a spot to take a drink when we reach the top?' Hannah said, pausing beside some wild apple trees.

Grace took off her sunglasses, pushed back her straw hat and wiped perspiration from her brow. 'That would be wise on a hot day like this. It's like summer. Let's find a place where the breeze will cool us down.'

It was a hilly walk along the cliff top, so steep and narrow in parts they had to turn their feet at an awkward sideways angle to keep their balance. In one place the ground had given way at a burrow and they gripped the high bank to get past. They leapt over a tinkling stream. Brambles, gorse, fern and the windswept landward-veering trees often hid the sea from view. They carried on until the cliff dropped into a hollow and bare rock left the sea naked to their eyes. A strong breeze cooled their bare arms and their lower legs exposed by their shorts.

Hannah sat down on a grassy tussock, pointing out a similar one to Grace. They took their bags off their backs, Hannah's an old crib bag of Matt's, Grace's a smart sturdy haversack.

'You must say when you want to turn back, Hannah,' Grace said, pouring herself lemonade and passing the bottle. 'I mustn't be selfish and forget you have a family to care for.'

'There's no hurry. Matt's at sea and Aunty Janet won't like it if I pick up Nathan too soon.' Hannah smiled. 'And Mrs Penney will be glad to have the house to herself for a while.'

'I suppose this must be a welcome break for you,' Grace observed. 'You seem to get on well with your mother-in-law. That's good as you live in her house.'

'It's Matt's house actually. His father left it to him. But I do get on well with Mrs Penney. I'm happy to leave the house as she's always had it. As Matt says, our turn will come if we want to make changes. Would you like one of these shortbread biscuits? Mr Patrick at Roscarrock made them.'

'Thank you. Mmmm, delicious. It's curious how some people do things that don't appear to suit them.'

'Oh, in what way?'

'Well, Patrick Opie doesn't seem the sort to be good at baking and you, if I may say so, don't look at all like a seamstress. You seem the outdoor type.'

'I am. I would have liked to work on the boats but that of course isn't allowed, it's entirely a man's domain.' Hannah gazed dreamily at the sea. 'I used to live with my aunt and she set her heart on me following her trade. Who else were you thinking of?'

'On, no one really,' Grace replied quickly, remembering there were bad feelings between Hannah and the man she had been thinking about. 'I was stopped from doing what I wanted to do too, by my father. I wanted to go to university and become a doctor. He wouldn't let me do either, no matter how much I begged him. As far as he was concerned, women were meant only to be wives, mothers or servants. He was most disappointed in me for not trotting off dutifully and getting married to provide him with grandchildren. Every time we sat down to dinner there seemed to be some young man, usually squirming with embarrassment, put there for me to consider. I didn't meet anyone I really liked and domesticity has never been attractive to me. I've noticed the way you and Matt look at each other,' she went on, talking in the easy manner the two women had fallen into. 'If I met a man who moved me in the same way . . .'

'You'd willingly change your name,' Hannah finished for her.

'Yes.' Grace turned her face, afraid Hannah would read her thoughts. Out in the sea was a huge lump of land called Shag Rock and through her field glasses she watched a group of the distinctive crested birds that had colonized the rock and given it its name. She listened to the wash of the sea, loud, heavy, constant. At the bottom of the cliff the rock reached out in long fat fingers, its submerged depths lurking in greenish-white shadows. Two gulls stood on the orange-coloured lichened top of the boulder directly below them, then flew down and bobbed about on the water. 'I think the bay is particularly beautiful. I do envy you living here all your life. My mother wouldn't leave her birthplace. My father's family was Cornish but there's no one left here now except for Aunt Adela. You're lucky coming from a large family. I saw your older brother the other day. I hope you don't mind me asking, but was he born with his condition?'

'No, Josh was like any other man until two years ago.' Now Hannah looked away. 'He had an accident.'

'I'm sorry.'

Hannah fell quiet, eating shortbread biscuits and sipping lemonade. It was the talk of the village that Grace had been to Daniel's new house again and again. There were many who had warned her that an association with him would lead to disaster but she had assured them that it was only out of charity that she was bothering with him. Hannah thought Grace foolish but considered it none of her business. But now that their friendship was becoming established, should she tell her that Daniel had been involved the night Josh had received the brain damage that turned him into an imbecile? It was a family secret that her other brother, Mitch, had beaten Josh into his idiotic state for attacking his bride-to-be. That was no concern of Grace's, but should she tell her that Viv had been seduced by Daniel, that he'd forced the sixteen-year-old girl to seek an abortion and when she couldn't go through with it he had cruelly told her to keep out of his life? Daniel had stopped Josh from doing his worst to Viv, but he was still responsible for the condition that had made her stepfather throw her out on the street and turn to Mitch. If Grace knew this, would she give up her quest, her belief that Daniel deserved a second chance? Grace was not naive, stupid or easily fooled, Hannah guessed. She sensed Grace had a slightly wicked sense of humour; perhaps she was amusing herself and enjoyed shocking the villagers. Hannah decided Grace was old enough and sensible enough to look after herself. And if Daniel's good looks were what was attracting Grace to him, she was probably a lost cause anyway and criticism would only send her rushing more eagerly into his

49

arms. She could never mention Daniel's attack on herself to Grace, it was far too personal.

Grace was thinking about Daniel again. She was curious to know why there was animosity between him and Hannah. Aunt Adela had told her that Daniel and Matt Penney had once been partners on the abandoned boat and had publicly fought over Hannah in the chapel forecourt. Strange that Hannah hadn't added her voice to the warnings about Daniel.

She couldn't stop herself from asking, 'Why do you hate Daniel Kittow?'

Hannah was shocked at the sudden question. She packed up the crib bag. 'He's evil.'

'That's a rather simplistic statement, isn't it? I can't agree with it,' Grace returned shortly, standing up so she could see Hannah's face more clearly.

'It's the truth,' Hannah said rather tartly, looking at her squarely. 'No one has been closer to Daniel than me. You should believe what people are telling you about him.'

A shaft of cold air blew up from the sea, sweeping away with it the close friendship that had been forming between the women. Hannah was vexed at Grace's superior tone. Grace felt jealous that Hannah should have been so close to Daniel.

'We'll walk on to Portloe, the next village, then turn back,' Hannah said. 'You can see Nare Head from here, the other end of Veryan Bay. It's a clear day, soon you'll be able to make out Falmouth on the horizon.'

'Really? How interesting.'

They went on their way, talking like a tour guide and holidaymaker.

Mrs Skewes hastened to her husband's study that afternoon. 'David, can you leave what you're doing? I want to talk about Grace again. I've just been down to the village and Miss Peters told me that Grace is still seeing Daniel Kittow, after all we've said to her. What shall we do?'

The Reverend Skewes abandoned his sermon. 'I don't think there is anything we can do, Adela. Grace is infatuated with the man. The warnings she's received have only served to make him more attractive to her. If we continue to berate her I fear she'll move out. Then she'll be entirely at Kittow's mercy. If your brother hadn't been so strict with her she wouldn't be letting her freedom go to her head now. We must hope and pray she won't let him take things to the extreme. If he hurts her, we'll be here to pick up the pieces.'

'But she's making a laughing stock of us, David. People are saying we shouldn't allow it.'

'None of us are immune to foolishness, Adela. We're setting an example, standing by Grace and loving her no matter what she does.'

'I suppose so.' Mrs Skewes wrung her hands. 'But it's terrible to think she might throw her future and happiness away on that odious man.'

Lily walked to chapel that Sunday and, forewarned by Hannah, Jowan met her on the forecourt. Shyly and awkwardly he invited her to sit next to him for the service.

After the service, Janet invited Lily to stay for dinner. She approved of her son's choice.

'Thank you, Mrs Rouse,' Lily said, blushing prettily. 'I'm afraid I'm expected back at Roscarrock very soon.'

'Well, perhaps another time. Jowan will walk you part of the way home.' It was settled, as far as both Janet and the villagers were concerned. Jowan and Lily were officially walking out together.

Hannah watched smiling as Jowan stuck out his arm, Lily put hers through it and the young couple walked away.

'Thank you, Hannah,' Janet said.

'What for?' Matt asked, emerging from the chapel with Nathan wriggling in his arms.

'She knows,' Janet said in the mysterious way women sometimes have of communicating.

Matt grinned and kissed Hannah's cheeks. 'What have you been up to?' He laughed when she explained. 'Think she'll make a fisherman's wife?'

'Yes, of course.'

Nathan held out his arms to Hannah and she took him from Matt. Grace passed them, offering a brief good morning and going straight to the Manse.

'That didn't seem very friendly,' Matt observed. 'You haven't fallen out, have you?'

'We didn't hit it off as well as I'd hoped.'

'Why not? Is she a snob?'

'No, not at all. She's still seeing Daniel. It's put a barrier between us.'

Matt slipped his arm round her waist and led her up the hill. 'It's just as well then. I don't want you involved with him in any way at all.'

Clicking heels were heard behind them and a hand touched Hannah's shoulder. 'Please wait a moment,' Mrs Skewes puffed, her plain face pinched and anxious. 'Mr Skewes said I shouldn't but I must ask a favour of you, Hannah. You see, I'm desperately worried about Grace. She won't listen to me. I don't know what to do.'

'About what?' Matt asked, frowning at what he saw as another piece of female illogicality.

'I think I know,' Hannah said to Mrs Skewes. 'You're worried about Grace seeing Daniel Kittow. I'm afraid it would be a waste of time me saying anything to her. I've told her Daniel is evil but she didn't believe me. I'm sorry. You'll just have to hope she'll tire of him or go home to Kent.'

'Or wait for him to chuck her over,' Matt said bluntly.

'You shouldn't have said that,' Hannah remonstrated with Matt as they walked on. 'Mrs Skewes was thunderstruck.'

Matt was unrepentant. 'She might as well brace herself for the inevitable. That man is spreading poison through the village, you can smell it, breathe it.'

It wasn't like Matt to be melodramatic, but Hannah couldn't disagree with him.

Poison and evil influences were far from the minds of Jowan and Lily as they walked towards Roscarrock. At Turn-A-Penny Lane, Lily stopped and looked at Jowan. 'You'd better go back for your dinner now,' she said reluctantly.

'When do you next have time off?' Jowan asked, his chest thrust out confidently now that the initial part of the courtship was over.

'Wednesday afternoon,' she answered, looking coyly at the ground.

'Oh.' His fresh face creased in disappointment. 'I'll be at sea then, unless the weather takes a bad turn.'

'I can get away on Saturday evening.'

'That should be all right. Would you like me to meet you at the gates of Roscarrock? At seven o'clock? I'll think of something we can do.'

'I'd love to.' Lily looked modestly over his shoulder.

Jowan shuffled his feet on the dusty lane, then bending forward quickly he put a soft peck on her cheek and turned for home, whistling cheerfully.

Lily watched him until he was out of sight then skipped along like a happy little girl. She was conjuring up a vision of standing in the Rouses' doorway, waving goodbye to Jowan as his boat put to sea; Mrs Rouse herself.

When she reached Roscarrock's tall wrought-iron gates, a smartly dressed man was there, staring at them. 'Good morning,' she chirped gaily. 'Can I help you, sir?'

He turned and took off his hat, uncovering his thick red hair. Daniel gazed down on Lily, his eyes widening in pleasure at what he saw. She was just his type, exactly what he needed. He liked making love outside.

'Good afternoon,' he replied in a soft lazy drawl. 'I was just curious to see the pair of gates here. I haven't been about locally for several months and they weren't here then.'

Lily was puzzled. He looked a bit like a gentleman, stood straight and confident as if he was someone of importance, but his voice and the ruggedness of his face suggested a working man. 'Mrs Opie had them put up just before last Christmas. I think they're very grand.'

'I agree with you, Miss . . .?' He raised a quizzical eyebrow.

'Miss Lily Andrews,' she said with a nervous giggle.

'You have a connection with Roscarrock, Miss Andrews?'

'I work there, as under-housemaid.' She blushed harder under his piercing gaze than she had at her meeting with Jowan earlier this morning. He was so very good-looking, with an appealing sternness about him, like the heros in the romantic books she read in her room. 'Well, I must run along or I'll be late helping with luncheon.'

Daniel didn't move. It looked as if he wouldn't be able to talk her into taking a walk along the cliff with him now, but maybe another time. 'I wouldn't have taken you for a servant. You're not from Porthellis, are you?'

'No, from Gorran Haven. Do you know it?'

'I've been there once or twice. I've just walked the cliff path from Porthellis and I'm going back by the road.' He glanced up at the pale blue sky, scattered with light clouds. 'It's a lovely day to be outside stretching your legs.'

'Yes, it is. Listen, I don't mean to be rude but I really must go.'

'Perhaps I could ask you to go for a walk with me some time, Lily.'

'Oh, no,' and as his face darkened she explained quickly, 'You see I have a boyfriend. He lives in Porthellis. He's a fisherman, his name's Jowan Rouse. You might know him.'

'I was only thinking of a little company, Lily,' Daniel said, moving closer so he towered over her. 'I'm sure he wouldn't mind that.'

Lily was out of her depth here. The stranger was staring at her. He might be a friend of the Opies and she didn't want to offend them. Desperation made her add to her excuse. 'But his cousin Mrs Penney wouldn't like it. She brought us together and she comes to Roscarrock ever such a lot and Mrs Opie treats her like one of the family and if Mrs Penney thought I was being forward with men and told Mrs Opie, I could be dismissed.' She finally stopped for breath, close to tears, fearing she might have upset someone of importance.

'I completely understand,' Daniel said in a polite voice. 'I won't keep you any longer.' He moved aside and opened the gates for her.

Lily rushed through them and ran halfway down the drive before stopping and trying to calm herself. She didn't know who the man was but thought it best not to mention him to anyone.

Daniel strolled along the way she had come from Porthellis. He looked casual, a man enjoying the fresh air and quiet lane, but his brain was busy turning over everything the girl had said. He had assumed that Mrs Opie would have wanted nothing more to do with Hannah when she learned she was pregnant and must marry quickly. How very strange that Hannah went often to Roscarrock. Her shy little sister might have married the arrogant grandson, but that wasn't what Lily had meant when she said Hannah was treated like one of the family. He'd seek Lily Andrews out again, but not for his original reason. He wanted to know what was going on at Roscarrock.

At the end of the following week Hannah was awakened in the early hours by the sound of loud boots marching down the street. It sounded as if an army was on the move. She met the owners of the boots a little later on when she went outside to fetch milk from Farmer Teague's horsedrawn cart. A group of men spilled out of the new house. Daniel was striding in front of them.

Hannah couldn't help staring at them, her jaw sagging. There were four strangers, all hard and mean looking, roughly dressed, generally unkempt. One was of huge proportions, a human barn door of solid muscle, his head too large for the rest of him, hands like sledgehammers. The breath caught in Hannah's throat. Had Daniel invited demons into the village?

'Mornin', m'dear,' a toothless man with a flat nose and torn ear roared raucously at her, encouraging his companions to make lewd noises with him. 'You look like you've never seen a stranger in yer life before. Give 'ee a 'and with that milk can, shall I? A pretty maid like you shouldn't—'

'Shut up!' Daniel snapped. 'Don't talk to her.' He turned on all the men. 'I don't want any of you talking to her, not ever, understand?'

The huge man mumbled, 'Yes, Skipper,' and his companions echoed his words.

A shiver ran up Hannah's spine. Daniel was clearly in charge of this band of rogues. What on earth was he up to? She forgot the milk and scampered back to the door. Daniel swept his eyes over her, possessively, she felt, as if he was telling her that if anyone was going to insult her or be familiar with her it would be him.

'Rum-looking lot,' Henry Teague said, coming for her milk can.

'What?'

'I'm not surprised you ran for cover, Hannah. They gave me the jitters too. What d'you think they're doing with young Kittow?'

'I hate to think.' She watched as a woman, her face concealed under a large headscarf, slipped inside the new house. It was Nan Trebilcock, an attractive widow in her early forties, beguiled by the generous amount of money Daniel was rumoured to be paying her as cleaning woman. Working for Daniel was harming her reputation but people remembered she had been a 'flighty piece' before her marriage. She was now shunned by some, treated with suspicion by others, considered unwise by the most charitable and pumped for information about Daniel Kittow, his habits, his home, by the nosiest. Henry Teague handed Hannah her milk. She thanked him and went inside quickly.

The news spread round the village faster than a gorse fire on a dry summer's day. Daniel Kittow had installed the four ruffians in his old cottage. A workman and his son from St Austell had been renovating the interior and two of the men living at the cottage were put to work on the exterior, whitewashing the walls, repairing the slate roof, painting the doors, while the other two worked on the boat with Daniel. Their conversation made it clear that the four outsiders were to be the *Sunrise*'s new crew.

Hannah was worried about Prim having these rough men as next-door neighbours and she called on her later in the morning. She winced at the bad language passing between the two men whitewashing the cottage. Neither of them spoke to her but she felt some of their talk was meant for her ears.

'What d'ya think of this place then, Brinley? Think we'll get much fun out of it?'

It was the toothless, torn-eared man who had spoken and Hannah was surprised that the gentle sounding name of Brinley belonged to the giant.

He threw back his thick bull neck and laughed loudly. 'Skipper says we can, Eric.'

'We'll drop in the pub later on, wet our whistles,' Eric guffawed, slapping whitewash about with abandon, 'after we've seen what the women are like. So far they don't look bad.' He made a crude gesture. 'Skipper said most of 'em are ready 'n' willing and he should know.'

'Watch where you're sloshing that bleddy whitewash,' Brinley boomed at him. 'Skipper said he wants a proper job done. We'll forget the women till the work's done. I want t'get this over and help on the boat.'

Eric howled with laughter. 'The day you forget women, you bleddy old goat, will be the day you turn up yer toes.'

'Have you heard them out there?' Hannah demanded from Prim the moment she was in the shabby dark kitchen where not one thing had been changed or updated since her childhood expulsion; there had been no money for improvements. She was burning with indignation. 'They've got the foulest mouths I've ever heard. To think he's brought those creatures to live next door to you. Where's Josh? They had just better not tease him. I'm not bringing Nathan here while they're about. Goodness knows what Matt will say.'

'Calm down, Hannah,' Prim said, 'or you'll make my bread drop. There's a postcard from Leah on the mantelpiece. Anyway, I'm used to living with swearing inside this house with your father, and outside with having old Rufus next door for so many years. That huge fellow mended my washing line just now and he said he'll cut down all my brambles when he's got a spare minute. They probably aren't as bad as they look.'

'Mother!' Hannah looked at Prim as if she was a turncoat. She took the bowl of dough from Prim and put it on top of the oven to prove, covered it with a tea towel then watched with mounting anger as Prim poured out tea in two extra mugs. 'Mother!'

'I have to live next to 'em,' Prim said quietly. 'Most of the time it's just me and Josh here. When your father's not working he spends most of his time with Maggie Curnow. I'd rather be on friendly terms with them than at loggerheads.'

Hannah declined to help Prim carry the mugs of tea out to the men and sat down grumpily at the table. Her mother couldn't see it but she was certain that Daniel was going to pick the village up in his fist and shake it to its foundations.

Chapter 6

'Your crew are making a frightful noise again, Daniel,' Grace said, holding out the cherry cake she had bought at the bakehouse to him. Jealous of Nan Trebilcock becoming his cleaning woman she was at the new house more often than before, trying to appear useful to him.

'None of your business,' he replied bluntly. He smiled to himself as he thought about what Brinley and the others were currently up to. There was no work for them to do this afternoon and he had told them to make a nuisance of themselves in the village. He despised its inhabitants. They had shown no forgiveness over the way he had tried to pitch Matt Penney into the harbour, after Matt had been missing at sea for several hours and believed dead; the day of his arrest when Hannah had publicly humiliated him as she'd protected Penney from him. Daniel was deliberately appearing to live a faultless life in Porthellis but through his crew he'd show these self-righteous people he had no pity. He was on his way out but glanced at the cake and said harshly, 'I don't like boughten cake.'

'Well, never mind, I'll give it to Aunt Adela.'

Daniel shook his head wryly. He liked Grace's responses; she never let him put her down. 'I'm about to go to Mevagissey to buy some new oilers. Fancy driving me there?'

'I'd love to,' she smiled enthusiastically. 'Just give me a minute to get rid of this cake.'

He took it from her. 'Leave it here. I daresay I can force down a few crumbs later.'

Aunt Adela tutted in disapproval as they got into Grace's car outside the Manse, but Grace didn't care. To show Daniel she wasn't stilted in any way she drove far too fast for safety along the lanes. They reached Mevagissey unscathed, however, and knowing Daniel would prefer to be alone among the fishing fraternity while he visited a chandlery, she spent time in a tea shop. On the way back she drove slowly, wanting to spend as much time alone with him as possible.

Daniel was quiet. Grace would have been pleased if she knew he was thinking about her. He had appreciated her thoughtfulness at the fishing port, and because she didn't chatter unnecessarily he rather enjoyed her company. Keeping her around was one way of getting back at Hannah; it had spoiled their friendship, and he loved the way it shocked the villagers. He trusted Grace, he was sure she would prove useful in looking after his interests at Porthellis when he wasn't there.

He followed the actions of her trousered legs on the clutch and accelerator. Her perfume was strong and feminine in the confines of the car. Her complexion glowed, her eyes sparkled, and she looked younger than her thirty-three years. In his arrogance he knew it was himself who was having this positive effect on her. She probably thought she was in love with him. He didn't doubt that with a little persuasion she would go to bed with him. At times he had touched her innocently and she'd liked it. He had liked it. When they got back a slice of the cherry cake and a large helping of Grace would round off the little outing nicely. But as they neared Porthellis he decided against it, still considering it best to keep his sexual encounters – and he had been making up for lost time – out of the village.

As they pulled up outside the Manse he thanked Grace for the use of her car and insisted on going home alone. He was still thinking about her.

Feena sent Patrick to collect Hannah, Matt and Jeff for Leah and Greg's homecoming dinner. Hannah was as excited as a child when they drew up outside Roscarrock, hopping out of the car, running up the steps and into the house. She rushed into the drawing room and there was Leah, looking radiant after her four-week honeymoon.

Leah sprang up from the sofa and they hugged. 'It's so good to see you.' Hannah clasped her hands. 'You look superb. You must have had a wonderful time.'

'Of course she did. Don't I get a welcome?' Greg said, feigning a small, lost voice. He looked most attractive in his dinner jacket and black tie. He kissed Hannah's cheek. She kissed him back. 'How's Nathan? Bet he's grown like a weed since we last saw him.'

'He has, he's walking around holding on to the furniture and has his hands in everything,' she replied proudly. 'It's so good to have you both home, Greg.'

'She's been like a cat on hot bricks all day,' Matt said, kissing Leah and shaking Greg's hand. 'Anyone would think she hadn't seen Leah for ten years. Glad to see you enjoyed your honeymoon.'

'It was the greatest success,' Greg said, winding his arms round Leah's tiny waist. 'I've got the loveliest bride in the world. It's a good thing Patrick's gone back to Porthellis to collect Miss Treloar or he'd be terribly embarrassed by all this romantic talk.' He started to serve drinks. 'Grandmother will be down in a minute. Good evening, Mr Spargo. I'm pleased you could come.'

'Dad!' Leah ran to Jeff. Engulfed in his big arms, her small pink face pressed against his chest, the image of a mature woman left her and Hannah was reminded of how childlike she was. 'Why didn't Mum come?'

'You know your mother, my handsome,' Jeff said. 'She never was one for socializing.'

Greg was studying Hannah. 'That's a lovely frock you're wearing, Hannah.'

'Thank you.' She gave a pert curtsy. 'Mrs Opie had it made for me.'

Matt frowned. He did not like the way Feena showered Hannah with gifts but looking at her now, he realized with a familiar longing how beautiful and desirable she was in the low-backed, full-length satin gown that was closely moulded to her body. Most women wore their hair short and he was glad Hannah kept hers shoulder length. Whenever he could he brushed it for her – he had done so tonight as they'd got ready. He had put the row of pearls round her slender neck, and wished the night was already over and he could take her in his arms. Hannah knew his mind and a secret look passed between them.

'How are things in the village?' Leah asked Jeff, her eyes, too, on Hannah, envying her sister her tall figure and natural grace.

'Aw, a lot's happened since you've been away, maid. We've got a houseful of rowdy louts living next door.'

'Where? Surely you don't mean the Kittow cottage? Has a new family moved in?'

Jeff explained about Daniel's release from prison and his boat's new crew, perfectly at ease in the plush surroundings. 'They don't bother me, your mother and Josh much but they've been terrors to the Joses. Broke Fred's model yacht, the one he made himself and was so proud of, and Mrs Jose is at her wits' end with they throwing rubbish in her garden and making rude remarks. They're drunk as lords down the pub nearly every

61

night then they make a hell of a racket on the way home. The Reverend Skewes called on 'em and asked 'em to behave. They said, well, I won't mention what they said t'he. John Jacobs had to warn one of 'em off for hanging around Lizzie. I thought the bloke was going t'break John's jaw, but John's a good fighter, laid un out on the quay like a jellyfish. Course, you won't know either that 'tis Daniel who owns the new house. Arranged it all in prison, he did, bold as brass. Got that fancy piece, Grace Treloar, eating out of his hand too. You remember her at your wedding? Well, she's with him at every whip 'n' turn, so they say. Mind you,' Jeff said with an element of pride, 'a good-looking man never has any trouble drawing women to un.'

'Crumbs,' Leah said. 'Nothing happens for years and the first time I go away I miss all the excitement. Lily's told me she's courting with Jowan. I'll go down to see Mother first thing tomorrow.'

'Be careful of those men,' Hannah warned grimly. 'They aren't at sea yet. Someone stole some vital parts of the *Sunrise*'s engine while Daniel was in prison and they're waiting for new parts to be delivered – she won't be seaworthy until next week apparently. With nothing to do, they're hanging around trying to cause trouble. Mrs Trudgeon swears they're stealing cakes from the bakehouse. Constable Burt has been called into the village nearly every day for one thing or another but he can't find anything to prove against the men.'

'And you've got Daniel living in your street, Hannah?' Leah said, her eyes wide. 'What's he doing while all this is going on?'

'Nothing,' Hannah replied bitterly. 'He's goes about his business on the *Sunrise* as if he was a law-abiding citizen. He rarely speaks to anyone and never goes to the pub. But it was him who brought those men into Porthellis; he hates all of us and they're doing his dirty work for him.'

'Crumbs,' Leah said again.

'Let's forget him,' Matt said sternly. The atmosphere was getting sombre. 'We're here to celebrate your homecoming, Leah.'

Lily appeared to ask Greg to help Miss Benson escort Mrs Opie down the stairs. Then Grace, well-groomed in blue silk taffeta, arrived with Patrick and after the formal greetings were over there were a few awkward minutes of small talk. Grace asked the newlyweds about their honeymoon. Patrick engaged Matt in talk about the gardens. Feena beckoned Hannah to sit beside her on one of the sofas by the fire.

'Your mother wouldn't change her mind about coming, I take it.'

'No, but she wouldn't come to this sort of thing anyway.' To avoid Feena's keen gaze Hannah sipped from her glass of lime cordial. Feena must have known Prim wouldn't come to Roscarrock again; they would loathe each other all their lives, but Hannah had not been prepared for Prim's violent reaction.

'I had to go there on Leah's wedding day so I wouldn't look a blooming fool in front of the village but that's the last time! I'll not give that bitch another chance to lord it over me. How could you have thought for a moment I'd go, Hannah? You can tell her to stick her invitation up her perfumed bottom!' Prim was hurt and angry that Jeff had gone tonight. Hannah regretted passing on the invitation to her parents but her father seemed to be enjoying himself.

Jeff moved about the room, studying the paintings, stopping at the satinwood grand piano to run his fingertips over the ivory keys. Every so often he glanced at Feena. He was impressed. Dressed in a black suit with gold frogging over the hip-length jacket, she cut a dramatic figure. Her hair was softly curled close to her head and diamonds glittered at her throat, her wrists and on her fingers. Her make-up was expertly applied, she looked years younger. Moving close to her, he sniffed her strong musky perfume; he remembered it from his days as her lover.

Feena met his dark eyes, and there again was the superior, haughty look he'd been attracted to. She said, 'I was saying to Hannah it's a pity Prim didn't come tonight but it does mean we will have even numbers round the dining table.'

'It was kind of you to invite us to welcome Leah back,' Jeff said.

'My house is open to Hannah's family at any time.' She watched his lips as he put them to his glass.

Feeling embarrassed at the rather intimate looks passing between the couple who had sired and conceived her, Hannah looked away, glad that Miss Benson appeared at that moment and announced dinner was ready to be served.

Patrick sprang away from Matt and stood in front of Hannah. 'May I have the honour of escorting you in, Mrs Penney?' he said gaily.

'I'd be delighted, Mr Patrick,' she laughed, putting her hand on the arm of his shabby suit.

Feena spoke up before other arrangements could be made. 'Mr Spargo, I'm sure you'd like to escort Leah. Matt, will you take Miss Treloar in? And Greg, dear, you can take me.'

When they were seated round the huge mahogany table, set with cut-glass candlesticks and bowls of scarlet camellias, Hannah said, 'And what will we be feasting on tonight, Mr Patrick?' There was a subtle change in her voice, as if she was trying to sound more cultivated. 'I dare say you've been working hard in the kitchen all afternoon.'

Matt raised his dark brows impatiently; Feena saw it and pursed her lips.

'Oh, we're going to be very cosmopolitan tonight. We're having minestrone soup, veal scaloppine and Marquise Alice,' Patrick said proudly across the table from her, rubbing his hands together in anticipation.

Leah leaned round Matt to Greg seated at the bottom end of the table and whispered, 'What did he say?'

'Veal cooked the Italian way and a French dessert, darling.' He blew her a kiss.

Sitting at the head of the table Feena raised a toast to the couple back from honeymoon, waited for the good wishes to die down, then turned to Hannah. 'I knew that gown would suit you, dear. The sequins match the colour of your eyes. You look gorgeous. Don't you think so, Matt?'

'Hannah would look gorgeous in a filthy sack,' he replied shortly.

Hannah shot a vexed look at him. Patrick started off about the gardens again, taking it for granted Matt was listening to him. Leah concentrated on her food. Greg watched her fondly.

'You look charming too, Miss Treloar,' Feena went on. 'Such a refreshing change to see evening trousers. I must get something like it for myself. You must tell me afterwards who your fashion house is. How are you enjoying your stay in Cornwall? You've been with us a month now. Have you decided to stay?'

Grace glanced at Hannah before answering. 'Yes. I'm thinking of opening up a little gift shop. I thought I could also sell wool and stationery to keep it open all year round.'

'What a novel idea,' Feena said. 'In Mevagissey? It's the biggest place locally to attract holidaymakers.'

'No, in Porthellis. I'm told quite a few people are about in the summer. It's for something to do really. It's not as if I need to make a massive profit.'

'Have you thought about costume jewellery?' Feena said. 'That reminds me of something. Hannah dear, how would you like to have your ears pierced? It's quite the thing these days. I could get someone to come to the house and we could both have it done.'

'Hannah doesn't need holes in her ears,' Matt said tartly.

'That's for Hannah to decide, isn't it?' Feena returned.

All eyes were on Hannah for her reaction. 'I would like to have my ears pierced,' she said quietly.

Matt let the fork fall from his hand and clatter on the plate. He gulped water from a glass and glared at his wife.

Leah was eyeing Mrs Opie but she was ignored.

'Yes, well, I thought I'd plant some Virginia creeper on one of the outside walls of the walled garden at the end of the year, then we'll have a blaze of autumn colour,' Patrick said to no one in particular.

Jeff accepted second helpings of everything, content to listen to the conversations, speaking only when spoken to. Halfway through the meal he suddenly became aware of the white damask napkin at his side; unperturbed, he unrolled it and tucked it into his collar.

Grace was intrigued by Matt. He had pulled his facial muscles in so tightly it was a wonder he could eat and drink. What an interesting specimen he was. He obviously adored Hannah but he had a moody streak in him. Grace wondered why Mrs Opie and Hannah were so close; odd for the mistress of a big house and the girl who'd been her housekeeper for a few short months, leaving in disgrace. Aunt Adela hadn't come up with an answer to this mystery. Mrs Opie obviously didn't mind about the baby, in fact she doted on him. Hannah behaved differently in these surroundings, she had publicly gone against her husband's express wishes. It wasn't surprising he didn't want her receiving attention from her old employer. Had anyone noticed that Mrs Opie was ignoring the quiet little bride? And Leah was wife of the heir to the property. Grace looked again at Matt. He noticed and stared back blatantly. A stubborn, tough individual, she thought. He and Daniel hated each other; sparks could easily be made to fly between them.

'Have you found somewhere to ride yet, Miss Treloar?' Feena asked.

'I have approached a couple of farms but they didn't have any suitable mounts. Hemmick Farm has an empty barn that could be quickly converted into a stable. Mr Henry Teague has said he's willing to do that and rent it out to me if I send for a couple of my own horses. I would employ a capable stable boy.'

'I have a better idea,' Feena said, her eyes firmly on Hannah again. 'Install your horses in my stable. The stable boy could use the old coachman's cottage. You could teach Hannah to ride and go out together.'

'I'd be pleased to,' Grace said, turning to Leah who looked as if she was trying to shrink in her chair. 'I'd be happy to give lessons to Hannah and Leah.'

'Of course, but I expect Greg will want to teach Leah, won't you, darling?'

'Yes, Grandma.' He smiled at Leah. 'It will be fun, darling.'

Leah tried to return his smile.

'Don't you like horses?' Greg was at once concerned about his wife's lukewarm response to the idea.

'Yes,' she said and concentrated on her dessert.

The meal was completed in a strained atmosphere. When everyone was back in the drawing room, Feena said brightly, 'I've recently purchased a new board game that's very popular in America. It's called Monopoly. One has to acquire the most property to win. Who would like to play?'

'Sounds interesting,' Grace said.

'I've read about that,' Jeff said enthusiastically. 'I'll have a go.'

'Thank you, Mr Spargo,' Feena said regally. 'How about you, Matt? I'm sure you could master it.'

'Yes, all right,' he answered, glancing restlessly at the clock on the mantelpiece.

Greg set up the folding card table for the board game. When he stood back, Leah nudged his arm. 'I don't want to play, Greg.'

'Don't worry, darling.' He kissed the top of her head. 'It's not difficult. I'll guide you.'

'I don't want to play,' she hissed, her small round face turning hot and red.

'Why not? What's the matter?' He slipped a protective arm round her.

'Nothing,' she said sullenly.

Shrugging his shoulders, Greg excused himself and Leah, saying she was tired and they would go to bed early. Leah kissed Jeff and Hannah and bid the others a quiet good night.

'Understandable I suppose,' Jeff smiled after them. 'They haven't been married long.'

'Mmmm,' Feena said vaguely.

She had studied the rules of the Monopoly game and the others soon picked it up. It was fought long and hard by all. Jeff was the first to lose when he overreached himself and flamboyantly bought all the property named on one side of the board. Feena was out next and then Patrick; he excused himself and left for the bathroom. The three younger people were left to battle it out. Hannah and Grace forgot their differences over Grace's friendship with Daniel and enjoyed themselves as they had at their first meetings.

'Can I pour you a nightcap, Feena?' Jeff said softly, going to her where she was sitting on the sofa. 'Do you still take a drop of brandy and water?'

'I do, but I don't want anything now, thank you.'

'You look beautiful,' he said.

It took all her willpower not to flush with pleasure at the unexpected compliment. 'Still feeling the need to try out your old charm, Jeff? I don't expect it works as well these days.'

'I meant it. You look as good as the day I first saw you, out there in the woods. 'Tis no wonder Hannah's turned out to be so beautiful,' he ended proudly.

Feena nodded demurely. 'She means everything to me. Matt doesn't like me.'

'Of course he doesn't. We're all jealous of the people who have pulls on the one we love the most. Matt feels threatened but he's a good man. Hannah couldn't have married anyone better, even from your class.'

Feena observed Matt as he threw the dice, a look of intense concentration on his face. 'I hope he won't go astray like you have always done.'

'So do I, but he's not likely to if Hannah looks after him properly. He's a different sort of man to me. He's not proud of his good looks. I was never born to be faithful to one woman.'

Feena looked Jeff fully in the eye. 'Out of mere curiosity, how do you and Prim get on now?'

'She keeps my house, cooks my meals, looks after Josh, but we don't share the same bed, if that's what you mean. Haven't done so for a couple of years. Have you had someone else since we parted?'

'No. You destroyed my trust in men.'

'I made you bitter. That's a shame. A woman like you, still quite young and desirable, shouldn't spend all her nights alone.'

Feena was flattered but the next moment she asked herself if this persistent womaniser was amusing himself with her feelings. He couldn't be trusted. He had ended their association, shunning her plea that they go away together and start a new life with the baby she was expecting. If he wasn't sharing a bed with Prim, there would be another woman seeing to his needs, perhaps more than one.

A flurry of excitement at the game table caught Feena's attention. Grace had just secured a lot of property. There was another woman attracted to a handsome rogue of lower birth, but in this case the man concerned was much more callous and conniving than Jeff Spargo. There was no use advising Grace to drop Daniel Kittow; Feena knew how impossible it was to use one's common sense where such men were concerned. It would end when Kittow had no more use for her or was bored with her; then he would crush her, trample over her feelings, ignore her pleadings and thrust her heartlessly out of his life. Feena felt unsettled and resolved never to ask Jeff here again.

The game ended close to midnight, with Grace winning nearly all the property on the board. 'I shall go to St Austell and buy Monopoly for my aunt and uncle. You must come up to the Manse and play with us,' she said to Hannah and Matt.

Upstairs, Greg was having a hard time extracting from Leah why she had suddenly become unhappy. 'Everything was fine in Paris and Scotland, darling,' he said as they climbed into the fourposter bed. 'Did someone say something to upset you?'

'It's nothing,' Leah repeated for the umpteenth time. Greg would think her silly if she told him she was seething with anger at his grandmother. Throughout their engagement Mrs Opie had paid more attention to Hannah than to her. Leah had accepted it but she had thought she would become more important when she became Mrs Opie. But the lady had all but ignored her when she and Greg had arrived home this afternoon. Throughout the dinner Leah had felt she didn't exist as far as Mrs Opie was concerned. She knew she didn't have Hannah's confidence and poise but she felt she should be treated at least on an equal footing with her sister.

Greg kissed her, nuzzled her neck, pulled at the silk ribbons on the front of her nightdress. 'I love you, darling,' he murmured huskily.

Her body tightened. She became frigid. Her lips did not respond to his. She felt she didn't belong here, lying in this over-sized bed.

'Darling, what's the matter?' He smoothed her hair from her face and tenderly kissed the top of her nose.

She was near to tears. 'I–I don't want to, Greg. I'm tired.'

'It's all right.' He kissed her hot, damp forehead. 'It's been a taxing time for you these last few weeks. You can relax now we're home.' With his arms round her, he settled down to sleep.

It wasn't taxing away from here, she thought miserably, the tears hot on her cheeks. She had made love with Greg almost every night on their honeymoon. It had been unsuccessful on their wedding night and Greg had kissed away her tears of disappointment, reassuring her that she was only tense because of the wedding, that it would be all right next time. He had been right. But now they were back at Roscarrock, living under his grandmother's roof, she was tense again.

All the guests from Porthellis squeezed into the car so that Patrick would have to make only one journey. The evening had ended on a happy note and Hannah was not pleased to find that Matt was in one of his moods.

'Grace and I have forgotten our differences,' she said, watching his grim profile in her dressing-table mirror as she unclasped her pearls. 'It was a good evening so why are you looking grumpy?'

'You haven't got a clue, have you?' he accused her, his tone exasperated.

'What have I done?' she said crossly, keeping her voice low so as not to wake Nathan. 'I'm fed up with your attitude towards Mrs Opie. She's my mother, remember? I have the right to go to Roscarrock and I don't think it's too much to ask you to behave in a reasonable manner about it.'

'And what about Leah?' he retorted darkly.

'Leah? What about her? I don't know what you're driving at.'

'Of course not, because you've always got your head in the bloody clouds when you're in that damned place or with that damned woman. You were so busy standing in your own light tonight you didn't notice Leah was left out of all Feena Opie's schemes. She wasn't given an evening dress to wear tonight. She wasn't asked if she wanted to have her ears pierced. She wasn't included in the ruddy horse riding. How do you think she must have felt? Left out, that's what. That's why she went to bed early. Even Greg didn't notice the real reason. She'll be living there from now on. What's she going to think with Feena Opie lavishing all her attention on you?' He stabbed a finger towards her. 'Leah hasn't been told the woman is your mother, has she? Even though she's Greg's wife, an Opie now herself. Your selfishness is going to make that poor girl feel very uncomfortable.'

Hannah was mortified but she was also furious at Matt's outburst. 'You're not concerned about Leah in all this, you're only ranting and raving at me because you hate Mrs Opie.'

Throwing his suit jacket on a chair, Matt charged across to her and caught her arms. 'When are you going to see that woman for the manipulating bitch she is? I forbid you to take Nathan to Roscarrock again.'

'You have no right to do that.' She struggled to get free. 'You're jealous that I'm close to someone else.'

'Too right I am, you foolish woman.' He pulled her against him. 'I'm worried about anyone who would come between us and I'm convinced Feena Opie's trying to break us up.'

'You're being ridiculous. Let go of me, Matt.'

Gripping the back of her neck, he pulled the evening gown off her shoulders. 'Take this off. I don't want to see you in it.'

'Stop behaving like this.' She beat his chest. 'Who do you think you are? Daniel Kittow?'

He let her go so abruptly she nearly fell on the floor. 'I'd never try to rape you,' he said icily.

Hannah gulped. Her last remark had been cruel and undeserved. 'I'm sorry I said that but I don't like being shouted at and pulled around.'

'I'm sorry. I got carried away,' he said quietly. 'But it's difficult to make you see sense over Feena Opie.'

Hannah stepped out of the evening gown, put it on a hanger and placed it in the wardrobe. They undressed silently, avoiding each other's eyes, and got into bed.

She recalled the few moments he had imprisoned her, pulled down the dress, exposed her breasts to his eyes. She knew Matt would never hurt her and she felt strangely excited. She put a hand on his chest. His skin was hot, his heart was heaving, he was still in a passion. She kissed his shoulder, stroked his hair. He rolled over to her and they made love fiercely.

Patrick had escorted Grace to the Manse but the instant he'd driven off she went down the hill and turned into Cobble Street. She could hear the *Sunrise*'s crew whooping it up down in the harbour. The lights were on in Daniel's house and without hesitating she went inside. She was all dressed up, she knew she looked good, and she wanted Daniel to see her, to find her attractive.

He was in the kitchen rubbing oil into the new set of oilskins. 'You'll ruin your reputation coming here this late at night,' he said, wiping his hands and lighting a cigarette. 'You could have been embarrassed. I could have had a woman here.'

'I've come here night and day and I haven't seen anyone.'

'That's only because I'm not laying anyone from the village,' he smirked, coming to her. 'How did the dinner go?'

'It was quite boring.' In fact she had found it stimulating observing the tensions and interactions of her fellow guests. 'Feena Opie offered me the use of her stables. I shall send for my horses and employ a stable boy.'

'Definitely staying here then?'

'Yes. Going back to Kent or moving elsewhere doesn't appeal to me.'

'Where will you live?'

'I'll stay at the Manse until I've found something in Porthellis or close to it.'

'You like this house, don't you?'

'Yes, very much.'

He blew a smoke ring above her head. 'I'm taking the train to Plymouth tomorrow. Would you like to travel up and meet me there?'

'For what people call a dirty weekend?'

'No, we'll get married. I'll make my conditions plain. I've always gone my own way and always will. Nag me, try to tie me down, interfere with anything I do and I'll make you suffer. The house is mine but you can do what you like with it. I'll be up there for a few days. You can think it over.'

Grace did not know why or where this proposal had come from. She did not care, and with the greatest sense of excitement she had ever felt she said at once, 'I don't need to think about it, Daniel. I'll take what's on offer.'

Chapter 7

It was the Sunday School's anniversary and there was a special service in the chapel on Sunday. A bigger than usual congregation attended, packing into the pews, spilling over into wherever there was a bit of space. Some were attracted by the promise of well-rehearsed singing, others by the fact that one of the county's best-loved circuit preachers was invited. It was an honour to hear him, most people agreed afterwards; he made the Gospel come alive, he was good Wesleyan stock. After the benediction, pronounced by the Reverend Skewes in a voice suitable to the occasion, the congregation, old and young, filed out of the chapel in respectful silence.

The next day was an even greater occasion, planned meticulously and looked forward to by all but those in a sick bed. The Chapel Tea. The long trestle tables were hauled out of their resting places and put up at one end of the Sunday School room. They were covered with calico and a feast was spread out on them for all to enjoy. Hannah was among the aproned women who arranged platters laid first with crocheted doilies then heaped high with richly buttered scones, golden splits, yeast cake, saffron cake, seed cake, black soda cake, thickly cut sandwiches filled with home-cured ham, and wedges of savoury pies. Pots of strawberry and blackberry jam and crusty-topped clotted cream, jellies and trifles and vases of polyanthus, tulips, daffodils and lilac added to the magnificent colourful display.

Those attending the teatime feast arrived dressed in their best finery. New feathers and strips of silk titivated the women's hats, watchchains jangled on the men's waistcoats. The older men wore bowlers, the younger ones trilbys; the swains among them tilted their trilbys slightly to the side. There was a feeling of oneness among the villagers, a sense of eagerness, anticipation and joy. Hannah was particularly light-hearted because Daniel had left the village a few days ago. She didn't know how long he would stay away but a heaviness had lifted from her, she felt the air was fresher, easier to breathe.

Miss Peters sidled up to her. She looked like a surly-featured doll in a red velvet coat and matching bonnet tied under her pointed whiskery chin. Hannah raised her brows to see the old lady had brought her horsewhip with her. 'You got the tea ready yet? And I want a comfy place to sit. Me old bones can't manage a hard form.'

'I've put aside a stool with a thick cushion on it specially for you.' Hannah's eyes gleamed.

'No need t'talk t'me like I was a little child,' Miss Peters said grumpily. 'Where's this stool then? Or have I got t'fetch it meself? And put it where I can see what's going on. Better make it near the door. You can fetch me a cup of tea and plate of food.'

Miss Peters didn't usually demand to be waited upon but Hannah was happy to do it. When she was seated near the door, out of the draught, as if it was her duty to check on who was coming in, Hannah helped the other elderly folk to comfortable seats.

'I'm thinking of asking for tuppence off people as they arrive so they can touch the top of her head for luck,' Matt whispered in her ear, motioning towards the inscrutable old lady.

Hannah dug him playfully in the ribs. 'Don't let her hear you saying things like that. You'll get her whip across your legs, and serve you right.'

He laughed and popped half a triangle of ham sandwich into his mouth. 'Look who's come in. Constable Burt.'

'He must be worried the *Sunrise*'s crew will try to cause trouble.' It was all too easy with the villagers constantly on their guard and ready to retaliate.

The words were hardly out of her mouth when Brinley, Eric and their two mates, Tippy and Merv, burst through the doors. They pushed Hamlyn Innis and Mrs Trudgeon, who were discussing the rising cost of raw materials, out of their way. The chatter stopped, heads twisted in their direction. Mothers gathered their children to them. Hannah checked that Nathan was safely with Aunty Janet and Mrs Penney. She felt her stomach knot.

The Reverend Skewes and Constable Burt stepped forward.

'You're welcome to join us,' the minister said, smiling weakly.

'As long as you don't cause any trouble or bother the ladies,' the constable added in his most official voice.

'Whad'ya mean?' Eric scowled, his small, mean eyes disappearing in the loose folds of his heavy features. 'Since when did we cause trouble?' He made a gobbling sound and the others joined in. 'We don't never bother the women, 'tis the other way round. They get lonely when their men's out at sea.'

'If you're going to talk like that you can get out right now,' Matt fumed, pushing in front of the minister and the constable.

'Leave this to me, Matt,' Constable Burt said sternly, heaving the irate fisherman back behind him.

'We'll behave,' Brinley said gruffly, pushing his bulk towards the food tables. People cleared a path for him like a field of corn parting before a violent wind.

Prim quickly put some food on a plate and offered it to him. 'Please don't ruin it for the kiddies,' she appealed.

'We won't bother no one if they don't bother us.' He winked at her. Brinley had a soft spot for Prim. The skipper had warned him and the others to leave the Spargos alone, saying he alone would deal with them, but Prim reminded Brinley of his late wife whom he had loved dearly and he would have been disinclined to cause trouble for her anyway. He spied Fred Jose, however; the skipper wanted him to be given a dog's life.

Pressing two long slabs of yeast cake together, he munched them and advanced on Fred who backed away from him until he was wedged into a corner of the room. Then Brinley turned round and leant his massive frame against the hapless fisherman until Fred could hardly breathe. Eric, Tippy and Merv headed for the tables and piled so much food on their plates they threatened to leave nothing for anyone else.

Without Daniel there to warn him off and punish him for it, Eric cut a jibe at Hannah. 'That's your husband, ain't it? He with the big mouth. Just lookin' for a fist t'smash it in.'

Before Hannah could reply, Matt pushed her gently behind him. 'Speak to my wife again and it'll be your face that'll end up looking like it's been hit by a brick wall.' There was something powerfully menacing about him, and Eric backed down from further confrontation.

'What's so special about you and your pretty little missus, eh? The skipper says you're his.' Eric shrugged. 'He's welcome to 'ee.'

'What did he mean, Matt?' Hannah clutched his arm, suddenly feeling faint.

'I think it was obvious, darling.' Matt patted her hand. 'Try not to let it

75

spoil the day. Hopefully they'll go soon.'

Hannah clamped a hand to her mouth, muttering urgently between her fingers. 'Take me outside, Matt. Through the back door. I think I'm going to be sick.'

As they hurried out through the back door of the room, Leah came through the front door on Greg's arm. Grateful to have something to take their minds off the troublemakers, the villagers crowded round to greet them. Stuffing food into his mouth, Tippy shoved his way through the press of people until he was facing the young couple.

'Well, look 'ee here,' he roared at the top of his rough voice. 'We've gotta toff and some sweet little lady with un. I think you've come to the wrong place, m'dears. This is a village tea treat. Not for the likes of you.'

Greg frowned with annoyance and tried to lead Leah away. Tippy grasped Leah's arm. Leah screamed. Greg put up his fist but Jeff got to the offender first and yanked him backwards then lifted him up, making him gag on his food.

'You lay a finger on my daughter again and I'll . . .' Remembering there were women and children present, Jeff ran out of words.

Constable Burt sprang forward to do his duty and for a few minutes a pandemonium of argument and accusation broke out. Then the sound of a whip cracked through the air and people scattered.

In the silence that followed Miss Peters strode up to Brinley. Her tiny hobgoblin face held all the malevolence of an enraged bull. He stared at her, open-mouthed, food spilling down over his chin and on to his jersey. 'I reckon you're the leader of this rabble, matey. You can get them out of here right now, before I whip the skin off your backs. We edn't afeared of you in this village. There's many a good man who've kept his fists in check but not any more. We've had enough. When he gets back you can say up against that heathen rogue Daniel Kittow that he don't scare none of us.' She sliced the whip expertly through the air, swiping a split out of Brinley's hand. 'Now get! Before I get really mazed.'

Brinley looked as if he'd been struck by all the forces of nature. He turned as red as blood, air hissed out of the sides of his mouth, gurgling sounds came from his throat. His fists clenched and children hid behind their mothers' skirts while adults blanched. They fully expected the huge man to order his cronies to tear them and the room apart.

John Jacobs stood at Miss Peters' side and was quickly joined by Jeff, Roy Rouse and several other fishermen. 'You may be a threat when you single out one of us or our women but you can't take on all of us together. If we have to take the law into our own hands to protect the village, we will, you can count on that. Now, as Miss Peters said, get out, and stay out of everywhere but the pub from now on.'

Brinley was smouldering, a hair's breadth from totally losing his temper. 'You might put up a fight, you might even beat us, but we'd make sure some of you weren't fit t'put t'sea for several weeks.'

Prim crept up nervously to him. 'Please don't fight in front of the children. They've done nothing to you. My grandchildren are in here.'

She had given Brinley a reason to step down without losing face. 'All right, we'll go, but only for the sake of the kiddies. You men with the big mouths had better watch out in future.' With a snarl he stormed out and the other men followed him, muttering angrily.

Jowan and Lily had sneaked outside several minutes earlier for a kiss and cuddle. They were interrupted by Tippy on his way to use the outside toilet. His cloddish face gleamed with a malicious grin. 'I'll have some of that,' he guffawed, grabbing Lily from Jowan's arms and planting his ragged lips on hers before she could fight him off.

Jowan shouted in fury and grabbed at Tippy's grubby shirt collar to free his sweetheart. He had help. Constable Burt had left the Sunday School room hard on the heels of the troublemakers. He had seen Brinley and the other three men amble off down to the quay and had decided to follow the man who had broken their ranks. In one efficient movement he bent Tippy's arm behind his back and yanked him away from the distraught girl.

'I'm arresting you for—'

Tippy gave forth an ear-splitting yell and butted his head backwards, splitting the young constable's bottom lip.

With blood spurting down his face, Constable Burt continued calmly, '—assault, breach of the peace and striking a police officer. You're off to a cell, mate.' He swiftly put the handcuffs on the miscreant and hauled him off towards the public telephone to call for a police van.

Lily rubbed at her mouth with her hanky as if she'd been contaminated with a deadly poison. 'I need a drink of tea,' she said, her voice muffled as she kept up her ministrations.

Fear was making Jowan's light grey eyes seem twice their normal size. He was terrified she would refuse to marry him if she thought this sort of thing went on in Porthellis every day.

'What's the matter with you?' Lily giggled, her merry nature driving out the unpleasant moments. 'You look like a big fish out of water.'

Blinking, gulping, taking a deep breath, he asked Lily there and then to marry him.

The hotel in Plymouth wasn't as superior as Grace was used to but it was clean, the surroundings were pleasant and it did have room service. She tipped the porter who brought the tray of champagne and chocolates generously. Daniel had checked in with her during the afternoon, then promptly left, saying he wouldn't be back until late. Grace didn't mind. She'd stood calmly at his side as he'd signed the register Mr and Mrs D. Kittow. The long sloping letters told the truth; she was Mrs D. Kittow, by special licence. Her stay here was above board, she wasn't here for a grubby liaison and she looked the little desk clerk straight in the eye. The desk clerk knew a lady when he saw one and his manner was impeccable as he handed the porter the key.

Grace unpacked her suitcase. She hadn't brought many day clothes with her but had been sure to include all the expensive, luxuriant underclothes and nightgowns she had bought soon after her mother's death, a reaction against the strict life she had been forced to live. After a leisurely bath, her skin left satin-smooth by the fragrant oils she had tipped into the water, she tried on the three different nightgowns resting on the bed. She twisted and twirled in front of the cheval mirror, deciding, with a sense of burning excitement growing in the pit of her stomach, on the sheerest creation. Her mother would have called the dusky pink, low-cut, lace-trimmed nightgown wanton, disgusting, too sinful for even a husband to see. She would have had a seizure at her daughter's choice of husband, too, but Grace could not have been happier. Even with her wealth, she knew she was considered too old and plain to secure a young, good-looking husband like Daniel, or one as exciting.

It was almost ten o'clock. The chambermaid had turned down the bed. Grace had closed the dark paisley curtains and lit the bedside lamps. She waited patiently. Every few minutes she stuck out her left hand, as she had done repeatedly since leaving the registry office, to gaze at the thick gold ring Daniel had put on her finger. Having learned that fishermen considered wearing gold was lucky, she had given him a ring too. She had no idea why Daniel had married her. It couldn't be entirely for her money. He had ways of making his own and he didn't seem the sort of man to sponge off a woman. She would have slept with him, as often and for as long as he'd wanted her, but now she could have him, lose her virginity to him, legally and morally.

Before leaving Porthellis, two days after Daniel, she had written to her lawyer. Despite the fact that she loved Daniel desperately, she did not believe it likely their marriage would last for ever, and she instructed her lawyer to set aside her property in Kent and tie up several thousand pounds where Daniel could not touch it. It gave her security, a sense of peace which would help prevent her from been overwhelmed and destroyed by Daniel. She had kept enough of her wealth afloat to live comfortably off the interest and she would open the gift shop in Porthellis.

She went to the dressing table and smoothed her hair, its dull colour a golden sheen in the lamplight, and studied her make-up. It was perfect. She dabbed on a little more scent, for the first time putting some down her cleavage. She had a good figure, firm and youthful. She felt confident Daniel would like what he saw when the nightgown came off.

There was the sound of a key turning in the door. She sprang up from the dressing table and stood beside the tray of champagne on the bedside cabinet. Daniel entered and locked the door after him. His business had gone well and he was in a very good mood. He smiled at Grace before taking off his hat and sports jacket.

'Hope you haven't been bored.'

'Not at all,' she said smoothly, disguising the fact that her pulse was racing and she would die of shame and disappointment if he didn't notice her very soon. 'I had dinner downstairs. It was rather good. Have you eaten?'

'Yes, with a friend of a friend.'

Picking up the bottle of champagne and two glasses, she moved towards him. 'Would you like some champagne?'

He noticed the provocative nightgown, saw what it revealed. He took his time answering. 'I'll open it.'

They sipped the champagne. She watched his eyes. They were sliding over her as if she was wearing nothing. They put their glasses down at the same time.

He came to her, put his hands on her. 'You're a brazen hussy for a woman who's never been with a man before.'

She slid her hot palms up over his broad chest and round his neck, bringing herself as close to him as she could. 'Only you have this effect on me, Daniel.'

He thought about it, smiled. 'I'm honoured.' Then he didn't waste any more time.

Used to very early starts, Daniel woke before his bride. She did not stir as he sat up in bed, switched on the table lamp and lit a cigarette. He was totally relaxed. Rarely had he felt more fulfilled than he had last night. Grace had allowed everything he'd wanted to do, with her nightdress off, the lights left on. There had been a special sweetness in her first time, yielding, not tense or demure, totally uninhibited. A long, lazy smile passed across his rugged features. He didn't want Grace's money, it would keep her independent from him and make it easier if he wanted to be rid of her. With the deal he'd clinched yesterday, via prison contacts, he'd be an able provider and still be in funds.

He looked down at Grace's bare neck and shoulder. For all his womanizing, a full married life with her had not really crossed his mind. He would never have guessed at the passion he'd quickly gentled out of her. If last night was repeated often, perhaps he wouldn't stray too soon. He stubbed out the cigarette and woke her.

Later, in the small, comfortable dining room, they ate a large fried breakfast and several rounds of toast. They were both ravenously hungry.

'How long are we staying here?' Grace asked.

'Brinley's ringing me later today,' he said piling marmalade on the slice of toast on his plate, amused at the demure way Grace spooned marmalade on her plate before spreading it. 'No point in going home until the parts for the boat engine turn up.' In the meantime Brinley and his mates could make their presence felt in the village.

'Are you looking forward to going out to sea and fishing again?' Grace wondered why a man with Daniel's talents wanted to continue working as a fisherman. He could soon finance and set up a little business of his own; she overlooked the fact that the initial outlay would almost certainly be obtained unlawfully.

Daniel's eyes shone. 'I can't wait to throw out the nets. I can make more money doing other things but it's in my blood, the thrill of the chase, finding the right spot in a big shoal. I might not do it for ever but I want to keep on with it while I'm young and fit. Have you phoned your aunt yet to tell her about us?' he ended, smirking.

'No. I'll do it when we leave the table.' Grace wasn't looking forward to the call. She'd left it until today because she had not wanted anything to spoil her wedding night. Gazing across the table at the muscular red-haired man she'd given herself to with complete abandonment, she didn't really care if Aunt Adela disowned her.

Daniel was looking out across the waters of Plymouth Sound. There was a longing in his voice. 'If Brinley's phone call says there's no parts for the *Sunrise* we could hire a boat and sail round the bay. The wind's just right. Are you game?'

'That would be wonderful,' she enthused. 'I might have to slip out and buy something suitable for sailing.' She hoped they could stay here for a few days' honeymoon, that for a while she could have him all to herself before he went his own way again.

Chapter 8

Grace's horses arrived at Roscarrock before she returned to Porthellis. Feena Opie telephoned Mrs Skewes from her suite to say the thoroughbred animals were safely stalled in the stable and inquired about the whereabouts of the stable boy.

'I'm sure I don't know anything about it, Mrs Opie,' Adela Skewes' voice came back hurt and aggrieved. 'Grace doesn't tell me what she's doing until after she's done it. I received a telephone call from her two days ago. She's been staying in a hotel at Plymouth. She rang to tell me she's got married.'

'Congratulations,' Feena cut in quickly to stop the woman prattling on about missing her niece's wedding, presumably the reason for the agitation.

'No, Mrs Opie, congratulations are not in order. Grace has done a very foolish thing. She's ruined her entire life.' Mrs Skewes began to sob and Feena held the telephone away from her ear for a moment. There was much sniffing, then, 'I–I'm sorry about that. You see, Grace has married someone very much beneath her. A criminal who has wild men at this very moment in Porthellis disrupting the life of the village.'

Feena knew at once who Mrs Skewes was talking about. 'You mean she's married Daniel Kittow? How extraordinary. I didn't think he was the marrying kind.'

'Nor did I,' Mrs Skewes gulped and wept. 'There's only one reason why he's married Grace. He's after her money. I don't know what I'll do.'

'There's not much you can do,' Feena said unsympathetically. 'I'll see about getting someone to look after Grace's horses, you're obviously in no state to make arrangements. Mrs Skewes, could you do something for me in return?' An order.

'Y-yes, of course, Mrs Opie.' Adela Skewes blew her nose into her hanky.

'Slip down the hill and ask young Mrs Penney to come up to Roscarrock as soon as she possibly can.' Feena put the telephone down. Having Grace Treloar's horses in her stable would have meant Hannah being more often at Roscarrock, and in time Nathan would have been taught to ride on her property too. It was a different matter now that the young lady had married the Kittow scoundrel; that horrid individual must never have reason to come to Roscarrock. As soon as Grace returned from Plymouth she'd be told to stable her horses elsewhere and so as not to disappoint Hannah, Feena would buy her own stock. First, though, Hannah must be advised of this marriage.

Hannah couldn't understand why Grace's horses coming to Roscarrock should necessitate her immediate presence at the big house; Mrs Skewes had made it sound vital. She hoped Feena hadn't thought up another extravagant idea to celebrate Nathan's birthday in a week's time.

'I would have sent Patrick or Greg to fetch you but they've gone to look over a timber yard. Greg wants a little summerhouse built for Leah in the garden,' Feena said.

'Has Leah gone with them?'

'No, she's about somewhere. Patrick felt it was strictly a man's thing.'

'I'll go find her and we can all have tea together,' Hannah said eagerly.

'What I'm about to tell you isn't for Leah's ears. Anyway, I expect she's quite happy pottering about in Greg's study. She sees herself as a sort of secretary now she's learning to type.'

It was said rather unkindly and Hannah was about to take issue with Feena when she swayed on her feet, clutched her throat and sat down suddenly. She had become pale and was shaking a little.

'Hannah, dear,' Feena gasped, not knowing whether to reach first for her daughter or the bell. 'What is it? Shall I send for someone?' She ordered Pogo who was pestering for attention away from Hannah.

'No, I'll be all right.' She waved a hand in front of her face. 'It's perfectly normal. I was like this with Nathan. I think I'm pregnant again.' The child had been conceived, Hannah was sure, on the night of the dinner party; both her babies had come about in a time of intense loving after an angry scene with Matt.

Feena limped to her and kissed her hot cheek. 'That's wonderful news. When is it due?'

'I'd say the end of next January. Could I have a drink of water, please?'

'Of course, my dear. I'll ring at once. Why don't you lie down on my bed for a little while?'

'No, I'll be fine in a few minutes.'

Feena was stroking Hannah's back when Lily appeared and was sent away for the water. When the under-housemaid had gone, Hannah said, 'Why did you want to see me?'

'It doesn't seem as important now but I thought you ought to be told something I learned this morning. Mrs Skewes said Grace has married Daniel Kittow.'

'Married!' Hannah exclaimed, forgetting her sickness. 'We'd gathered she must have gone off somewhere with Daniel, it was too much of a coincidence them disappearing within days of each other. But married? What on earth is Daniel up to now? He can't possibly be in love with Grace. He couldn't love anyone but himself. Oh, well, maybe she'll be able to stop him causing trouble.'

'For the village or you in particular, Hannah?'

'Both, I hope.'

'I'm very concerned that that man may harm you. You never know what might happen with his thugs in Porthellis. I want you and Nathan to move in here until things settle down.'

'I can't do that.' Hannah was astounded by the idea. 'My place is with Matt.'

'Not if there's a threat to you or his two children,' Feena stressed vehemently. 'You'll be company for Leah and you can go home when Matt's there.'

Lily tapped on the door and entered with a glass and jug of water on a tray, saving Hannah from having to answer. Lily looked at her quizzically and Hannah found a bright smile for her.

At the bottom of the stairs Lily went straight to the study-cum-library. Leah was sitting at the antique desk Greg had placed opposite his. With the tip of her tongue at the corner of her mouth in intense concentration, her glasses perched on the tip of her nose, she was tapping out a letter on the newest model typewriter bought exclusively for her use.

'Hello, Lily,' she said without looking up. 'Is Mr Greg back yet?'

'No, Mrs Greg.'

'That's good.' She carefully tapped out the word 'attention' and muttered to herself, 'I want to get this finished first, ready for him to sign.'

'Mrs Greg, I come to tell you that your sister, Mrs Penney, is upstairs

85

with Mrs Opie. Your sister looks like she's been took poorly and they both look worried. I thought p'raps you'd like to know.'

'Oh. Thanks for telling me, Lily.' Leah was disappointed to have to leave the letter unfinished but she got up immediately and ran upstairs. She knocked on the double doors of Feena's suite and waited to be bidden entry. She could never enter straightaway as Hannah and Greg did.

Mrs Opie called out, 'Come in.'

It sounded impatient and Leah entered timidly.

Hannah was putting the empty glass down and she smiled at her sister. She saw at once Leah was alarmed. 'It's all right, Leah. I'm feeling a little unwell because I'm pregnant – well, I'm pretty sure I am. How are you? I hear you've learned to type.'

'Lily told me you'd been taken ill,' Leah hastily explained her presence, feeling Mrs Opie saw her as an intruder. 'I'm glad it's good news and not bad. What does Mother say about it?'

'She's pleased. She guessed before I did.'

Feena was overcome with jealousy; presumably Matt's mother and Hannah's aunt also knew she was expecting. She snapped at Leah, 'You run along and carry on with what you were doing. Hannah and I are talking privately.'

Hannah couldn't bear the crestfallen expression on Leah's face. Despite feeling dizzy, she stood up abruptly. 'You've told me the news, Mrs Opie. I must get back to Nathan, and I've got sewing to do. Leah, will you walk me to the gates?'

'You're in no fit state to walk home, Hannah,' Feena protested.

'The fresh air will do me good,' Hannah replied firmly, linking her arm through Leah's and leading them out of the room.

'Don't let her upset you,' Hannah said as she and Leah walked down the drive, still arm in arm. 'Mrs Opie's always been bossy. It's just her way.'

'She's very fond of you but she doesn't like me,' Leah said gloomily. 'She behaves as if I don't exist. If Greg and I have a baby I bet she won't take any notice of it.'

'She will,' Hannah said soothingly, knowing she must have a word with Feena about her lack of warmth towards Leah. 'She's probably giving you and Greg time and space to settle in. Greg's always lived a separate life, all the Opies have. It's better than having her interfering in everything you do, isn't it?'

'I suppose so,' Leah said uncertainly. 'I wish we lived somewhere else, on our own.'

'Why don't you tell Greg?'

'Greg loves Roscarrock. He's got his work here, all his books and things in their own places. Most girls would kill to have what I've got. I don't want him to think I'm ungrateful.'

'He's your husband, Leah. You've got the right to tell him how you feel.'

'But you wouldn't dream of living anywhere else but at Seaview Cottage. Matt owns it and one day Greg will have Roscarrock. It doesn't seem right trying to drag him away from the place.'

'You're bound to find it strange for a while, Leah. You're being too hard on yourself. I think you're very clever learning to type. Concentrate on that. I'm sure Greg is very proud of you. You'll probably have a baby of your own soon and then you won't have so much time on your hands to feel . . .' The expression was 'left out' and she remembered that Leah didn't know why she had been called to Roscarrock. 'Mrs Opie phoned Mrs Skewes to tell her Grace's horses have arrived.'

'Have they?' Leah said sharply. 'I didn't know that.'

Oh, damn, Hannah thought, this is making things worse. 'Well, that's not the point really. Mrs Skewes said Grace has gone to Plymouth with Daniel and they've got married. Because of the way things are between Matt and me and Daniel, Mrs Opie wanted me to know about it.'

'Why?' Leah said sulkily, drawing away from Hannah. 'Daniel wanted you once but it doesn't really involve you any more than it does anyone else in Porthellis. If you ask me, it's just another ruse to get you here. Mrs Opie seems to want to rule your life.'

Hannah felt at that moment that she had no choice but to tell Leah about her true relationship with Mrs Opie. Matt was right, keeping the truth from her was hurting her, and it was unnecessary. As Greg's wife, in fact as Hannah's niece by marriage, she had the right to know. Halfway along the drive was a wrought-iron bench. 'Let's sit down. I've got something to tell you.'

Leah didn't say a word as Hannah recounted the story of her birth, of the real reason she'd been offered a job at Roscarrock. 'I hope you'll understand why Mrs Opie and I are so close, why she takes so much interest in Nathan. I'm sorry you weren't told before. You will have to keep it a secret. It wouldn't affect me very much and everyone knows what Dad's been like, but the scandal would destroy Mrs Opie.'

'I see it clearly now,' Leah said, stunned, her heart lightened. She resolved that from now on she'd try to live with Greg under Roscarrock's roof almost as if Feena Opie didn't exist. She had no wish to be mistress of the big house, she wasn't ready to run it; Greg would one day inherit Roscarrock and she'd cross that bridge when she came to it. She'd take Hannah's advice, concentrate on her typing, on becoming the perfect secretary and helpmate for Greg. She had suddenly grown up. 'I'm glad you've told me, Hannah, but I think you ought to be careful. Mrs Opie's obsessed with you. I can see why Matt's so wary of her now.'

'There's no need to be so dramatic, Leah,' Hannah said, relieved it had gone so well. She was feeling better and was looking forward to the walk home. 'Mrs Opie's not going to keep Grace's horses here but she's going to buy her own.' She grinned and put her hands out in front of her in a wide arc. 'We could have some fun learning to ride together before I'm too big with this baby.'

Leah thought of all the times she had pushed Greg away from her in bed since coming home from their honeymoon. She had a sudden longing to see his stern attractive face, feel his arms round her. She laughed happily and patted her flat tummy. 'I'll soon catch up with you then we can push our prams round the gardens together.'

They kissed each other goodbye. Hannah strolled home, humming cheerily. Now that she had sorted out the problem over Feena's behaviour towards Leah, the fact that Daniel and Grace had married seemed none of her business. Next time something like this happened she would phone Feena for the news and not go rushing to Roscarrock.

Leah skipped back to the study to finish Greg's letter to a researcher for his latest novel, a little troubled that she had so very nearly allowed her sistership with Hannah to be spoiled. If only Feena Opie and Daniel Kittow did not exist, she reasoned, they could live in peace.

Chapter 9

The crew of the *Misty* had shot their long line, stretching seven and a half miles, north to south, over the reach of water called Hurd Deep but known to the fishermen as the Ray Pits. They were hoping for a good catch of ray and skate. Other boats from Porthellis, and some from Looe and Mevagissey, were also trying the Ray Pits while the rest had headed down to the Lizard.

Matt was taking the last watch with Graham Chellew, the chatty half of the middle-aged brothers. 'We'll do better here, I reckon. Weather's not foxy. If the tide slackens off and the breeze keeps northerly we'll have just the right conditions to haul 'em in,' Graham said as if Matt didn't know this. He pulled off his woolly hat and scratched an itchy spot amid his spiky white hair. It made a noise like a piece of leather being grated. His uncomely features were screwed up in his habitual expression of over-compensating for the harshest weather. Matt never talked much. Graham took this for granted and his tongue carried on. 'Jeff's worried about they buggers back on shore. What they'll get up to next. Me and Malcolm have a mind like some of the other men, we'd like to see 'em run out of Porthellis. What do you think, boy?'

''Tis a good idea,' Matt said grimly. 'A man could get himself into a lot of strife attempting it, but we've got to protect our families.'

Jeff came out of the wheelhouse and joined them. 'Malcolm and Alan are still sleeping. You talking about Kittow's ruffians?'

'Aye,' Matt said, noticing his father-in-law was rubbing his chest. He'd had a heart attack two years ago. 'You in pain?'

'Nah.' Jeff lit a cigarette, his dark good looks clearly illuminated in the glow of the match. He looked his normal self. 'Got a bit of a cold, could be going down on me chest. I'll keep me eye on it. I'm more concerned with getting those bastards out of the village. Some of us men think if the

89

p'lice don't do something soon some of us should remain behind while the boats are out, p'raps one man from about four or five boats. Be harder work for the rest of us but it'd put our minds at rest.' He began to cough and, cursing, threw his cigarette into the waves. His chest wasn't painful but it was uncomfortably taut.

'You can be one of the first t'stop behind,' Graham said, examining him anxiously.

'Shouldn't be much longer before Kittow's engine's made ready for sea,' Matt said. 'I know about one of his men, the one they call Merv, from my uncle in Gorran Haven. He's worked on every coast, a drifter but a top engineer. Would've got the engine working ages ago if it hadn't been well and truly buggered up. We'll be able to keep an eye on them once they're out here.'

'If it would help, I'd pay for the bleddy engine t'be repaired meself,' Jeff said tetchily, spitting over the gunwale, then leaning back instinctively with the other two fishermen as the crest of a tall wave pitched over the side. 'It was Fred Jose what wrecked Kittow's engine, no one else would do such a mean thing. Kittow must know it too. He'll tip Fred in the bleddy water one day and won't let un come up for air. Pity that little runt didn't drown backalong instead of my boy. 'Tis he what's brought this extra trouble on the village. That Eric's threatened to get hold of his mother. If he tries his hand, Fred and Curly won't be able t'stop him. Mrs Jose is a good woman, bin a good neighbour all these years. We can't let that happen to her.'

'To her or any other woman,' Matt barked, gnashing his teeth, suddenly fearful for Hannah. He was thankful Kittow was currently out of the village. He'd had enough talk of his enemy. Jeff was skipper of the *Sunrise*, but he gave the order, 'Let's see about hauling in the line.'

After nearly seven hours of long, hard work, all the lines were coiled and stowed away in the baskets, new hooks and stops attached where needed. Jeff had taken his turn at hauling, coiling, unhooking the fish, steering the lugger, his chest growing tighter, face getting whiter under its weathered veneer, breath coming harder. He said nothing. Matt had noticed but knew if he mentioned it, Jeff would swear at him for being a fussy old woman.

They headed back home, drinking tea, eating the last of the allowance, ruminating that they would have done better than the two hundred and ninety stone of fish in the fish berth if they had shot further out and if five baskets of line had not failed. Jeff sat down thankfully on his bunk in the cabin, glad for once to be out of the freshening winds that threatened to cut off his breath. If he could find the money he'd consider going to Mevagissey tomorrow to see the doctor, just to be on the safe side. If the doctor recommended a few days' rest he'd take it, and look after the local women.

Jeff walked to Roscarrock the following afternoon. It was raining hard. He had his coat collar turned up, head down, trying to stop a bout of coughing.

Lily answered the door to him. 'Yes, sir?'

'I've come to see Mrs Opie,' he said, his voice gruff, eyes watering. 'Mrs Greg Opie.'

'If you wait inside the porch, sir, I'll see if Mrs Greg's home. Who shall I say is calling?'

'It's Jeff Spargo.' He coughed, searching about in his breast pocket for a handkerchief.

'Oh, of course it is. I recognize you now. I am a silly fool,' Lily laughed. 'You're Mrs Greg's father. Come along inside, Mr Spargo, and I'll fetch her from the study.'

Jeff waited in the vestibule as Lily hastened to the hall and tapped on the study door. She disappeared inside. Jeff heard her say, 'Tis your father for you, Mrs Greg.'

A moment later, Leah, feeling important to have a visitor, was helping Jeff off with his coat. She gave the coat to Lily, led him into the drawing room and stopped dead in her tracks. Mrs Opie was there. Leah had thought her grandmother-in-law was up in her suite.

'Sorry,' she mumbled, pulling on Jeff's arm to hurry him away. Since Hannah's confession she didn't feel quite so in awe of Mrs Opie and rather than trying to court her favour she chose to avoid her.

'I came to see Leah,' Jeff said charily, meeting the challenge in the stubborn lift of Feena's chin. She was sitting in her wheelchair, writing a letter. 'You said her family could come here any time.'

'And I meant it,' Feena said coolly. 'You are wet, Mr Spargo, and you look poorly. Do sit down.' She turned narrowed eyes on Lily who had followed Jeff and Leah into the room. 'Lily, fetch a tray of tea and hot scones. And next time someone calls at the door, don't cackle like a giddy hen when you answer it.'

'Yes, Mrs Opie.' Lily breezed out, her face twisted in amusement. Her employer never fazed her in the way she did Mrs Greg.

'I don't want to intrude,' Jeff said obstinately, not moving from a spot on the Turkish rug.

'Did you want to speak to Leah alone?' Feena asked haughtily.

'Well, no . . .'

'Sit down then. I shall be going to the little parlour at the back of the house presently. I'm busy today, but perhaps I may be permitted to take a cup of tea with you both before I leave.'

'Yes, of course.' Jeff cursed the woman for making him feel awkward even though she was being sociable, but he secretly admired her elegant appearance as he sat down on one of the sofas.

Leah sat close to him. 'How come you're here today, Dad? I thought you'd be getting the *Misty* ready to take out again.'

Feena watched him keenly as he replied. 'I saw the doctor today. He says I've got an infection on my chest and should stay home in the warm. He gave me some pills.' Jeff produced the bottle of pills as if he wanted Feena to see he was telling the truth.

'What a pity you had a wet walk, Mr Spargo.' There was a note of suspicion in Feena's voice.

'It wasn't raining when I started out,' he replied smartly.

'I'm glad you're being sensible, Dad,' Leah said, shifting about, wishing she could develop Mrs Opie's grace and poise. No matter how hard she tried, it didn't come naturally to her as it did to Hannah.

Lily arrived with the tray and automatically carried it to Feena. She waved it away. 'Mrs Greg is hostess today.'

The little bit of confidence Leah had achieved vanished with the task of having to pour tea in polite society. Even with her rough and ready father here it seemed as mammoth a task as climbing a mountain. Her hand shook as she gripped the silver teapot. She remembered to pour the milk first and then the tea to protect the delicate china. The teacup rattled on its floral saucer as she held it out to Feena. A mistake. The old woman couldn't possibly reach it unless she moved closer in her wheelchair. Leah's bottom lip quivered as Feena stared at her. Jeff saved her further embarrassment by taking the cup and saucer and handing it to Feena himself.

'Thank you,' she said graciously. 'I don't want a scone, Leah.' How like her father Leah looked, Feena thought, when he sat down again. She shouldn't be unkind to the girl. After all, she was Greg's choice, he adored her and she made him very happy. She was also Hannah's sister and Feena had noticed Hannah's irritation with her over Leah. There was no point in causing bad feelings.

She said conversationally, 'Do you happen to know if Grace Treloar, now Mrs Daniel Kittow, is back in the village, Mr Spargo? We're waiting for her to take her horses away from the stable so we can buy our own. Greg is going to teach Leah to ride. That is if you can tear him away from the study, Leah.' She gave a pleasant little laugh.

Leah was surprised and pleased at this change in her attitude. 'I shall do my best. Greg needs more fresh air and exercise.' She poured two more cups of tea while her father and Mrs Opie chatted generally about horses. Then Leah blushed furiously. She was suddenly reminded that her father had been Mrs Opie's lover. Had they spent time together in this room? In Mrs Opie's bedroom? Was that where Hannah had been conceived? She thought she'd drop her cup and saucer but at that moment Greg popped his head round the door.

'Good afternoon, Mr Spargo,' he said. 'It's good to see you. Would you mind if I steal Leah away for a few moments? I'd like her to go over something with me. Then we'll both come back and join you.'

'You carry on,' Jeff said. 'They get on well,' he remarked to Feena when they were alone.

'One would never have thought it, but they do seem suited. I understand Hannah is to have another baby. I hope it's safe for her in the village.'

'What do you mean?'

'I'm referring to that dreadful man, Kittow, and his cohorts. Kittow lives very close to Hannah. There could be some unpleasantness, especially if Matt loses his temper. I'm worried about Hannah, Nathan and the new baby.'

Jeff sipped from his cup demurely. 'Don't be. Us men are taking measures to protect the women and children. We could easily throw the troublemakers and Kittow, too, out of Porthellis.'

Feena was not impressed and said disdainfully, 'Brave talk invariably leads to cracked heads.'

Jeff smiled wryly. Stuck-up cow, he thought. There was a strong tickle in his throat and he began to cough.

Feena wheeled herself towards him. 'Let me pour you some more tea. It will help soothe your throat.'

'Thank you,' he said as he mopped his streaming eyes. 'Sorry about that.'

'It looks as though you ought to take the doctor's advice, Jeff. You didn't answer me about Grace Kittow. Is she back in Porthellis?'

'I haven't heard anything. I could ring you when I know something, if you like.'

Feena was looking into his dark eyes. She felt a moment of panic. It would be all too easy to fall under their spell as she had many years ago. 'No, thank you,' she said in a tone that would not be argued with. 'If you'll excuse me, I must get on.' Retrieving her notepaper and pen, she made for the door. Jeff stood up respectfully and opened it for her.

In the small parlour Feena couldn't settle to writing her letter. She was disturbed at Jeff Spargo turning up here today, and flattered herself into thinking it wasn't only Leah he had come to see.

While waiting for Leah and Greg to return, Jeff looked thoughtfully out of one of the tall windows at the wood on the edge of the cliff. Feena had been too afraid to let him into the house when they'd been lovers in case the servants saw him. They had met in the old coachman's cottage at the back of the house and in the woods. Now he had an open invitation to the house and a legitimate reason to go on accepting it. If he got bored while he was off work he might pay another visit here.

Chapter 10

The villagers didn't realize the Kittows had come home until three mornings later when Daniel appeared on the boat with three of his crew; the fourth, Tippy, had been sentenced to twenty-eight days for breach of the peace. Janet Rouse was the first to spot Daniel's red head bobbing in and out of the wheelhouse as he shouted instructions to his men. Soon their swearing resounded up and down the quay, making the oldest male inhabitants of Porthellis consider taking their daily cogitation elsewhere. Janet went straight to tell Hannah.

'Oh, Aunty Janet,' Hannah groaned as she charged across the kitchen to stop Nathan pushing his cereal bowl off his highchair. 'I'm trying to forget that man exists. Anyone would think nobody but him matters.'

''Tis a bit hard to ignore un with his men kicking up their heels every night. You don't live down by the waterfront and hear 'em when they've left the pub. Noisy beggars. They can't be earning anything so Daniel must have left them in plenty of funds before he went away. Not that Maggie Curnow'll mind. She looked after him and he's looking after her by putting all that extra money in her till. Still, at least we've got rid of one of 'em for a while. Hope they keep him locked up for months.'

'You make those men sound like a band of outlaws,' Hannah said in vexation. The morning sickness she'd suffered since she'd got up had only just subsided and she didn't want anything to upset her delicate tummy. Wetting a flannel, she cleaned up her messy child and the equally messy highchair after his clumsy and joyful attempt at feeding himself.

Janet wasn't about to change the subject. 'You going down the street to welcome the new Mrs Kittow to the neighbourhood? I suppose she's in the new house.'

Taking off his soiled bib, Hannah lifted Nathan out of the highchair, kissed his clean and shiny face and put him down on the floor to crawl about. 'I wouldn't know, Aunty, and I won't be setting foot inside Daniel Kittow's house to find out.'

'Strange, him marrying her,' Janet said, her face working as she thought over this conundrum again. 'But then I s'pose his money must've run out with the way he's been splashing it about. He's got a big supply he can lay his hands on now. Women are silly enough to sell their souls for his sort. She'll last till he's got his hands on all of it.'

'Daniel's not like that,' Hannah said, surprising herself at this sudden surge of loyalty for her childhood friend. 'I mean,' she added quickly to counter the astounded expression her aunt turned on her, 'I've never known him to wheedle money out of a woman before.'

'Well,' Janet snorted, 'with all his other vices, what makes you think he wouldn't?' Nathan was leaning on her feet, trying to untie the stout laces of her flat brown shoes. 'Mind you, if only he could settle down with Grace she might manage to persuade him to get rid of those blokes.'

Hannah had endured enough talk about the Kittows and put the dishes in the sink. As she attacked them with the dishcloth she thought about her father, glad to have the small worry about his health to distract her.

Janet lifted Nathan to make a fuss of him. He was cross at being picked up and he smacked her shoulder and tried to bite her cardigan, but she hardly noticed; she was still thinking about Grace and Daniel Kittow.

Down on the waterfront Daniel was tight-lipped as he watched the engineer working on the thirty-horsepower Ruston diesel engine of his boat. 'You got all the right parts, Merv?'

'Aye, Skipper. Should have her sorted out in about four hours.'

'You should've made a start yesterday,' Daniel snarled. 'Not waited for me to get back. What were you all bleddy doing?' He looked at Brinley for an explanation.

He shrugged his enormous shoulders as if he had forgotten the reason. Eric and Merv looked away sheepishly.

'Well?' Daniel bawled, his harsh voice echoing round the harbour.

Jeff, who had telephoned Feena Opie to inform her that Grace Kittow had arrived at her new house, was sitting on a mooring stone some feet away, nonchalantly carving the figure of a mermaid out of a piece of whalebone, half his mind on the persistent questions from an ice-cream-licking, camera-clicking holidaymaker. He glanced up when Daniel shouted and grimaced. Most people saw those men as roughnecks whose behaviour disgusted them. He agreed with Hannah, that Daniel was biding his time to get revenge on the whole village. If he was in a filthy mood he might start wreaking it sooner rather than later. Apart from Fred Jose, who would suffer the most?

'Merv was worst for wear, Skipper. Me and Eric didn't dare touch the engine.'

'I want it finished today and no excuses,' Daniel said savagely. ''Tis time you started earning your keep. Is the coal on board?'

'Yes, Skipper,' Brinley said meekly. 'A hundredweight's safely stowed away, the fuel tanks are topped up and the new nets you ordered are aboard. You can see for yerself we've scrubbed her down prop'ly, scraped 'n' oiled her mast. Long line's coiled 'n' ready. All we gotta do is put the grub on board 'n' net the bait. We can go out with the fleet t'morrer.'

'I should bleddy well think so,' Daniel said irritably. 'I'll get the food myself. Eric, you can be the cook. I won't have a drop of drink on board. If I find some, the man responsible will be over the side. You carry on working, Merv. Eric, you can stand by in case he needs help. Brinley, you clean up the cottage. It's like a bleddy pigsty in there. It's my home, remember.' He lit a cigarette, not offering the packet round. When he spoke next he had dropped his voice. 'I'm talking seriously now. We'll occasionally be sailing upcoast to Plymouth and be dropping off something to another boat or I'll be meeting someone in the port myself. Sometimes we'll be passing on something downcoast or locally. I'll tell you when, and then I want you really quiet and sober. I don't want the police sniffing around. Got that?'

'Yes, Skipper,' his crew answered like children reciting at school.

'Good. There will be extra in your pockets then. Tippy's not coming back. He overstepped the mark by getting arrested. Get on with your work.' He reached for the paint pot and brushes he'd brought with him.

'Skipper, can we have something for t'night?' Brinley asked with a boyish grin. He pulled out his trouser pockets to show they were empty.

'I'll give you something later.' Daniel leapt on to the quay and knelt at the side of the lugger to begin touching up the name *Sunrise* and the boat's number in black. He baulked at giving these ruffians more of his money, which had dwindled to just a few pounds in his savings account, but it would be wise to keep them sweet until he wanted to get rid of them.

Brinley put in an hour's elbow work at the Kittow cottage. When the overflowing sinkful of dishes was washed, ashtrays emptied, bottles thrown in the dustbin, heaps of discarded clothes picked up and the clutter packed away, all that was needed was a quick sweep over the flagstoned floors downstairs and the linoleum ones upstairs.

Brinley had a thing about hygiene from his army days when he had to share latrines with hundreds of other men and he took a bottle of disinfectant outside to the closet. He lifted the bucket out from under the wooden seat and emptied its contents in the hole dug ready in the earth, rinsed out the iron receptacle at the outside tap then swirled neat disinfectant round inside it. He wasn't content to use squares of old newspaper and checked that his supply of soft toilet paper was intact in its hiding place behind the tools and sundries up on the high shelf. A quiver of fear ran through him. A huge hairy spider scuttled across the low galvanized sheeting which served as the roof. He shot out of the toilet into the bright sunshine, settling his ragged breathing by gazing up at the pale blue sky with its adornment of woolly clouds.

'Morning, Brinley. You expecting rain?'

It was Prim, spreading her starched whites over the scrubby bushes in the next garden. Putting the disinfectant down on the ground, he went over to her, rubbing his massive paws self-consciously down his twill shirt.

'Got the kettle on, Prim?' he asked, hoping today she'd invite him inside to drink the mug of tea instead of bringing it outside to him. But of course Prim was a respectable woman.

'Give me a few minutes,' Prim said, laying Jeff and Josh's collars in a neat row on her overgrown privet.

'You should get yer old man to trim that, give un something t'do instead on spying on we.'

That the giant had seen through Jeff's real intention for idling his sick leave away on the quay made Prim blush. 'He has to take it easy, Brinley. Has to watch his heart.'

There was a frightened cry from inside the kitchen. 'Josh!' She dropped the enamelled bowl, her best small tablecloth spilling on to the ash-covered path, and hastened indoors; in a moment of despair she had once nearly smothered Josh but now she was as protective of her brain-damaged son as if he was a newborn baby. Brinley ran after her.

Wearing a sackcloth apron, Josh was standing on the rope mat at the fireside, whimpering and coughing. He was black with soot from head to toe, the long flue brush dangling limply from his hand. 'Aw, Mu-um.'

Prim suppressed a kindly laugh. Josh became upset if people made fun of him but he looked so comical with only the whites of his narrowed eyes gleaming like beacons on the darkest night. 'Just stand still, son. I'll get you cleaned up in no time.' She said to Brinley, 'He was cleaning out the flue of the range. I should have known it was too hard a job for him.'

Brinley fetched the large tin bath hanging up outside on the back wall. With deft movements he gently helped Prim strip Josh naked and cover him with an old horsehair blanket. They filled the bath with hot soapy water from the copper, left over from Prim's washing, and the young man was scrubbed pink and clean.

'The soap's not too harsh for him,' Prim said to Brinley, furiously rubbing a flannel round her son's ears while he protested about the indignity of having a bath during the daytime. He'd forgotten about his mishap with the soot. 'Good job I didn't do all my washing on Monday.'

Brinley was carefully cleaning up the soot with damp rags. 'Poor bugger. He didn't know what hit un. Well, at least yer flue's cleaned out. Yer fire will draw like a wild stallion.'

'Thanks, Brinley. Jeff would only've shouted at the boy and frightened him. And he wouldn't have helped me clean up the place.'

''Tis my pleasure, Prim. Tell 'ee what, when we're done, why don't I go up t'the bakehouse and get us all some cream buns to have with that tea?'

'We'd like that, wouldn't we, Josh?' Prim said, tipping clean water over her son's head.

Grace knocked on the front door of Seaview Cottage. She was planning a house-warming party. Thinking Daniel would not be interested in this sort of entertaining, she had been pleasantly surprised when he had agreed to it. He'd had a twinkle in his eye when she said she would invite every neighbour in Cobble Street. Nan Trebilcock, who had agreed to become Grace's daily help, was to do the catering; Grace would pay for the extra hours.

She had written a formal invitation to the Opies. On arriving home she had found a polite letter from Feena Opie awaiting her, concerning her horses; not a friendly gesture, and she had had to take up her original arrangement with Henry Teague, but she hoped someone from Roscarrock would attend the party. She thought some of the people from the village would come, if only out of curiosity, and hopefully she'd be able to persuade her aunt and uncle to join in. She was more doubtful about Hannah Penney but as she had been the first friend she had made here, and they were close neighbours, she wanted to ask her first.

Hannah answered the door and invited Grace inside. She led the way to the kitchen where she had been sewing at the table. Mrs Penney exchanged pleasantries with Grace and promptly brought out the biscuit barrel and set about making coffee.

'I'll come straight to the point,' Grace said when seated at the other end of the table. 'Daniel and I are giving a house-warming party on Saturday evening. I'd like to extend an invitation to you, Hannah, and Matt and Mrs Penney.'

'What's a house-warming party?' Mrs Penney interjected before Hannah came out with the refusal written bluntly across her face. 'I've never heard of such a thing.'

'It's what people do when they move into a new house, Mrs Penney,' Grace said. 'I do hope you'll come.'

Hannah repeated what she'd said to her Aunty Janet not many hours since. 'I will never set foot inside Daniel Kittow's house and neither will Matt.'

'That goes for me too, but thank you for thinking of us,' Mrs Penney said politely.

'Look, I know there are bad feelings between your family and Daniel, but coming to the party could change that,' Grace coaxed.

'You have my decision,' Hannah said, her blue eyes cold.

Grace rose, leaving her coffee untouched. 'I see. I hope we can still be friends, Hannah.'

'Of course. I'll show you out.'

'This is silly,' Grace exclaimed. 'I'm holding out an olive branch to you. All the unpleasantness of the past could be left there. I don't know what it is that Daniel's supposed to have done—'

'Never mind the past,' Hannah said sharply. 'You may choose to overlook his true nature but if you'd open your eyes you'd see what he's doing now. He's terrorizing all of us with his band of thugs. One of them is locked up for assaulting my cousin's fiancée. Half the children in the village have learned the vilest swear words, women have had to clean vomit off their doorsteps after those men have been drinking. The door of the barkhouse was kicked in. Do I have to go on?'

'No, you do not,' Grace said. She wanted to say something in her husband's defence but could only feel ashamed because she knew what Hannah was saying was true. 'Good morning to you both.'

She saw herself out. Drawing in a deep breath of salty air, she listened to a pair of gulls perched on the roof of Seaview Cottage squawking raucously at each other and she knew she and Hannah had come close to an open quarrel. She had to find out exactly what had happened between her and Daniel. He must have known the Penneys wouldn't come to the house-warming; it must have amused him to think of them being asked. Only on one occasion had he spoken of Hannah and it had been with loathing. Their mutual hatred had come out of a once very close relationship and that made Grace feel uneasy. She did not have the heart to go up to the Manse at this moment. Aunt Adela had sobbed down the telephone when she'd called yesterday to say she would be seeing about having her things delivered to the new house. She went home; perhaps Nan Trebilcock would be forthcoming about what she was burning to know.

Later in the morning Daniel saw Lily Andrews enter the Rouses' house. He'd wanted to see her again and now he would make the opportunity. Lily must have heard about him but she hadn't seen him in the village. Not wanting to risk being pointed out by her mouthy future mother-in-law, he finished his work quickly, went home, washed and dressed smartly. He told Grace he had some business to see to, then walked towards Roscarrock.

Lily had only a couple of free hours and it wasn't long before she was walking back along the lanes, re-reading a romantic poem Jowan had written for her. Daniel had hidden behind the hedge of Turn-A-Penny Lane. When she passed by, he climbed over the hedge and quickly caught her up.

'Oh, good morning.' He doffed his hat. 'Miss Andrews, isn't it?' He sauntered along at her side as if he had all the time in the world.

'Yes, sir,' Lily said politely. She looked at him sidelong; if she hadn't taken up with Jowan she would have made a point of walking the lanes more often in the hope of meeting this handsome stranger. The pale gauntness of his face had gone, replaced by a healthy colour. ''Tis fair weather.'

'Yes, indeed. Perfect for walking. Are you hurrying back to work?'

'I've got half an hour to spare,' Lily replied artfully; she might as well enjoy talking to him and she wanted to know who he was. 'Um, are you on holiday, sir?'

'No, I live in the area,' he said. He swept his practised eye over her comely figure – pity he had to keep his hands off her, but she was connected to Hannah. 'I understand a family called Opie live at Roscarrock and didn't you mention a Mrs Penney when I saw you last?'

'Oh, she was the housekeeper before I come to Roscarrock. Mrs Opie owns the property. She got very fond of Mrs Penney and she still comes to visit every week. Dines there sometimes. Her sister, Miss Leah, married Mrs Opie's grandson.'

'So there is a family connection?' Lily had mentioned before that Hannah was treated like one of the family. He wanted to draw out what she'd meant.

'Yes, but Mrs Opie makes more fuss of Mrs Penney than Mrs Greg. Sometimes I think Mrs Greg gets a bit jealous. Well, you can't blame her. Mrs Opie gives Mrs Penney presents all the time and treats her baby boy as if he was her grandson.'

'What a curious arrangement,' Daniel commented to encourage the under-housemaid's runaway tongue.

''Tis when you think that Mrs Opie had no dealings with anyone from Porthellis for years until Mrs Penney came to work for her. Makes you think.'

'Think about what?'

'Well, Mrs Opie doesn't go out and mix much. I s'pose she could be afraid of spending a lonely old age. But then Mrs Penney is ever so pretty and such a nice woman, anyone would get very fond of her.'

'Would they?' Daniel replied rather sourly.

Feeling that she was losing his interest, Lily became indiscreet. 'Course, there could be another reason.' Abruptly she closed her mouth. It was one thing to exchange rumours with other folk in service but quite another to gossip to a stranger.

'You were saying?' Daniel prompted, fearing she was about to clam up. He quickened his step and stood in front of her, smiling kindly.

Realization suddenly hit Lily. How could she have been so stupid? Why had she not realized before who this man was? She'd heard enough about him, he was the talk of the area. Tall, handsome, striking red hair. He'd made the effort to speak nicely but his accent and his rough hands had told her he was not a gentleman. Panic raced up her spine. Daniel

Kittow was said to be devious and dangerous, and he preyed on young girls. For some reason he wanted to know about the set-up at Roscarrock, and Mrs Penney in particular; it was said he hated her. Lily was alone with him and he wanted an answer from her.

The rush of colour clouding her pert, chubby face and the way her body stiffened alerted Daniel. So the game was up. He said coldly, 'What do they say about Hannah Penney and the Opie woman?'

'Nothing. I . . . let me past. I should have got back ages ago.'

A cruel twist came to his wide mouth. 'You're going nowhere until you answer me.'

Remembering how Tippy had forced a kiss on her, Lily was terrified she'd be dragged off to a field and raped.

'I – if I tell you, will you promise not to hurt me?'

'Well, if you don't tell me, Lily, I will definitely hurt you, very badly.'

Lily began to cry. 'Th-there was a nurse, sh-she nursed Mrs Opie. My m-mother knows a woman who works at another big house where the nurse was employed. She said the nurse found out that Mrs Penney is really Mrs Opie's . . .' Lily swallowed the bile in her throat.

Daniel caught her arms and shook her impatiently. 'Yes, go on.'

'M-Mrs Opie's d-daughter.' Lily broke into uncontrollable sobs.

The subtle difference he had noticed in the Hannah he'd known for so many years fell into place, her haughtiness, the way she wore her clothes, her love of Roscarrock. Now he had the reason why she had suddenly been offered the job as housekeeper at a very young age, why Greg Opie seemed uncommonly fond of her, and why the Opie woman had been going to take her off to Torquay when she got pregnant. They'd be living there now if Matt Penney hadn't nearly perished in the sea, making Hannah realize how much she loved him. The last thought made him feel sick.

'The bitch,' he snarled under his breath, terrifying Lily. When had she found out she was Feena Opie's daughter? While they had still been friends?

He tightened his grip on the quivering maid. 'You're not to tell anyone else this, do you understand? I'll know if you do and I'll come after you and then I'll break the legs of the silly little bastard you're engaged to.'

Now he had something he could use to wipe the smug expression off Hannah's face. He had the knowledge to cause a scandal that would upset her cosy little world and perhaps deny her an inheritance she was no doubt looking forward to. She was fond of the Opie woman and might do anything to protect her real mother's reputation. He'd use the knowledge when it suited him.

Throwing Lily against the hedge, he left her there weeping bitterly.

Chapter 11

The Porthellis fleet left for the pilchard drive in July, staying at Newlyn, the men travelling home by train at the weekend to save time and fuel. Wives, mothers and sweethearts had long lonely hours to endure but at least they had respite from the *Sunrise*'s vulgar crew.

The *Sunrise* caught marginally better catches than the other boats, not because its crew were more experienced or more skilled but because their skipper drove them relentlessly. They made more money per week because they often fished on Sunday like some of the Newlyn men and their up-country rivals. The consensus was that Daniel Kittow was out to prove himself superior at his trade because of his enforced absence. Some people hoped he'd wear himself, his crew and the boat out permanently, others asked what good it would do if they foundered while out fishing in risky conditions.

Hannah's pregnancy was beginning to show and bowing to the exhortations of Matt and Nathan's four 'grandmothers', the riding lessons she had begun with Leah under the tuition of Greg and the able young stable boy came to a halt all too soon. She had taken to the saddle as if she had been born to it and looked forward to resuming the lessons after her confinement. She still went to the stable every week so that the pony she had ridden, an even-tempered chestnut mare called Bonny, would not forget her.

Jeff had been a regular visitor to Roscarrock during the days he spent recovering from his chest infection. Leah missed his visits now that he was back at work and she went more often to the village. She sat in the various homes of her family, hardly changed from the quiet, loyal girl she had been before her marriage. Greg lavished attention on her but neither Feena nor Patrick showed the same fond interest in her as they did in Hannah. Sometimes she felt miffed at being overlooked, but usually she was content to keep in the background. She spent many hours daydreaming or reading in the summerhouse erected specially for her. Very occasionally Mrs Opie joined her and the lady trusted her to take Pogo for his walks. All three women had their ears pierced.

While Leah prayed she would get pregnant, Grace made sure she did not. Having escaped the first month of her marriage, she visited her doctor and had a contraceptive fitted. She had no idea whether Daniel wanted children, he never mentioned the subject. If it turned out one day that he did want to be a father, she would consider having just one to please him.

Her gift shop was now up and running. She had taken the premises next to Phineas Brown's butcher's shop, renovating and enlarging the poky, long-deserted building. Its shelves were stocked with ornaments made from seashells, felt piskies, models of tin mines, cheap china animals for the less discerning mantelpieces, scenic postcards, Cornish wall plaques, pretty boxes of stationery, notebooks, pens and pencils. She approached local craftsmen and craftswomen and soon had lacework, knitted garments and pottery on display, together with good quality costume jewellery, wools and embroidery silks. She did not want to work in the shop full-time and for twenty-five hours a week she employed a middle-aged spinster, Miss Faulkner, who lived in a small wayside cottage not far outside the village.

Her fear that Hannah would shun her was unfounded. Hannah was not as friendly but she was one of the first customers in the shop on its opening day to wish her well and she bought some embroidery silk. Although none but the nosy turned up for Grace's house-warming party, the villagers accepted her presence among them. They never mentioned Daniel; it was as if they overlooked the fact that she was his wife. The Opies had declined her invitation but Feena called on her one afternoon and promised to come again. It took Adela Skewes six weeks to settle her nerves and come to terms with her niece's ill-advised marriage and visit her home. It now bore Grace's choice of name in a flourish of wrought iron near the front door – Chynoweth, meaning new house. There Adela encountered the only family Grace desired: two pure white kittens called Crystal and Jade.

Porthellis lived in a restless quietness, concentrating on catering for the growing holiday trade. Mrs Trudgeon opened part of the bakehouse shop as a small tearoom and Hannah's elder sister Sarah in River Street took in bed and breakfast. Like wary observers watching the tide for dangerous undercurrents, the villagers watched Daniel Kittow for signs of what he might do next, and the European nations watched Adolf Hitler.

One weekend after Daniel had been home, Grace left Miss Faulkner in charge of the shop and took a walk along the cliff to assuage her loneliness. The women spoke of how bereft they felt when their men were away, not knowing if they were safe and sound until the following Saturday, and although Chynoweth was on the telephone and Daniel occasionally rang her, she found the emptiness in her heart almost too much to bear at times. She loved him hopelessly.

She walked to the Dodman, stopping a moment to read the inscription at the foot of its towering cross: IN THE FIRM HOPE OF THE SECOND COMING OF OUR LORD JESUS CHRIST AND FOR THE ENCOURAGEMENT OF THOSE WHO STRIVE TO SERVE HIM THIS CROSS IS ERECTED A.D. 1896. She said a prayer for Daniel's safety.

She trekked on until she was, according to her pathfinder's map, looking down on Vault Beach. It was a picturesque spot. High sloping fields and cliff looked down on the sea passively lapping the sand. Seaweed bobbed in the surf. In shallower areas the water was a beautiful aquamarine green which she likened to the eyes of her kittens. Above, an unseen lark trilled. On the banks, foxgloves and cow parsley grew with sloe. Orange insects with black wingtips hovered over five-foot-high thistles with many deep purple heads on their stems. Pretty pink flowers brightened the brambles. There was honeysuckle and elderberry. On the gorse bushes, spiders had spun webs as fine as muslin.

Her spirit lifted. If Daniel felt a pull for the sea in the same way as this place tugged at her heart, she understood why he kept on as a fisherman. Every now and then he sailed up to Plymouth or caught the train there. She knew women weren't allowed on the boats except for the annual picnic but he wouldn't let her accompany him on the train either. She hoped he would come home next weekend.

She moved on to Gorran Haven. Just before she reached the fishing cove famous for its crabbing, she saw a colony of kittiwakes nesting on the rocks. Honking and squawking, they made a glorious noise. Lower down, near the water, sat a row of shags. The water was busy with small craft.

She took tea at an outside table of a small cafe, sharing it with a charming elderly couple on holiday from Newcastle who promised to drive round to Porthellis and visit her shop. Then she ambled back across the cliff, thinking her life was near to perfect.

* * *

Hannah was carrying a bag of groceries up Porthkilt Hill. Striding down towards her in a businesslike fashion was a woman dragging along with her a small girl. The girl's faltering steps couldn't keep up and she stumbled, hitting her knee on the hard ground. The woman slapped her leg. Hannah frowned at hearing the smack of flesh on flesh. As they got closer, she saw they were scruffily dressed and none too clean.

'Can you tell me where Danny Kittow lives?' the woman asked her in a rough voice.

Hannah saw she was near her own age but harsh lines round her sallow eyes and mouth made her appear older. Her face was heavily made up. Hannah glanced down at the little girl and was dismayed at her filthy face, runny nose and stick-thin arms and legs. Blood trickled down her knee where it had scraped the ground; if Nathan had received such a fall he would have bellowed long and hard. The girl hung back, dry-eyed. A ragged cotton bonnet was rammed down over her head, the scrap of blanket she was clutching as a comforter was black with dirt. Her eyes were red-rimmed and had dark shadows under them. There was a strong smell of urine, mould and cheap scent emanating from their direction.

Hannah was curious as to why this shabby woman should want to see Daniel. 'He lives in the same street as me,' she said. 'I'll show you the way. You'll have to turn round, you've just passed it.'

'Bugger.' The woman pulled the girl round with her, making her worn-out shoes scrape the ground. 'Is he likely t'be there?'

'No, he's away with the boats on the pilchard drive. Won't be home till Saturday, if he comes home at all.'

The woman swore more soundly. 'I've come all the way from St Austell. I didn't want t'go back until I'd finished my business with him.'

'Mrs Kittow might be there,' Hannah said, feeling sorry for the girl who stared vacantly up at her. She had some chocolate in her bag but felt the hostile woman wouldn't appreciate her offering some to the child. 'She owns a shop in the village but she isn't there today.'

The woman glared at Hannah suspiciously. 'Are we talking about the same man? He told me his mother was dead years back and his cottage was on the waterfront.'

'He's got a new house now, down here.' Hannah turned into Cobble Street, thinking she had never met a more aggressive woman. 'And I was talking about his wife.'

'Wife? You mean that bastard's got married?'

Hannah wished the woman wouldn't keep swearing in front of the girl. 'Yes, a few weeks ago.' She pointed to Chynoweth. 'That's his house there.'

'Bloody hell, the jammy bugger! But if he fell in a cesspit he'd make sure he got up smellin' of roses.' The woman snorted and strode off without saying thank you.

Hannah went inside Seaview Cottage via the front door. She wasn't usually given to twitching the net curtains but she peeped out of the parlour window as the woman approached the new house.

Grace had only just arrived back from her walk and was making herself a light lunch. Wiping bread crumbs from her hands, she answered the urgent thumping on the front door. She raised her neat brows at the unkempt woman on the doorstep and assumed she was a Gipsy.

'Are you Danny Kittow's missus?' the woman snarled, her rank breath hitting Grace's face.

'Yes, can I help you?'

'Yes, you bloody well can. Come here!' Her hand shot out and she pulled at something Grace couldn't see. The next moment a little girl was pushed over the threshold into the hallway. 'I've brought somethin' for that bastard, his kid. She's Danny's. I've brung her up for four years on my own without a penny piece from him. Now I can't cope any more and he can have her.'

'But—'

'Here's her things.' The woman thrust a small cloth bag at Grace. 'Her name's Melanie. You won't have any trouble with her if you give her a good clout round the ear.'

Grace was outraged. 'You can't turn up on my doorstep and leave your child here.'

'You mean Danny shouldn't face up to his responsibilities?' the woman jeered. 'I'm not the first girl he's got into trouble. If word gets round I've left her here you'll have a queue outside your bloody door all the way down the road.'

'You can't prove Daniel's the child's father,' Grace said angrily. She was about to say she was going to call the police when the woman snatched off the girl's bonnet.

Grace recoiled. The girl's hair was thick with scurf and something was crawling through it, but her tatty mane was the rich red colour of Daniel's.

She peered closely at the girl to see if she bore a resemblance to Daniel but her face was so marred with ingrained dirt it was hard to tell. She had sores at the corners of her mouth. The girl pouted and backed away from her. She looked like a Dickensian street urchin and Grace was stung to fury for a different reason. How could someone neglect their child in this way?

'I never doubted Danny would end up in prison,' the girl's mother said bitterly, 'but I never thought he'd get married. You're a lot older than him. Married you for your money, did he? For this grand house? I was a virgin when I met him. I was going to marry a boy in the same street,' she snorted, 'live happily ever after. Then I met Danny while out shopping for me mother. Right away I was dazzled by his good looks. It wasn't long before I chucked Sidney over and let Danny have his way with me. When I told him I was pregnant he told me t'go to hell. My mother threw me out and all that was left for me t'do was work the streets. He's welcome to his bastard. Her birth certificate's in the bag.'

Grace stood speechless as the woman advanced on her daughter. The child looked frightened and ducked out of her reach. 'You're staying with this lady from now on. Be a good girl for her.' She said no more to bid her child goodbye and gazed icily at Grace. 'I wish you well with Danny Kittow. I hope he doesn't destroy your life like he has mine and others'.'

Grace and Melanie stared warily at each other, not knowing what to do or say. Then to Grace's horror she saw wetness trickle down Melanie's legs. When the girl came out of her stupor and realized what was happening, she ran into the space under the stairs and curled herself into a tight ball. The eyes that stared up at Grace were filled with fear.

Grace was mortified that Melanie should be frightened of her. She crouched down before her. 'It's all right, Melanie. It was only an accident. I'll get you cleaned up.' Grace had no idea how she would do this, only that she needed help.

Chapter 12

Grace hurried down the street and knocked on Hannah's front door; she hadn't got used yet to the more usual practice of going round to the back of a house where the door was always open. Hannah had stopped looking out of the parlour window when the woman and girl had gone inside Chynoweth. She put aside the little shirt she was making for Nathan and opened the door to find Grace very red in the face.

'Hannah, please can you come with me? I need your help,' Grace implored her.

Hannah was alarmed to see this refined woman who was usually in total control of herself wringing her smooth white hands on her doorstep. 'Why? What's happened?' Her first thought was that the aggressive woman had attacked her.

'A woman came to the house a short time ago. She had a little girl with her and she's gone away and left the child with me.' Grace's worry had made her as breathless as if she had run ten miles.

'Left her with you?' Hannah frowned, puzzled.

Grace went even redder. 'Yes, she said the girl is Daniel's child. Now she's wet herself and seems terrified of me. She's obviously been ill-treated. I don't know what to do. Please will you come and help me?'

Stepping over Daniel Kittow's doorstep would be like committing sacrilege to Hannah. 'I don't know . . .'

'I know how you feel but I don't want to ask my aunt, she would fuss so. Please come, for the girl's sake. She's wet and smells awful.'

Hannah was reluctant but she couldn't dismiss the plea; she had seen for herself how neglected the girl was. 'Just give me a minute to ask my mother-in-law to mind Nathan.'

The two women walked the short distance to Chynoweth together. Grace ushered Hannah inside ahead of her.

The little girl was crouching like a rat in a corner, her red-rimmed eyes enormous in her thin, dirty face. 'Poor little thing,' Hannah said. 'She probably thought you were going to beat her for wetting herself. We must find her something else to wear.'

'Her mother left this.' Grace picked up the cloth bag which she'd put down on the bottom step of the stairs.

'Look inside it then,' Hannah prompted her.

Grace picked up the bag and gingerly loosened the ragged drawstrings. She pulled out a dress. It was washed but creased and in no better condition than the shapeless one on Melanie's back which looked as if it had been cut down from an old curtain. A shrunken grey cardigan, a grubby nightie and two pairs of hopelessly stretched knickers made up her wardrobe. 'There must be more than this surely.' Grace dug about inside the bag but found only Melanie's birth certificate. She looked at Hannah helplessly.

It was obvious Grace had no intention of touching the child if she could help it; she probably had no notion about children anyway. Sighing impatiently, Hannah approached the little girl, kneeling close to her and using a soothing voice. 'It's all right, my handsome. We're not going to hurt you. We're not angry that you've done wee-wees. My name's Hannah and this is Grace. What's your name?'

The girl gazed back from large startled eyes.

'Her name's Melanie,' Grace said, then looked at the birth certificate. 'Melanie Wicks. She's four years old.'

'She's very small for her age,' Hannah observed. 'Listen, Melanie, you must be uncomfortable in your wet clothes. Grace and I want to give you a wash, a nice warm bath, and put you in clean clothes. Would you like that?'

Melanie did not respond.

'Do children talk by the time they're four?' Grace asked, keeping well back and hoping Hannah would lead the child upstairs to the bathroom.

'Most children can form short sentences by the time they're two,' Hannah replied shortly, peeved that Grace was hanging back and showing her distaste so obviously. This wasn't her responsibility.

'I'll pop upstairs and run the bath water and put out fresh towels. I'll tip in some bath foam, that should help things along.' Grace went upstairs, her mind busily ticking over what she should do with the child after she'd been made more presentable.

Hannah gently touched Melanie's arm and the little girl allowed herself to be pulled to her feet. Hannah had expected her to fight against her but Melanie meekly climbed the stairs with her. Too afraid not to cooperate, Hannah thought sadly, poor little soul. She tested the bath water for the correct temperature with her elbow.

'You need to undress her,' she said pointedly to Grace as Melanie stared down nervously into the frothy water. 'She's probably never had a bath in her life.'

'Would you mind, Hannah? I know I've no right to encroach on your time but I've never done anything like this before. I'm afraid I might hurt her.' Grace's concern for Melanie was as genuine as her disgust at actually touching such a filthy individual.

'Very well,' Hannah said resignedly. 'You'd better go downstairs and wipe some disinfectant over your hall carpet.'

'Oh, yes, of course,' Grace said, much relieved. She didn't mind that, she had had to clean up after her kittens a few times.

Melanie made no protest as Hannah stripped off her clothes but when she tried to take the comfort blanket from her to lift her into the bath, Melanie let out a piercing shriek and struggled violently. Hannah calmed her down and decided to put them in together. The comfort blanket smelled of vomit and other indescribable odours; it might as well be washed too. Melanie was terrified of the bath and clung to Hannah as she tried to lower her into the water. Her thin body was scratched and bruised and dotted with open sores. Hannah was afraid she would cause even more damage if Melanie struggled.

At last, after much gentle persuasion, Melanie allowed herself to be lowered slowly into the water. Gradually she relaxed as Hannah, all the while speaking kindly, gently swirled it round her battered body. 'Would you like to smell this soap, Melanie?' She put the bar of sandalwood scented soap under her nose and Melanie gave it a tentative sniff. 'I'm going to lather up a flannel and wash you all over. You'll smell just like the soap and you'll feel good.' She hoped the bath would soothe the girl's neglected skin. She used Grace's Amami shampoo to wash her hair twice, commandeering her tooth glass to rinse it with clean water. Melanie blinked and wriggled, clutching at Hannah and soaking her, but she made not the slightest protest. She seemed fascinated with the bubbles. As the top layers of dirt washed away, Hannah was struck by how much she looked like Daniel; in fact she was the image of him even without her telltale mop of thick red hair. She had a defeated air about her, heartbreaking to see in one so young. She had probably been bullied and abused all her young life. Hannah was seething; it didn't seem to have occurred to Grace that Daniel was partly responsible for his daughter's distress. How she loathed the man.

Grace came back as Hannah was wrapping a blue fluffy towel round Melanie's shivering body, the comfort blanket dripping water on to the tiled floor. 'It seems a shame to put her other dress on her,' Grace said compassionately. 'It doesn't smell very sweet. Is there something we can do?'

'I could pop along to my cousin Lizzie. She mentioned the other day she's got some clothes her stepdaughter has grown out of. She was going to pass them on to my sister Naomi but I'm sure she'd let me have some.'

'That would solve our immediate problem. I'll give you some money to pay for them. I'll fetch my purse.'

'Lizzie won't want paying, she'll be only too glad to help,' Hannah said drily. 'Shall I take Melanie downstairs?'

'No, my bedroom's across the landing. She'll be more comfortable there until you get back.'

Until she put Melanie on the Kittows' bed, Hannah hadn't really taken in how fine Daniel's house was. The bed was a small reproduction fourposter in golden oak, matching the rest of the sturdy suite – rather masculine, Hannah thought. The bedspread was blue-green in watered silk. The bathroom had been impressive too, she realized. It was modern with brass fittings and a wall heater. Ceramic pots of delicate ferns trailed from glass shelving holding an enormous array of male and female toiletries.

'I'm just going to pop out for a minute, Melanie,' Hannah said after gently towel-drying the little girl's hair and rolling her comfort scrap in the end of her towel. 'If you want to go wee-wees, ask Grace and she'll take you to the bathroom.'

While Hannah was away, Grace tried to amuse Melanie by showing her the things on her dressing table. Melanie peeped somewhat mystified out of the confines of the towel. Grace showed her the teddy bear that had been hers as a girl. That had no interest for her either. Suddenly her tiny face lit up. Crystal and Jade, the kittens, had crept into the room and jumped on to the bed, seeking attention. They sidled up to Melanie and she let out a hollow giggle, then looking guiltily at Grace she shrank back inside her towel.

'It's all right,' Grace said quickly. 'These are my kittens. They're called

Crystal and Jade. Would you like to hold one?'

Melanie looked uncertain but nodded. Grace picked up Jade, distinguishable from her sister by a dark smudge on the top of her nose, and nestled her into Melanie's arms. Crystal followed but both kittens soon wriggled free. Shrugging off the towel for better mobility, Melanie began to play with the kittens on the bed.

Grace's mind was in a whirl about how one should treat a child. Then she remembered that children were invariably hungry or thirsty and Melanie looked as if she hadn't ever eaten well. 'When we've got you dressed you shall have something nice to eat and a glass of milk,' she stated, feeling more confident.

Melanie glanced up at her with a look of such longing Grace thought her heart would melt. 'You stay with Jade and Crystal, my dear. I'll run downstairs and fetch you some biscuits.'

Melanie was making crumbs all over the bed as she frolicked naked with the kittens when Hannah returned with a bundle of clothing. She was glad to see that Grace didn't seem to mind that her immaculate bedroom was getting messed up. There was an empty glass that had contained milk on the bedside cabinet.

Melanie came reluctantly but instantly to Hannah's call to get dressed. Hannah wiped the crumbs from her face and put her into a good white vest and pair of knickers, a blue print dress and white cardigan. An old pair of sandals from Lizzie's stepdaughter fitted her quite well. A pained expression crossed the girl's face. 'Do you want to go to the toilet?' Hannah asked.

She nodded.

Hannah carried her there swiftly, feeling she might not make it in time if she walked. Melanie was nonplussed by the toilet and Hannah had to help her on to the seat. She clutched Hannah's skirt when she pulled the chain then stared down amazed as the bowl flushed.

Grace was waiting for them on the landing. 'Shall we go down to the kitchen? I'll make something for her to eat. Perhaps some scrambled egg on toast.' She was learning to cook with advice from Nan Trebilcock and a number of cookery books but she hadn't mastered very much yet.

'That's right, Grace, you're getting the hang of this,' Hannah said mischievously.

Grace made a wry face.

As Grace bustled about the kitchen and Melanie sat stiffly at the table,

Hannah looked round in amazement at all the latest equipment designed to take the drudgery out of housework. There was an Electrolux refrigerator and a washing machine – she had only seen such items before at Roscarrock. She wondered whether Grace or Daniel had supplied them.

'You'll have to ask Melanie frequently if she wants the toilet,' Hannah said. 'I should burn her old clothes to get rid of the lice. You'll have to get some lotion from the chemist to kill the lice in her hair and some boracic acid to bathe her eyes. She's got pinkeye. You'll likely as not find her eyes will be stuck together tomorrow morning by the heavy discharge. You'll have to bathe them with cooled boiled water.'

Grace was sickened. 'Poor little girl, but she won't be here tomorrow.'

'Why not?' Hannah challenged tartly.

'Well, I . . . I can't look after her. She can't stay here. I'll phone the authorities and they can come and collect her and find her somewhere to live.'

'Why can't she live here?' Hannah demanded savagely. 'She's Daniel's child. You don't dispute that, do you? Look at her, can't you see the resemblance?'

'Yes,' Grace said lamely; she had been trying not to think about it. 'But I'm not capable of caring for a child.'

'You mean you don't want to.' Hannah faced her with the cruel truth. 'It would upset your cosy little world, wouldn't it? How can you think about sending her away? Her mother's a despicable creature, she doesn't want Melanie. Are you going to throw her on the scrapheap too?'

Grace was nearly in tears. The eggs she was scrambling were beginning to burn and she hastily piled the good bits on to the toast and put it in front of Melanie. Melanie was white and pinched. Grace smiled at her, hating herself. 'There you are, darling. Tuck in and you can have some ice cream for afters.' Melanie ignored the knife and fork and began to eat using her hands.

Hannah felt she had said enough. Saying goodbye to Melanie, she made for the front door. Grace raced after her. 'Hannah, I feel sorry for the girl but it's not my responsibility to bring her up.'

Hannah whirled round. 'Yes it is. She's Daniel's daughter, you're Daniel's wife. It's as simple as that. Or are you as rotten to the core as he is?'

'Daniel's not rotten,' Grace exploded.

'Then he won't mind being presented with his child, will he? Or are you afraid of that, Grace? That he'll insist on turning her out like he turned his back on her before she'd even been born. It's not the first time he's left some poor innocent girl in trouble, you know. He seduced the girl my brother Mitch married. She came to Porthellis looking for help from Mitch and then Josh tried to force himself on her. Daniel saved her from that and afterwards Mitch beat Josh until he turned stupid. It was all Daniel's fault in the first place. He leaves a trail of hurt and destruction behind him wherever he goes. Don't worry about Viv's baby turning up to stake a claim on its real father, she lost it after what happened. If I want to see Mitch and Viv I have to go to Portmellon because they won't set foot here again, and all because of Daniel. I hope that's given you something to think about. Good morning, Mrs Kittow.' Hannah swept out of the new house on a tide of indignation and anger.

Grace stood for several minutes in stunned humiliation then she picked up the telephone. She asked the doctor to call. When she went back to the kitchen, Melanie was raiding the biscuit tin. Grace could see that she had hidden biscuits inside her clothes and the damp comfort blanket but she did not say anything.

Melanie sat on the floor and played with the kittens until she nodded off to sleep. She looked comfortable so Grace left her on the floor and sat at the table, pulling at her nails as she waited for the doctor. She tried not to think about Hannah's cutting remarks; instead she wondered how best to get out of this predicament. Melanie was Daniel's responsibility and only to a lesser extent hers. The answer came quickly – boarding school. Until Melanie was old enough to attend, she could live in a nursery. She would see to it tomorrow. She would pay. Daniel couldn't grumble. It was a pity he had to know about this.

When the doctor came he wanted to inform the authorities of Melanie's neglect but Grace assured him that she would take care of the child's future. She paid for a taxi to collect the prescriptions of boracic acid and treatments for head lice and scabies from a chemist in St Austell. Bribing Melanie with chocolate, she got her to lay her head on a towel on the kitchen table and clumsily bathed her eyes and treated her skin and hair, using the fine-toothed comb the doctor had said she'd also need to dislodge the nits. Again, Melanie did not complain.

There was a nightie in the bundle of clothes Hannah had brought and Grace changed Melanie into it at seven o'clock when she looked sleepy. The other three bedrooms were fully furnished with items Grace had sent to Kent for. She put Melanie into the single bedroom next to hers, complete with the damp and crumby comforter. Digging out a storybook from her childhood days, she read *Goldilocks and the Three Bears* to her. Melanie stared at her blankly. She probably had no notion of fairy tales. Grace went downstairs after telling Melanie where she was going; she only had to shout if she needed her.

Grace poured herself a large gin and tonic and curled up on the sofa. She hoped Hannah would say nothing about the girl to anybody. With any luck she would be able to get Melanie out of Porthellis without any fuss.

She was awakened in the middle of the night by the most terrible screams. Dashing to Melanie's room, she found her sitting up rigidly in bed, screaming as if she was being burned to death. Grace shook her gently, then more forcefully until she woke up fully. Her little body shook with sobs. Grace didn't know where the words came from but she gradually soothed her night terrors away until Melanie went quiet, resting her sharp chin on her shoulder. Suddenly filled with emotion, Grace hugged her close. The bed was soaked with sweat and urine.

'Out you come, darling. Now, don't worry. I'll put dry sheets on the bed and find you something else to wear.' Taking off the soiled nightie, she washed Melanie in the bathroom then improvised, feeling rather pleased with her effort, by putting a short-sleeved cotton cardigan of her own on her. She pulled off the wet sheets and scrubbed the bed with disinfectant. Her mother had been incontinent towards the end of her life and one of the rubber sheets had been mixed up with the good linen sent down from Kent. She put this at the dry end of the bed, put on a fresh linen sheet and tucked Melanie in a second time. The rest of the night passed quite peacefully but Melanie wet the bed again.

First thing in the morning, Grace bathed her sticky eyes and put her in the bath. Her repugnance for these tasks had gone and her actions were gentle. When Melanie was dry she smoothed ointment on her sores and dressed her in more of Lizzie Jacobs's hand-me-downs. As they ate cereal at the breakfast table, Grace didn't have the heart to send Melanie away – not until the signs of her neglect had healed. She didn't want her ostracized for something that wasn't her fault; people, particularly other children, could be so unkind.

She phoned her aunt. Adela Skewes immediately buzzed down the hill and agreed that the child must be sent to a nursery. She would have preferred straight away. 'After all, she is a . . . you know.'

Grace wanted to go to St Austell but Mrs Skewes declined to mind Melanie for a couple of hours. Nan Trebilcock was more sympathetic. Grace confided in her fully and she was happy to help. She started on the soiled linen and offered to cut Melanie's hair tidily. Nan could be trusted. She'd been hurt when the villagers had shunned her for working for Daniel and she felt a loyalty towards the Kittows. She had willingly responded to Grace's probings about Daniel and the Penneys, informing her that it was jealousy over Hannah that had caused the estrangement. This was as much as Grace had learned before; it hadn't settled her, she felt Daniel must have loved Hannah very much to hate her like he did now.

'There's a box of my old toys in the smallest bedroom and Melanie likes to play with the kittens,' Grace said, pulling on her light cotton gloves then reaching for her clutch bag and car keys. 'She can play in the back garden if she wants.'

'I'll watch her with me life, Mrs Kittow, never fear,' said Nan amiably. 'She's the dead spit of her father, right enough. Feed her up and put some flesh on her bones and I'll reckon she'll be a pretty little maid.'

'She is pretty,' Grace declared. 'Be sure to ask her regularly if she wants to use the bathroom, but if she does have an accident you're not to chide her. There are clean clothes in her room.'

Grace drove back and forth as fast as the narrow lanes and other traffic allowed her. She staggered into the house with armfuls of bags and packages. Nan helped her to spread the dresses and sets of underclothes, pairs of socks and shoes bought for Melanie over the sitting room furniture. She tried to add up in her head how much her employer must have spent but soon lost count. 'Got something for every day of the week here, missus.' She twirled a beribboned straw hat on her red-varnished fingertips.

'Goodness knows she deserves it, Nan. I don't expect she's ever had anything but rags in her life. I want her to have nice things for her new start. Actually, I quite enjoyed myself. You've done a good job on her hair, a fringe suits her. I must pay you extra for that.'

Melanie was playing on the floor with the kittens, unaware that the clothes were for her. Grace smiled down at her. 'Some of her habits are rather anti-social but she's quite manageable. Has she spoken since I've been out?'

'Not a word. She didn't come near me unless I invited her to, like as if she's used to having to keep out of the way of grown-ups. When I started singing she got a bit upset. I think she thought I was shouting at her.'

'Poor little dear. She's had a dreadful start in life. Well, I'll make sure she's well cared for from now on. I've written to the authorities. I'll make sure her appalling mother can never claim her back.'

In the afternoon, Hannah knocked on the door. 'You've still got her with you then?'

'Yes,' Grace replied coolly. Hannah had been right to attack her yesterday over her uncaring attitude but she was still smarting. 'Do you want to come in and check on her?'

'No.' Up went Hannah's chin. 'Not if you're going to put it like that. It's really none of my business.'

'That's right. It's mine and Daniel's business.'

'I doubt if he'll think it's his. I'll leave you to it.' On this dour tone, Hannah departed.

'I forgot to thank you for your help yesterday,' Grace called after her grudgingly. 'I'm grateful to you. I'll send back the clothes borrowed from your cousin.' Then she muttered under her breath, 'Don't come here again.'

Holding her hand tightly, Grace took Melanie out into the village the next day. Her new crisp cotton skirt and blouse couldn't hide her shameful thinness. The good food, milk and vitamins Grace had pumped into her had made the dark circles under her eyes a little less obvious and her nose didn't run as much. Her straw hat obscured most of her hair but its colour was commented upon. Every now and then Grace had to discourage Melanie from scratching her healing sores.

They paid a visit to the gift shop where Grace told Melanie she could chose anything she liked from the shelves. Miss Faulkner's high bust bristled at her lack of manners as Melanie snatched a three-inch felt piskie and wrapped it inside her comfort blanket. Grace bought sweets for her in the grocery shop where Hamlyn Innis looked down on Melanie in disdain. Grace decided she'd sell sweets in her shop in competition with Hamlyn. In the tea shop Mrs Trudgeon was kinder, giving Melanie a free cream bun. She asked straight out, 'Belongs to Daniel, does she?'

Grace replied stoutly, 'Yes, and I'm glad to be looking after her.'

After walking along the quay, afraid Melanie would tire easily, Grace led her to sit down in a quiet spot on an upturned rowing boat near the beach. A fresh breeze fanned their faces and Grace thought it would do Melanie good. They were joined by Lizzie Jacobs, her two stepchildren and her two natural children, the youngest a three-month-old baby.

'So, this is the little maid Hannah told me about,' Lizzie said good-naturedly. 'You've got her looking a treat compared to what Hannah said.' Lizzie's older children scampered away to play on the sand. 'She's welcome to join mine if she likes. She'll need friends.'

Grace was about to say Melanie wouldn't be in the village long enough for that but a painful lump in her throat prevented her. She looked at Melanie, sitting so very close, leaning into her, ramming her fingers into the sweet packet, a slightly aggressive gleam in her deep blue eyes telling she wouldn't share them. An unknown force grew in Grace, a feeling she found comfortable and natural, and which she did not want to fight. She put her arm round Melanie firmly, kissed the top of her head. 'Thank you. I think she's rather shy at the moment. Tell me, Mrs Jacobs, do you think the villagers would shun Melanie because she's Daniel's and was born out of wedlock?'

'Well, there may be some that would be prejudiced but most of us wouldn't take it out on a child. 'Tisn't her fault how she came into the world. Besides, she's the minister's great-niece.'

Grace gazed thoughtfully at the white sparkles of water where the breeze disturbed the reflection of the sun on it. The cliff of the dark side was bathed in light today. 'Yes, she is,' Grace agreed softly.

On the fourth night that Melanie had the night terrors, Grace took her into her own bed, putting the rubber sheet over the mattress as added protection to the nappy she'd put on her – a piece of advice from Nan Trebilcock. Melanie slept with one hand on her comfort blanket, the other clutching Grace's nightdress. Grace wrapped her arms round her. 'There you are, darling. Grace is going to make everything better for you.'

Daniel got home late on Saturday night, after personally passing on a package of jewellery, stolen in France and brought across the Channel, to his fence in Plymouth. Grinning at his wife's bare arm stretched across the bed, he tore off his clothes, eager for her after the week's absence. He yanked back the bedclothes and it seemed to him all hell broke loose.

A child was sitting up, stiff as a ramrod, screaming her head off in his bed. 'What the bloody hell's going on?' he shouted.

'Daniel, for goodness sake, put something on,' Grace hissed. 'You mustn't let her see you naked like that.'

As he grabbed his shirt and held it to his waist, the child slithered out of bed and ran past him, blubbering loudly. 'Grace, for goodness sake—'

'Explanations will have to wait. I must go to Melanie. You've frightened her out of her wits.'

'She's frightened? Who is she?' he demanded incredulously, but his wife had disappeared after the offending child. Next moment he howled in rage, 'The bed's bloody wet!'

It was half an hour before Grace returned to him, half an hour in which, clad in his underpants, he had smoked and ground his teeth and paced up and down the bedroom carpet. 'It had better be good,' he snarled at her.

'Don't you recognize her, Daniel?' Grace sought to make light of it as she pulled the wet sheet off the bed, but she was nervous.

'What's the kid got to do with me?'

'She's your daughter.' Grace rubbed her arms to stop her trembling. She felt vulnerable and a little fearful as he loomed over her. 'Her mother brought her here five days ago. She's been terribly ill-treated, Daniel.'

'Are you out of your sodding mind? Some bitch turns up on the doorstep and you take in her brat? The bitch saw you for a rich woman and leapt in with both feet to get rid of the kid and you fell for it. She's out of the house first thing in the morning.'

Grace fought to stay calm. 'I'm positive she's your child, Daniel. She's the living image of you. Her mother's name is Janie Wicks. She lives at St Austell. Do you remember her? She said you seduced her.'

'Name's familiar,' he growled. 'It doesn't prove nothing.'

'Look at Melanie tomorrow, Daniel. You'll see she's yours.' Grace employed a softer feminine note, running her hands over his chest in the tantalizing way he liked.

'Supposing she is. What're you doing with her?'

'I've been looking after her. At first I thought to send her away but I've grown very attached to her. I'm thinking about raising her as mine.' She thought it wise not to say 'ours'. 'I want to see she gets a good education, all the benefits of life she deserves.'

He snorted. 'What about your shop? Got bored with that already, have you? I got the impression you didn't like kids. Or are you going to get a nanny or something?'

The cloud of worry that had hung heavily over her for the past five days evaporated and words she'd never thought she'd say tumbled out of her mouth. 'Miss Faulkner has said before that she'd run the shop full-time if the occasion arose and I could employ a part-time girl to help. I don't think I'll get a nanny. I want to give Melanie all my time, to help her live a normal life. She's four years old, Daniel, and she doesn't talk yet and she still needs nappies.'

'All right, I don't want to hear any more about it. Do what you like with the kid. Just make sure you keep her out of my way and remember it's your idea not mine.' He pulled her to him roughly. 'Now do you think you can forget about being a bloody mother and concentrate on being my wife?'

Chapter 13

With Nathan napping in his cot, Matt working on his allotment and Mrs Penney invited to Gorran Haven for tea with her brother and sister-in-law, Hannah took the opportunity to put her feet up. Taking off her apron, she carried a cup of coffee and the latest issue of *Woman's Weekly* into the parlour and rested against the cushions on the black horsehair sofa. It was a comfortable room, one of the few carpeted parlours in the village; her wedding presents were added to Mrs Penney's porcelain in the bow-fronted cabinet. She glanced at the regulator clock on the wall; it was two thirty, she could get an hour or two to herself.

Her eyes grew heavy and laying the magazine on the small bump of her tummy, she nestled down for a snooze.

She was out in Rufus Kittow's tosher, the *Wynne*, with the other children many years ago. Daniel was rowing towards Hidden Beach, his muscular arms easing them through the grey unfriendly water as if he had the strength of twenty men. Edwin, Hannah's toddler brother, and Eileen Gunn were floating dead in several inches of green putrid water in the bottom of the boat. They were no more than skeletons, with remnants of purple-blue stinking flesh hanging off them. Their eyes were intact and staring at Hannah, malevolently. Why had she let them die? they silently accused her. She was the oldest girl there, why hadn't she stopped Daniel's foolhardy scheme?

'Forgive me,' she cried over and over again, but her words were snatched away by the roaring wind that suddenly whipped and lashed about the boat, tossing it round and round as if it was a twig in a whirlpool. Then she saw that it was Daniel scouring the sea with his big rough hand that was making the waves leap and rise, making the boat spin and lurch until it tipped its cargo, dead and alive, into the enveloping water. Hannah gripped the upturned boat. Her elder brother Mitch, Fred Jose, Lizzie,

125

Leah and Jowan were all trying to cling to her, shrieking in terror, 'Don't let us die, Hannah!' In a sweat of fear she tried to grab them but they were dragged away, one by one, to their doom.

There was nothing she could do now but swim for the shore, try to save herself. Her arms and legs wouldn't move, they were dead weights and she began to sink. A surge of high-pitched diabolical laughter drew her feverish eyes down into the inky-black depths. Daniel was down there, his mouth opened wide, twisted and cruel, laughing as if he was mad. 'It's your turn next, Hannah. I'm going to take you down with me, all the way down to the bottom, down, down, down . . .'

Hannah woke with a dreadful start, sweating and burning, gasping in air to calm her raging heart. The horror of the nightmare clung to her and, with painful clarity, as on Hidden Beach a few months ago, she had the horrible feeling that someone was watching her.

She sat up and turned her head towards the door, then clamped a hand to her mouth to hold back a scream. Daniel was sitting close to her in an armchair, his long arms resting on the upholstery, his face filled with the hate and desire for vengeance that always marked his face when their paths crossed. He was dressed in lightweight slacks and a pale blue open-neck shirt.

It was some moments before she could get any words past her dry throat and when they did emerge, they were little more than a nervous squeak. 'What are you doing here? How dare you walk into my home.'

The smile on his face was false. 'I've come to say exactly the same thing to you, Hannah, dear,' he sneered. 'Don't ever set foot inside my house again.'

She struggled to her feet, the magazine hitting the carpet and making her blink nervously. She felt less intimidated standing up but only for a moment for he, too, rose and loomed over her. 'Grace asked me to go there,' she said hastily, 'to help her with your little girl. She was desperate to know what to do about Melanie. Surely you can't object to that. I didn't want to go inside your house.'

'I can't stop her having who she likes in her blasted shop but she had no right to ask you into my house. I've made that plain to her now.' Despite her own fears, Hannah felt a twinge of worry for Grace; had he beaten her? He leaned towards her. 'Go there again for whatever reason and I'll come and wreck this bloody place. Understand?'

She didn't know what made her do it but suddenly she was gripping his arm. 'Please, Danny, let's stop this now. There's no need for there to be a rift between us. We're both married, have a child. We probably can't be friends again but let's put an end to all these bad feelings now. What do you say?' She was looking up at him with the tender pleading eyes she'd used on him when they had been friends.

It seemed to drive him wild. He grabbed her arms. 'Never! I'm going to make your life as wretched as I can.'

'But why? Because I married Matt?' His vicious grip hurt her and she felt she was suffocating. His mouth, open and threatening, was almost on top of hers, his blue eyes blazed.

He tightened his hold. 'Because I love you, Hannah.'

His words made no sense to her. 'But if you love me, Danny, why do you want to hurt me?'

'Because I spent every damned moment in that stinking hellhole of a prison yearning for you, that's why!' he snarled. 'No matter what I did I couldn't get you out of my head. I had visions of everything we'd said and done together, how we'd kissed in Roscarrock's stable and nearly made love in the coachman's cottage.' He was trembling now, as if some kind of raw malevolent energy had overtaken him, drained his reason, his humanity. 'You used me, Hannah, and all because you weren't sure of your feelings for Matt. You kept us both dangling on a string while you lived the life of a lady in the big house, you bloody bitch. Then you chose him, you jumped into his bed like a common whore! We'd been friends all our lives and when the police arrested me you scorned me in front of the whole sodding village. I want you to feel as lonely and as empty as I do.'

He must have felt the furious beating of her heart against his chest, heard her laboured breathing. Her shock and fear seemed to satisfy him. A wicked shadow flitted across his face, then his manner softened. Hannah didn't trust the sudden change. She struggled but it was futile. 'There is a way I could forgive you, Hannah,' he breathed.

'What do you mean?'

He looked deep into her soul. 'You can leave Penney and go away with me.'

Tears coursed down her cheeks. She couldn't lie to him, even if it cost her dearly. 'I–I couldn't do that, Danny. I love Matt. He and Nathan are my life.'

'You can have me or nothing! I'll take everything else away from you.

I can hurt you, Hannah, in a way you'd never expect.'

She was petrified, certain he was about to rape her, hurt her cruelly. The world seemed to exist only around the two of them and the fact that Daniel had her totally in his power.

He let out a long, shuddering breath, as if he had made a decision, a judgement. Then suddenly he let her go and was gone, disappearing from the room like a wraith, leaving behind such a strong sense of malevolence that she felt it could yet reach out and destroy her.

Shaking violently, the taste of sour plums in her mouth, she stumbled to the kitchen for water. At the sink she swayed on her feet, her legs seemed to turn to pulp, her head buzzed. She had an overwhelming feeling she was going to be sick. Her vision blurred, blackness came in thick suffocating folds and she hit the floor with a resounding thud.

Matt found her half an hour later. 'Hannah!' He was alarmed but not scared at first as he rushed to her for she had fainted once while pregnant with Nathan. As he lifted her into his arms, his heart missed a beat in a long, sickening pause. He felt the unnatural heat emanating from her, he heard her forced, shallow breathing. She seemed to be in a deep coma, about to slip away from him for good. Nathan started crying upstairs but he did not hear his son. In a moment of blind panic, Matt screamed, 'For God's sake, someone please help me!'

Fred Jose had Hidden Beach all to himself. He had been fairly sure he would. On Sunday afternoons most of the adults took a well-earned nap and few children ventured here on the Sabbath; their superstitious parents forbade it as it had been on a Sunday that the boating tragedy had occurred, and Brinley and his mates never came here.

Fred had brought a week's copies of the *Daily Mirror* with him. He had been ogling the cartoon drawings of Jane, a scantily clad, curvaceous, leggy blonde, and he was now lying down with his head on an old rolled-up towel, his eyes closed, picturing himself as part of the mildly catastrophic adventures which always befell her just as she was dressing or undressing. There was a huge grin on his scrawny face.

'What are you looking so pleased about, Jose? But then I suppose gawping at those pictures is the nearest you'll ever get to having a proper woman.'

Fred nearly wet his faded serge trousers. He'd rather face the most perilous sea than Daniel Kittow. 'I–I was j-just . . .' he blubbered.

Daniel kicked the newspapers away; they caught on the sea breeze and scattered down the beach. 'You're leaving the village. Get on your feet.'

'B-but I—'

Fred howled as Daniel hauled him to his feet and shook him violently. Daniel looked out of control, his colour high, eyes narrowed like a reptile's.

'A-all right, I'm g-going,' Fred whimpered.

Daniel whipped him close, making Fred's twisted collar cut into his neck. 'Let me make myself clear, Jose. You're going now, right this minute, and you're never to come back. If I see you again I'll kill you with my bare hands.' He pushed Fred away so roughly the weaker man hit the sand in a heap. 'Now get!'

'But my things,' Fred wept, his small work-scarred hands held out as he pleaded. 'I haven't got my clothes, no money.'

'That's right, Fred.' Daniel kicked him viciously. 'You're going out the same way you made sure I did. Without even your dignity.' He lashed out with his foot again and Fred scrabbled away. 'Go before I drown you in the sea. It's all you're fit for. You're not even a good fisherman,' he taunted. 'Your father won't miss you, he's ashamed of you. You should have drowned that day my grandfather's tosher turned over.'

Sobbing like a stricken infant, Fred tore up the beach. Daniel chased him until he crashed through the gorse bushes, ripping his clothes and flesh. Only then did Daniel slow down and stop. He caught his breath and let his rage subside. It was some time before he made his way to an outcrop of rock where he sat down and lit a cigarette. His expression was unmerciful. His revenge had only just begun.

Dozing in her threadbare easy chair at her kitchen hearth, Prim was gradually awakened by a low tapping noise. At first she thought it was Josh tilting his box of draughts from side to side. He would do this over and over again, taking out the last black or white piece to slide down until he had an eventual winner. The clicking sounds sometimes drove Prim crazy but it kept Josh contentedly occupied for hours.

'It's not the boy, he went up bed t'sleep,' she told herself, reluctantly dragging her plump body out of the chair. ''Tis someone at the door. Probably Mrs Jose forgot to buy in enough for tea again and wants to borrie something.' As Jeff never spent a second longer in her company than he absolutely had to and Josh was unable to hold a conversation, Prim, still trying to come to terms with the unnatural solitude caused by nearly all of her large brood having left home, had developed the comforting habit of talking to herself. The gentle knocking on the door persisted; Mrs Jose wouldn't walk straight in on a Sunday, believing it was impolite. 'I've got plenty in the cake tin,' Prim mumbled wryly as she pulled down the latch on the back kitchen door.

The shape of a man filled the doorway, blocking out the sunlight. 'Oh, 'tis you, Brinley. Summin' up?' Prim patted her grey bun hoping it was tidy and wished she had taken off her apron.

Brinley had brilliantined his sparse hair down on his lumpy scalp. Prim had only seen him in working garb before but today his paunch was spread out like a huge lump of dough over a tight pair of pinstriped trousers. He tugged nervously at his stiff collar and navy blue tie which seemed to be threatening to cut off his air supply. He stuck out the tin mug in his thick hand. 'Afternoon, Prim. Could 'ee lend me a cup of sugar?'

Like a shy maiden encountering an awkward youth, Prim asked him inside. She knew he didn't really want any sugar and she was flattered, unnerved and excited by his arrival. She went to the built-in cupboard in the kitchen and took out the sugar packet. Taking the tin mug from Brinley, she filled it to the rim. 'That should keep you going for a while,' she said, her face on fire, patting her hair again.

'Thanks, Prim. I'll go up to the shop first thing tomorrow and reimburse you.' Brinley felt pleased with the word 'reimburse'. What else could he impress Prim with? 'Merv 'n' Eric are sleeping off a skinful. I didn't go out last night.'

Prim already knew this. The antics of the *Sunrise*'s crew were discussed daily; today after chapel. Merv and Eric had drunk themselves stupid in the Ship Inn last night and had roamed through the streets loudly singing bawdy shanties until Miss Peters had poked her elfin head out of her bedroom window and emptied the contents of her chamberpot on them. Before the drunkards could gain retribution, Matt, John Jacobs and Hamlyn Innis, who were taking their turn at providing a watch for the village, had forced them on their way. Porthellis was hoping it was a good sign that the big man had stayed home.

Her shyness suddenly gone, deciding she might never get another chance, Prim whipped off her apron. 'Jeff's in the pub, with Maggie Curnow,' she said meaningfully. 'Josh is upstairs. He'll sleep all afternoon.'

Brinley smiled at her, the same warm, loving smile that split his broad, brown-weathered face every time they met. Prim hadn't been filled with desire for over thirty years but she burned with a sweet longing for the man who'd come courting her in her kitchen. Jeff had broken his marriage vows a thousand times. Surely the Lord would understand if she did the same, just this once.

She said tenderly, 'Why don't you put that mug of sugar down, Brinley?'

Grace was in the kitchen with Melanie, who trotted round after her everywhere she went, when Daniel returned home. 'Oh, good, you're just in time for tea, darling,' she said cheerily, hoping he had recovered from the dark mood he'd been in since she had told him about asking for Hannah's help. He had sworn at her over it last night and again this morning, pointedly ignoring Melanie who shrank away from him nervously whenever he came near her. He had barely looked at her when Grace had introduced him to his daughter this morning.

Muttering something unintelligible, Daniel lit a cigarette and stalked off to the dining room, seating himself at the head of the oval-shaped table already laid with Grace's finest embroidered linen cloth, plates and cutlery. She made no mention of his smoking at the table while she put down plates of tiny sandwiches, scones, sausage rolls, a Victoria sponge, a bacon and egg flan and fancy biscuits. Melanie, dressed in a silk frock that hung off her skimpy frame, stayed in the kitchen until Grace brought her in with the last plate of food.

Grace lifted her on to a chair at the side of the table, fondled her head gently then sat down opposite Daniel.

'Where's the tea?' he asked sulkily.

Grace frowned, perplexed. 'This is the tea.'

'I meant a cup of tea or are we only to have these bloody glasses of water?'

Grace had never been served a cup of tea at a meal table before. 'I thought I'd make it after we've finished,' she smiled, 'if that's all right.'

His answer was a snort and he helped himself to food. Melanie had surreptitiously taken a pink wafer biscuit off a plate and was nibbling it with her head down. Grace didn't chide her. She must have fought for a share of food in the past and manners could be taught later. 'Have a

131

sandwich next, sweetheart,' she said, putting a tongue triangle on the little girl's plate.

Daniel picked up a piece of flan, chewed, swallowed, and stared at Melanie. He felt no emotion but he did not doubt she was his child; she resembled him too closely to be anybody else's. He said to Grace, 'Have you told her I'm her father?'

'Not yet,' Grace replied, pleased by his acknowledgement of Melanie's existence and his paternity of her. 'As she doesn't speak I'm not sure she'd understand. Do you want her to call you Daddy?'

'Father's more usual around here,' he said drily, 'but I'm not fussy. She's not backward, is she?'

'Dr Makely doesn't think so. It's likely that she can speak but has been told to shut up so often she's too afraid to. She'll talk in her own good time when she's learned to trust us.' She turned to Melanie. 'Do you want to go to the bathroom, sweetheart?' Grace was proud that she had got Melanie's 'accidents' down to about one a day. Melanie shook her red head and continued eating.

'She knows how to tuck in,' Daniel observed.

'She should soon reach her proper weight. She likes storybooks,' Grace said, cutting the Victoria sandwich while Melanie watched closely. 'Would you like to read to her later?'

'Christ,' he swore irritably, doubly offending his wife.

When Grace went to the kitchen to make the pot of tea which would be drunk in the sitting room, he followed her there. Melanie climbed down off her chair and stayed by the table. She stuffed food into her mouth and into her pockets, then clutching as much as she could hold in her two little hands, she sneaked upstairs to hide some in her bedroom. She had been left alone in various homes for anything from a couple of hours to a few days before.

Grace was about to pick up the silver-plated tea tray when Daniel wound his arms round her from behind. He nuzzled her neck and she responded by leaning her head against his chest. 'I'm glad you like Melanie, darling,' she said.

His hands moved to caress her intimately and she moaned with pleasure. She shivered as he ran his tongue round in a tiny circle behind her ear. 'I don't want her sleeping in our bed tonight.'

'I'm sure I can get her settled down.' She put a peck on his chin but when she tried to turn and kiss him properly on the mouth, he clamped his arms tighter, keeping his lips to her ear.

He hissed, 'I don't know what you're doing to prevent you having babies but you'd better stop it as of today. I want kids, sons, and lots of them.'

Chapter 14

It was a wet Tuesday afternoon and Matt, unable to rest on the *Misty* with the remainder of its crew before sailing again that evening for the pilchard grounds, was mooching around Newlyn's ancient narrow streets. His mind was not on last night's poor catch or the nets they had lost, or even on the fact that so far this week they hadn't broken even with expenses.

He had not long ago phoned his mother, as prearranged yesterday morning when he'd reluctantly allowed her to talk him into going off to work. He had spoken to Jeff about his worries over Hannah as they'd walked together to catch the bus to St Austell railway station.

'There's nothing you can do, boy,' Jeff had said, surprised that Matt had thought about staying home. 'Course you got t'go t'work, you'd only be in the way. 'Tis a woman's thing. Your mother, Prim and Janet will look after her and the little 'un. 'Tedn't as if the doctor says you've got anything to worry about, is it?'

'No, but there's something strange about Hannah, different. As if she's cut herself off from everything, even me and Nathan. The doctor said she must have fainted yet he says she seems to be in shock. I don't understand it. What could have upset her?' Matt did not mention that he'd feared she was dying as he'd run to the front door to alert a couple of boys out playing to get their mother to phone for the doctor.

Jeff put a firm hand on his son-in-law's shoulder. 'Tedn't for we to understand. 'Tis for we t'work and keep a roof over their heads 'n' leave the childbearing to the women.' Jeff gazed gravely at the heavy grey sky, wet his finger and put it up in the air. 'Betterfit you concentrated on this poor weather.'

On the phone his mother had said that Hannah was fine, she was up and about, a bit quiet, but seeing to Nathan as before and doing a little sewing. Matt couldn't help thinking his mother had kept something from him. He shook his head ruefully, trying to comfort himself with the thought that his worry was only natural; he loved and adored Hannah so much.

Rainwater dripped off his woollen hat and fell uncomfortably down his neck but he did nothing about it. He left Newlyn behind and was on the road to Penzance, a restless sea and Tolcarne beach to his right where a couple of bleak-faced elderly holidaymakers strolled in mackintoshes. Not wanting to be close to people, he turned round and headed up a quiet back street, lighting a cigarette. He was so deep in his own melancholy, a trait in his character that surfaced occasionally in spite of his happy marriage and settled life, that it took several seconds for a loud yelping to register with him.

Down a narrow alley he saw a young burly man in ragged colourful clothes, probably a tinker, kicking a small black and white mongrel dog. 'Hey! Stop that!' Throwing his cigarette down, Matt raced up to the man and pushed him away from the pathetic, cowering animal.

'Bugger off! What's it got t'do with you?' the man snarled. 'I'll do what I damned well like, it's my dog.'

'You're not fit to keep a dog. Keep away from it.' Matt squared up to the man, making it clear he was prepared to fight if need be in the dog's defence.

The tinker stank of stale alcohol and he lurched for Matt's throat with outstretched meaty hands. 'I'll teach 'ee to interfere!'

Matt raised his fists and the tinker, seemingly suddenly afraid, let his arms fall to his sides, but he wasn't looking at Matt, he was staring directly over his shoulder. Cautiously, Matt glanced round. His dark features tightened to see Daniel Kittow there. The little mongrel had scampered away and Daniel was holding it against his chest.

'You heard what he said,' Daniel snarled at the tinker. 'Sod off now if you don't want your face stamped into the road.'

The man had lost his indignant bravado. He adjusted the wide-brimmed black and green hat on his greasy dark curls and said slyly, 'Well, if you've taken a liking to the dog, gents, I'd be willing to sell un to 'ee.'

Matt put his hand into his coat pocket to dig about for a two bob piece, thinking that if the dog proved good-tempered it would make a playmate for Nathan. It might even cheer up Hannah. He was sure she wouldn't be able to resist its tiny pointed face and forlorn brown eyes.

Daniel marched up to the tinker, kneed him viciously in the crotch and kicked him smartly on the chin as he keeled over. 'We're taking it,' he spat at the man, finally grinding the heel of his boot into his hand. Matt was sickened as he heard the crunch of broken bone.

'There was no need for that,' Matt remonstrated with Daniel.

'I'm not a good chapel man like you, Penney,' Daniel said through clenched teeth. 'I sort things out my own way.' He kicked the man writhing on the ground. 'Clear off or I'll give you some more.'

The tinker didn't have to be warned twice. Using the nearby wall to help him to his feet, he shambled off, murmuring profanities under his breath.

Daniel turned and went back the way he'd come. Matt walked at his side. 'I suppose you're proud of what you've just done,' he said contentiously.

'Of course,' Daniel retorted. He eyed Matt sideways. 'Heard you had the doctor to your house on Sunday.'

'I did,' Matt replied stonily, not offering any more information. He held out his arms. 'I'll take the dog now.'

'I'm taking him,' Daniel said, halting his long stride.

'Hand it over, Kittow,' Matt argued stubbornly.

'Go to hell.'

'I'll not ask you again.'

'You're right about that, Penney, you won't.' A strange gleam entered Daniel's eyes. 'You can't have the dog because where you're going you won't be able to look after him.'

Instinct warned Matt to brace himself. 'What're you talking about?' A snigger and a cough made him look round. As if they'd materialized out of the hostile air, Brinley, Eric and Merv were ranged behind him. Brinley was rubbing a palm over his clenched fist. Eric was stabbing the wall with the point of his gutting knife. Merv was swinging a giant-sized wrench.

Matt turned his eyes back on his arch enemy. 'Are you too afraid to face me fair and square, Kittow?'

'No,' Daniel returned almost gaily, tickling the dog under its matted ears while it tried to lick his fingers. 'But when you can afford to pay for help, why dirty your own hands? It's something my dear wife has taught me. Now your wife is a different matter.' He smiled dangerously. 'Hannah's taught me other things.'

'Why you rotten . . .' Matt lunged for his foe but Brinley grasped his arm and twisted it behind his back until he cried out in pain. Matt struggled but he was no match for the massive fisherman.

'Don't finish with him until he begs for mercy,' Daniel ordered his mob before walking off with the little dog.

'Let go of me!' Matt shouted as the three thugs slammed him against the wall. Brinley and Merv stretched out his arms and put their feet between his ankles to keep him off balance.

'Aw, we will,' Eric gave a toothless guffaw, breathing foul breath into Matt's face, 'when we've done what the skipper said. And me 'n' Merv owe you for Saturday night.' His knife flashed and a sharp pain seared Matt's cheek. Blood splashed down the front of his coat and jersey. 'Do 'ee reckon that pretty little missus of yourn will still want 'ee if we rearranges yer handsome face?'

Matt strained against his attackers but to no avail. His one shout for help was cut off as Brinley smashed his fist into his mouth. He howled in agony as the wrench slammed into the pit of his stomach. The knife, the fist, the wrench were used again and again. His guts felt as if they'd exploded, burning, twisting; his chest as if it had caved in. Blood obliterated his sight. The pain was torture.

'Oh, God, help me . . . this can't be happening . . . oh God, stop them . . .'

His woollen hat was snatched off, his head jerked back by his hair. He felt a sting on his neck. Desperate fear that he'd never see Hannah again overrode his pain.

'Don't cut his bleddy throat!' Brinley bellowed savagely, thrusting Eric away from the attack as if he was a piece of flotsam.

'Skipper said not t'finish with un until he begged for mercy,' Eric hissed like a barbarian, scrabbling for his knife where it had been sent clattering several feet away. Raising it in his fist, he rushed for Matt where he'd sunk to the wet ground, his hands instinctively trying to shield his head.

'He didn't mean it literally, you stupid bastard,' Brinley thundered. He was feeling sick to his stomach. So far he'd been happy to follow all Daniel's orders but he'd just remembered that Matt was Prim's son-in-law, and by the way she spoke of her children he was married to her favourite daughter. If Prim knew he was partly responsible for the bloodied scrap they'd reduced the young fisherman to she'd turn against him and there would be no hope of them going off together with Josh as they'd planned after making love on Sunday afternoon. Brinley raised his fist at Eric and Merv. 'He's had enough. He won't be fishing for weeks, maybe months. We've done our job, now let's get back t'the boat before we're seen.'

Too afraid to argue with Brinley's iron fist, the other two men wiped the blood off their weapons, hid them and started off down the alley. Brinley stood over Matt. He was doubled up against the wall, clutching his body, his dark eyes blazing with pain while he struggled to breathe. Blood smeared all his visible flesh; it made red rivulets down his clothes and was spreading out over the ground. Brinley shuddered; it he hadn't stopped the assault, he and the others could have been running away from a murder charge.

Matt could just make out the looming figure, standing there, staring down at him. 'Help me,' he pleaded, his voice barely audible, gurgling with the blood in his mouth.

'I'll phone for an ambulance,' Brinley said then he hastened away after his mates.

The attack had been witnessed by a housewife taking a short cut to the next street. When the huge man had disappeared from sight, she ran to Matt. Taking off her headscarf, she crouched down and dabbed at the blood on his face. 'Try to stay calm, dear. I've phoned for help and the ambulance will be here soon. I saw who did it. I've called the police too. They'll soon be behind bars.'

It seemed as if a fullscale war was being fought inside Matt's head. Pain racked his body, waves of agony surged through him, making him cry and groan. He tried to bring a hand to his throat. 'I c-can't breathe . . .' He felt icy-cold, frightened.

'Hold on,' she said soothingly as if she was talking to a child. She took one of Matt's battered hands in hers; there was nothing else she could do for him. 'Help will be here soon.'

Although the alley had been almost deserted earlier, a crowd of onlookers now quickly gathered, as if some primitive signal had been responded to.

'Bloody hell,' an old man gasped. 'He looks like the sharks have had un.'

It was Lily's birthday that day. Hannah had left Nathan with Prim and was on her way to Roscarrock with a present for the under-housemaid. Prim and Mrs Penney had advised against it but she was desperate to get away from the village, to shake off the crushing bleakness that had enveloped her since Daniel's harrowing visit. She hadn't told Matt about it, fearing an ugly confrontation between the two men. She had appeased Prim and Mrs Penney by phoning and asking Greg to collect her.

'Thank you, Greg,' she said as he opened the front passenger door of his black and cream Railton saloon for her.

'Are you all right, Hannah? You look rather peaky.'

She met the concern in his soft grey eyes with a quiet smile. 'You know what I'm like, Greg. Pregnancy doesn't suit me like it does most women. Remember how I scared you at Roscarrock when I was expecting Nathan?'

'I shall never forget it.' He rolled his eyes playfully. 'Well, don't faint again until we get there.' He smiled mysteriously before getting in behind the steering wheel.

Hannah recalled ironically how she and Greg had shared a mutual dislike of each other when they had first met. She hadn't cared for his pompous ways and what she had seen as his unhealthy interest in Leah. He had been suspicious of why Mrs Opie had favoured her so much. Now they were the best of friends. And Daniel, who had been the closest friend she had thought she could ever have, hated her for spurning him and she hated him for his assault and his threats.

He had put a different connotation on their brief dalliance. She had seen it as a few kisses with little chance of there being anything permanent between them. Daniel had always stressed he wasn't the marrying kind. It had been good being close to him, nothing more. There had never been the sensuousness and unfolding desires she had experienced when she'd been with Matt. They had not nearly made love in the little cottage as Daniel had stated. She had allowed his hand to wander a little but had quickly stopped him. How could a man who had ruthlessly used whatever young girl took his fancy call that nearly making love? Hannah realized that she had never really known Daniel's mind.

'Good heavens, Hannah, don't look so fierce,' Greg said, thoroughly alarmed. 'Anyone would think you wanted to murder someone.'

'Sorry,' she sighed. 'I was just thinking.'

'What about?'

'Oh, nothing really. You know how we women—'

'Get when you're pregnant?' he finished for her. 'I hope I do.' The smile was there again and Hannah felt that any minute now he'd give a burst of cheerful whistling. He caught her eye then raised his fair brows and grinned.

'You're trying to tell me something, aren't you?' she exclaimed. Her spirits lifted. 'Leah's pregnant! Oh, Greg, that's wonderful. Congratulations. You must be thrilled.'

'I am, but don't let on to Leah that you know. She wants to tell you herself.'

'Does Mrs Opie know?'

'Yes.'

'What did she say?' Hannah hoped Mrs Opie had shown Leah joy over her baby.

'Grandmother was thrilled to bits. She's going to throw a party for us to announce the news.'

The moment she was out of the car, Hannah popped down to the kitchen and gave Lily her present, a box of lace-edged handkerchieves on which she had embroidered Lily's name. Lily thanked her with her usual gusto and proudly displayed the bead necklace Jowan had given her.

'Pity he isn't about so he can come to the little party I'm having this evening,' she said excitedly. Just for today Miss Benson was overlooking her high-pitched voice. 'Never mind. I'll save him some of the cake Mr Patrick baked for me. Isn't everyone here nice, Mrs Penney?'

'Yes, they are,' Hannah agreed, and she was consumed with a fierce sense of homesickness for the big house where she had once lived. 'Well, I'll leave you to it and go up and see Leah and Mrs Opie.'

Leah was hovering about on top of the servants' stairs, waiting for her. 'Hannah, are you feeling better now?' she asked sympathetically.

'Yes, thank you, Leah.' Hannah looked closely at her younger sister. Leah had a peaches and cream complexion and looked every bit the radiant mother-to-be. Overwhelmed with joy for her and suddenly full of emotion, Hannah burst into tears and wrapped her arms round Leah's slim shoulders. 'Oh, Leah,' she sobbed.

'Hannah, what is it? Are you ill again? Come and sit down.' Leah led her to a chair in the hallway. She produced a hanky from her dress pocket. 'Now, my love, tell me what's the matter. Do you want the doctor?'

'No.' Hannah forced a watery smile. 'I'm fine really. I'm just being silly.'

'No, you're not.' Leah stroked her sister's soft blonde hair. 'You must have had a fright fainting like that. You'll feel better at the end of the week when Matt comes home again. I've got a marvellous idea. I'll ask Greg to drive us down to Penzance tomorrow, in time for when the boats come in. I'd love to see that myself. Would you like to go?'

'Oh, Leah.' Hannah burst into fresh sobs. 'I'd like nothing more right now than to see Matt.'

'Leah! What's happening here? Have you upset Hannah?' Feena Opie had wheeled herself out of the drawing room and was heading towards them.

Leah was offended that she was thought to be the cause of Hannah's distress. 'Of course I haven't,' she snapped. 'Hannah and I were having a private conversation.'

'Don't you speak to me like that, girl,' Feena bristled, shocked that her timid granddaughter-in-law had addressed her crossly. 'Bring Hannah into the drawing room then run and fetch some tea.'

Leah was even more offended to be ordered about like a servant. She was thinking of a suitable frosty retort when the front door suddenly burst open and Jeff rushed into the vestibule.

All three women froze in horror. His presence here now, on a working day, in his working clothes, spelled very bad news which his harrowed expression only served to confirm. Hannah clutched Leah's hand. It had been to this same house that her father had come unexpectedly before to tell them Matt was missing, feared drowned. A terrible wailing sound came from her throat, making the hairs on the back of Leah's neck stand up stiffly. The wail became a scream and Hannah thrashed her arms together until Jeff caught hold of her and shook her into stillness.

'He's in Penzance hospital. He's hurt quite bad but he's going t'be all right,' Jeff shouted through the fog he was afraid had blocked off her mind.

'Was it an accident on the boat?' she whimpered.

'No.' Jeff glanced worriedly at Leah and Feena. Hannah was in such a state, should he tell her the whole truth?

Hannah gripped his neck and swung his head round to her. 'What happened to him? Was it Daniel?'

Jeff nodded grimly. All Porthellis had been waiting for Daniel Kittow to hurt Hannah or Matt and he had managed it in a particularly nasty way. News of the attack had filtered down to the moored boats at the same time that the police had swooped on the *Sunrise*. After a violent fight, Brinley, Eric and Merv had been taken away in a van. Daniel had sat on a mooring cleet on the quay and watched, seemingly totally unconcerned, while he fed a small dog on his lap with scraps of meat and bread. One of the policemen had spoken to him but had soon left as though satisfied he had had nothing to do with the crime. Jeff was certain the cocky red-haired man had ordered his crew to beat Matt.

One of the fish buyers had offered to drive Jeff to Porthellis so that he could tell his daughter the bad news in person rather than over the telephone. Jeff had accepted gratefully but regretted it hadn't given him time to wipe the smirk off Daniel Kittow's face.

He prised Hannah's grip from his neck and held her hands firmly. 'He was set upon by Kittow's crew and they've been arrested and taken off by the police. They tried to deny it but the police said they were given their descriptions by more than one member of the public.'

'Never mind them.' Hannah was hardly aware that the hall was now full of people, including Greg, Patrick and all the servants. 'How badly is Matt injured?'

Jeff had glimpsed Matt's wounds before getting into the fish buyer's car. He would let her see the awful truth for herself. 'Cuts and bruises mostly, a couple of broken ribs, the ambulance men said.'

'But he can come home?' Hannah asked hopefully. She looked pleadingly at Greg. 'Can we fetch him home?'

'I don't expect he'll be able to come home for a few days, Hannah,' Jeff said. 'But you can go and see him.'

'I'll get the car ready,' Greg said quietly. The look he gave Patrick said that he sensed Jeff was holding more back. Patrick nodded, and before Feena could push herself forward and organize things as best suited her, he joined Jeff kneeling before Hannah and squeezed her arm. 'I'll slip down to the village and fetch Mrs Penney. I daresay she'd like to see her son. Where's Nathan?'

'He's with my mother.'

Hannah needed Patrick's gentle strength and loyalty now more than Feena's overbearing fussiness and Leah felt no compunction about pulling Feena's wheelchair further away from Hannah. Feena was incensed and took it out on Miss Benson.

'Go and order tea or something,' she snapped.

'Yes, Mrs Opie.' Miss Benson hastily gathered an abnormally quiet Lily and a weeping Angie back to the kitchen.

Greg returned and beckoned Hannah to him.

'Dad, tell Mum to fetch anything she needs for Nathan and you'll stay with her and Nathan, won't you?' Hannah asked in a worried voice.

Jeff patted her chilled hand. 'Course I will, my handsome. You can trust me.' He stood aside to let her rise.

As Hannah made her way towards Greg, her body was gripped by an agonizing pain.

143

Chapter 15

It seemed a terrible weight was crushing her. Her tongue felt stuck to the roof of her mouth. She couldn't move, swallow or breathe without pain. Each time a glimmer of light threatened to seep into her hazy black world, Hannah allowed the sweet darkness to engulf her again. She didn't want to see the shadowy figures that moved about her, she didn't want to respond to their touch or gentle voices. Then something important impressed itself upon her fleeing mind, something so dreadful it demanded her immediate attention and she began to resist the darkness that beckoned her.

'Matt . . . Matt!' As her eyes slowly focused, her memory returned sharply and she pictured herself in terrible pain soon after her father had told her Matt was badly hurt and needed her.

'Hush now, Hannah, dear. You're going to be all right.'

It was Mrs Opie's voice and she realised with a start that she was lying in her old room at Roscarrock. She moved her eyes from the ceiling and met the sympathetic gaze of her real mother. Wetting her dry lips, she moaned, 'Matt . . . he needs me.'

'Yes, dear, but you're too weak to go to him now,' Feena said soothingly, patting her hand. 'You must get your strength back first.'

Hannah tried to sit up but pain surged through her body. 'Why do I feel so weak? What am I doing in bed here? Matt's hurt. I must go to him.'

'You became ill, dear. Too ill to be taken home.'

Hannah closed her eyes in the effort to think. Had she fainted again? Instinctively her hands reached for her stomach. It was flat. She let out an anguished wail. 'I've lost my baby.'

'I'm sorry, dear.' Feena stroked her face tenderly. 'We called the doctor and midwife but there was nothing they could do.'

Hannah was filled with panic. She had to forget her terrible loss for the moment. 'But Matt! I should be at the hospital. What's happening to him? How long have I been lying here?'

'You must be brave, dear. It took thirty-six hours for the baby to come away and since then you've slept deeply for two days. Mrs Penney and Patrick are staying at a hotel in Penzance and have kept vigil at Matt's bedside. They've been phoning regularly with news.'

Hannah wanted to scream and protest that it wasn't fair that she couldn't be with Matt, that he couldn't be with her when she needed him, that their baby had perished through the shock of the news. Choked with tears, she murmured, 'What did those men do to him to make him stay in hospital for so long?'

Feena held her hand tightly. 'Matt's got a fractured skull and broken ribs. One of his lungs collapsed but the doctors have treated it successfully. He's been sedated for most of the time so he's not in much pain.'

'Oh, dear God.' She licked her dry lips. 'Is he asking for me?'

'Yes, dear. Mrs Penney has explained you're poorly and that you'll see him as soon as you can.'

'How long will he have to stay in hospital?'

'For a few weeks at least.'

'Weeks!' Becoming frantic, snatching her hand from Feena's, Hannah tried to push back the bedcovers. 'I have to get up. Will Greg take me to the hospital?'

She was so weak Feena needed little effort to cover her again. 'Wait for a little while, dear. The doctor's coming later this morning. He'll tell you when you're well enough to travel.'

'It's not fair.' Huge tears rolled down her flushed cheeks. 'Matt and I really need each other and we've been kept apart. Daniel Kittow must have had something to do with those men beating him.'

'Don't think about that now, dear. Those men are in prison and they'll be given a long sentence. If Kittow is involved, he'll be arrested too. Just concentrate on getting your strength back.'

'Where's Nathan? He must be missing us both.'

'He's staying with your Aunty Janet. She'll bring him here to see you when you're a little stronger. She and Prim are taking turns looking after him and Prim and your father have called here regularly to see you.'

Hannah was desperate for sleep again. She couldn't bear being separated from Matt and Nathan. It was Daniel Kittow's fault. He had terrified her in her own house and weakened her. And she was being forced to lie in the bed where he had nearly raped her. She hated him, oh, how she hated him.

A strange sense of strength flowed through her. She would use that strength to get well and reclaim the two most important people in her life. Then she would go after Daniel Kittow and get even with him.

'The doctor said I can get out of bed today, Mum.'

'I know,' Prim smiled. It was the following day and Hannah did seem stronger. Prim put another log on the fire crackling in the wide fireplace. 'Just for a little while. You lost a lot of blood. You must take things easily for a long time.'

'But I'm feeling so much better,' Hannah said almost brightly. She had put the tragedy of her own situation to the back of her mind and thought only about recovering enough to see Matt. 'I had a good night's sleep.' She watched her mother tidying up the large bedroom, straightening the towels at the sink, sweeping back the long curtains to let in more light. She seemed perfectly at home. 'I hope you and Mrs Opie are getting on all right.'

Prim was keeping busy because she could hardly bear to look Hannah in the face. She had received a letter this morning, written on prison notepaper, from Brinley.

Their lovemaking had been a fumbling lumbering affair but Prim had thought him satisfied and she had felt a little of what drove Jeff to seek that side of life so often. Then he had asked her to go away with him and take Josh with them. Prim had overlooked his raucous behaviour, believing a gentleness lay hidden under his wild exterior. But that man had been responsible for the death of her grandchild and the near murder of her son-in-law. Now he was asking for her forgiveness and understanding, writing that he regretted attacking Matt and had called an ambulance. He pleaded with her to go away with him after he had served his prison sentence, promising that he would reform and live a settled life. But she would never forgive him. She had torn up the letter and burnt it. As well as her distress over Hannah's plight, there was a personal heaviness in her heart. She had looked forward to starting a new life away from her loveless marriage. She was also a loser in what Brinley had done.

'Mrs Opie has been very civil to me,' she said, using her hanky to wipe at an imaginary greasy mark on the window pane. 'She was good enough to suggest I sleep here the first two nights. In times like this you forget your differences. I've sat with Leah a lot of the time. We didn't want her being upset.' Prim coloured and fussed with Hannah's dressing gown.

'Come on, my handsome. I'll help you into this.'

'Poor Leah,' Hannah said as she sat up gingerly and Prim pulled back the bedcovers. 'Greg told me she's pregnant and I ruined the lovely surprise she had for me. I must talk to her when she pops in to see me next. Because I've lost my baby I don't want her to think I'm not interested in hers.' When she was settled comfortably in the armchair at the fireside she said, 'I'm looking forward to seeing Nathan this afternoon. I've missed my little boy.'

'He's missing you and his dad but he's been good as gold,' Prim crooned, smoothing the damask cover on the bed.

'Tell me again what the hospital said about Matt this morning,' Hannah said anxiously.

'His breathing is a little easier and he's progressing slowly.' Prim picked up Hannah's brush to attend to her hair.

'That doesn't tell me much,' Hannah complained miserably. 'Let me have my hand mirror, Mum. Good heavens! Look at me. I'm so pale and the bags under my eyes are enormous. I look at death's door.'

Prim brushed her hair with a grim expression; there had been one or two anxious moments when the doctor thought she might slip away from them.

'I must look better than this when I see Matt. It'll frighten him.' She put the mirror down on her lap. 'Mum, does Matt know about the baby?'

'No, 'twas thought better not to tell him until he's stronger. Wouldn't do him no good to be worrying over you.' Tears prickled Prim's eyes and she was glad she was standing behind her daughter. Matt had occasionally cried out Hannah's name but he'd been unable to understand anything anyone said to him.

'Mrs Opie wants Nathan to stay here in the nursery but I've said you'll soon we well enough to go home.' Prim and Feena hadn't quarrelled but had exchanged strong words over the matter. Prim had argued that Hannah would probably recover more quickly in her own home. Feena had made the point that with Mrs Penney away, Seaview Cottage would be cold and empty. 'Course, it's up to you, Hannah. Nathan's your son. I could stay with you at home for a while. Josh would be useful keeping Nathan occupied.' Prim didn't think her own cottage was a good option; it didn't have a proper bathroom or inside toilet.

'I can't think that far ahead, Mum. I just want to see Matt and have

Nathan near.' Hannah knew it would be a hard decision, both options had their advantages and one of her mothers would be disappointed.

Two days later Patrick Opie entered her room carrying an enormous bunch of roses. 'From the walled garden, Hannah,' he beamed at her. 'Summer's slipping away from us but they're still at their best.'

He put the roses down on a table for Mrs Opie to arrange them in a silver bowl, then he sat down opposite Hannah. She was dressed in a skirt, blouse and cardigan and, because it was a cool day, a lightweight coat. In a few minutes Greg, Leah and Mrs Opie were going to drive with her down to Penzance.

'Thank you, Patrick,' Hannah smiled, the first smile she'd given in six days. 'You must have missed your garden. It was good of you to stay at Penzance and run Mrs Penney to the hospital each day.'

'I was pleased to be of service to her, Hannah,' Patrick said humbly, twiddling with his moustache. 'I made sure Mrs Penney had someone to talk to and that she ate regular meals.'

'How is she?'

'Rather tired. She says she won't come home until Matt is properly conscious.' Patrick shifted uneasily and his weathered face suffused with colour. 'Um, I hope you won't be offended if I bring up the subject of money, Hannah, my dear, but can Mrs Penney afford to stay long at the hotel?'

'She has some savings, Patrick. They should last a week or two longer. I'm going to join her.'

'Do you think that's wise?' Patrick frowned. 'I mean, are you well enough?'

'Didn't they tell you? Mrs Opie, Greg and Leah are going to stay too. Mrs Opie says she could do with the change and Greg will drive me and Mrs Penney to the hospital. Patrick,' she became quietly serious, 'I want to know the truth about Matt's condition. All I'm told is he's progressing slowly but I'm convinced the others are keeping something from me. If Matt is still in a critical condition I need to know. I don't want to receive another shock. I don't think I could stand another one now. It's been nearly a week and he's still unconscious.'

Patrick was a man of few intimate gestures but he reached forward and clasped her hands. 'You mustn't read anything into that, Hannah. People who have received blows to the head have recovered fully after being unconscious for several weeks. Matt was given a terrible beating and you must prepare yourself, my dear, for the fact he may never be as fit and well again.'

'What do you mean by that?' Hannah's lips trembled and she gripped his warm, rough hands.

'Matt's ribs were badly broken, one was in splinters and had to be removed. He received internal injuries and the surgeon had to remove his spleen and one of his kidneys. It's doubtful he'll ever be strong enough to pull in a netful of fish again.' Hannah was weeping but he felt she ought to know everything. 'My dear, his face was badly cut. He'll be scarred for life.'

'Oh, God,' she sobbed. 'How could they do that to my Matt?'

Sitting on the arm of her chair, Patrick held her close. 'That's the worst of it, Hannah. Matt's face is bruised and swollen at the moment but it probably won't look so bad as time goes by. Great-aunt Feena thought you shouldn't be told but I think you're entitled to have your questions answered honestly and it's best you have a little time to get used to the extent of Matt's injuries.'

'Thank you, Patrick,' she sniffed, drying her eyes. 'Your way is kinder in the end. I'd better wash my face before Greg comes for me.'

'I'm sorry about the baby, Hannah,' he said sadly as she made herself presentable for the long journey. 'You will take care of yourself?'

'Don't worry,' she smiled bravely. 'I know I must get well and strong for Matt and Nathan's sakes.' She looked wistfully into the dressing table mirror as she applied a little face powder. 'I'll miss Nathan while I'm away but I shall stay with Matt until he's ready to come home.'

'Perhaps your aunt and your mother would like to be brought down to the hotel to see you one morning,' Patrick suggested.

'You are so kind, Patrick.' Her gaunt face wore a severe expression as she looked out of the window at the blue strip of sea. Somewhere out there was Daniel, working as free as a bird, healthy and strong. 'The complete opposite of the man responsible for my troubles.'

'Don't you mean men?'

'Those men might have attacked Matt but I'd stake my life it was on Daniel Kittow's orders. I shall never forgive him.'

'I can understand that, Hannah, but it would be better if you could try to forget it.'

'There's nothing on earth that will ever make me forget it,' she vowed.

Leah and Mrs Opie stayed in the Castle Bay Hotel on the waterfront and Greg drove Hannah and Mrs Penney to the West Cornwall hospital. Greg remained in the waiting room while Hannah, clinging to Mrs Penney's arm, crept nervously along the ward Matt was in. For a moment she thought they had approached the wrong bed. The man lying there appeared too small to be Matt, his upper body and head swathed in bandages and dressings. Drips and tubes were attached to him. Only the earth-brown colour of his hair told Hannah this was the man she loved.

Informed earlier of her medical history, a nurse pulled out a chair for Hannah. 'Thank you,' she gulped between her tears. 'H-has he come round yet?'

'He opened his eyes for a few moments just before you arrived, Mrs Penney. He calls your name every now and then. Try speaking to him. We'll see if he responds.'

With her heart breaking for Matt, it took several attempts to clear her throat before her voice would come clearly. She took his limp, battered hand, his right hand with the top of the forefinger missing. 'Matt. Matt, darling, it's Hannah. Wake up.' She pressed her lips to his hand. 'Matt . . . Matt . . .'

Pale, weary and shaken, Mrs Penney sat on the other side of the bed in silence. She had spoken often to Matt but he had not stirred for her. If anyone could break through the mists engulfing his mind, it was Hannah.

Hannah was desperate for him to wake up before the visiting hour was over. In between calling to him she kissed his hand and stroked his forehead, still bearing bumps and bruises from the beating. She could see stitches peeping out from under his many dressings and she followed the line of the various tubes The nurse told her they were keeping his lung drained and monitoring his breathing which was sometimes ragged and noisy. Hannah could see for herself it would be some weeks before he'd be well enough to come home. She longed to hold him but knew it would only add to his horrific injuries. She wanted to cry and never stop but she had to be brave.

'Matt, it's Hannah, darling. Can you hear me?'

She kept looking at his eyelids, hoping they would lift and respond to her. She kissed the back of his hand once more and felt him trying to squeeze her fingers. Checking a rush of emotion, raising herself up from the chair, she gazed down on him. 'Matt. It's Hannah. Wake up for me, darling.'

Mrs Penney became alert and the nurse moved closer.

The slight pressure on Hannah's hand increased and Matt's eyelids flickered then opened. His dark eyes, mere slits under the puffy flesh, searched, blinked, found Hannah and remained still. They seemed to glaze over and she feared he would slip away again. 'Matt!' she cried desperately.

'Careful now,' the nurse warned.

His swollen lips quivered for long, agonizing moments. 'Han-nah?'

'Yes, darling,' she smiled down on him, her eyes misty. 'Do you want anything?'

His tongue, white and furred, awkwardly wetted his lower lip. The nurse asked Mrs Penney to move so she could administer a few drops of water to him. 'Han-nah . . .'

'I'm here, Matt,' she said, unable to keep a tremor out of her voice. She glanced hopefully at Mrs Penney.

'S-sorry, Hannah.'

'Don't be silly, Matt.' Tenderly she stroked his brow. 'You've got nothing to be sorry for. All you need now is plenty of rest and you'll soon be home.'

'They hit me.' His voice was a hoarse whisper and raw with emotional hurt. 'Cut me . . . went for walk . . . yesterday.'

Yesterday – Hannah was glad he had no conception of time. He didn't realise she had been ill and had not come straight to him.

'You're going to be all right, Matt. Nathan's being well cared for and I'm not going to leave your side.'

Tears slid from the corners of Matt's eyes and Hannah gently wiped them away. Under her breath, she murmured, 'Somehow I'll make him pay.' When she left here she would ask Greg to drive her to the police station.

Chapter 16

As she beat a Viota cake mix Grace glanced at the drawing Melanie was making at the other end of the kitchen table. Grace's fair eyebrows were rising steadily. A detailed picture of the beach, slipway and quay, not at all in the expected wobbly manner of a child, was appearing under the girl's swiftly moving hand, her small, strong features hardly creased in concentration. Grace was delighted at finding her stepdaughter had a natural talent.

'That's a lovely picture, darling,' she said, careful not to gush with enthusiasm; Melanie shied away from anything emotional. 'Shall we show it to Daddy when he comes home?'

Melanie nodded. A couple of days ago she had started to respond to Grace with nods and shakes of her head rather than her usual wide-eyed stares. Grace knew she was beginning to trust her and to like her. Occasionally she sought and gave affection by tentatively leaning against her or winding her arms round her neck for a moment. Grace had yet to see her smile.

'We could put it in a frame and ask Daddy to hang it on your bedroom wall,' Grace said. 'He's coming home later today.' She referred to Daniel as Daddy several times each day to get Melanie used to the idea and so she wouldn't forget him during his absence. Daniel had not been home for three weeks but had telephoned last night to say he was bringing the boat home now that the pilchard season was over. Grace wasn't looking forward to seeing him quite as much as usual.

She was growing fonder of Melanie every day. She played so quietly one could forget she was in the house and when Grace wanted time to herself, she stayed happily with Nan Trebilcock. There were still one or two social and behaviourial problems to sort out. If someone knocked on the door, Melanie would run away and hide and invariably wet herself.

Grace thought she was afraid her mother had come for her. If Grace didn't check her she ate hot or sticky food with her hands and she always had to be reminded to wash her hands before meals or after using the toilet. Food went missing from the larder and other oddments from the house and Grace or Nan would find them hidden in Melanie's room or comfort blanket.

A spark of interest showed in the deep blue eyes Melanie had inherited from Daniel. She turned the page of her small sketching pad over and started on another picture. Grace finished the cake and was washing the few dishes when Melanie shyly tapped on her waist. Grace smiled down on her.

'See?' Melanie displayed her new drawing.

At first Grace thought she was making one of her little piping sounds, then, with a lump in her throat, she realised Melanie had spoken. 'Yes, darling, I do see,' she answered calmly although her heart was thumping excitedly. 'It's a picture of Daddy's boat, isn't it?'

Melanie nodded.

Grace was overwhelmed. The picture of the *Sunrise*, coloured in blue and white, appeared to be perfect in every detail. Melanie had a rare talent that could set her up well in later life. Hoping to prompt another word out of her, Grace asked, 'Who's this picture for? Me?'

'D . . . daddy.'

Grace nearly burst into tears and she hugged Melanie's small body to her. 'I'm sure Daddy will love it, darling.'

An hour later Daniel came home and put the little dog in his arms down on the sitting room floor. 'You can't bring that dirty little creature in here!' Grace exclaimed indignantly.

'I'll bring what or who I like into my own house,' he replied, the smile on his face vanishing in displeasure. Grace hadn't rushed to embrace him as she'd always done before; there was an aloofness about her. He shrugged. 'I brought him home for Melanie. He's called Dumpy. I rescued him from a tinker who was kicking hell out of him.'

'Please, Daniel, I wish you wouldn't use language like that in front of Melanie.' She looked down at Melanie where she had been making a simple wooden jigsaw puzzle on a tray on the carpet but the little girl had moved. She was on her knees in front of the fireplace, cradling Dumpy against her white linen dress which the dog's paws were dirtying.

'She likes him,' Daniel said triumphantly. 'Be better for her than those stupid cats of yours,' he added sarcastically. He went closer to his daughter. 'Melanie, Melanie.'

It was some moments before she looked up apprehensively at him, moments in which Grace's stomach churned in worry that he'd get angry or offended if he was ignored.

'He's yours, Melanie. Would you like to go for a walk with me and Grace and Dumpy this afternoon?'

Melanie nodded shyly and quickly averted her eyes.

'We'll take a picnic to Hidden Beach,' he told Grace. 'I've treated Dumpy for fleas and worms and had him checked over by a vet. He's quite healthy. I've got a bed for him on the boat. He's a born sailor. I think I'll take him with me sometimes when I'm working.'

Grace looked at the ugly mongrel, mainly of terrier breed, she guessed, pleased to hear he was at least free of worms and fleas. 'Now, Melanie, you've got something for Daddy, haven't you?'

Carrying Dumpy clumsily so his gangly legs hung down and quivered, Melanie fetched the picture of the *Sunrise* lying on the side table and nervously proffered it to Daniel.

Daniel eyed her, puzzled.

'It's her present to you, Daniel. Take it,' Grace said proudly. 'She drew it herself.'

Making a wry face, he took the picture from Melanie and immediately jeered, 'She didn't do this.'

Not liking his tone, Melanie edged away to stand close to Grace.

'Oh yes she did.' Grace stood up and whispered darkly into his face, 'She's got a rare talent. I watched her draw it. You've upset her now. Say sorry to her and thank her.'

Daniel studied the drawing again. 'Did she really do this?'

'I swear to you, Daniel, it's the truth,' Grace said fiercely.

He whistled through his teeth. 'Bloody hell, but then I suppose I would produce clever kids.'

He went to Melanie and lowering his great height down to her level, he stroked Dumpy who was wriggling and yapping excitedly in her childish grasp. 'Thanks for the picture of my boat, Melanie,' he said a little awkwardly.

'Now you must say thank you to Daddy for the dog, Melanie,' Grace said, standing over them, hoping Melanie would speak.

'Thank . . . you,' Melanie squeaked, not looking at her father.

Daniel's head swung round to Grace. 'She's beginning to talk?'

'As from today.' Grace smiled down at Melanie. 'I think we'll go forward in leaps and bounds with her now. Daniel, could I pin you down to a Sunday when you'll be home for certain?'

'Why?' He straightened up and glared at her.

'I want to arrange to have Melanie christened. Uncle David said he'll do it in a small private ceremony.'

'I'm Church of England,' he said.

'Are you? I didn't think you had any beliefs but I assumed you were christened in the chapel.'

'Well, I wasn't. Old Rufus took me along to get dipped in the church at Gorran Haven after my mother abandoned me. By the way, she weren't married. I'm a bastard.'

Grace sighed. Yes, in more ways than one, she thought despondently. 'Well, as I believe in God and you don't is there any reason why she shouldn't be christened in the chapel and by a man who's agreed to be her uncle?'

'You mean Skewes thinks of her as family?' he inquired tartly, keeping up his aggressive tone because he was annoyed and disappointed by Grace's coolness towards him. 'He never comes here to see her or invites her up to the Manse.'

'Uncle David and Aunt Adela have called here to see Melanie and we've dined at the Manse occasionally,' Grace admitted, somewhat embarrassed under his penetrating glower; the Skewes wouldn't set foot inside Chynoweth while Daniel was here and he had never been invited to socialize with them.

'So why wasn't I told?'

'I didn't think you'd be interested. Usually when I've spoken to you about Melanie you don't seem to be listening.'

Daniel shook his head sourly. He'd given the girl the dog, thanked her for the picture and said they'd all go on a family picnic, but still his wife had to pick on him. With a grunt he went upstairs to bath and change his clothes.

Grace followed him, telling Melanie to stay with her new playmate.

Ignoring Grace and her frown, Daniel threw his soiled clothes on the bedroom floor and pulled clean ones out of the drawers and wardrobe. Then he smiled lecherously. 'Can't wait till I'm clean and smelling nice, eh?'

With an effort, Grace suppressed her natural desire for him. She didn't want his gorgeous body, his hungry expression to distract her now. She had something deadly serious on her mind. 'Did you have anything to do with it, Daniel?' she asked sternly.

'Do with what?' So there was a reason for her frigidity, but he knew how to make her yield, what turned her from a worthy lady into a sensuous siren. He moved to her and stroked her face.

Grace backed away from him. 'The attack on Matt Penney.'

'Oh that.' He smiled as if she had brought up a pleasant subject. 'Yes. I ordered the men to do it. They made a very good job of it too. You won't see him taking out a fishing boat again.'

Grace was deeply shocked, not just by his forthright admission but by the fact that he almost seemed to be boasting about it. 'How could you want to hurt another human like that? I knew you were a hard man but I didn't realise you could be so cruel.'

'Yes, you did,' he reminded her, pushing her towards the bed. 'I told you all about me right from the beginning. What I did was kill two birds with one stone. I wanted rid of that rabble so I informed the police of the attack while it was happening. The police keep questioning me, but Brinley and his mates know better than to snitch on me, and they can't prove a thing because some people I do business with will swear I was with them.' It seemed Matt had not told the police he was involved; had his beating wiped out that part of his memory? 'I've got a new crew. I've brought a nice respectable family back from Newlyn with me for the dogging season, a fisherman and his three sons. They're moving into the old man's cottage now. You can go down to 'em later and introduce yourself to Mrs Penrose. And in case you're wondering, I told Fred Jose to get out of the village. There's nothing mysterious about his disappearance as other folk believe.'

Her horror growing, Grace tried to pull away from him but he eased her down on the bed, lay over her and pulled up her skirt. Sickened, she turned her face away from him. 'Not now, Daniel. Melanie might come up.'

'She's happy with Dumpy.' He tugged on her blouse, making the top pearl button pop off. 'Now you make me happy. Did you go to the doctor and have that thing taken out?'

'Yes,' Grace said, regretting it now. She wasn't sure if Daniel was fit to be a father to Melanie with her humble background, let alone a child from her own body. She pushed on his broad shoulders, 'Please, Daniel.'

'There's no need to say please, Grace,' he mocked her. 'You can have me any time.' His hands had pushed her skirt up to her waist and were on her hips, his thumbs hooked into her silk underwear.

'Did you know the shock of what you did to Matt made Hannah lose her baby?' Grace said savagely.

He hesitated, his expression closed for a moment. He wasn't a bit sorry at the loss of the Penneys' baby. 'Yes, and that's all the more reason for us to bring new life into the village.'

'I don't want children, Daniel,' she pleaded, tears pricking her eyes.

He looked so angry she feared him for the first time. 'Then why do you want to play nursemaid with that brat downstairs? Are you too proud to bear my children?'

'No, it isn't that.'

She started to cry silently and Daniel lost his desire. He rolled off her and sat on the edge of the bed. 'What is it then?'

'I love you, Daniel.' She wiped her eyes with the heels of her hands and levered herself to sit close to him. 'God knows I'm a foolish woman but I love you with all my heart, no matter what you do. I just don't think it's right to bring children into the world until they can be guaranteed a stable home life. I'm not a maternal woman, and, well, a man who can arrange for someone to be beaten as Matt Penney was shouldn't—'

'I owed Penney that beating,' he muttered sulkily.

'Nothing can justify what you did, Daniel. He's lost his livelihood, his child and half his face.'

'He's not as bad as that!' he snapped. 'The bastards are exaggerating. I went to the hospital and took a peep at him myself.'

Grace felt ill as she visualised him gloating over Matt but she sensed a defensiveness in him and it made her bold. 'What about his child?'

'What about it? That had nothing to do with me. Hannah could have miscarried it anyway. I'll knock on her flaming door and offer my condolences,' he said coldly. 'Anyway, you're getting off the point. If you don't want children, why are you bothering with Melanie?'

'She's already in the world, nothing can change that. You're her father and I'm your wife. It makes us both responsible for her. I didn't want her at first but I'm growing to love her. We could do a lot for her, Daniel.' She put a beguiling tone in her voice. 'If we settled down like a normal family then we could think about having a baby of our own.'

He snorted and tossed his head. 'Are you suggesting I become a respectable citizen?'

'It's not that hard, Daniel.' She moved behind him and put her arms round his neck. 'You've made a start. You've got yourself a new crew. Good people, you said. I don't know what went on in the past but surely you've got the revenge you wanted on the Penneys. Leave them alone to get on with their own lives while we get on with ours.' She bent her head to kiss the side of his face. 'Please, darling.'

With a force that hurt her chest and cut off her breath, he pushed her away from him. 'Go to hell, you conniving bitch!' Standing and pointing at her, he shouted, 'You said you'd take what was on offer and I said if you nag me or try to change me I'd make you suffer. Go on like this and I'll keep my word. I'll make you wish you'd never been born. If you don't want my body there's plenty of women who do. And what I do to Hannah Penney is my business, not yours. Keep out of it.'

Leaving Grace in a frightened huddle on the bed, he snatched up his clean clothes and stormed off to the bathroom.

Downstairs, Melanie curled up in a corner of the living room and wet herself. When Daniel thumped down the stairs and out of the house, Dumpy deserted her for him and she slipped back into her shell.

Chapter 17

Miss Benson knocked and entered Mrs Opie's suite. 'Mr Spargo is here to see Mrs Greg, madam. I've told him she has gone to St Austell for a doctor's appointment and he's requested to see you.'

'Oh, what a nuisance,' Feena sighed. She had only just got back from Penzance and was painting a still life to unwind, the bronze figure of a ballet dancer, and although the light wasn't good on this early November day, she was enjoying her activity. But she was curious to learn what Jeff wanted. She put her palette down. 'Help me out of my smock please, Miss Benson, then you had better show him up.'

After the plain-faced housekeeper had left, Feena wheeled herself quickly to her bedroom and retouched her make-up. She flicked at her closely waved grey hair and smoothed at her slightly sagging jowls, wishing she had a way of holding them up permanently. Then she went back to the sitting room and transferred herself to a chair well away from the light of the windows. She called Pogo to her, patting her lap for him to jump up, then she awaited her old lover with an imposing expression.

'I'm sorry I missed Leah,' Jeff said the moment he'd been admitted. 'I thought that while I was here I'd have a few words with you, if that's all right.'

'Do sit down, Mr Spargo,' Feena said in her formal hostess tone. 'Would you like some tea?'

'Yes please, Mrs Opie, if it's no trouble,' he replied, glancing about the feminine confines of the room, admiring Feena's style and taste. Firelight gleamed on cut-glass vases and porcelain ornaments. A photograph of Hannah and Nathan in a silver frame was set discreetly amid those of the Opie family. He breathed in Feena's alluring perfume.

'It's no trouble. Miss Benson will see to it.'

When Miss Benson withdrew again he selected the chair nearest to

Feena. She noted that he was wearing his suit with the addition of a clean white handkerchief in the breast pocket, he had brilliantined his thick black hair and polished his shoes. In his hand he held his trilby hat rather than his working cap.

'What do you want, Jeff?' she demanded. 'When you were here last I clearly remember Leah telling you she had an appointment with the doctor today.'

'I haven't come to see Leah,' Jeff admitted, his dark eyes calmly sweeping over her. Pogo jumped down off her lap and cautiously sniffed his shoes. 'It's about Hannah. Matt's coming home soon and I'm worried about her. She hasn't had the chance to grieve over the loss of her baby yet and she's going to have her work cut out nursing Matt. He hasn't realised he'll never be fit to fish again. Could be really traumatic when he does. They're going to have to rethink their whole future.'

Feena nodded her head slowly. 'I share similar worries, but why are you discussing this with me?'

'We are Hannah's parents, Feena. Prim and I don't talk about nothing at all these days. I believe she'd leave me if she had somewhere to go.' I wish she would, he thought to himself. 'And I'm concerned that Hannah shouldn't be pulled in different directions by the two sets of people who figure in her life – you lot here and us lot in Porthellis. We worked it out well when she had the miscarriage and I want us to do it again. She doesn't need the added stress of us trying to make up her mind what's best for her, Matt and Nathan.'

Miss Benson brought the tea tray and neither of them spoke until she'd gone. Feena served the tea. 'You've changed,' she said, observing him over the rim of her teacup.

'How do you mean?'

'Your insight into Hannah's problems. You used to be such a selfish man, it wouldn't have crossed your mind in the past.'

'I told you I saw things differently when I stopped hating Hannah.' Jeff smiled wryly and dipped a biscuit into his tea. 'You obviously didn't believe me then.'

Feena felt a reciprocal smile coming on but kept her face straight. 'You can hardly blame me.'

'I s'pose I did treat you badly, leaving you to bear my child alone.'

Feena could have said a lot of bitter things but in the face of Hannah's tragic circumstances and the hard future she would have to cope with, they didn't matter any more. 'It's all in the past. There is no point in raking it up.'

'I did think about you.' Jeff put his cup and saucer down and gazed into her eyes with the same warmth and interest of many years ago.

'Did you? In what way?' Feena knew the sensible thing to do would be to stop this conversation but she couldn't help herself. She would have preferred to keep on loathing Jeff Spargo but he was weaving a little of the magic he'd used on her in the past.

He leaned towards her, his big rough hands spread out on his knees. 'You meant more to me than just the physical side. We had a few things in common, didn't we?'

Feena knew he was lying. Sex had always been the foremost thought in his mind. They hadn't shared any other experiences, not even a joke. He had hated her possessiveness and after the affair she had told herself she was a fool to have been captivated by him. If she hadn't been so lonely after her husband's death she probably wouldn't have fallen for his handsome face and slick tongue. But now Jeff had changed, and although she had Greg and Patrick in the house and had reclaimed a part of Hannah, she was still lonely.

'There were strong feelings between us, Jeff,' she said cagily. She wasn't going to let him think she was about to fall back into his arms. Not that I want to, she told herself. 'Now what about your suggestions for Hannah?'

'Well, I haven't got any actual suggestions. I think we should simply listen to her and help her to do what she wants to. I'll keep Prim in check and my eye on Janet Rouse. I'm not particularly worried about Mrs Penney. She's a sensible woman.'

Jeff hoped he had made his point. It had been a struggle to get Feena to leave the hotel and let Janet take her place for these last few days of Matt's ten-week stay in hospital. The villagers had raised a fund to help the Penneys with the expense of staying at Penzance. The money wouldn't cover the hotel fees and Hannah had wanted to move into a humbler establishment. Feena had offered to pay for the hotel but Hannah had wanted to utilize the villagers' generosity. Jeff didn't want his daughter to go on having these unnecessary struggles.

'I'll do my best to support Hannah in whatever way she wishes,' Feena said demurely.

'Good. How was Matt yesterday?'

'He still has difficulty sitting up and most things have to be done for

163

him. Those men should be hanged for what they did to him!' She was suddenly passionate. 'You'd think he'd been through the war. I get so angry when I think how Daniel Kittow has got away with his part in it.'

'He'll get his just dues,' Jeff mumbled. He wished he had a plan to get rid of Kittow but the ruthless young fisherman wouldn't easily be toppled from his perch.

'I hope so.' Feena had been thinking along the same lines. She had spoken to the Chief Constable but he'd said that without firm evidence there was nothing the police could do. 'Anyway, as I was saying about Matt. He can speak sensibly now but seems to have memory lapses. It's what his face will look like when all the bandages come off that worries me. The swelling has gone down but how badly will he be scarred? The doctor told me one side of his face was criss-crossed with slashes. It's not a pleasant prospect for a lovely young woman to have to look at a monster for the rest of her life.'

Jeff thought Feena's last remark callous. 'I'm sure Hannah will always love Matt whatever he looks like.'

'Yes, of course.' Feena coloured. In her opinion Matt would never be any good to Hannah and she didn't relish the prospect of her daughter having to care for an invalid for the rest of her life. 'As you've said, Jeff, Hannah and Matt have a lot to face together and we must help them all we can. More tea?'

He didn't like the vaguely scented insipid brew but he wanted to linger here. 'Yes, please.' He got up and wandered over to her painting. 'You still do this then. It's very good, Feena.'

'Thank you. Do you still make ships in a bottle, Jeff?'

'Yes. Used to get good prices off the holidaymakers until that Grace Kittow opened her shop. She sells cheap rubbish, but occasionally I meet someone who wants a real craftsman's work.'

'Have you made one for Nathan? I'm sure he'd love it when he's older. Perhaps you could teach Matt to do it. It will give him something to do while he's convalescing. I'd offer to see he had a proper rest period away somewhere with a nurse in attendance but he says all he's looking forward to is coming home.'

'We all feel better when we're at home. If the people there love us,' Jeff added as he picked up his second cup of tea.

Feena met his eyes and smiled. 'If you've nothing to rush back to you may as well stay and wait for Leah to come home. Greg's taking her shopping after she's seen the doctor. They should be at least another hour.'

'What do you think of this one, darling?' Greg was holding the white handle of a huge pram.

'I don't think I'd be able to see over the top of the hood.'

Leah knew she ought to be one of the happiest mothers-to-be ever to enter Scoble's in Fore Street. Girls of her background usually had to make do with battered handed-down contraptions to wheel their babies about in or carry them in shawls round their bodies. Hannah had been the only mother to have a new pram in Porthellis since the last minister's wife. Yet here she was, choosing from the pick of the latest models and not the least bit excited. And she wouldn't have to push her baby up a steep hill or bumpy cobbled street or struggle to get her pram in and out of small doorways and cluttered surroundings.

'Boo,' Greg laughed, thrusting a cuddly bear into her arms. 'Gus will like this.'

'Gus? We're not calling the baby Gus,' she said indignantly, putting the bear into the smaller pram she was looking at and giving it a push to test the feel of it.

Raising his brows in perplexity, Greg slipped his arm affectionately round her waist. 'This smaller pram is more suitable for you,' he said. 'You're so tiny you're not likely to give birth to a whopper of a baby. Are you sure you don't like Gus?' he added playfully, hoping to soften her mood. She had been down in the dumps for days. 'It's the name of one of my old university chums. Augustus Miners. He was quite a card.'

'I want Rhett, like the hero in *Gone With the Wind*,' Leah said, ready to sulk if he disagreed or laughed at her.

Greg didn't want anything remotely American for his child but said sportingly, 'That's rather nice. Rhett Augustus Opie. Well, we have plenty of time to decide.' A shop assistant was unobtrusively waiting on them and he told her they had chosen the pram and bear. 'Let's take a look at some baby clothes next, shall we, darling?'

When they had finished their shopping, they were laden with parcels. They headed back to the car, having arranged to have the pram delivered. Leah seemed a little brighter and Greg ventured, 'Would you like to go to a restaurant for a spot of tea, darling?'

'No, I want to go home and show Lily what I've bought.' At least in the cheerful under-housemaid she had one person who would be excited for her and not turn the subject round to Hannah's plight. It was all she had heard these last few weeks. As sorry as she was for Hannah and Matt, it was galling to be continually overlooked while she was about to provide a new heir for Roscarrock. Leah had endured a whole evening in the Castle Bay Hotel listening to Mrs Opie try to persuade Hannah to bring Matt to Roscarrock; she would hire a nurse for him and Hannah and Nathan could live there too. Leah had been relieved that Hannah had flatly refused. And she was the subject constantly on the lips of her mother and father, her sisters and Aunty Janet, and any of the villagers she met when down in Porthellis.

'The doctor did say everything was all right with the pregnancy, didn't he, Leah?' Greg asked.

'Yes, I told you. Everything's fine. I didn't need to see him really. The women in the village only see the midwife a couple of times in the later stages.'

'That may be all right for them, darling,' Greg said, darting a glance at her as he drove out of the town. 'But I want you and our baby to have the very best of care and attention.'

Leah squeezed his hand. 'Greg, when are we going to have the party?'

'What party?'

'The party your grandmother is going to give to announce that we're having a baby.'

'Oh that. Well, everyone knows about it now and in the circumstances it would be rather thoughtless, don't you think?'

'Of course, how silly of me. Because of Hannah.' Leah turned away and gazed despondently out of the window.

Chapter 18

The wind was gusting into Porthellis when Matt came home. Greg pulled up his car outside the cottage. Wearing his pyjamas and dressing gown, Matt hauled himself up on weak legs from the back seat and with his arms round Greg and Hannah's shoulders, he hobbled inside. A crowd of well-wishers had gathered outside Seaview Cottage, many bearing bags of black grapes which they believed would make good blood for the invalid. ''Tis a crying shame such a fine young man should be brought to that state,' they commented before dispersing.

Prim and Josh were inside with Janet, and although Josh wasn't sensible in the head, he was strong as an ox and Prim gently instructed him to help Greg carry Matt up to his bedroom where a roaring fire was lit. Hannah took Nathan out of his highchair and followed them up with Mrs Penney. Once Matt's dressing gown had been removed and he was tucked up in bed, Greg led Josh downstairs.

'How is he?' Prim asked her son-in-law.

'A bit emotional, I think, but glad to be home,' Greg answered self-consciously, running a hand through his hair. Although he saw Hannah and Leah on the same level as himself and had a lot of respect for Matt, he had never felt comfortable in working-class surroundings. He didn't think of the Spargos as family. 'He was talking about going back to sea before Christmas. I don't envy the person who has to tell him it's out of the question.'

'The doctor should do that,' Prim said, guiding Josh away from the highchair where he stood, his head lolling to the side, puzzled why the toddler was no longer there.

'No, it'll be best coming from Hannah,' Janet said stoutly. 'And she ought to tell him soon, and that there's no new baby on the way, before some well-meaning visitor puts their foot in it.'

'Matt won't want no visitors yet,' Prim retorted tersely. 'He needs all the rest he can get.' She looked at Greg with pursed lips. 'I suppose your grandmother will be getting you to drive her down here tomorrow.'

'Perhaps,' Greg replied, knowing full well she would. Feena had wanted to come today but he had persuaded her to let Matt settle in first. He didn't want to get involved in any female wranglings and glanced at his watch. 'Well, if you'll excuse me, I'd like to get back to Leah.'

'Thank you for bringing Matt home,' Prim said.

'Have you finished that little baby's coat you said you were knitting for her, Mrs Spargo?' Greg couldn't bring himself to address Prim informally.

'Not with all this going on,' Prim said as if astounded he'd asked such a thing. 'There's plenty of time yet.'

Upstairs, Hannah carefully placed Nathan beside Matt where he sat up against the pillows. Matt took his son's little hand but Nathan pulled it back and seemed nervous of him. 'He doesn't recognise me with this dressing on my face,' Matt said with grief in his voice. 'You'd better take him away.'

Nathan kicked out with his leg and Matt yelped as it hit his tender ribs. Nathan was disturbed and began to whimper, his chubby arms held out to Hannah. She passed him to Mrs Penney. 'Daddy can play with you when he's better,' she said, sounding more cheerful than she felt.

Mrs Penney leaned forward and kissed Matt's forehead. 'It's good to have you home, son. I'll take Nathan downstairs and make some tea for Prim and Janet. I'll bring you up some later, but just shout out if you want anything.'

'Thanks, Mum,' Matt murmured. Weary from the long, uncomfortable journey, he dozed off.

Hannah took off her coat and placed a bottle of analgesic tablets and a urinal bottle beside the bed, then sat down on it, waiting for Matt to open his eyes.

When he did, he was confused where he was for a few moments. 'Sorry,' he mumbled, wanting to smile at her but remembering it would hurt his face. 'Don't know what's the matter with me.'

'You've had a terrible shock to your system, Matt, as well as a savage beating. At least you're home now. It's a big step forward.' She lifted his hand, kissed it then placed her lips gently on his brow, the only area on his face that would not hurt him. He had a strong clinical smell on him.

'You are going to sleep with me tonight?'

'I shouldn't really. I could roll over and hurt you.'

'I'll take the risk. I so badly want to feel you close to me.'

Matt's body was beginning to heal but he was still weak and extremely sore and because of an infection in a cut on the left side of his face there was a large dressing yet to be removed. On the other side were two livid red scars where he had been slashed and a small scar on his chin. His eyes had retained their puffiness.

He raised a hand and indicated the dressing on his face. 'When does this come off?'

'The district nurse will call tomorrow and change it. Shouldn't be much longer now.'

'Have you seen what it's like underneath?'

'No, they wouldn't let me stay and watch in the hospital while they were tending to you, remember?'

'I can't remember anything like I used to.' He looked like a young, frightened boy.

'It'll take time before you're your old self again.' She smiled to encourage him.

He went rigid, reliving again, as he did every day, the way Daniel had ordered the attack. When he was well enough he would go to court and give evidence against the three thugs; with several villagers giving witness about their riotous behaviour, they would receive long prison sentences. Matt hoped they would rot in there. If only he could break Daniel's cast-iron alibi and have him locked up too, but with his known hatred of Daniel, and his memory of the beating and the events leading up to it patchy, the police were unlikely to believe Daniel ordered the attack. He had yet to face him. What he would do when it happened he didn't know. He did not want the sort of revenge that would physically hurt his enemy. He wanted Daniel brought down, utterly shamed, his ego ground into the dirt. He wanted him to know how it felt to fear for the future.

He gripped Hannah's hand tightly and said bitterly. 'We'll really see what damage Kittow's men have done to me when my face is bare. I'll probably look so ugly the children in the village will run away from me. Nathan might always be afraid of me.'

'No, he won't, darling. You'll always have scars as a reminder of what happened but you'll still be just as handsome. If anything, the scars will make you look more manly.'

'That's what one of the doctors said,' Matt sighed ruefully. He gingerly touched his nose. 'I lost a couple of teeth but at least they didn't break my nose.' He couldn't smile but a twinkle came into his dark eyes. 'I wish I could make love to you.'

'So do I. We'll be able to soon.' Hannah gazed down at the rug on the floor. She didn't want to spoil Matt's good spirits but she had to tell him some of the news she'd been holding back. When she looked at him he was gazing out of the window at the sea which was just visible from this room.

'Wind's getting stronger all the time,' he said. 'Must be rough for the boats out there today. I expect they'll be back early. Looks like a gale's blowing up. Will you ask Jeff to come and give me a report on the . . .' His mind went blank for a second. 'On the, um, *Misty* when he gets back? With me being laid up for so long and the expenses we've had, I'll have to sort out our finances.' He sensed a heavy quietness in Hannah and began to panic. 'What's the matter? Nothing's happened to the *Misty*, has it?'

'No, and I'm not worried about money. We'll get by. I'm afraid I've got some bad news for you. I've waited until you were home to tell you.' She swallowed heavily to stop the tears lurking dangerously behind her eyes. 'Matt . . . I–I lost the baby.'

He stared at her blankly for a minute then looked down at her middle. 'You mean . . . I hadn't noticed . . . I . . .' Suddenly he groaned so loudly that those below looked up over their heads in anguish. 'My God, Hannah, when did it happen?'

She clasped his hand tightly in both of hers and now she couldn't stop the tears from falling. 'It was on the day you were attacked. You were so ill you didn't realise that I wasn't able to be with you for nearly a week.'

Weeping angry, frustrated tears, Matt cried, 'I was looking forward so much to our new baby. I'm sorry, Hannah. Sorry I wasn't there for you.'

They couldn't hold each other but she crept up beside him and placed her face against his shoulder.

'That bastard Kittow has a lot to answer for,' Matt muttered after a while. 'He struts around like he's got the world by the throat while ruining other people's lives.'

'Let's forget him for now,' Hannah said, drying her eyes. 'Let's just enjoy being like this together.'

A little later when Matt had fallen asleep, Hannah looked out of the window at the new house down the street. Hatred was burning in her heart.

Chapter 19

The night was lashed by a fierce south-easterly gale and torrential rain. It battered the boats against each other and the harbour wall. Huge waves thundered into the cove. The howling wind, like a demented, vengeful spirit, gusted through the narrow streets and alleys, whipping tiles off roofs, blowing off shutters, bringing down chimney pots, electricity and telephone lines, rattling windows and doors, demolishing chicken coops and scattering loose objects about the village.

Matt slept fitfully and Hannah cradled his head against her breast. Nathan woke up crying and she brought him into bed with them and he slept in the crook of her arm. She wasn't comfortable but having her two men close against her body at long last brought balm to her troubled soul.

Further down the street, lying fearfully in her bed as the storm raged, Melanie screamed when the door of an outside closet somewhere close by was wrenched off its hinges and sent crashing to the ground.

Grace hastened to her room and searching about in the darkness found her curled up in a tight ball under the covers, clutching her comfort blanket. 'There's nothing to worry about, sweetheart. It's only the wind.' Grace felt about to see if she'd wet the bed. It was dry. 'I think you'd better pay a visit to the bathroom before you settle down again.'

'Here, I've got a light,' Daniel said from behind her, holding up his lighter.

'Thank you.' Grace shivered. She was nervous herself, having never experienced weather like this before, and she was heartily relieved Daniel was home. With Melanie gripping her nightdress, she led her to the bathroom.

When they were out on the landing again, a sweep of grit hit the long narrow window on top of the stairs and Melanie screamed in terror. Grace picked her up and whispered, 'I'm frightened too.'

'There shouldn't be any damage to this house,' Daniel said confidently. 'It's new and strongly built. Get Melanie back into bed before she gets cold.'

Melanie had a vice-like grip on Grace's neck and her face was buried in her shoulder. 'She won't be able to settle with all this noise going on, Daniel. I usually bring her in with me. I'll sleep in her bed for the rest of the night.'

'There's no need for that. There's plenty of room in our bed,' Daniel said. Putting his arm round Grace, he led them into the master bedroom.

Grace was pleased at his thoughtfulness. He hadn't ignored Melanie since he'd stalked out with Dumpy but he hadn't been very friendly towards his daughter either; with Grace he'd alternated between indifference and hostility until she'd assured him she wanted him as much in bed as ever. One small incident stuck in Grace's mind. Daniel had stretched past Melanie on the sofa to stop one of the kittens scratching at a cushion. Melanie had flinched and retreated to the floor, her little face dark and closed. Daniel had seemed appalled by her reaction to him.

'I wasn't going to hit her, Grace,' he appealed to her. 'Tell her I wasn't going to hit her.'

'Why don't you tell her, Daniel?' Grace replied warily. 'Obviously the men in her mother's life used to hit her. She doesn't trust men.'

Daniel glared at Grace for a moment, then picking up Melanie's sketchpad and pencils he held them out to her. 'I'm sorry if I frightened you, Melanie. Will you draw a picture for Daddy?'

Melanie nodded and complied apprehensively, taking her pad and pencils away to a chair and sitting there while she drew a picture of the kittens sleeping in their basket. She showed Daniel the finished picture from where she sat.

'Very nice,' he said shortly, then sighing impatiently he had left the house.

The incident had not brought father and daughter much closer but Melanie did seem a little less in awe of him now.

Grace put Melanie in the middle of the large bed then they all lay down together. Melanie turned to her and snuggled into her body. All three listened to the wind whistling round the house.

'I was afraid of the wind when I was a kid,' Daniel said suddenly.

'Were you?' Grace was astonished. 'I didn't think you were afraid of anything.'

'Old Rufus used to tell me the dead rose from their graves on stormy nights and took naughty boys back with them to be their slaves. One night the old bugger rattled on my bedroom door and put on an eerie voice, saying he was a spirit come for me because I'd put a pile of gull droppings on Mr Nunn's doorstep. I was brave enough in normal circumstances but not with the wind threatening to blow the roof off.' He caressed the back of Melanie's head. 'I've hated the thought of children being frightened in storms ever since.'

Melanie responded to his touch by moving on to her back. 'Dumpy,' she said feebly.

'He's all right,' Daniel said. 'I brought him off the boat when we battened it down. He's in his bed in the kitchen.'

'Dumpy fri-tened,' Melanie whimpered.

'She's worried about him being all alone,' Daniel said, getting out of bed. 'I'll go and fetch him.'

Grace didn't like the idea of having the scruffy little dog in the bedroom but she didn't dare protest.

Daniel lifted the covers and put Dumpy into Melanie's arms. Then he got back into bed and stretched out his arm, cuddling her and Grace into him. 'This is cosy,' he said, sounding satisfied.

Grace stroked the bulging muscles on his arm. 'Yes, it is.'

As dawn broke, the gale eased off a little. Melanie was sleeping soundly. Daniel carried her back to her own bed and tucked Dumpy in with her.

'Are you going down to see if the boat's damaged?' Grace yawned when he returned.

'Wind's still too strong to be able to do anything yet. Should blow itself out in a couple of hours. Then the village will need all hands to mop up. It'll look like we've been in a war.'

Getting back in bed, he took Grace in his arms. She wrapped herself round him, revelling in the closeness of his hard, lean body. She expected him to make love to her immediately but he lay still for some moments. 'I shouldn't have taken Dumpy away from Melanie before. She likes him. He's happy on the boat but I'll bring him home when we're moored up.'

'Melanie will like that.' Maybe he'd keep a check on his temper when he was at home, too. It had taken her four days to coax a word out of Melanie after he'd shouted that day and she was usually tense when he was around.

Leaning over her, Daniel kissed her, his passion rising quickly. Grace returned his caresses and was eager for him. Suddenly he stopped and she opened her eyes to see a serious expression on his handsome face. 'Are you still dead against us having kids?'

She ran her fingertip down his cheek. 'I didn't go back to the doctor, Daniel.'

'Why not?'

'I thought I'd leave it to fate.' Despite his wickedness, Grace was so frightened of losing him she'd have a dozen babies to please him.

He grinned down at her. 'So you could be pregnant now?'

'I could be.'

He kissed her lips and muttered huskily, 'Let's make sure of it then.'

The wind turned and blew the heavy purple clouds out to sea, remaining in occasional spiteful gusts to re-distribute the litter and exacerbate the destruction it had wilfully created. There was little fuss as the villagers picked their way over the debris and surveyed their property for damage. The recklessness of the weather had left Porthellis looking like a battlefield many times before in even the youngest fisherman's lifetime and no doubt would do so again. Neighbour began to help neighbour good-naturedly with the necessary repairs.

Windows had been smashed, including one in Grace's shop. Leaving Melanie happily with Dumpy and Nan Trebilcock, she teamed up with her uncle and they went round the village making a list of people's requirements for repairs – from those who could afford it. Then they drove to St Austell to buy the materials and report the loss of the electricity and telephone lines.

'How will the other people manage, Uncle David?' Grace asked as they navigated the roads strewn with foliage and branches, occasionally having to stop and clear the way ahead. 'The ones who haven't got the money for repairs?'

'They'll get by no matter how tight the fit but the villagers are very adept at knocking up chimneys and things,' the minister replied as he looked cautiously upwards out of the windscreen for loose branches that might be about to fall on the car.

'I could organize a fund-raising event for those who are really in hardship,' Grace said. She was thinking particularly of the Rouse family whose lugger had been ripped free from its mooring and hopelessly smashed on Slate Rock.

'The villagers won't want charity,' the Reverend Skewes said soberly, thinking how his flock wouldn't countenance anything organized by Grace no matter how well-meaning; they were not hostile towards her but she was first and foremost Daniel Kittow's wife. 'We usually have a Christmas bazaar and social evening in the middle of December. We could bring it forward. I'll get your aunt on to it and I'm sure she'll be glad of any ideas you can come up with.'

At mid-morning Daniel was walking home with Colville Penrose, his new engineer and father of the rest of his crew, to collect some tools from his garden shed.

'I thank the Lord the *Sunrise* didn't fare badly,' Colville said in his deep accent. He was a short man with a solid look about him, squinting eyes, iron-grey hair under a flat cap and side whiskers. He compressed his thick lips as some people they passed on the quay bid him a gruff good morning but ignored Daniel. 'Won't take us long t'put her t'rights, I reckon.' He stepped over a section of split wood, realised it was part of the Ship Inn's sign board and handed it over to Maggie Curnow who was glaring at both of them.

'Stupid mare,' Daniel snorted. 'She don't like us because we don't use the pub.'

Colville wondered why his skipper, who frequented all the pubs at Newlyn, spurned the local drinking establishment, but he didn't question his employer.

'The *Sunrise* is a fine craft,' Daniel said proudly, pausing to pick up some sharp-edged broken roof tiles and put them safely against the barkhouse wall. Colville helped him. 'Some of the others won't be able to put to sea for at least a few days.'

'Pity about the Rouses' boat. Roy's son'll have to postpone his wedding. Me and the boys didn't own the *Prudence* but 'twas a tremendous blow to we when she sunk off the Wolf a few weeks ago. The Lord delivered us from the sea then.' Knowing Daniel's amoral nature, the deeply religious Colville couldn't bring himself to give the Lord the credit for what he said next. 'Good job for we you offered us work straightaway. Wonder what the Rouses'll do now.'

'Who cares?' Daniel shrugged as they carried on. He stepped into the doorway of Grace's Gifts out of the strong wind to light a cigarette.

Colville's long slanting eyebrows furrowed into a frown. 'You shouldn't think like that,' he quietly admonished his skipper. 'Mind you, Porthellis isn't a very friendly place. Don't matter too much to me and the boys, we're working most of the time, but the missus has been getting a bit upset. She's always been a good chapel woman but she feels out of place here. She hasn't been invited to join none of the women's groups. That woman Spargo next door can hardly put two civil words together to her.' Mrs Penrose had argued strongly against her menfolk taking up Daniel's offer of work and a cottage. Colville felt a pang of guilt at his insistence that they should; his sweet-natured wife pleaded constantly that they go back to Newlyn where they had friends and family.

''Tis nothing to do with you, Colville,' Daniel told him. 'You're working for me and the whole village hates me. Prim Spargo is Matt Penney's mother-in-law and they think I put my old crew up to attacking him.'

Colville felt like a man failing in his Godly duties as he recalled how he'd overlooked the rumours about Daniel's involvement in the Matt Penney incident, rumours which he knew were probably true. He was concerned, too, about packages that had changed hands between Daniel on the *Sunrise* and an unfamiliar sailing yacht off the Dodman last week. Daniel had made it clear he expected his crew to keep silent about it. Colouring self-consciously, Colville said carefully, 'Aye, we heard that.'

'Well, that's all in the past now. At least the *Misty* wasn't damaged so Penney won't have nothing to worry about there.'

'You think 'tis true he won't never be able t'fish again?'

'Sounds like it.'

'That's a terrible thing.' Colville shook his head grimly.

'Cut the bullshit, Colville,' Daniel snapped, tired of his engineer's subtle attempts to get him to see things his way. He began to walk up the hill. 'You'll never have any luck trying to convert me and you know full well I hate Matt Penney and couldn't give a sodding damn if he's down on his luck.'

Colville was quiet for some moments, then he risked, 'The tide goes full circle, Daniel.'

Daniel wasn't listening. They had turned into Cobble Street and just up ahead was Hannah, sweeping debris off her doorstep. He hadn't seen her since he'd terrified her in her parlour, and his only thoughts about her had concerned his knowledge that Feena Opie was her natural mother and that he could cause her further torment whenever he desired it. He was shocked by her appearance. Her long blonde hair hung lankily on her shoulders. Her face was gaunt and bore a sickly colour. She had a coat and scarf on but it was obvious she had lost a lot of weight and she didn't

176

seem to have the strength to finish her task. She looked as desolate as she had on the day of the boating tragedy, when as a ten-year-old girl, she had been thrown out of her home, and he had rescued her from a vicious beating from her father.

He quickened his step as she put aside her broom and stooped to pick up a long piece of splintered wood. 'Hannah, let me help you.'

She straightened up rapidly with the piece of wood in her hand. Her expression was fiercer than the worst of last night's gale. 'Don't you speak to me, Daniel Kittow,' she hurled at him indignantly. Then suddenly the dam of hurt and hatred for him burst inside her and she strode up to him, wielding the piece of wood like a weapon. 'How dare you speak to me after what you did to me and Matt, you evil callous swine! I know you ordered Brinley and the others to attack him and I begged the police to lock you up.'

As Daniel stood stunned, she lashed out with the wood and brought it down viciously across his shoulder. 'I hate you with all my heart for that and for making me lose my baby. You said when you came out of prison you wanted revenge on me. Well, you've had it in full but now it's me who's going to get revenge on you! I'm going to make your life as miserable as I can. You and your threats can't hurt me any more but I'll do anything I can to hurt you, to bring you down to the gutter where you belong. I wish you were dead!'

Her next blow was aimed at Daniel's head. He ducked just in time to escape it but he was trapped against the wall.

Colville tried to grab her flailing arms. 'That's enough of that. Calm yourself down.'

Hearing the shouting, Mrs Penney rushed outside and appealed to her to stop. Such was Hannah's fury she shoved Colville away from her and brandished the piece of wood at Daniel's face.

'Hannah, for pity's sake!' he cried, holding his blood-soaked shoulder which was impaled with splinters. 'Stop it.'

'Pity?' she screamed like a madwoman, tears streaming down her face. She lunged at him again. Daniel threw himself to the ground, raising his hands to defend himself. 'What do you know about pity?' Hannah yelled. 'Or decency? Or kindness? Or love? You're not fit to be part of the human race, Daniel Kittow. You think because you have a bigger house than the rest of us you're ruddy marvellous. You think you're so masculine, so clever, but you're no better than anyone else. You're not a better fisherman

177

than anybody else in Porthellis. You have to lie, cheat and steal to make more money. You're a rotten husband and a rotten father. It's a shame that woman ever brought Melanie here. When she grows up she'll learn her father is nothing but the scum of the earth.'

There was a loud hum inside Hannah's head and she was gasping for breath. She had said her piece and meant every word. Her strength left her and her fingers let go of the wood, now stained with his blood. A black mist threatened to overwhelm her but she heard Matt calling to her, his voice strained and worried. She stumbled but shook off the helping hand Colville put out and allowed Mrs Penney to take her indoors.

Up and down the street neighbours had come outside to stand on their doorsteps. As Daniel got to his feet, he felt over a dozen accusing pairs of eyes on him, all agreeing with Hannah's sentiments, while Colville looked down, embarrassed, at the cobbles. Never in his life had Daniel been the slightest bit concerned over a fight or angry words, but Hannah's hate-filled tirade had pierced his hard exterior and lodged in his soul. Keeping his eyes on the ground, he continued on his way home.

Hannah's face was blood-red, her limbs were shaking, her eyes glazed over. Mrs Penney was so alarmed she didn't know what to do first. Matt kept calling, his voice weak and hoarse, and she decided the best thing was to take Hannah upstairs and hope Matt could calm her. Somehow she got Hannah up the two flights of stairs to the bedroom and propelled her into the room. Matt was trying to get out of bed.

'For goodness' sake, Mother, why didn't you stop her?' he bellowed, making himself fall back feebly on the mattress and clutch his ribs.

'I couldn't, Matt. It was as if she wanted to kill Daniel. I'll put her in beside you. It's a good thing the district nurse is coming this morning. I'll ask her to look at Hannah too.' Mrs Penney was near to tears, wondering how she was going to cope if Hannah was taken seriously ill and Matt had a relapse. 'Hannah needs as much rest and recuperation as you, Matt. It took it out of her going to the hospital every day when she was hardly over the miscarriage. I need some help. I'll take Nathan with me and pop down the hill and ask Prim and Josh to move in with us.'

'I'll be all right,' Hannah gasped. 'I just need a lie-down.'

'You need more than that, darling.' Matt held his hands out to her.

When she was settled beside Matt, Mrs Penney hastened away to interrupt her grandson's morning nap.

When her breathing was finally under control, Hannah turned to look at Matt. His dark eyes were rooted on her, gleaming unnaturally in his deep concern for her. 'I'm sorry if you were worried, darling.' Her voice was low and rusty. 'Did you hear what was happening?'

'Every word, you were shouting so loud,' he answered sombrely.

'I couldn't help it.' She snuggled closer to him for comfort. 'He offered to help me clear up. As if he hadn't done all those terrible things to us.'

'I understand, Hannah. But what's all this about you getting revenge on him? I hope you didn't mean it.'

She couldn't bear the anxiety in his face. 'Of course I didn't. I just got so angry.'

Matt slowly brought her hand up to his lips. 'Perhaps it's a good thing you got it out of your system. Now we can settle down and start again.'

Soon he fell asleep and Hannah watched him, tracing a gentle finger down the outline of his face, now greatly altered by Daniel's act of malice. And she cried. They couldn't start again, not in the way Matt assumed. Her heart ached as she thought of the anguish he had ahead of him when he realised he would have to give up the livelihood he loved despite its harsh conditions. Her love for Matt grew to a new depth of passion but she felt a part of her was not with him. A sense of unreality engulfed her, and her love for Matt was equalled by her hatred for Daniel Kittow.

Chapter 20

There were more serious discoveries as the day wore on. Old Mr Nunn was discovered dead in his bed; he had died peacefully in his sleep. And Jowan Rouse, standing despairingly on top of the cliff to view the wreck of the family lugger through his telescope, spotted a body down at the bottom.

The body was wedged in a cleft in the rocks and stayed there despite the relentless bombarding of the sea which sought to dislodge it. The locals speculated on its identity but had to wait two days for conditions to settle sufficiently for the Coastguard and a party of rescuers to scramble reasonably safely down the cliff and retrieve the corpse. A French cargo ship had been wrecked off Fowey with some crew lost and a yacht was reported to have foolishly put to sea on the evening before the storm and was still missing, so it was commonly held the body belonged to 'one of they poor souls.'

A crowd gathered to watch as the body was hauled up on to Roscarrock land. The Coastguard told Patrick and Greg it was that of a man, a young man by his clothing. When Curly Jose got to hear of it he contacted the authorities and his and Mrs Jose's fear that the body might be Fred's was tragically realised.

'We couldn't understand why he suddenly disappeared like that,' Mrs Jose cried when Jeff and Prim called at her cottage to offer their condolences. It was a lament she had repeated many times since Fred had gone missing. She was a humble, rather solemn woman, given to quiet acts of charity, slow to utter a word of unkindness against another, and well-respected in Porthellis. It unsettled the Spargos to see her placid, round face bereft of all hope. 'It doesn't make sense,' she sobbed in her tiny front room where Curly had lit a hearty blaze for her comfort, the cavorting flames offering no cheer. 'Fred going off and not taking nothing with him. No clothes, no money. He didn't even leave a note. The police have asked us if he'd been unhappy before he disappeared. But Fred had no reason to kill himself, if that's what they were inferring.'

Prim didn't know what to say to her now childless neighbour, not while she was blessed with six living children, umpteen grandchildren and two or three more on the way. She patted Mrs Jose's chilled hand. In a few moments she would set about making tea to add to the batch of hevva cake and scones she'd brought to help refresh the expected stream of sympathisers.

'He wasn't much of a son, was always three scats behind everyone else,' Curly said as he drew Jeff aside in the little cold passage for a smoke. 'But he was all we had.' He wiped away his tears. 'He didn't deserve whatever happened to un, Jeff.'

'I know, Curly.' Jeff shook his dark head at the vagaries of fate. 'Did you say the police are still making inquiries?'

'Aye. The missus don't know it yet but there's something a bit strange about Fred's death. Apparently he'd only been in the sea about twenty-four hours but he'd died several weeks before.'

Jeff shivered. 'That is strange. S'pose the experts will be able t'work out what happened to un.'

'I hope so. The missus is expecting to put him to rest soon, but they won't release his body till all their inquiries have finished.'

Jeff sighed mournfully. 'I don't know, Curly. The village hasn't been right since that Kittow bastard come back among we. No matter what he does he's got the luck of the devil with un. While the Rouses lost their boat and everything in it, his was one of they that got off practically scot-free.'

'He hated Fred,' Curly said bitterly, balling his fists then splaying out the fingers of his rough stubby hands and mentally gripping Daniel Kittow's neck. 'Never missed a chance at taunting un. He made sure that rotten lot what used t'live next door made life a misery for all of us. I wouldn't put it past that evil bugger to . . .' A queer look came over Curly's face. The unspeakable thought passing through his mind was plain to see.

Jeff opened his mouth in shock to disagree but shut it abruptly. In the circumstances, it wasn't such an unlikely possibility.

Accompanied by Leah, Feena Opie paid her fourth visit to Hannah since Matt had come home. Greg carried his grandmother up to the first floor where the district nurse had ordered Matt and Hannah to share a room with separate beds. Although Hannah didn't need a lot of bed rest, she stayed in the room most of the day to be with Matt. Nathan was playing on the hearth rug where his father could see him.

Settling his grandmother in the one small armchair at the fireside, Greg left, saying he'd come back in an hour or so. He did not want to crowd the room or tire the convalescents. Matt's bandages were off and Leah couldn't bring herself to look at his scarred face. It reminded her too painfully of her own injury and after mumbling a greeting and offering a half smile, she sat quietly beside Hannah on her bed.

With her nose slightly in the air, Feena asked. 'Is that fireguard safe enough for Nathan, dear? Can he pull it over?'

'It's perfectly safe,' Hannah said, trying to keep her patience; she'd answered the same question more than once before. 'Josh has fixed it to the wall.'

Feena knew Matt was watching her keenly and she turned her fur-hatted head away so he couldn't see her disapproving frown; she hated the thought of Hannah's idiot brother near her grandchild.

'I noticed the boats are out,' she said, interested only because it affected Jeff. On the evening after the storm, he had come to Roscarrock and told her about Hannah's verbal and physical attack on Daniel Kittow. Feena had been alarmed until Jeff assured her Hannah really was being made to rest under proper medical supervision. She had hoped Leah and Greg would find some excuse to leave her alone with Jeff, but they had stayed put in the drawing room, almost stubbornly, she'd felt.

'Perhaps now that Daniel can see she's not frightened of him any more, he'll leave her alone in future,' Leah had said hopefully.

'Was she frightened of him?' Jeff's handsome dark features had sharpened, his eyes becoming unnaturally alert, hinting at the brute strength he still had, one of the qualities that had first drawn Feena to him. He looked younger as restless energy buzzed through him. 'I knew she was intimidated by un like the rest of us, worried about what he might do, but what exactly do you mean by afraid?'

'Didn't you know?' Leah said, smirking for the benefit of Mrs Opie; these days she did all she could to annoy her. 'Hannah was certain Daniel would hurt Matt sooner or later. Thank God he didn't do anything to Nathan.'

'I'll break his bloody neck!' Jeff stormed.

'Steady on, Mr Spargo,' Greg appealed to his father-in-law. 'If you confront Kittow, he might start something else against Hannah. You wouldn't want that, would you?'

Some of the rage left Jeff and he sagged a little under the effort to breathe normally. He found his temper quickly exhausted him nowadays. 'He'd better just watch it, that's all.' He apologised very sweetly to Feena.

Greg watched her muted reaction, wondering what her true feelings for the fisherman were. He knew she and Jeff Spargo had been lovers.

Now Nathan rose to his feet and leaned on Feena's knees, kneading the fur muff on her lap. She opened her clutch bag and took out a little toy she'd brought for him, a rubber duck. 'You like that, don't you, darling? Bubsie will bring you something else next week. If you came to Roscarrock you could play with all the toys in the nursery.' Acutely jealous of Prim living here, she went on, 'Why don't all three of you come to Roscarrock for a few days, Hannah? A change of scene would do you and Matt both good. You should soon be strong enough to go for a gentle ride, Hannah. The exercise and fresh air would perk you up.'

'Don't start that again,' Matt muttered testily. 'Our home is here, not in yours.' Sitting up in bed in his pyjamas, he felt at a disadvantage with two female visitors.

He was offended that Leah wouldn't look at him and he'd noticed how Feena Opie had given him no more than a quick glance as she'd entered the room in Greg's arms. His face was scarred but he wasn't a monster. It wasn't a handsome sight but it would improve in time. Nathan came to him happily and even napped in his bed. The biggest test had been Hannah's reaction when the district nurse had taken off the dressing. His eyes had been glued to Hannah's face. He knew her completely and a brave reaction, a suppression of horror, wouldn't have fooled him. She had raised her brows at his scabbed flesh where Eric had wielded his gutting knife. She had looked angry, indignant, then she had wrapped her arms round his neck and tenderly kissed his lips. She'd whispered something intimate and he knew she still desired him. It was one of the few things that kept him from falling into despair.

'It was just a suggestion, Matt,' Feena retorted as if she had the right to be offended. The bedroom was at the back of what she saw disparagingly as a quaint house. The linoleum was faded and cracked in places, the heavy wood furniture ugly and the beds didn't match. The walls were painted grey and the plain ceiling had turned a grimy-looking ochre with age. The window was small and thick-paned, making everything dark and shadowy, slightly oppressive. Mrs Penney's attempts to brighten the surroundings by hanging yellow frilled curtains struck Feena as being like putting a jam jar of buttercups on a grave. She was angry; how was her dear girl expected to get back to her old self in conditions little better than a hovel?

Hannah's heart was sinking. She liked to see Feena but her visits invariably gave rise to a strained atmosphere both while she was here and after she'd gone. Matt was getting more and more frustrated because he felt he should be stronger by now but he could still hardly make the short journey to the bathroom unaided. Hannah understood why he became short-tempered and uncooperative but she was often in no mood to deal with it. Her body was growing stronger, her skin had regained some of its healthy glow, the shadows under her eyes were gone, but her patience was limited and for some reason she felt afraid to go far from this room. Afraid her sanity would desert her and she would actually enact one of her maudlin fantasies about doing something cruel to Daniel.

Nathan looked at his mother uneasily as if he sensed everything was at odds in the room. Leah sought to relieve the heavy atmosphere. 'Guess what, Hannah. I'm having piano lessons. You know how I've always wanted to play.'

Suddenly tired, depressed, wishing the visitors would go, Hannah could only smile wanly.

'The arrangements for the fund-raising evening are going well, I understand,' Feena cut in as if Leah had not spoken. 'Your minister's wife wrote to me and I shall do what I can to help, not that I shall be attending the bazaar thing, of course. A lot of generosity will be required if the Rouses are to replace their boat and the other boats and houses are to be fully repaired.'

'The village will do it,' Matt remarked sourly. He kept back the further comment that the Opies had not sought to help the villagers in the past and they didn't need their patronising help now.

Leah fell into a furious silence. So, she was ignored again. What she did was of no interest to anyone in the room. Her baby wasn't mentioned and her health wasn't asked about. She wasn't showing much yet but the fact that she was wearing a stylish new maternity smock with a lace-trimmed collar hadn't been noticed. Her hairdresser had plaited lengths of her hair and arranged them in a becoming Grecian style but it counted for nothing to anyone but Greg. She hadn't been thanked for carrying in a huge bunch of flowers sent by Patrick. Well, she wouldn't waste her time coming here again. Without excusing herself, she stamped down the stairs to talk to Prim and Josh.

'Why don't you take Mrs Opie down to the parlour for tea?' Matt suggested to Hannah as if he had grit between his teeth. If he had to endure another moment of the older woman's meddling in his marriage, her fawning over his son, her patronising attitude towards the village and its inhabitants, he'd bellow at her to get out of his house for good. 'I want to answer the letter from the Salvation Army captain in Plymouth.'

Matt had forgotten one important detail. 'I'll have to find Greg to carry Mrs Opie downstairs,' Hannah said wearily. She knew Feena would never allow Josh to touch her.

'Hannah's very tired,' Matt went straight in on the attack the moment she'd left the room.

'And you want me to go?' Feena replied tightly, stroking Nathan's silky fair hair. He had lost interest in the rubber duck and was chewing on a glass button on her dress.

'Go and never come back,' he snarled.

'It's you who should go, or better still tell Hannah and Nathan to leave this horrid little house.' So as not to alarm Nathan, Feena didn't raise her voice but her tone was as cold as ice. 'What good are you going to be to them from now on? Hannah should never have married you. It's an old cliché but you're not good enough for her. Now you'll only drag her down. If you were a real man, if you loved her as much as you say you do, you'd do the honourable thing and let her get on with her life.'

'You manipulating bitch.' Matt nearly choked as his anger rose. 'You'd do anything to come between us and I wish I could get Hannah to believe it. Hannah and I love each other, too deeply to ever allow you to hurt us. Our lives will be back to normal very soon and I'll do my level best to cut you out of it. If I had the strength to get out of this bed now I'd throw you down the bloody stairs.'

The truth about his physical condition was on the tip of her tongue but Feena knew Hannah would never forgive such spite. Never mind, she told herself, her day would come, when the proud, uncouth brute realised his masculinity, his ability to earn a living, had gone along with half of his good looks.

Hannah guessed Greg would be wandering about the harbour. Eager to get Feena away from Matt, she hurried down Porthkilt Hill. She hadn't been out of doors very often since Matt had come home and although she would have been pleased to see her neighbours at any other time she was vexed at being continually stopped by their good-intentioned inquiries. She was nearly at breaking point when Miss Peters tried to coax her into her tiny house and wait while she fetched a homemade remedy for Matt's aching ribs.

She spied Greg's tall fair head on the quay and waved and called to him. He waved back and she sighed with relief when he started towards her. Then Grace Kittow came out of her shop with a big cardboard box in her arms and Hannah froze. She wanted to whirl round and stride away but a heavy numbness spread through her limbs. The very sight of the woman was anathema to her. She couldn't cope with it now.

Grace smiled cautiously. Many times she had wanted to call on Hannah to say she was sorry she had lost her baby but she knew the door would be slammed in her face. And who could blame Hannah? Many people, including her Aunt Adela, had voiced their disapproval and astonishment that she could stay with such a cruel, heartless man. Jeff Spargo had forbidden his family to step inside her shop and he hurled abuse at her, even when she had Melanie with her. Grace wanted to turn on her heel back into the shop but Hannah was grimly facing her.

Taking long strides, she approached her foe. 'It's good to see you out and about, Hannah. How are you?' Her words were obviously unwelcome; in fact Grace wondered if they'd sunk in. There was something odd about Hannah. She'd never seen anyone look so fierce and yet the girl seemed to be looking straight through her.

Hannah stayed motionless and Grace came to a halt a few feet away, unsure if it was wise to walk past her.

Afraid there would be unpleasantness, Greg ran up the hill and took Hannah by the arm. 'Come along, Hannah. Let's go back.' He tried to lead her away but she was rigid and did not move. She was glaring at Grace but Greg had the chilling sensation she was not totally with them.

In a flat, toneless, hate-filled voice, Hannah said, 'Your husband nearly killed Matt and he killed my baby.'

Grace involuntarily took a step backwards. The box of unsold summer stock was growing heavy in her arms, making them tremble. 'People say Daniel was involved in Matt's beating but there is no proof. You lost your baby, Hannah, at the shock of hearing about Matt.'

'No, I didn't,' she continued in a monotone. 'Before that he came to me. He came into my house. He terrified me. He said he loved me and if I didn't leave Matt for him he'd destroy everything I had. He imprisoned me in his arms and I thought he was going to attack me.' Then, as if she had come partway out of her trance, her voice softened and she gave a smile that chilled Grace and made Greg blanch. He had to get Hannah home and call the doctor. 'I feel sorry for you, Grace. You love Daniel with all your heart, as I do Matt. You'd do anything for him, wouldn't you? But you mean nothing to him. Poor Grace. Don't you think you ought to go away and take Melanie with you? He's a dangerous man. He'll only bring unhappiness to Melanie. She's just a child. You mustn't risk him hurting her.' She stopped speaking and stared into space.

'You'd better go on your way, Mrs Kittow,' Greg said urgently. 'I'm sorry, Hannah isn't herself at the moment.'

Her face as white as a sheet, Grace skirted round them and hurried home, the box a dead weight in her arms.

Greg wound his arm round Hannah's waist and after some moments he led her up the same route.

'Oh, Greg,' Hannah said, as if waking up suddenly. 'I was just coming to get you. Your grandmother wants to . . .' She felt a dreadful need to cry. A sob came into her voice and she clutched him in panic. 'I saw Grace . . . I . . . what did I say to her? I feel all strange. Oh, dear God. Greg?'

'It's all right, Hannah,' he said soothingly, holding her very close as they climbed the hill, not caring what the few people about, staring curiously at them, thought of his attentions. 'Seeing Grace brought home the enormity of all that's happened to you. I'm going to get your mother to put you to bed and call the doctor.'

'No!' she wailed, the sound like the cry of a tortured child. 'It would upset Matt. I'll be all right. I'm tired, that's all. I just need a little rest.'

'You need help, Hannah,' he insisted.

'I'm not mad, Greg,' she said angrily, trying to pull away from him. He refused to loosen his grasp, 'Matt and I just need to be left alone to get better. Take your grandmother home. It's her fussing that upsets us. What did I say to Grace?'

She was staring at the new house now. There were moments when she hated its mistress simply because she was married to Daniel, then her mood would swing when she remembered that the difference in their class had not stopped Grace from befriending her, that her kindness had caused her to take Melanie into her home and then her heart. And she couldn't hold her responsible for being in love with Daniel – he had such a terrific attraction for women. It was not just his fine physical attributes; they were drawn to his reckless spirit, his contempt for goodness and justice. They lost their common sense the instant they knew him. All the way down through the centuries women had fallen for absolute bastards like Daniel. Women who scorned kind and faithful men. They didn't want a doormat but a hero. But they mistook depravity for boldness.

Would she love her kind and gentle Matt so much if he didn't possess a quirk of moodiness, sometimes for no real reason? He was quick to defend his rights as aggressively as was required. He demanded his opinion, could be obstinate, unyielding if the mood took him. Would she have fallen in love with Matt, desired him so much that she threw all caution to the wind and made love to him when she wasn't even sure she wanted a future with him if he was perfect? No. Women didn't love or like perfect men, they needed the badness in them.

Greg gave her a little shake. 'We can't stand here all day, Hannah.'

'Did I say terrible things to Grace?'

'No, you told her how you felt and exactly what Daniel had done to you. You mentioned he'd come into the house and terrified you, that he told you he loved you. Is that true?'

'Yes, it's why I fainted. I felt the evil in his soul when he touched me. Promise me you won't tell anyone. Matt would be distressed and my father keeps threatening to thump Daniel. I'm afraid he'll do it and he'd be no match for him.'

'I promise on one condition, that you'll let me call the doctor. You'll never get over this if you don't seek professional help.'

'But Mrs Opie will start fussing about me seeing a top specialist again.' Her blue eyes were huge and imploring and Greg had to control the urge to hunt down Daniel Kittow and beat the living daylights out of him himself.

Tenderly he stroked Hannah's chin. 'You have my word that I'll keep Grandmother in line. Do we have a deal?'

The fight had gone out of her. 'Yes.' She wept at last, the quivering hot tears bringing a little relief, but she was more frightened than she'd ever been; her reason seemed to be slipping away from her.

Chapter 21

Drawing heavily on his cigarette, Daniel stood, feet astride, swaying unconsciously with the movements of the boat, waiting silently until Colville had finished a few words of prayer. He had scoffed the first time Colville and his three sons bowed their heads to ask for a blessing on the catch before they'd shot the nets. Other times he'd shown his impatience, then demanded they stop their mumbo-jumbo on his boat. Now he stayed quiet, for at times the prayers seemed to work. The number of fish in the fishberth often had the edge on the other local boats. He hoped it worked today. The dogging season was over and they'd been fishing for pilchards for two weeks. Bad weather had often kept them in and when they had gone out, the nets more often than not were only half filled.

Daniel was tempted to ask why, if their faith could influence the size of the catch, God had allowed their last boat to sink. Why hadn't they been blessed with a boat of their own? Or their own house instead of having to rent? Their last accommodation had consisted of two cramped rooms in a shared tenement. But he shied away from the inevitable sermon that would follow. He'd never understand how anybody could love and worship a being that sent such hard times.

Porthellis shunned Daniel, folk made a point of crossing the street when he was about, but the Penroses were beginning to fit in. This had more to do with the eligibility of the three young brothers than the Penroses' good nature and respectability. Aged between seventeen and twenty-four, Andy, George and Colville Junior were being sized up as potential husbands. If he hadn't currently been keeping his extra-marital activities away from home, Daniel would have broken in some of the better females on offer before they ensnared a pious Penrose.

When his crew had finished their prayers, Daniel gave the order to shoot the nets. They were approximately two miles south-west of Polperro, under an indigo, starry night sky, the wind bitingly fresh, the sea tipping the boat from side to side. The shore could be seen clearly, a comfort to the fishermen to know they weren't far from home. George Penrose, the middle and smallest of the three brothers and the strongest, shot all fifteen nets, while Colville Junior steered them behind him. All the Penroses were expert at each job on the boat and carried out the work good-naturedly. There were few mistakes and very little lost tackle. His grandfather would have been proud of the lugger's present crew, Daniel mused.

He didn't have time to ponder more. There'd be no long watch tonight. He eyed the dark water beneath the bows in awe, excitement running down his spine as a massive quantity of phosphorescent, silvery pilchards appeared as if in one body and then separated and spread out in the nets. It was a supernatural sight, he conceded. 'You've done it this time, Colville!' Daniel shouted jubilantly to the engineer in the wheelhouse.

They hauled the nets in as quickly as they could. It was ten-thirty and they worked all through the night until early morning to clear the nets, their backs and arms strained to breaking point. Their tally was over nine 'last', nine thousand pilchards. The crew were in a sparky mood. Daniel tolerated the continual prayers of thanks as they started for home.

'We'll go up to Rame Head with the rest of the fleet next week and hope we'll have as much luck there.' Daniel mopped the sweat from his brow in the cabin, hoping Andy Penrose had said his last 'Praise the Lord' as he pulled out the remaining food in the allowance bags.

'Can't put it down to luck, Skipper,' Andy beamed, rubbing his aching arms as he surveyed half a thickly curranted saffron cake, six rounds of beef sandwiches, a hunk of cheddar, a pasty the size of a battleship and a packet of shop-bought biscuits. 'Plenty t'keep us going till we get home for dinner. I'll take something out to George and Col.'

Daniel snorted irritably. He'd had hopes for Andy, the youngest brother, thinking he would be the bad penny in the family and share some of his own, more natural, traits. On reflection, old Rufus would have hated the present crew.

Colville joined Daniel in the cabin and sat without speaking on the end of his bunk to eat and drink. At least he was now leaving God in peace. A pasty in one hand and a mug of tea in the other, his expression was serene. He was probably contemplating something deep, Daniel thought, like the birth of the universe, his mortality, or the purpose of being alive. Silly old bugger. Lately Daniel's emotions had veered between anger and regret and a terrible aching longing, and he brought anything into his mind rather than dwell on the cause. Now he was recalling Melanie's christening. He'd stood in the chapel, a little apart from the party at the font, his hands stuck idly in his suit trouser pockets. He had not listened to a single word as an ugly, mannish female friend of Grace's who had travelled down from Kent, Adela Skewes, and Colville – his own choice, an obvious one because he had no other – sincerely repeated the vows of godparents. Because of Methodist sobriety, cups of tea and a little cider were to be served with an iced cake in his house immediately afterwards and he had been concentrating on how quickly he could get away and take Dumpy for a walk across the cliff, to get the smell of all this damned holiness out of his nostrils.

Then he'd caught a glimpse of Melanie's face. She looked scared, her pale skin puckering around her eyes which were darting left and right, upwards and downwards as if she was desperate to escape. Clutching Grace's hand as if it was her only hope of preservation, she was dressed in a white silk dress, a white bow in her red hair. She looked very pretty. Grace had carefully explained to her that this was her special day, rabbiting on about God and Jesus and the manger and the Cross and Heaven and belonging to the chapel family. Meaningless ritual, a bloody farce, Daniel wanted to shout out. It's frightening the child as much as going into hospital for an operation would.

The Reverend Skewes motioned for Melanie to be brought forward so he could sprinkle her head with the blessed water. The little girl gulped and pleaded mutely with her stepmother not to make her do this fearful thing. 'It's all right, darling,' Grace assured her, smiling brightly as she steered her up to the font, and Daniel was consumed with furious indignation that his stupid wife didn't realise how terrified Melanie was.

Then Melanie looked directly at him and those large blue eyes, so like his, appealed to him to help her. His heart lurched. He wanted to tear her away from Grace and run out of the chapel with her. He moved towards her, even stretched out his hand, but at the last moment some tiny part of him, born of primitive breeding and superstition, or so he angrily berated himself later, made him let her suffer the ministrations of the ceremony. The instant the Reverent Skewes was finished with her, he pushed through the party and took Melanie's hand, lifted her up in his strong arms and held her tightly.

The feel of her small body against his, her face coming to lie on his shoulder, the fresh smell of her, her trusting him for the first time, helped blot out the memory of someone else he'd held in his arms. But not always. Too often he recalled Hannah's pregnant body as he'd crushed her in his arms, her soft feminine scent, the sensation of her hair falling over his forearm, and he almost groaned in despair.

He wasn't sorry she'd lost her child. He wouldn't care if the brat she did have suddenly died. He had one regret, that Matt's beating had not totally disfigured him. There was sentimental talk in the village about how he had enough good looks left to overcome the scarring to his face. He should have ordered the bastard blinded and his back broken so he was crippled and couldn't make love to Hannah. That hurt Daniel the most, the thought of them being together intimately. To him sex had always been the means of his own gratification. Women had always given themselves to him willingly and he particularly enjoyed the delicious moments when he had taken a young virgin. But he had never really given himself to them, not even to Grace who, strangely, fulfilled him the most despite the fact that his union with her was within marriage and lacked the wild sensation of forbidden fruit. He knew with a bleak heaviness, a vile numbing feeling, that he could only truly give himself to Hannah and then only if she wanted him as much as he wanted her. And that would never happen.

He had meant it when he said he loved her. The longing for the one thing his good looks, overt masculinity and devil-may-care attitude to life had failed to give him had tortured him in prison. He couldn't stand her rejection. The hurt, the overwhelming feeling of loss and despair had boiled away inside him like an evil brew, giving him no peace, no hope, until he felt he must punish her or go mad.

Having the new house built close to her home to torment her had been easy. Causing havoc in the village had amused him. Ordering Matt to be attacked had satisfied him. Threatening Hannah, being hostile to her, scaring her out of her wits had meant nothing to him. Seeing her actually suffering had been totally different. He would never forget the look of pain and bewilderment which had turned into a terrible madness, her beautiful face corrupted as she'd attacked him with the piece of wood. She didn't fear him any more. She would never again plead for his understanding, that they make a fresh start, as she had in her parlour. She hated him with all her heart. She would never forgive him. His revenge had hurt him more than it had her.

194

He was worried about Hannah. A doctor, not known to the village, called regularly at Seaview Cottage and rumour had it that he went there to see Hannah, not Matt. Prim and Josh Spargo had been living there for over a fortnight now. What was the matter with her?

Daniel had let his tea go cold and blinked when Colville plonked a fresh mug down in front of him. 'Are 'ee going to the bazaar on Saturday evening?' he asked conversationally.

Daniel needed a cigarette before he could answer and he searched about for his packet and lighter. Colville pulled them out from where they had slipped under his thigh on the bunk and handed them to him. Grunting his thanks, Daniel lit up and heaved a sigh as he blew out the smoke. 'What did you say?' He rubbed his eyes and yawned.

'Are 'ee going t'the bazaar? The missus have knitted a jersey for the sale of work. You went find a better knitter than she. And she can run up a jersey or cardigan quicker than any other woman I know.' Colville could see he was boring Daniel and would soon be bawled out of the cabin. He hastily mentioned something Mrs Penrose needed to know. 'She'd like to knit a little something for your little maid for Christmas, if that's all right with you.'

'Course,' Daniel nodded. The boat heaved suddenly and he clung to the edge of the bunk to prevent himself being thrown to the floor. The movement made him cry out and he pulled up the sleeves of his jersey to reveal a chafed area on each wrist. 'Should have worn my gloves,' he grimaced.

'Got some flannel in my locker,' Colville said, fetching the three-foot lengths of red flannel and handing them to Daniel. Grumpily Daniel wound the bandages round both wrists then pulled his sleeves down. 'Have to watch they don't turn to boils,' Colville said.

'I'll bathe 'em when I get home.' Daniel stretched his shoulders and his eyes landed on the bunk opposite. It had been Matt's bunk when he'd been a partner on the *Sunrise*. A partner and a mate. Changed because of Hannah. Hannah . . . No! Think of Melanie.

He said abruptly, 'I'll take Melanie to the bazaar. 'Tis time she mixed with the other kids. Grace keeps her under wraps. 'Tisn't good for her. She won't feel she fits in when she starts school after Christmas.'

'You're a wise man,' Colville said approvingly. He viewed the top of Daniel's bowed head and said carefully, 'The way to happiness comes when you put others before yourself.'

Daniel looked up. 'Think me selfish, do you, Colville?'

'Don't really matter what a man thinks others think of un, but what he thinks of himself.'

Narrowing his eyes, Daniel spat, 'All right, Colville. I'm a selfish bastard! Not only that, I'm cruel and evil. When I want something I'll do anything, and I mean anything, to get it, no matter who it hurts. Satisfied, you sanctimonious piece of shark shit?'

Colville didn't bat an eyelid. 'And now you want to do right by your little maid. That's good.' He headed out of the cabin. 'Drink up your tea while it's hot. We'll be home in under an hour.'

Daniel's jaw dropped but no words came out. He closed his mouth and picked up the mug of tea. 'Conniving old bastard,' he breathed out loud. Colville hadn't said so but it did help, thinking about Melanie. He'd make plans to secure her future. And next year he might have another child. Grace was probably pregnant. She had been rather tetchy lately, not quite so eager to come to him, even more protective of Melanie. Women got like that in pregnancy, susceptible to mood swings, nest building – she was having some of the rooms in the house redecorated. Perhaps one was to be a nursery. He was suddenly looking forward to going home.

When they'd finished with the fish buyer and washed down the lugger, Daniel made his way up the hill on a quicker step than normal. Melanie never said much but sometimes, when he was in a good mood at home, she gave him a sweet little smile when he looked at her. He wanted to see that smile every time he walked through the door. He wanted her to look forward to him coming home, run to meet him, like other kids did their fathers.

Dumpy was trotting at his feet, seemingly eager, too, to see the little girl who always made a fuss of him. As they passed Seaview Cottage that horrid sinking sensation overwhelmed Daniel again. He'd never get used to Hannah hating him. Somehow, he would have to change the way she felt. She'd never trust him again but he couldn't bear to think of her meeting him with hostility for ever.

Once inside his own door, he called out softly, 'Melanie.'

Nan Trebilcock appeared at the kitchen door shushing him with a finger to her bright red lipsticked mouth. 'The dear little soul's just dropped off to sleep in the sitting room. I'm just doing a few little jobs for Grace in here.'

Moving to the kitchen, Daniel threw his allowance bag on the table. 'Where is my wife?' he asked.

Nan was putting the kettle on the range. 'She's down at the shop. She'd just come in from riding not ten minutes ago when Miss Faulkner came here in a right state. A water pipe's broken in the shop and the stock's getting all wet. Most of the wool's ruined. Grace phoned for a plumber then took the mop and some cloths down there to help clean up. Be some time before she gets back, I should think. She's taken her car to pile the ruined stock in.'

Daniel made a face but he wasn't much concerned for the condition of Grace's shop. 'I'll go upstairs and wash and change.'

Nan pulled at a curl of her recently permed hair. 'Would you like me to heat up your dinner? It's a nourishing lamb stew, with my own herb dumplings.'

He nodded, holding her gaze. He knew Nan's little game with him. She wanted his body. He would have given it to her right at the beginning but that would have caused complications. The signals she'd been throwing at him had been getting stronger the past few weeks. Sly, lingering looks, knowing smiles, swaying hips. She'd pressed her breasts against him as they'd passed in the passage where the space had been made narrow by the delivery of a new dressing table Grace had ordered. He'd come across her straightening the seams of her stockings, and knowing he was watching, instead of pulling down her skirt she had kept it up for several moments. It was time he did something about it.

When he came back down the stairs, smelling of soap and aftershave, he was smiling smugly.

'Oh, there you are,' Nan said. 'It's all ready.' She tilted her head to the side and simpered at him. 'Can I get you anything for afters?'

'Perhaps.' After she'd put his meal on the table, he came close to her. 'You look very nice today, Nan. That a new hairdo?'

'Yes.' She patted her head coquettishly. 'Do you like it?'

He dropped his voice to a low husk. 'I've noticed you like to take care of your appearance.'

'Well, I think a woman should look her best, don't you?' Her eyes travelled along his shoulders, down over his muscular chest and arms, lingered on his large hands. 'Your wrists look sore. You should do something about that.'

'Would you bathe them for me?'

'I'd be glad to, Daniel.'

He put his hands on her waist. 'I get the feeling you'd like to do a lot of things for me, Nan.'

'Well, I am a widow.' She thrust her lower body against him. 'People already say we're closer to each other than we are.' She put her arms round his neck and raised her face to kiss him with open lips. The next moment she cried out as Daniel pushed her roughly back over the draining board.

'You bloody disgusting whore! You look after my daughter and want to romp with me. Get out of my house and never come back. And never go near Melanie again or I'll make sure every man in Porthellis knows what easy meat you are. I'll tell my wife you're seeking a job elsewhere.'

He let Nan go and, sobbing, one hand on her hurting back, she snatched up her coat and scarf from the hall and ran out of the house.

Daniel peeped into the sitting room and saw that Melanie was still sleeping, curled up on the sofa with the two cats. He ate his meal then made three phone calls in the hall. The last was to his contact in Plymouth. 'We'll be up your way next week. Tell the Frenchie I'll meet him, usual place, Monday night, to see if he's got anything for me. How much have I made? Cheeky bugger. A tidy sum or I wouldn't be bothering to do it, of course. How about you? Really? No, I'm keeping my head down this way. The coppers are watching me for other reasons. What?' He laughed. 'Nah, I'm too old to change my ways now.'

He sat on a chair and watched his sleeping daughter. Melanie was softly flushed, her lips slightly pouting, cat in either arm. A red-haired angel, he thought proudly.

When she woke she was confused and whimpered to see him there.

'It's all right, sweetheart. It's only Daddy. I've got Dumpy in the kitchen for you.'

The cats wriggled out of her arms and she sat up, grabbing her scrap of blanket, eyeing him warily. 'Nan?'

'She's gone home and Grace is down at the shop. Listen, Melanie, I've rung for a taxi. How would you like to ride in it with me? All the way to St Austell? We could look round the shops. You can choose a new dolly or something. Then we'll buy a huge cream cake for Grace and bring it home and all share it for tea. Would you like that?'

Melanie looked uncertain and he repeated all that he'd said. Then he smiled at her and finally she nodded. 'Right then, you're looking smart enough but you'd better run along to the bathroom before we go. I'll fetch your hat and coat.'

There was a man in Gorran Haven who ran a small taxi service and about fifteen minutes later, dressed in his suit, a black silk tie and a cashmere overcoat, Daniel handed Melanie into the back of the car and sat beside her. Their first stop in St Austell was a solicitor's office.

'It was good of you to see me,' Daniel said across the desk to a thin, severely suited man with a meticulously trimmed grey moustache and full head of wavy grey hair. Melanie sat on his lap, leaning shyly against his chest.

'It was fortunate that I had a cancellation this afternoon, Mr Kittow.' The solicitor, Mr Sobey, smiled widely, revealing big teeth. 'How may I be of assistance to you?'

'I'll be frank with you, Mr Sobey,' Daniel began, totally at ease. 'This little girl is my daughter. I did not marry her mother and her existence was only brought to my notice a few months ago. My wife and I wish to legally adopt her so she can take my name and inherit from us. Also we wish to stop her real mother from reclaiming her,' he said as if he'd taken a high moral stand. 'She's turned into a thoroughly undesirable sort. She suddenly left Melanie with my wife one day, saying she wanted nothing more to do with her. The one thing that might go against me is that I've served a short prison sentence but my wife is the daughter and niece of Methodist ministers. She is a lady by birth, has her own means and has an exemplary character.' Daniel looked the solicitor in the eye. 'She has helped me to reform. We both love Melanie very much and can give her a good life.'

'I see, Mr Kittow.' Mr Sobey leaned forward to view Melanie closely. She turned her face into Daniel's coat.

'Is there any proof that the little girl is your daughter?'

'She's proof enough surely. She's the image of me and I'd hardly be claiming somebody else's brat, would I?'

Mr Sobey nodded. 'Do you happen to have her birth certificate? If not, we could request a copy.'

Daniel put an envelope on the desk. 'It's in there.'

'Good. The adoption should be reasonably straightforward, Mr Kittow. It should only take a few months and a short court appearance. I would recommend in the meantime that you and your good wife make a will to protect the child.'

'I'll make mine now,' Daniel said, taking it for granted that Mr Sobey's time was at his disposal.

When business had been satisfactorily concluded, Mr Sobey promised to be in touch shortly and Daniel left. He carried Melanie down the steps leading from the office and put her down on the pavement in Fore Street. The sky was overcast and it was getting dark, but it made the Christmas decorations in the shop windows sparkle beguilingly. Melanie stared about her with a child's eager hope. Daniel took her hand and smiled down on her. 'Now, sweetheart, let's find a toy shop.'

Grace was peering out of the sitting-room window, wringing her hands, when the taxi pulled up outside the house. She rushed to the front door. 'Daniel! Where have you been for so long? I've been worried sick.'

'I left a note for you.' He kissed Grace's forehead and lifted Melanie out of the taxi before Grace could. He paid the taxi driver and tipped him heavily to carry their shopping into the hall. When the family was assembled in the sitting room and he was helping Melanie off with her hat and coat, he said to Grace. 'I've been to see about us adopting her. I thought it was time something was done about it.'

Grace stared at him. There was a subtle change about him. Were his intentions good? Could they be after what Hannah had told her? 'That's wonderful. Perhaps she could start calling me Mother. I'd like that.'

Free of her outdoor things, Melanie ran out of the room. She hadn't said a word to Grace. 'She wants to show you our shopping,' Daniel explained, grinning.

The door of the sitting room received a hard whack from something as Melanie came back.

'Daniel!' Grace shrieked. 'You can't buy a child so many toys at once.'

Melanie was proudly pushing a smart doll's pram which was nearly as big as one for a real baby. Piled inside it were a big porcelain-faced doll with golden hair, a golliwog, a teddy bear, a beach ball, various boxed games, jigsaw puzzles, storybooks, a sketchbook and paints, and a huge variety of doll's clothes and pram covers.

'Why not?' Daniel said as the pram arrived in front of him and Melanie sat on his knee. 'I have a lot of birthdays and Christmases to make up for.' His expression darkened for a moment and he swallowed hard. 'I've a lot to make up for.'

Chapter 22

Matt buttoned up his shirt, tucked it into his trousers and pulled on his jumper. He pushed his feet into his shoes and raised each foot carefully on to a chair to tie the laces. He bent over to look into Hannah's dressing table mirror and raised his arm to comb his hair. He accomplished all this without letting himself think about the odd twinge of rawness as he moved about. Finally he stared at his stony reflection for a full minute. He did this every day, to prove to himself that his scars didn't bother him – that the man who had ordered the mutilation didn't bother him.

Fingering the rough pits either side of his face, Matt attempted an encouraging smile at himself. Who was he fooling? He had hardly begun to get over his injuries and was still getting terrifying flashbacks to the attack when Hannah had suffered a nervous breakdown. Greg had been wonderful. When he'd brought Hannah home he'd taken his protesting grandmother immediately to his car then contacted a specialist he knew. Hannah had forlornly agreed to see Dr Adam Bennett, not knowing, and still unaware, that he was a psychologist. She was much improved after her talks with him but he had warned Matt that she would be vulnerable for some time.

Matt went downstairs, ignoring the fact that he had to moderate each step to avoid the occasional stab of tenderness about his ribs. In the kitchen Hannah was sitting at one end of the table, her head bent over her sewing, one of the numerous orders for Christmas presents that she and Janet were making. She looked up and smiled at him. He kissed her cheek and she kissed him back, then he automatically sat down opposite her.

Laying aside her work, she stood up. 'I'll get your breakfast, darling.'

Matt couldn't get used to Hannah rising each morning before he did; he never woke up until an hour or so later. While she was busy sewing, he

201

hadn't brought money into the house for weeks; he didn't count his share of the *Misty*'s profits which were anyway meagre because of the poor catches. He said, 'I can do it, darling. I don't need someone to wait hand and foot on me every day.'

'I don't mind, Matt.'

She watched him for physical trauma as keenly as he looked for signs of mental distress in her.

'I'd like to do it, Hannah,' he said, making his voice lively. 'It's not good for me to stay idle. Have we got any bacon left? You can fetch that for me if you like while I get the frying pan ready.'

When she came back from the cold cupboard with three rashers of bacon on a plate, he asked, 'Where's everyone to?'

'Mum and Josh have gone home today and your mother's taken Nathan down to Naomi's to play with her three. She's going to help pack up Mr Nunn's house with Mrs Skewes. Shame, he not having any relatives, but his will left everything to the village. The seventy-eight pounds and the proceeds from his bits and pieces when they're sold off at the bazaar will be an enormous help to the storm fund.'

'Mr Nunn would have been pleased about that,' he said, pushing the melting dripping around the pan as Hannah returned to her sewing. 'I've been thinking about the bazaar. I've got heaps of things I could turn out for it. Someone might like to buy my old sailing magazines.' When the rashers were sizzling in the frying pan, he added, 'I'm missing Nathan but it's good having the place to ourselves for once.'

'I was thinking the same thing.'

'Want a cup of tea?'

'Yes, please.' She dropped her sewing again and fetched her cup from the cupboard. She watched Matt, sadly noting how he had to restrict his movements. But it was peaceful and comforting to have him all to herself. It felt warm and safe in their home while a bitter-cold wind battered the walls outside. She had a sudden need to be close to him and nestled against his side where he stood at the range.

Matt put the fork down and turned to hold her, saying tenderly, 'Everything's all right, Hannah.'

'I know.' She snuggled in closely. 'Sometimes I just have to reassure myself you're really here.'

This time she didn't shed any tears as she so often did and it gave him hope. Gently tilting back her head, he kissed her lips and very soon their embrace became passionate. 'Do you believe I'm here now?' he grinned into her eyes.

'Oh, yes, Matt,' and she squeezed him so tightly it hurt him.

After he'd eaten, and insisted on washing and drying the dishes, he stood behind her as she worked and put his hands on her shoulders. He kissed the top of her head. And caressed her neck with his fingertips. And kissed the hand she raised to him.

'We haven't been alone for ages,' he said huskily.

'No.' She rested her head carefully against his chest. 'It's lovely.'

'We ought to make the most of it,' he murmured, sending tingles coursing through her as his hands slid down to rest on her breasts. They hadn't made love since their double affliction but took comfort and pleasure from touching each other.

'Shall we go upstairs?' she said eagerly and gave a girlish laugh. 'We've got the perfect excuse. If anyone comes we'll say we're both tired.'

'You're reading my thoughts, darling.'

A week ago, Dr Bennett, realising their special closeness was more healing than anything he could prescribe or suggest, gave permission for them to return to their own double bed. A fire was kept lit day and night in their room. They undressed quickly and got into the warm cosy bed.

To show she was not repelled by his scars, Hannah kissed the ones on his face, then those on his body. He sought her lips and they took delight in each other for a long time.

'I could stay like this for ever,' Hannah purred dreamily, her eyes closed as she breathed in the wonderful familiarity of him.

'Me too. I wish I wasn't so shy.'

'Shy? You?' She giggled, raising herself to look down on him. 'You've never been shy with me.'

'I mean I wish I'd had the nerve to ask the doctor if it's all right for us to make love properly. I want you so much I could die,' he ended.

'Do you think you're strong enough?'

'I wasn't thinking of myself. If it hurts me I'd only have to stop. I was thinking of you, whether we ought to take the risk of you getting pregnant again. I don't want you getting upset.'

Hannah moved to lie facing him on the pillow. She swallowed hard. 'Matt, I've been waiting for the right moment to tell you something. Dr Bennett suggested it, to help us get over the grief of losing our baby. It sounds a strange thing to do, really, but he's sure it will help us both.'

'What is it?' He took her hand and interlocked their fingers.

Tears glistened in her eyes. 'He said that we should name the baby. I know it was a girl. Mother told me. Then we . . . should picture holding her in our arms, say hello to her, then goodbye. Then, as we've a strong faith, we –' she was sobbing now and tears fell from Matt's eyes too, ' – we should p-picture ourselves giving her to God to look after for us, until we meet again in eternity.'

Matt held Hannah close. It was some moments before he could speak. 'Catherine Ellen Penney. Hello, Catherine . . .it's your mummy and daddy . . . we–we just want t-to say we love you and g-goodbye, for now. Dear God, please t-take care of our little girl for us.'

They cried until the tears would no longer come.

'Are you all right, darling?' Matt asked softly.

'Yes,' Hannah nodded, giving him a watery smile. 'I love you so much, Matt.'

He kissed her very tenderly. 'I love you with all my heart, Hannah.'

Their lips met and in a short time they were consumed with desire. 'I want you, Matt,' she whispered desperately. 'I need you so much. If we make another baby it will be conceived with all the love we can give it.'

'If you're sure you're ready,' he whispered back. 'All that matters is that we have each other and Nathan, that we are a family.'

That afternoon Matt told Hannah and his mother he wanted to rest, but after five minutes lying on the bed he got up and began turning out cupboards and drawers. As he put aside items for the bazaar, which was to be held in two days' time, he felt useful again. Soon he had a pile of things on the bed, his sailing magazines, his collection of tin soldiers and cigarette cards, his Flash Gordon books. He added novels by Rider Haggard, Conan Doyle and R.M. Ballantyne. He would have liked to give some of his old toys to Nathan when he was older but the village was too badly in need to be sentimental. From his chest of drawers he donated his favourite tiepin and cuff links made of nine-carat gold.

After a while he sat on the bed to rest. What else could he give? He thought of his late father's collection of gramophone records. Knowing he would have contributed if he'd been alive to do so, Matt decided they could go too. The only snag was that they were in an old suitcase, up on the top shelf inside the wardrobe. The suitcase was heavy and it wouldn't be wise to try to pull it down from such an awkward angle. He couldn't ask Hannah or his mother to do it. A stubborn part of him wasn't going to wait for Josh to be fetched.

Opening the wardrobe doors, he steadied his feet and taking hold of the suitcase handle he braced himself. Counting, one, two, three, he pulled the suitcase out and swung it down towards the floor. An agonising pain tore through his body. He was forced to drop the suitcase the last few inches and it thumped on to the floor at the same time as he cried out. Clutching his ribs he doubled over, leaning against the wardrobe.

Hannah and Mrs Penney came rushing into the room together. 'Dear God, Matt, what were you doing?' Hannah rushed to him, climbing over the suitcase. 'You shouldn't have tried to take that down all by yourself.'

'Why not?' he howled, his twisted features showing inner torment as much as physical pain. 'It doesn't weigh a ton. I should be able to do that by now! I should be out there fishing with the other men, not stuck in the house like a bloody invalid!' As he stared at Hannah, he saw her chin tremble and she looked away. 'Oh, no,' he groaned, a sound that came from deep within him. He sank to the floor. 'That's it, isn't it? I am an invalid! I'm not going to get better. I'm nothing. I'm not a man any more.' A great sob wracked him, he clenched his hands to his face and his shoulders shook as he wept.

Hannah knew she must break through his despair. She knelt before him and wrenched his hands away. 'You look at me, Matt Penney!' she bellowed passionately. 'And you listen to me. You are a man, the best man this village has ever known. You are not an invalid and you won't always be as weak as this. You will get better but it will take a long time and you'll have to be patient. I know I should have told you before but things haven't been easy. Matt, the doctors said you won't ever be strong enough to be a fisherman again but you're a young, intelligent man. You've been to grammar school, remember? You've lost some of your strength but you've been blessed with brains. You must sit down and take stock of yourself and plan a new future for yourself and us.' Running out of breath, she sat down close to him, still gripping his hands, afraid he'd put them back to his face and cut himself off from her.

His eyes wide with horror, he looked across the room. 'It's true, isn't it, Mother? I'll never fish again.'

Mrs Penney nodded grimly, dabbing her anguished eyes with her hanky. 'I'm sorry, son. I felt it was Hannah's place to tell you but Hannah was ill herself.' She spread her hands in a helpless gesture. 'I suppose we were hoping you'd realise it yourself.'

Matt shook his head as if he was trying to clear his mind. 'I knew it deep down. But I didn't want to believe it.'

Hannah tried to feel his ribs but he pushed her hands away. 'I'm trying to see if you're hurt, Matt.'

'I'm not hurt. I've just bruised myself a bit. Just leave me alone,' he said loudly, then lowered his voice and pleaded, 'Please, both of you. I need to be alone for a few minutes. I have to think.'

Hannah was about to protest but Mrs Penney intervened. She held out her hand. 'We'd better do as he says, Hannah. You come along with me, dear.'

Downstairs, Hannah sat beside the kitchen fire, staring blankly into the flames. Would there be no end to the agony Daniel Kittow had inflicted on them?

'He'll be all right, Hannah,' Mrs Penney said, preparing one end of the table for a large flasket of ironing. It was as hard for her as it was for Hannah, her only child disfigured, weakened, his working life brutally snatched away; the loss of her second grandchild; Hannah's illness; the disruption to her home. She, too, had a stake in what Matt made of the future.

'How can you be sure?' Hannah muttered glumly. 'I've been dreading this moment. You know how Matt can sink into low moods. Fishing was his life. He won't want to do anything else.'

'He won't waste away, if that's what's on your mind,' Mrs Penney said confidently, putting the iron on the range to heat up. 'Matt's a proud man and it'll be hard for him to adapt but his family is more important to him than anything else. When he's got used to the idea he'll do exactly what you told him, plan for a new future.'

'I hope you're right.' Too many terrible things had happened for Hannah to be optimistic. She couldn't bring herself to sew; all she could think about was Matt, sitting on the bedroom floor, facing the fact that one of the biggest parts of his life was over. Was he angry with her for keeping it a secret from him for so long? She couldn't bear it if he blamed her.

Nathan had fallen asleep where he'd been playing on the floor. He was in a warm, draught-free spot and Hannah had left him there, covered with a pram blanket. Now he woke up and crawling out from under the blanket he toddled to his anxious mother.

Holding out his arms, he gave her a broad, dribbly smile. 'Hello, sleepy-head.' She swept him up into her arms, kissing him and clinging to his sturdy little body. Nathan patted the top of her head, gurgling and chuckling. At last Hannah smiled. She sat on the mat with him and played with his wooden building blocks. It eased the emptiness and worry inside her; she knew it was vital not to disturb Matt.

The two women prepared the food for tea. They laid the table, cut bread and butter, fetched Matt's favourite pickle from the larder. Nathan was put in his highchair. They always ate at the same time. Hannah and Mrs Penney exchanged a questioning look. Would Matt come down? Should they call up to him?

His tread was heard coming down the stairs. Mrs Penney lifted the baked stuffed potatoes out of the oven. Hannah forced herself to turn away from the door, busying herself by cutting slices of bread in half and putting them on the tray of Nathan's highchair.

Matt came into the kitchen. Closed the door. No one spoke. The women kept busy. Matt sat at the table. His face displayed the marks of bitter weeping. Hannah's eye crept to something he put beside his plate. Paper, a fountain pen, their savings book and other documents. On the top piece of paper he had been doing sums.

Matt reached out and stroked his son's head. 'Well, boy, we might be going into business together one day.' His voice was hoarse, emotional. He looked at his mother. 'Tea smells good. I'm ravenous.' Then he stretched out his hand to Hannah. 'Like I said this morning, darling, all that matters is that we have each other.'

Chapter 23

From the cover of the giant oak tree in the middle of Roscarrock's lawn, Jeff watched Leah, Lily, Miss Benson and the stable boy drive off in Greg and Patrick's cars to the bazaar. Then Jeff crept round to the back of the house and, seeing no lights on in the servants' hall, as he'd hoped, he let himself into the house. He knew from Leah that Angie Miller, the housemaid, would stay at home to attend her mistress, but she would almost certainly be upstairs in her comfortable attic quarters.

The servants' hall led into the main kitchen and he stole carefully through the darkness in both rooms by the light of a small torch. He tried a couple of doors, finding himself first in the walk-in larder and then a broom cupboard before he found the right one to the servants' stairs. Despite his efforts to tiptoe, his shoes tapped on each stone step and he halted a moment here and there so as not to make a regular noise. Once at the top, he had his bearings and switched off the torch. By the gentle illumination of the subdued electric lighting, he held his breath and made his way up the two flights of stairs, along the long corridor, to stand sheepishly outside Feena's suite. He undid his overcoat, straightened his suit and tie and tidied his thick black hair with his hands.

Alerted to the stealthy noises outside his mistress's rooms, Pogo began to growl low in his throat. Cursing softly, Jeff tapped quietly on the double doors before Feena became alarmed.

'Come in, Angie,' Feena called, her voice sounding curious; she obviously wasn't expecting to be disturbed.

Jeff went into the suite quickly, closed the doors behind him and stood just inside them. As Pogo yapped about his feet, he grinned bashfully, 'Hello, Feena.'

She was sitting in her wheelchair by the fire, a book resting on the crushed velvet of her dress. Her curved eyebrows shot up but that was the only sign of surprise she gave. Jeff watched, somewhat amused, his confidence gaining, as first anger flickered across her handsome, made-up face, then resignation. 'You've got a nerve, Jeff Spargo,' she hissed.

She called off Pogo and he obediently trotted to lie at her feet, clad not in comfortable slippers as might be expected at this time of day but high-heeled court shoes.

'I know,' he grinned. 'I thought I'd take the gamble on you throwing me out.' He was awkward for a moment, clutching the new trilby hat he'd treated himself to and not casting it casually aside as he'd first thought when this scheme had come to mind. 'You don't want me to go, do you?'

She put the book on a nearby table and looked him up and down, keeping him on tenterhooks. 'Seeing as you've dressed up to come here, you may stay for a little while,' she said finally.

Jeff was unsure from her tone whether she was pleased or simply tolerating him, but he wasted no time. He strode up to her, knelt down, took her face gently in his hands. 'I couldn't keep away, Feena.'

The romance of his sudden appearance and unexpected declaration filled her with emotion. He brushed her lips with his. Starved of intimate male contact for over twenty-two years, Feena gave a nervous and clumsy response. Then making herself relax, she put her arms round his neck and allowed her feelings to stir.

When he took his lips away, she stroked his rugged face, smiling girlishly; his tenderness had made the years fall away from her. 'I never thought we'd be doing this again, Jeff.'

'Me neither,' he whispered huskily, gazing into her eyes. 'Do you think we could start over again? I realized a little while back that although things turned nasty between us, you really did love me. Prim hasn't loved me since the early days of our marriage. Now we're like strangers sharing the same house, with only an idiot son holding us together. I owe her no loyalty, Feena. Nor to the other women who've kept me happy in bed. But things with you are different. I mean that. Apart from Hannah, I think there is something special between us. Don't you?'

Feena wasn't sure whether to believe him. It didn't matter right now. A need that had lain dormant for too long burned inside her. 'Oh, Jeff,' she murmured.

He understood. Lifting her up into his arms, he carried her to the bedroom.

Later, when her breathing had settled, she opened her eyes to see Jeff looking down on her anxiously. 'Was it all right for you?' he asked softly. 'I was afraid I'd hurt you. It's a long time since you've made love and . . .'

'And I'm an old woman?' Feena said, hoping he would still her fears that the years had been cruel to her body, fears that had made her stay almost fully clothed.

'I didn't mean that,' he said hastily, his face reddening. 'You're beautiful, Feena. You'll always be beautiful to me. I was thinking of your arthritic hip.'

'It's easier for you men as time goes by.' She ran a fingertip down his sweaty neck. 'I enjoyed it, Jeff. The young think they have dominion over the physical side of life but at times I've found it hard, not having someone to touch me, give me comfort.' She stared into his dark eyes. Jeff had changed. Before, he had cared only about his own gratification.

He lay down beside her and cradled her to him, careful not to hurt her delicate body. 'We don't always have to end up in bed, Feena. I'm quite happy just being in your company.'

'That's even more comforting.' She gazed up at the canopy of white silk cascading down from its gilt crown high above the bed. She had longed to take Jeff to her bed when they'd had their affair instead of skulking in the woods or the coachman's cottage but she had been terrified they'd be discovered. She had even more to lose now if their new liaison was discovered. 'We shall have to be very careful. Greg would be shocked and outraged and Hannah would never forgive us. I couldn't bear that.'

'Don't worry. I've thought of that too. I'd hate Hannah to be hurt again.'

'Where do they think you are tonight? Won't they expect you to be at the bazaar?'

'The family's used to me going my own way. As long as I show my face before the evening's over.' He gave a grin. 'I'll help pack up the hall and sweep the floor. That'll keep 'em happy.'

'I've hardly seen Hannah since she had the breakdown,' Feena said wistfully. 'Greg insisted I give her time and space. He said I can be overbearing and I was upsetting her. I don't mean to interfere. But my son and daughter are dead. I've got Greg and Patrick but they lead their own lives. The rest of you have lots of relatives to fuss over, to fill the empty spaces. Hannah's my only child now and Nathan may be her only child.'

'You'll have a great-grandchild when Leah's baby's born,' Jeff pointed out.

'Yes, and I'm looking forward to it. But it's not quite the same.' Feena looked at Jeff earnestly. 'I don't worry about Leah and Greg and the coming baby. Their future here is secure but what has Hannah got to look forward to?'

'I can take one worry off your mind.' Jeff kissed the scented skin of her wrist. 'Matt's been told he'll never fish again but instead of moping about he's planning to start up a little business.'

'What sort of business?' Feena was careful to keep a scoffing note out of her voice. 'He hasn't got much capital.'

'He's got some savings and he owns his house. He could put that up for mortgage to raise the money. He's looking into starting up a boat's chandlery. He could store all sorts of things to save we from going over to Gorran Haven or Mevagissey. With him we fishermen would know we'd get a fair deal. He'll still be in the fishing business and Hannah will be much more settled knowing he's safe on shore.'

'I see. And when did he decide this?' she asked tartly.

'Only a couple of days ago. Hannah's going to tell you herself next week. She said something about coming up here again.' Jeff frowned, wishing he'd kept his mouth shut. Feena was hurt at being excluded from Hannah's life for so long.

'It's about time she came here,' she muttered, sitting up and straightening her clothes. 'Greg could have collected her to come for a short while. I would have been careful not to be overbearing,' she stressed sarcastically. 'This is all very interesting about Matt starting a business but it doesn't take away my main worry. Daniel Kittow lives just down the street from Hannah and Nathan and he could hurt them at any time.' She began to cry softly and when Jeff touched her she leaned into his arms.

'Kittow's gone quiet lately, Feena.' He caressed her back. 'I don't think we have anything to worry about now.'

'I don't agree' she sniffed, pulling away. 'Daniel Kittow may be quiet for a reason. He could be planning something diabolical. If we value our daughter and grandson's future we've got to get them away from that evil man to where they will be safe. We simply must. Jeff, promise me we will.'

Chapter 24

Matt insisted he was well enough to attend the bazaar. When he entered the small, wooden-planked hall next to the chapel, the buzz of excited voices stopped and a spontaneous round of applause broke out. Feeling alive and energetic on the good wishes, he nonetheless took a seat next to the toy stall which was close to a paraffin heater; Hannah had extracted a promise that he'd take it easy and keep warm. People smiled indulgently as she wrapped the black and yellow woollen scarf he'd taken off back round his neck.

'Hannah,' he mouthed urgently, restraining her hands. 'I'm not a baby. You'll make me look a fool.'

'Sorry,' she grinned. 'I just don't want you catching a chill.' He stuffed the scarf into his coat pocket, together with his gloves. Hannah had already put her contributions on the various stalls – three lace tray cloths and a duchesse set she'd made, a large fruit and cherry cake and a batch of scones. She sat down beside Matt. 'See anything on the stalls you'd like to buy?'

He was pleased to see his own things on display; Josh had carried them here in the afternoon when the stalls had been set up. He was feeling part of village life again. 'There's a painted wooden engine there which would be nice for Nathan for Christmas. It looks as if the wheels move. And we'd better look for something for Mother and your parents.' He slipped his arm round her and gave an affectionate squeeze. 'Choose something for yourself too, darling.'

Hannah glanced round the stalls, making mental notes of what she might buy when the minister announced the bazaar was open. She had a white envelope containing a one pound note, tied with thin ribbon, in her hand. She'd add it to the others hanging on the decorated fir tree standing proudly on the raised platform. At the end of the evening, with great ceremony, Mrs Skewes would snip the ribbons, or pieces of wool or string, and pass the envelopes to Miss Peters who, as Porthellis's oldest inhabitant, had been given the honour of opening the envelopes and calling out the amount of money each contained.

Prim and the Rouses joined them, all wrapped up against the dense fog outside. 'Hope enough's raised to start you off with another boat, Roy,' Matt said as Janet engaged Hannah and Prim in conversation. Jowan looked longingly towards the door for Lily to appear while Ned, his lame younger brother, amused some children by letting them jump over his walking stick.

'Thanks,' Roy replied thinly, standing restlessly with his hands in his pockets. His agreeable face was pale and haggard and he'd lost weight. The wrecking of the *Echo* had taken the heart out of him. The boat had belonged to his father and uncles and he had taken it for granted that after his sons, it would belong to his grandsons one day. It had been his means of livelihood, his pride, and although he, Jowan and Ned earned a little money helping out on the other boats and labouring, it was damned hard watching his wife sewing every minute of the day to bring money into the house. He knew he should be sorrier for Matt than for himself, at least he could go to sea again, but Roy couldn't bring himself to feel anything much.

'Uncle Roy's still looking down in the dumps,' Hannah observed, her spirits taking a dip in concern over the man who had been her caring foster father. She'd have jumped up and given him a hug but Roy would be mortified at such a public display of affection.

'Aye, I've never known him to be so miserable,' Janet sighed. 'Even Ned's not as sparky as usual. Poor Jowan, he was looking forward to getting married and I was looking forward to having a daughter-in-law and grandchildren in the house.'

Hannah knew how hard it was to look on the bright side when things had gone so terribly wrong, but she took her aunt's hand and smiled. 'Well, hopefully tonight will put all that right, Aunty Janet.'

Mrs Skewes said there's been some very generous donations,' Prim remarked. Now that Hannah and Matt were re-establishing their lives, she was enjoying the social contact, glad Jeff wasn't here yet. Since her disappointment over Brinley, she couldn't bear the sight of her husband. She had lost her one chance of a new life but he was still enjoying himself.

'There's a lot of folk wanting good hard cash to repair their boats and houses.' Janet shook her head despondently. 'There's not going to be enough left over for a whole boat and tackle. We'll have to borrow some money whatever happens. It's been a rotten year. Matt and my menfolk will all have to make a fresh start somehow.'

'At least they're still alive,' Hannah said vehemently, suddenly remembering that the Joses weren't coming this evening. 'Fred Jose isn't.'

The hall lights had always been dim and on mentioning this to Grace, Mrs Skewes had been delighted at the wealth of superior quality candles her niece had donated to brighten up the occasion. No one would know how much Grace had contributed to the evening. Mrs Skewes thought this a shame, but the villagers would baulk at her generosity because she was Daniel Kittow's wife. Having begged candleholders and spare saucers from nearly every household, and added bits of tinsel and holly to them, Mrs Skewes went round the hall lighting the candles. The seasonal glow increased the sense of expectation that the bazaar would raise a goodly amount of funds; people from all round the area, not just those in the fishing industry, had pitched in to help.

'Looks very cheery, dear.' The Reverend Skewes caught up with her as she blew out the last match. 'Most people seem to have arrived. I think I'll make a start.'

'Grace isn't here yet, David.' Mrs Skewes looked hopefully towards the door. 'It wouldn't be right to start without her after all she's done. And all except Mrs Opie are coming from Roscarrock this evening.'

'Oh, getting esteemed company, are we?' David Skewes muttered drily, studying his pocket watch. 'It's two minutes past six. They're late.'

Mrs Skewes frowned. Her husband had no time for the Opies, not so much because they were church, but because he saw their aloofness as snobbery. He was offended that he and Adela hadn't been invited to the big house since Leah's wedding.

'Gregory Opie has taken some interest in the village since he married Leah,' she reminded him. 'He's been very good to Hannah, don't forget, dear. It will be interesting to have Patrick Opie among us. We must be sure to give them a warm welcome.'

'Of course,' the minister replied a trifle irritably, shaking his pocket watch to emphasize his earlier point. 'As long as they spend lots of money – they've got more to spare than us more humble mortals.'

The Roscarrock party entered a minute later and David Skewes was one of the last in line to greet them.

Prim went to her pregnant daughter, passing Patrick who was making a beeline for Hannah and Matt. To cover the awkwardness he felt at public occasions, Patrick was more garrulous than usual and flapped his overcoat about, causing a draught. 'Ah, Hannah, my dear, how are you? You're looking a lot brighter than the last time I saw you. And how are you, Matt? Good to see you're well enough to come out. I take it the little man is at home with Mrs Penney. And how is Mrs Penney? You know, I was thinking that in a little while I could sit with Nathan if he's asleep, so as to save one of you going home to relieve her.'

Hannah bade him sit down next to her so he'd feel less conspicuous and answered his questions. 'Mrs Penney will be as pleased as we are for you to mind Nathan.' Knowing Patrick's circumstances, it was unlikely he'd have much money to spend. It was his kindness that had prompted him to put in an appearance tonight.

Matt respected the unassuming gentleman and asked Hannah to change places with him so he could tell Patrick something about his proposed business venture.

Hannah kept her eyes on Leah but her younger sister either hadn't noticed her or, Hannah felt, was ignoring her. She shrugged it off; she had too much on her mind to worry about that now.

People eager to buy certain items were jostling each other to keep their place in front of the stalls, the stall attendants were becoming anxious to begin, children were dying to hand over their pennies and get their mitts into the barrel of sawdust and pull out a lucky dip, and David Skewes had run out of patience. Telling his argumentative wife that it wasn't fair on everyone else to wait any longer for Grace, he climbed the three steps, which always seemed dusty no matter how much attention they got, to the small platform and called for hush. Silence fell like a warm blanket and all eyes turned to him. He didn't waste time with a long boring speech. He offered a brief welcome, reminded the throng why they were here, said a prayer and then declared the bazaar open.

The proceedings began in a noisy, good-humoured jostle. Money and goods changed hands, a small pond of tea and a mountain of food were consumed. Children chased about with their lucky dip treasures and sticky halfpenny lollies. Hannah tried unsuccessfully to catch Leah's eye as she brought the wooden engine and an armful of purchases over to Matt for safekeeping.

Mrs Penney was sitting beside him. 'Isn't it kind of Mr Patrick? Now we can both stay, Hannah.'

'Yes, Mother,' she smiled happily. 'Looks like the bazaar is going to be a great success.' The next instant her smile turned into a scowl. Grace, sleekly but plainly attired, had walked into the hall and with her was Daniel, holding Melanie's hand.

Grace had deliberately waited for the bazaar to begin before arriving. She was sure her own and Melanie's presence would not cause a stir, but she'd been worried about the reaction to Daniel. She was acutely embarrassed to be proved right. Hannah's stormy eyes were targeted on them, and it seemed as if everybody else in the hall turned at the same moment to express their disapproval of the man most hated in Porthellis coming among them. Voices petered out, cups being carried to lips halted in mid-air, the buying and selling ceased. There was an unnatural quietness. It was as if Grace had brought a terrible smell with her.

'G-good evening,' Grace said to Miss Peters who was the nearest to her.

'Evenin'' the tiny old lady barked, looking past her to glower at Daniel. 'What've 'ee brung he for?'

'Daniel is part of the village, Miss Peters,' Grace said, blushing furiously.

'Not to us, he isn't.' Miss Peters had said her piece – the whole village's piece judging by the mutters round the hall. She turned away and pattered off to get another cup of tea.

Smiling as if he was heartily amused, one hand placed nonchalantly inside his trouser pocket, Daniel led Melanie to the toy stall. He was very close to Hannah but did not look at her. As Mrs Skewes hurried over to rescue Grace from standing alone and looking foolish, Hannah watched him, her back rigid, as he lifted Melanie up so she could view the toys. She pointed to a furry rabbit in a knitted outfit and a large fairy doll and Daniel handed over a five pound note to pay for them. Not having enough change, the woman serving at the stall became flustered and Hannah ground her teeth when Daniel said loftily, 'Keep it, Mrs Hoskins. The village's needs are greater than mine.'

Taken by surprise the woman didn't thank him but Melanie, looking sweet and pretty with her red hair framed inside a blue fur-trimmed bonnet, clung to his neck and said, 'Thank you, Daddy.'

Hannah stared in amazement as Daniel kissed his daughter's cheek. 'You're welcome, sweetheart. Let's try the lucky dip next.' He moved slightly, bringing Hannah into his line of vision. He met her hostile eyes and smiled briefly before walking away.

217

'Did you see that?' Janet gasped. 'Well, I never thought I'd see the day when Daniel Kittow showed he cared about someone. I thought he hardly had anything to do with the little maid.'

'You have seen the day, Janet Rouse,' Miss Peters interjected, her sharp chin jutting out. 'I got no time for un now but he weren't such a bad boy backalong.'

'We don't want to talk about him,' Matt snapped at the old lady, furious that she could find a good word for Daniel Kittow. He tugged on Hannah's hand to attract her attention; she was still gazing after Daniel. Matt was tense, his head was aching. He was trembling and feeling sick, all brought on by the sight of Daniel Kittow. He was raging inside. The most primitive part of him wanted to tear the arrogant fisherman asunder with his bare hands. A greater part was ashamed that he'd sat still and said nothing.

Seething that Daniel had smiled at her, Hannah turned to Matt. 'Do you want to go home?'

'Of course not. All I want is to enjoy the evening.' He loosened his grip on her hand and although he didn't feel like it, he smiled at her. He wasn't going to let Daniel Kittow or anyone else see he was bothered by his arch enemy's presence here. Their paths would cross for the rest of their lives and somehow, for Hannah's sake, he would have to make sure there was no more conflict. But how could he allow the man who ordered his brutal beating to get away with it scot-free?

Miss Peters stalked off and later, when Matt was talking to a group of men, including Greg, about his new scheme, Hannah joined the indignant old lady and some other women to help wash dishes in the kitchen.

'Sorry about Matt getting cross with you just now, Miss Peters,' she said, picking up a tea towel. 'The trouble is, we never saw Daniel's bad side when he was younger.' She was speaking calmly and all the women were particularly interested in what she had to say on the subject.

'Well, you knaw un better'n most,' a chubby woman wearing an old-fashioned cloche hat and busy at the stone sink commented. 'And goodness knows you've suffered the most.'

'Perhaps not,' Hannah said, wiping a plate and putting it on top of the growing pile of dry dishes. Mrs Penrose was beside her, similarly armed with a tea towel, and Hannah was looking intently at the engineer's wife who had now become the Kittows' daily help. Mrs Penrose's broad pink features twitched uncomfortably.

'What do 'ee mean, maid?' Miss Peters demanded, rising on tiptoe to lower a stack of teacups into the sink of steaming sudsy water. 'Who else have he had a go at?'

'I was thinking of Fred Jose.' Hannah wiped a plate very slowly. 'Daniel made it plain he wanted him out of the village. Fred simply upped and left, but the circumstances don't suggest he went of his own free will.'

'You think Daniel told un t'get out or else, do 'ee?' Miss Peters nodded as if she agreed with this. 'Some of us have thought so, including his poor mother 'n' father who'll be scattering his ashes out at sea on Wednesday.'

'Well, it would hardly be surprising,' Hannah answered, glancing from woman to woman. She looked composed and not even Miss Peters' sharp wit detected the mischief glinting behind her eyes. 'Fred's death is the most mysterious one we've had in the village. It's believed Fred fell down the cliff, probably the day he disappeared as he wasn't seen elsewhere, and his body was trapped in the rocks, only coming to light when the sea was running higher than usual because of the storm and the poor soul was bobbed about. The coroner recorded an open verdict. He could see no reason why Fred should kill himself. What's strange is why Fred, who was too afraid to trespass, should wander on to Roscarrock land and try to climb down a very dangerous part of the cliff. Fred had no head for heights.'

'Surely it was an accident,' Mrs Penrose said abruptly, aghast at what she felt was being hinted at here.

Hannah turned to her. 'You tell us, Mrs Penrose. The whole village would like to know for sure.'

There was a long, thoughtful silence while crockery was washed, dried and taken back to the hall to replenish the refreshment table. Miss Peters changed the subject by asking what Matt had in mind now he was no longer a fisherman. Mrs Penrose crept away from the kitchen with a tray of cups and saucers and tried to locate her husband.

Daniel, still with Melanie in tow, spoke to her. 'Enjoying yourself, Mrs Penrose? The social will be starting soon. There will be games and a singsong. Grace will find them rather quaint.'

'Oh, Daniel, you startled me,' she panted, a hand clasped to her throat. Her flesh crept; was she talking to a cold-blooded murderer? 'I–I was looking for Colville.'

'He's there.' Daniel jerked his head towards a gathering of men and women who were up on the platform removing a variety of musical instruments from their cases. 'I didn't know Colville played the fiddle.'

'Yes, yes, he does. Since he was a boy.'

Annoyed at the woman's obvious nervousness of him – or was she ashamed to be seen talking to him with the villagers looking on – he added sarcastically, 'Should be in for a bit of hymn singing then.'

'Yes, um, please excuse me, Daniel.' Mrs Penrose blushed and hastened away.

Daniel was bored but he was not going to let the ill feeling towards him chase him away. Melanie was still too shy to run about and play with the other children and he had the feeling the mothers wouldn't encourage it anyway. He had to present an amiable front for her sake, and if he hadn't been disinclined to upset Hannah he would have enjoyed baiting Matt. Crafty glances at Matt's face showed the scarring was livid and unsightly but it was true that in time his dark face wouldn't be too spoiled.

He looked over his shoulder at the rattling of more crockery. It was Hannah carrying another tray of reinforcements. He thought she'd glare at him or make a point of ignoring him but as their eyes met, she held his gaze. She smiled. Not at him. Secretly, to herself.

Chapter 25

Feena was astonished to see Matt was with Hannah when she was shown into the drawing room the following Wednesday afternoon. They were still dressed in black from Fred Jose's funeral, for which the whole village had come to a standstill. Matt was solemn but looked and felt invigorated after the short trip on the boat just outside the harbour with the other men, to watch Fred's ashes being scattered. His anguish at losing his ability to fish had lessened; at least he had a future to look forward to, unlike Fred.

'Matt! How good to see you,' Feena said, quickly recovering her composure. Smiling at Hannah, she tilted her face and Hannah gave her an affectionate kiss on the cheek.

'Good afternoon, Mrs Opie,' Matt said politely, and she was immediately suspicious. He had warned her he was going to try to come between her and Hannah; did he intend never to leave them alone together? She was relieved when he added, 'I've come hoping to have a word with Greg.'

'Just tap on the study door and go in, Matt,' Feena smiled at him. When he'd gone she gave Hannah a loving peck. 'I've missed you so much, my dear.'

Hannah sat beside her on the sofa. 'I've missed you too. Please don't think it was personal. I needed to be alone with Matt for a while.'

'I understand.' Feena was careful to keep the jealousy out of her voice. She stroked Hannah's hair. 'You look your old self again, that's all that matters. How's Nathan?'

'I was going to bring him today but he's a bit teasy, he's cutting a back tooth. Perhaps you'd like to come and see him tomorrow. The fog we've had for the past few days is beginning to clear at last. We could go down to the quay and see my uncle's new boat.'

'Goodness! Has he got another one already?'

'Yes,' Hannah replied excitedly. 'The bazaar raised over five hundred

221

pounds! We still can't believe it. There was enough to cover everyone's repairs and the entire cost of a lugger that was for sale in Mevagissey. It's seven years old, has all the latest equipment, and is called the *Renewal*. Uncle Roy sees it as a sign and he's a lot happier now. They're sailing it round tomorrow. It means Jowan and Lily can get married after all so you'll be losing her in the New Year.'

'I'm so pleased for your uncle and aunt. Do give them my regards. Their house will be a cheerful one with Lily in it. Things are looking up again in Porthellis.' Then Feena said deliberately, 'If only Daniel Kittow didn't live there.'

Lily bounced into the room with a tray of coffee. Piping hot liquid shot out of the spout as she put the tray down, making Feena glad that the girl would soon be leaving and she could replace her with a more dignified servant.

'Begging your pardon, madam,' Lily chirruped, making no move to leave the room.

'Yes?' Feena said sharply.

'I heard something about Daniel Kittow when I was down seeing Jowan last night. I thought p'raps you'd like to know.'

'Oh? What have you heard, Lily?'

''Tis going round the village, madam, that he might have done away with Fred Jose. People seem to believe it. If Constable Burt gets to hear of it he might be taken in for questioning and justice will be done.' Lily vehemently hoped this would be the case. She still suffered nightmares from Daniel's threats in Turn-A-Penny Lane.

Feena was dismayed. She didn't doubt for a moment that the red-haired fisherman was capable of murder and she knew that Fred Jose had been one of the main targets for his revenge. With Matt pulling himself together, her hope to get Hannah and Nathan away from him and Porthellis lay with the fisherman remaining their neighbour and continuing to cause trouble. 'That's just malicious gossip,' she snapped. 'You shouldn't listen to it, Lily.'

'I only thought you and Mrs Penney might be interested in what's being said.' With a disrespectful twist to her full lips, Lily bounded out of the room.

'Really,' Feena complained as she served the coffee. 'Calling the man a murderer is going too far.'

'I don't think so,' Hannah said, biting into a Lincoln cream biscuit.

'The sooner he's locked up again, the better.'

'He would be hanged for murder, Hannah.' Feena couldn't prevent a little shiver; she didn't like Hannah's smile.

'Hanged?' Her head swung round to stare at Feena. 'I hadn't thought of that.'

'Would you care?'

Hannah was quiet for a few moments. Daniel hanged? Dead? Did she want it to go that far? Did she hate him that much? Feena was looking alarmed at her expression. She shrugged her shoulders. 'If he killed Fred, he deserves to hang.'

Feena changed the unhealthy subject. 'What does Matt want to speak to Greg about?' adding in a slightly hurt tone, 'Or is it a secret?'

'Oh, that's what I've come specially to tell you. Matt's going into business by himself and he thought Greg might be able to give him useful advice about finance and so on. He's going to start a chandlery for the boats, supply rope, hooks, lanterns, tar, oilskins, that sort of thing. We've talked about it at length. He could sell woolly hats and jerseys, most wives and mothers make them for their men but holidaymakers would probably like to buy them. And he's going to run a line for the sporting fishermen too – rods and reels. All he needs is some premises, and he's already inquired about an empty cottage down on the waterfront. It's been empty for years and could never be made habitable again but it wouldn't take much work to turn it into a shop. It belongs to Mr Brown the butcher and he's said Matt can have it for a song.'

Hannah's enthusiasm made Feena unwillingly pleased for her for a moment. 'That sounds ideal for Matt. He probably won't believe it but I'm very pleased for him, and you too, dear. How is he going to raise the capital?'

'Our savings will pay for the cottage. He'll have to mortgage half the value of the house for the repairs to the property and for the stock. The initial outlay will be costly but we think it will be worth the gamble. Matt should have plenty of regular customers.'

'Well, you've both been through a terrible time and you deserve all the success in the world.'

'Thank you.' Hannah had finished her coffee. 'Where's Leah? I must have a word with her before I go. I didn't get a chance at the bazaar.'

'You'll have to hunt about for her, dear. Sometimes she pops outside to see her pony and she spends a lot of time in the nursery. She wanted to make changes to it. She and Greg had quite a quarrel about it. I'm afraid the girl's very sulky these days,' Feena ended disdainfully.

Hannah decided she'd get Leah's version of the story before she made a comment. 'I'm looking forward to riding again. I thought I'd come up on Friday afternoon if the weather's not too harsh. Nathan can stay with you.'

With that settled, Hannah went to the study and found Greg and Matt poring over pages of figures at Greg's desk. Greg told her that Leah had put her coat on and gone outside for some fresh air. 'Try the stable first,' he grinned, then the two men carried on with their deliberations. The anticipation and purpose on Matt's face gave Hannah real hope for the future.

In the cobbled yard, through the misty air, she saw a small mounted figure. 'Leah?'

'No, 'tis me.' Johnny, the stable boy, walked Leah's pony, Sable, up to her. 'You just missed 'er, Missus Penney. Mrs Greg's just gone indoors.'

She informed Johnny she'd be wanting her own mount made available at the end of the week, then leaving him to exercise Sable, she went up to the nursery.

A fire was lit behind the mesh guard and it was warm and cosy. Leah was sitting slumped, her long plaited hair damp from being outside. Her hands were lying protectively over her small bump and her face was fierce and closed. Hannah stood in the doorway and tapped on the door.

'Can I come in, Leah?'

She had heard steps approaching the nursery and guessed it would be Hannah. Expecting her elder sister to breeze in as if she owned the place, Leah was taken aback for a moment. 'Yes, of course you can.'

Taking off her coat, Hannah carried a sturdy child's stool over to Leah and parked herself on it. She tried to smile but Leah wasn't interested in being friendly. 'I know you don't want to see me, Leah, and I think I know what it's all about.'

'What?' Leah said edgily, staring across the room.

'You're at the same stage of pregnancy I was when I miscarried. You're worried it might upset me to see you getting bigger and naturally you're afraid for your own baby.'

Leah felt a little ashamed. After her terrible ordeals, Hannah was full of love and concern for her. But she was too resentful at being constantly ignored to admit the truth and she was smarting at Greg's refusal to spend time and money on altering this room. The old Victorian furnishings had been updated for Nathan, and he didn't even play in here because Mrs Opie insisted he stay in her suite. Nobody seemed to think her baby was important, or care that it was a future heir to the house and property. 'You must think me very silly,' she said tightly.

'No, I don't. I'm sure I'd feel the same. Married life between Matt and me is back to normal so I could have another baby soon and we could still be pushing our prams together.' Leah glared at her so intensely Hannah felt at a loss. 'Did Matt tell you why he wanted to talk to Greg?'

Leah nodded sullenly.

'We have a double celebration to look forward to. The birth of your baby and Matt opening his chandlery.'

'Matt won't be able to do the manual work renovating that old cottage,' Leah said spitefully. 'I suppose Dad and Josh, Greg and Patrick will be fussing round him, helping him to get it ready.'

Hannah blanched at the unkindness in Leah's words. 'Matt can't do all of it but he will most of it. He's gaining strength every day,' she said, guessing that Leah was feeling left out again. She remembered Greg telling her months ago, before news of the attack on Matt broke over them, how excited Leah was about the party they were to have. The party hadn't happened because of all that had taken place that day. Leah was pregnant, a time when a woman could go through an emotional minefield, when she needed to feel cosseted and important. Hannah attempted to rectify the imbalance her troubles had caused. 'Matt and I were wondering the other day what names you've chosen for the baby. Have you decided yet?'

'I want Rhett for a boy but Greg says it's a stupid name.' She got up suddenly and paced about the room like a caged animal. 'No one cares what I think, what I do or what I say in this damned house or in the village!'

'Oh, Leah, I'm sorry. My problems have overshadowed the joy of you expecting your baby.' Hannah reached for Leah but was pushed away.

'Just leave me alone, Hannah. Go downstairs and have a cosy chat with your mother. You're all that matters around here. And now that Lily can marry Jowan after all, I'll have no one who notices I flipping well exist. But when my baby's born I'll make sure he counts for something. It's he who will inherit Roscarrock, not your child! I'll make sure he knows that.'

Hannah was shocked by her words and would have remonstrated but she could see Leah was on the verge of a tantrum. Something had to be done before she became ill and risked her health and her baby's. Hannah was sure Greg was being loving and attentive, although perhaps not very perceptive. She withdrew, determined to have a strong word with Feena Opie.

Downstairs, Matt entered the drawing room and looked all round it for Hannah as if Feena was hiding her away from him.

'Finished discussing your project with Greg, have you?' Feena asked drily.

'Yes. Hannah's not back yet?'

'No. The coffee's still hot. Would you like some?'

Matt had drunk coffee with Greg but he was curious at her gesture of hospitality, and for once she wasn't fixing him with a piercing stare. 'Yes, please.'

Feena poured the coffee and he took it to the opposite sofa and sat down. 'I take it Hannah has told you about my business plans?' He was smiling, his dark velvety eyes shining like polished jet, and she could see why Hannah was still physically attracted to him. He was totally at ease, full of confidence.

'She has. I wish you well, Matt.'

'I find that hard to believe.' He sipped the strong brew, his dark brows raised.

'I know I said some harsh things to you in your house but I was as horrified as everyone else when I saw you in the hospital. You're obviously excited about your venture. Perhaps Daniel Kittow has done you a favour.'

'Nothing could compensate for losing my favoured livelihood but I'm not going to let Hannah and Nathan down. They are my responsibility. I shall provide for them. But yes, I am excited at starting something new.'

Feena looked him in the eye. 'We should be friends, Matt.'

He gave a wry laugh. 'You know that's not possible. I shall never trust you.'

Hannah came into the room and was pleased to see they weren't at loggerheads for once. Matt got up to go. 'Would you mind leaving me and Mrs Opie alone for a few minutes, darling? There's something I need to say to her.'

When they were on their way back to Porthellis, walking arm and arm, her head snuggled against his shoulder, Matt asked, 'So, my sweet, what did you say to the old lady? She looked as if she was spitting nails when she saw us off at the door.'

'I simply told her that if she doesn't start giving Leah her rightful place at Roscarrock I'll stop going there.' She explained how upset Leah had been. 'You warned me before about Leah getting hurt at my expense. I didn't mean it to happen, but until recently I haven't been able to think of anything or anyone but us. I'm glad I've put things right for her.'

'You think Mrs Opie will go along with it?'

'Yes. She hates being told what to do and was quite sharp with me at first, but she said she'd ask Leah to go shopping with her for the baby tomorrow. If there is any more trouble I'll tell Greg to buck up his ideas.'

'Good for you.' Matt took her into his arms, smiling down into her eyes. 'I love you, Hannah,' he said. 'As long as we have each other, no one can hurt us. While I was talking to Greg I came to a decision. I want us to go into business together. I don't want the chandlery to be just mine. We'll work it together, joint partners. M and H Penney painted on the sign. What do you say?'

'I say I love you too and I'd love to be your partner in the business as well as in our marriage.' She embraced him and they kissed passionately. 'Everything's going to be all right, Matt.' She wasn't just thinking about the business and Leah; the rumours Lily had brought up that afternoon gave her cause for satisfaction too.

Chapter 26

Daniel made his way through the bitterly cold weather and darkness to arrive at a smart address in Plymouth. He was expected and walked straight into the house through the back door. Striding along the passage runner, he tapped on the second door and went into the sitting room.

His brows rose. 'Where's Charlie?' he asked the woman sitting alone amid the highly polished furniture. Her rich perfume seeped into his nostrils. She was a long-bodied, figureless woman, aged about twenty-eight, with dyed red hair and a face shaped like that of a Dresden figurine. She was smoking a black cigarette in a gilt holder. Her green eyes surveyed Daniel's brawny body like a connoisseur of wine scanning an old, important label. While he waited for an answer he returned her look and ran his eyes over the smooth, crossed legs which were revealed by a tight skirt.

'My brother had to go out. He asked me to stand in for him. You have the package?' she asked in a syrupy voice which in any other circumstances Daniel would have found irritating.

'I came for a game of cards.' he said gruffly, turning away. 'I'll be going.'

'Charlie said you wouldn't trust anyone but him. He left this note for you.'

She held out a piece of paper. Daniel advanced, took the paper, unfolded it and read the message. Satisfied, he tapped his coat which had an inside breast pocket.

With slow, foxy movements she rose and stood close to him. Daniel had never seen a woman as tall as she was; she wore no shoes yet was still about three inches taller than he was. It was a new experience to have to look up to a woman. She rolled her shoulders, tossed her head. A strange gleam entered her eyes. She smiled with just the corners of her dazzling red lips. To Daniel, she seemed unreal. He sensed she was cruel. The smoke from the cigarette and her perfume were overpowering; he felt a little intoxicated.

He watched her parted lips as she put a hand inside his coat and felt about for the package. She took her time, pressing him, prodding him. When she finally had the package, she slunk away and locked it inside a walnut bureau. Toying with the tiny silver key in her long tapering fingers, she said, pouting, 'You are a good boy bringing this for Charlie. I'll make sure you're well-rewarded.'

'Why?' he challenged her.

'He told me you were my type. Strong, athletic, energetic, big.' If Daniel had been capable of blushing, he would have been bright pink as she gazed intently at a certain area of his anatomy. 'I'm delighted to see he was correct. Why don't you take off your coat?'

As Daniel did so, she glided to a drinks table. 'What's your name?'

Daniel made a wry face.

'Just your first name will do. You can make up one but you can trust me.'

Like hell, he thought. 'You can call me Charlie,' he said.

Her face remained expressionless. 'Well, Charlie, what would you like to drink?'

'Brandy.'

'I always think brandy's such a sensuous liquor.' She caressed the large brandy glasses before moving back to him. As he reached for his drink, she backed away. 'Not here, darling. Upstairs. The bed is absolutely huge. You will come?'

Daniel nodded, full of anticipation.

The first month of the New Year had passed and the boats had limped home from the seven-week stay at Plymouth for the herring season, which had been disappointingly lean again. For most of the fishermen the success of the bazaar was replaced with worry about how they'd get through the rest of the winter. And they had brought back tragic news with them. The day before, the lugger Curly Jose partnered had run aground off Rame Head and Ian Jacobs, the younger brother of Lizzie's husband John, and an older fisherman had been washed overboard and drowned.

A few hours later, in the early morning, Constable Burt turned up on the doorstep of Chynoweth. With him were two plainclothes detectives. A blast of freezing cold air followed them inside as Grace nervously showed them into the sitting room.

Daniel had arrived home bone weary and she had got up, wrapping her satin dressing gown about her, to answer the door. The policemen wouldn't tell her why they wanted to be admitted. Somehow she didn't believe there had been another accident but asked the question anyway.

'No, Mrs Kittow,' one of the detectives said sternly, removing his knocked-about trilby. Tall, middle-aged, dominant, his black mackintosh having seen better days, he eyed Grace balefully as she shivered in her fluffy blue mules. 'There's been no accident. We would like a few words with your husband, Daniel Kittow. I believe he should be home at this time. Would you rouse him, please.'

'Um, yes. Do sit down. We have an electric fire. Would one of you switch it on? It's cold in here. And please could you keep quiet. I don't want our daughter woken up.'

Grace dashed upstairs and shook Daniel violently. He fended her off, half asleep. 'Not now, Grace. I'm bloody whacked.'

'You have to get up, Daniel,' she hissed in his ear. 'Two policemen are here with the village constable. They want to talk to you.'

Daniel swore and sat up. He was wide awake and reaching for his clothes, groaning as his shirt hit the long deep scratches on his back. 'What do they want?'

'I don't know. They wouldn't say. Have you been up to something criminal, Daniel?'

'Course I bloody have. How do you think I've got so much money in my pocket? I thought I'd been careful though.' Had there been a raid on the house in Plymouth where he'd been three days ago? How had the coppers traced him? He swore again. He would get a heavy sentence for handling stolen jewellery.

He hurried into his clothes and went downstairs, leaving Grace still getting dressed. In the sitting room the two detectives were sitting idly, Constable Burt was standing to attention with his notebook and pencil. The electric fire had been switched on. 'You'd better have a good reason for getting me out of bed,' Daniel snarled. 'I've only just got to bed after bringing my boat in from nearly two months of almost useless bloody hard slog.'

'There's no need to take that tone, Mr Kittow,' the detective who'd spoken to Grace said in a hard tone. 'I'm Detective Inspector Keith Grant.

This is Detective Sergeant Tony Trewoon. Constable Burt I'm sure you know.'

'What's this all about?' Daniel kept up his hostility and lit a cigarette.

'Can you tell us what you were doing on the afternoon of August twenty-first last year?'

'Eh?'

Grace joined them and stood at Daniel's side. They glanced at each other with puzzled expressions.

'It was a Sunday,' the sergeant, an effeminate looking individual with a twitch in his right temple and a bad case of dandruff, added. 'A fine sunny day. Perfect for taking a stroll across the cliff.'

'So?' Daniel snapped irritably. 'Get to the damned point or get out! And I don't remember what I was doing on that day. Why should I?'

Inspector Grant looked at the constable. 'PC Burt has been making inquiries into the circumstances of the death of one of your fellow fishermen. Frederick Jose. It seems some of the villagers think you might have had something to do with it.'

Putting his hands on his hips, Daniel looked incredulous. 'Now you're being plain bloody ridiculous. I had nothing to do with that pipsqueak falling or jumping off the cliff. He couldn't stand up on a fishing boat without going ass over heels. No wonder he ended up at the bottom. Good bloody riddance. He wasn't good for anything.'

'Daniel!' Grace was horrified and not just because he was being unkind to the dead. She was thinking of his threat against Fred Jose on the first day she had met him.

'For your wife's sake if not for ours, I think you ought to curb your language, Kittow,' Inspector Grant said sternly. 'Go on, Constable.'

PC Burt read from his notebook, his fresh face pink now that he was the centre of attention. 'There was no investigation at the time of Mr Jose's disappearance because there was no indication of foul play. I made inquiries on learning that Mr Kittow had publicly threatened to get even with Mr Jose – it's thought Mr Kittow blamed Mr Jose for his prison sentence. He also encouraged his previous boat's crew to continually harass Mr Jose.'

'All hearsay,' Daniel scoffed, sitting down in an armchair and casually crossing his legs. He looked at Grace. 'You go back to bed, darling. There's nothing to worry about here.'

'I won't be able to sleep. I might as well stay,' she said, sitting on the arm of the chair. Daniel put his arm round her and grinned loftily at the three policemen.

Constable Burt cleared his throat and continued, 'The day following Mr Jose's disappearance, pages of the *Daily Mirror* were found on Hidden Beach and a rolled-up towel belonging to Mrs Jose. Fred liked to read the *Daily Mirror* and Mrs Jose believes he'd gone to the beach to relax immediately before he disappeared. Mr Kittow was seen coming down off the cliff in the direction of Hidden Beach the same day Mr Jose disappeared.'

'Were you there, Kittow?' Sergeant Trewoon demanded, walking about the room.

'I might have been.' Daniel shrugged. 'I can't remember what I do every Sunday.'

'Did you see Fred Jose that afternoon?' Inspector Grant pressed.

Daniel thought he had better tell the truth. The witness might be reliable and respectable, and if he backtracked later he would look guilty. 'Yes, I came across him on Hidden Beach when I went there to be alone. That's something I often do. The runt was leering over the Jane cartoons in the paper. I made fun of him and told him to bugger off. He's always been nervous of me and he scarpered like a rabbit, leaving his things behind. It's no secret I've always despised that pathetic little coward but I've not made any public threats to him and anyone who says I have is a liar. As for my old crew, they lived next door to him and they liked a bit of fun. He was an easy target for them.'

'Why did you get convicted criminals to man your boat? It's been suggested your motive was to get revenge on Porthellis.'

'I had to get a crew quickly and start earning again. I'd spent all my money on this house.' The detective's eyebrows rose. Before another line of inquiry started – Grant had obviously assumed Grace owned the house – Daniel reluctantly added, 'The money came from the insurance on my late grandfather. Anyway, I was broke and none of the self-righteous bastards in the village would've worked for me. As soon as I was able to arrange for a decent crew to take over, I sacked the other lot.'

'Sacked them? Was that before or after they were arrested for attacking another local fisherman, a man you are purported to hate? Why didn't you tell the Joses or the authorities you had seen Fred Jose on the day he'd disappeared?'

'I didn't care less what had happened to him. Any number of people could have seen him on any day after me. No one knows exactly when he died. According to the papers, there were no injuries on his body to suggest he'd been the victim of violence. The only reason you're here is because someone's been stirring up trouble for me. Whatever they're saying, you have no proof.'

'Is there anyone in particular who would want to cause trouble for you, Kittow?'

Daniel clamped his mouth tight. Hannah had vowed revenge on him. Was it her doing that the police were here? A terrible pain gripped his heart. He got to his feet, muttering thickly, 'Try the whole village. Now if you've finished—'

'Not quite.' Inspector Grant moved in front of him. 'We'd like you to come down to the station and make a statement.'

'What the hell for?' Daniel thundered, balling his fists.

'Hush, Daniel.' Grace caught his arm. 'You'll wake Melanie.'

'If you've got nothing to hide about Jose's death, you won't mind making a statement about your movements on the day in question, will you?' the sergeant said calmly, mockingly.

'All right, but not now. You can't drag me out of my house unless you arrest me. I'll come voluntarily during the morning. Now get out and let me get some sleep!'

'Ten o'clock, Mr Kittow,' Inspector Grant said, putting on his hat. 'Not a moment later.'

When the three policemen went into the hall, they saw a little girl with two armfuls of toys and a scrap of blanket huddled nervously on a lower step of the stairs. Daniel shoved his way through the policemen and picked her up, cradling her possessively. 'Bastards!' he said under his breath. 'She'll be too frightened to get back to sleep on her own.'

On the way back to St Austell, the policemen talked over the interview. 'Bolshy sod, ain't he?' Sergeant Trewoon remarked.

'I wouldn't liked to have tried to arrest him,' Constable Burt said from the back seat. 'He put up quite a fight when he was last taken in. Left me black and blue on the village quay.'

'Think he did it, boss?' Trewoon asked his superior.

'No. His venom alone would frighten a bloke like Jose to death. I reckon he told him to clear off, nothing more, and Jose was too scared to come back. If Jose was as timid as he's made out to be, he would've felt life wasn't worth living. My hunch was he jumped. And like Kittow said, there's no real evidence. Still, you never know what a second interview might turn up. I'm looking forward to giving him a hard time.'

Daniel carried Melanie upstairs and put her in his bed. When she was sleeping, relieved of all her toys except the felt piskie and curled in tightly to Grace, he said to his wife, 'I swear on Melanie's life I never touched the miserable little sod. Satisfied?'

'Yes,' she answered after a few moments.

'Had to think about it though, didn't you?'

'I don't think you could murder anyone, Daniel, but you are probably responsible in some way for that poor man's death.'

He turned away and thought about the woman in Plymouth, but her ruthless lovemaking, during which she had taught him a few tricks even he hadn't known, wasn't enough to keep his thoughts away from Hannah. He had to know if she'd started the rumours that he had killed Fred Jose.

Chapter 27

Matt tossed the last inch of the pasty he was eating out of the door of the old cottage. A batch of gulls flew down into what had once been the tiny front courtyard and squawked and fought over it. He laughed, enjoying the commotion. Lighting a cigarette, he took the pencil perched behind his ear and mulled over his plans.

It had taken more work than he'd expected to turn the two up, two down building into a shop. The gale had torn off most of the roof tiles. The floor timbers in the two bedrooms were rotten. The back wall needed shoring up. He had needed the help of tradespeople, family, and friends to complete the work, then they'd taken out the wall dividing the kitchen and living room and built a new wall lengthways to make a small storeroom and large shop floor. Most of the frontage had been knocked out to make way for a large display window.

He was now doing the electrical work. The dark pine counter and shelves he had designed were being made in the carpenter's shop; he would install them himself. Hannah was often here, doing what she could, making sure he wasn't over-exerting himself, but today he was alone and it was good to feel in control of his project; to dream about what the future might hold and wonder which of his two trades Nathan would follow.

He and Hannah would have to adapt to a new way of life, no longer governed by the departure and return of the fleet, the seasons, the peculiarities of the tide, sky and sea. His routine would be ruled by discipline and sound judgement rather than intuition, experience and hard graft.

He'd rig up a couple of movable lights over the shop window next, to illuminate the goods. Climbing the stepladder, he paused to gaze across the waterfront to the quay. All the luggers were out, long-lining down at the Lizard. The sky was clear, the wind blowing light northerly, perfect

237

for ray. The last time out, the *Misty* had caught one of the biggest turbots ever seen, well over thirty pounds in weight. And Alan Weekley had suffered the agony of being spurred by a weever fish. Matt would have liked to have seen the turbot hauled aboard; been there to dash Alan's hand into a bucket of salt water. He shook himself. No point in getting melancholy. Get back to the job in hand. He had a company rep calling later. Must telephone that paraffin supplier in St Austell, go up to the carpenter's shop . . .

Leah was turning the nursery into her own private little place where she could sit and daydream, something she had done all her life. She was making this room in the big house a nest for herself and her baby, a safe haven where they'd both feel pampered, important. It would help her endure life here while Feena Opie was alive. She'd considered Hannah's suggestion of a few months ago, to tell Greg she was unhappy and wanted to live in a house of their own. She'd thought about it then discounted it. She wouldn't be driven out. Her child belonged here even if she did not; it was unthinkable it should be born elsewhere. And just as her baby was daily growing stronger inside her body, receiving her love and nourishment, the cocoon she was creating was doing the same for her.

She loved Greg deeply, she was sure of his love for her, and although she did not regret marrying him she admitted people had been right to worry about their match. The differences in their age, background and personality made Greg a little remote from her. She was on her guard to make sure they didn't drift apart. He never made fun of her more common manner and speech, he only corrected her if absolutely necessary, careful not to make her feel a fool or inferior. Occasionally when he had been stubborn about something, he'd shower her with affection or bring her a thoughtful little gift. He doted on her, was kind and gentle. When she was older, she hoped he would love her as a mature woman deserved.

She wasn't pleased when Lily, working out her last week before her wedding, announced that Mrs Opie wanted to see her in her suite.

'Is Hannah here?' she sighed. Lately when Hannah came she was invited by Mrs Opie to join their tête-à-têtes. Leah wasn't fooled into thinking she suddenly counted to her grandmother-in-law; it was Hannah's doing.

'She is, but she's gone riding.' Lily wasn't fooled either. The first thing to impress her when she had started work here was the way Leah was disregarded. 'Mrs Opie want to see you alone first this time.'

'She can wait,' Leah muttered obstinately, sliding down in her chair, making her swollen middle mushroom out all the more noticeably. 'Have you got time to chat for a bit, Lily?'

'Can spare you ten minutes, Miss Leah,' Lily giggled, shovelling more coal on the fire. 'That's better, 'tis so cold today, the fire's burning blue.' Folding her apron carefully, she perched on the stool. 'Look at you, you dear little thing. Seven months gone and a belly stuck out like a molehill on a twig. You won't be able to walk soon. Wonder you can still climb the stairs up here.'

Leah joined in her giggles. 'Oh, I'm going to miss you, Lily. Anyway,' her face became fierce, 'you'll be able to come back to visit me any time you like. Just think, you can take tea with me like a lady, served by the new girl.'

'Like your Hannah, eh?' Lily preened, imagining herself sipping from the fine china in the drawing room. 'From servant to exalted visitor.'

'Not quite the same as Hannah,' Leah said cuttingly. 'Do you know the new girl? I caught a glimpse of her after Mrs Opie interviewed her. She seemed a bit stiff.'

'Never seen her before. She's called Mary Grayson, is twenty years old and comes from St Austell. She's a younger version of Miss Benson if you ask me. Well, I won't have to worry about she.' Lily saw the suppressed anger in Leah's great dark eyes. She looked relaxed but hot spots were burning on her cheeks. Lily sought to encourage her friend. 'You are glad, though, that Mrs Opie is showing some regard for you now, aren't you? And not just because the baby'll be an Opie. She seems to have grown a bit of a soft spot for you.'

'Has she? Huh! I'm not going to lick her heels and pretend I'm a grateful little idiot just because she's taken me shopping and doles out cups of tea when Hannah's here. I don't trust the woman and I don't want her interfering in the baby's upbringing.'

'Well, you can't blame her entirely if she does,' Lily said, hoping to dilute her bitterness. Leah would be isolated without her to confide in, to have a bit of a laugh with. Her life could become unbearable if she became eaten up with resentment and frustration. 'Grannies always make a fuss of their grandchildren. Be a crying shame if they didn't. You should see the way my mother drives my sisters up the wall harping on about their kids. I expect Mrs Rouse will do the same when Jowan and I produce a child, which,' Lily tittered, 'could be sooner than later.'

'Oh, Lily, you haven't,' Leah grinned, struggling to sit upright. 'Have you?'

'Well, we didn't dream of it till the wedding day was set.' Lily made a show of mock primness. 'But all the Rouses were out one evening, helping Matt Penney with his shop renovations, and we got carried away. Crumbs, what a performance! Neither of us had a clue what to do. In fact,' Lily roared with laughter, the cosy dark room seeming to vibrate with her gaiety, 'I could still be a virgin for all I know about it. Poor Jowan, you should've seen your cousin's face! He was more 'fraid than a cow going to the knackers. Now he's worried he'll never be a man. Well, we'll get it right one day, even if we have to break our backs trying. Here, I'd better get going or I'll be getting the sack.' Both girls fell about laughing.

Leah kept Mrs Opie waiting exactly ten minutes then waddled along slowly to her suite. She had been told there was no need to knock and she walked straight in, holding up her bump which was now a heavy weight bearing down on the top of her legs.

'That girl took her time,' Feena complained. 'I ordered her to ask you to come to me several minutes ago.'

'I was busy,' Leah said, closing her face but putting her wits on guard.

'Take the weight of your feet, dear,' Feena said sympathetically. 'It might be a blessing if you don't go full term. You're getting huge. I'm pleased to see you're wearing sensible shoes.'

When Leah was sitting, her arms resting protectively over her bump, Feena passed some colour charts and samples of materials to her. 'I've been thinking about what you wanted for the nursery. It's your first baby, you're starting off the next generation of Opies, and if I may say so I think Greg was a little unreasonable not allowing you to make the changes you wanted. Men don't understand about these things but it wouldn't have hurt him to take his nose out of his writing for once. Roscarrock is not his house yet. You may choose exactly what you want, my dear. I've written down the telephone numbers you'll need to order the work to be done.'

Leah was astounded. Mrs Opie had never before criticised Greg and Leah could hardly believe she was being allowed to contact the shops and workmen herself without any suggestions on the changes from Mrs Opie. For the first time she was being given free rein. Could Lily be right? Had this domineering woman developed a soft spot for her? 'Thank you,' she said, looking down at the charts and samples.

'I've also written down the number you'll need to advertise for a nursery nurse.' Feena smiled soothingly as Leah brought her head up to protest. 'I know you want to do most things for the baby yourself, dear, but you'll need someone to look after it while you're out riding or hostessing parties and dinners.'

'Hostessing?' Leah frowned suspiciously.

'Greg's a stick-in-the-mud and Patrick hates socializing but there's no reason why we shouldn't enjoy ourselves. You'll need to know about these things one day, when Greg inherits. He might not want to entertain much but it doesn't mean you should live like a hermit too. I know you probably feel nervous but I'll guide you. The first thing you'll need is a whole new wardrobe, befitting your station. I'm sorry your party was overlooked but we can have one to celebrate the baby's birth. If you like, we could get together with Miss Benson and arrange it now.'

Leah turned over the samples in her hands but she wasn't concentrating on them. She didn't trust Mrs Opie, but whatever her reasons were for treating her like an equal at last, she'd make the most of it. With Mrs Opie as her mentor, she could learn to make her mark as the future mistress of Roscarrock. She'd be comfortable in the role by the time it became a reality. Best of all, it might make Hannah jealous.

Hannah was exercising Bonny over fields that bordered Roscarrock. The blood was tingling through her veins, splashing healthy colour on her cheeks. Her eyes were brimming with energy. She had a new vitality for life now that Matt was contentedly occupied preparing the chandlery.

After a long gallop she eased up and made her way down a field leading directly to the cliff. The sea stretched out to the horizon, grey and still like the sky, as if nature was in a dull slumber, but she felt settled and alive. The wind was cold on her body but she didn't mind. When she got back to the house she'd soon be warmed through with hot tea and toasted crumpets and Feena's undivided attention.

A movement down at the bottom of the field caught her eye. A man was sitting on the stile, a big man in working clothes with a mop of red hair.

'Well, Bonny,' she kept the pony at a steady trot down through the patches of tall thistles made stiff with the hard frost, 'if he thinks I'll turn round and not face him . . .'

She reined in when she reached Daniel and stared into his beautiful blue eyes.

'I knew you wouldn't ignore me,' he said, gazing steadily back.

She raised her chin, eyes flashing. 'I'm not afraid of you.'

'I know. I'm glad.' He grimaced and Hannah sensed it was with difficulty he said next, 'Was it you who started the rumours that I murdered Fred Jose, Hannah?' He had accepted the humiliation of Inspector Grant's relentless interrogation with little aggression, knowing it was probably Hannah who had placed him in this position.

'Yes.' It was satisfying indeed that he realised it had been her ploy to send him to prison again.

He gave the smallest nod. 'You hate me that much? Want me to dangle at the end of a rope? I didn't kill him.'

'You as good as. You may not have actually pushed him over the cliff but it was you that did it.'

'I can't change that now.' He kept his stony expression. 'You've got your revenge, Hannah. The whole village thinks I killed him. I'll be branded a murderer for the rest of my life. But I've come to ask you to stop. Not for my sake. For Melanie's. You saw her before me or Grace. You touched her, helped her, before we did. You know what a rotten life she'd had. If she's shunned by the village she'll grow up miserable, never feeling she belongs anywhere. I swear you won't have any more trouble from me. Will you let things rest now? Please, for Melanie's sake?'

She looked at him, wondering if there was anything of the Danny of old left in him. There wasn't. Who exactly was speaking to her? 'Is this the brave, high and mighty Daniel Kittow pleading?'

'Yes. I love Melanie.'

'I see. Very well, for Melanie's sake I'll live as though you don't exist.'

The wind ruffled his hair. He sat rigid, eyes rooted on hers. 'We meant a lot to each other once. I'd like us to be friends.' He remembered how Hannah had made a similar plea to him that day he had walked into her parlour and found her asleep. 'But I suppose there's no hope of that,' he added.

'You're right. I despise you. I always will.'

He was quiet for some time. Hannah held her head high. She had no idea what was really going on inside his head. It did not matter. She had gained superiority over him. He could not hurt her again.

'There's something I want you to know,' he said softly. 'Hannah, I know that Feena Opie is your real mother.'

She could not deny it, or ridicule him; she could see he was sure it was the truth. 'How?'

'I got the information out of Lily – in my usual manner of doing things. It wasn't the girl's fault. It got back to her mother from that vile nurse Mrs Opie engaged when she broke her hip. I was going to use it against you. But not now. I want you to know it'll never pass my lips. You have my promise.'

'I thank you at least for that, Daniel,' she said in the manner of a dignified lady. She made to twitch the reins, to move on. She'd ride for another half hour, think over the conversation.

He put out his hand, touched hers. 'I love you, Hannah.'

'Don't tell me that, Daniel,' she replied quietly.

'It's the truth. I'll have to live out my life knowing you hate me, that I can never have you.' Then she saw his pain, the hunger that would never be assuaged. She even saw bewilderment.

'I believe you. I simply don't want to hear you say it.' She slipped her hand away. 'If I meant the same to you as the others you wouldn't have hurt me so cruelly, tried to destroy Matt. Even if Matt had been beaten to death, you wouldn't have destroyed our love. It's all very sad. You're sad, Daniel.'

He dropped his head. She trotted away, leaving him to his loneliness, the one emotion that was so often the worst to bear, and one he so richly deserved.

Chapter 28

On the second Saturday of March, Matt and Hannah stood proudly, arms joined, gazing at the sign over their shop, M & H Penney, Chandlery & Angling Supplies. The letters of their name, painted boldly in gold by Matt himself, curled into one another, proclaiming to the world their intimate, unbreakable relationship. Their eyes travelled down the fresh green paintwork of the low door – Matt had painted a sign above it, 'Beware, ye mortals, of these low portals' – then on to the window where a multitude of boat and angling equipment vied for space. Finally their eyes locked and their lips met in a kiss that would have lasted for half the morning, as Roy Rouse jovially put it as he clapped his hands on their shoulders.

'You going to stand out here all day, or are 'ee going to open up?'

The couple laughed when they saw they had an audience – all their relatives and a good number of villagers. Matt held up his key then smiled lovingly at Hannah. 'You do the honours, darling.'

'Are you sure? You put in most of the work, Matt.'

'Get on with it,' Jeff bawled good-naturedly. 'Or we'll have t'take the boats out dreckly with nothing on 'em.' Prim stood at her husband's side, moist-eyed, proud that her daughter should actually own a shop.

Hannah drew in a long sniff of fresh spring air, took the key from Matt and unlocked the chandlery while the others clapped. She led the way in, Matt followed her and they stood behind the counter while family and friends spilled inside to take a close look at the goods.

Miss Peters barged up to the counter. 'Be nice always to have paraffin at hand for my lamps in case of power cuts. There's always a neighbour who's run out.' She plonked a can on the floor and some coins in Matt's hand. 'You can fetch me up the can later.'

'Thank you, Miss Peters.' Matt beamed down on the tiny old lady as he handed her the change. 'Glad to be of service to you.'

Miss Peters eyed him coolly. 'Mmmm. Thought I'd have a few pence off, being your very first customer.'

'If you look in your hand you'll see I've knocked off threepence,' he returned. He knew Miss Peters would always find a reason to have a few pence taken off her purchases.

'Good boy,' and her wrinkled features broke into a smile.

The shop was busy all morning and although more people came to nose about rather than to buy, Matt was astonished to find they'd taken thirty-five pounds, eight shillings and sixpence by lunchtime. 'I guess the men ran their supplies down waiting for us to open up,' he ruminated gratefully.

During a quieter moment, Grace came in with Melanie. 'Is it all right if I look round?' she asked hesitantly.

'Fine by me,' Matt said, carrying on with the unnecessary polishing of a case of fishing reels.

'Are you looking for anything in particular?' Hannah said, joining Grace as she ran her hand down a navy blue jersey folded on top of a small pile of knitted garments. 'Or are you just browsing?'

Grace was pleasantly surprised that Hannah should be so friendly. 'I don't knit and I thought I'd buy one of these for . . . buy one of these.'

'You'll need a forty-four-inch chest,' Hannah said, pulling out the largest jersey at the bottom of the pile. She held it up for Grace to inspect. 'Mrs Penrose made it. She's an excellent craftswoman. It should last for years.'

'It looks splendid. I'll take it, please.' Melanie was gazing at a small ship in a bottle that Jeff had made. 'Perhaps we could have a look at that?'

'Certainly.' She held out the perfect replica of a galleon in full rig inside the thick glass. 'Do you like it, Melanie? The sailors used to sail boats like these in the olden days.'

Melanie shook her head. 'Not like Daddy's.'

'Well, how about one of these little boats then?' Hannah lifted down a rough shape of a lugger, carved in crude timber by Matt while he'd recuperated in bed and now only meant to give atmosphere to the shop. 'Would you like it, Melanie?'

She nodded shyly and Hannah placed it in her hand. 'Well, you shall have it, as a gift for being the first little girl we've served.'

'It's very kind of you,' Grace said as Hannah wrapped her shopping.

'It's my pleasure.' Hannah smiled as she took the money for the jersey.

Grace was not looking her best today. She was immaculately groomed, stylishly dressed as usual, but underneath her make-up her skin was lifeless, her eyes dull; the effort she had to make to maintain her standing in the village because of Daniel's behaviour was obviously taking its toll. Hannah was reminded that the other woman was kind and caring. Daniel wasn't the only one worried about Melanie's future.

Grace returned Hannah's smile, and at that moment seemed to stand several inches taller. 'I wish you well with your business, you and Matt.'

'You were very friendly,' Matt remarked, watching his wife's face closely when Grace and her daughter had gone.

'It's not their fault, what Daniel did. Now that Melanie's legally adopted and bears the name of Kittow, she's got something that won't be easy to live with. I don't want to make life more difficult for her.'

Colville arrived with his three sons and bought tackle obviously meant for the *Sunrise*. Matt wondered how he'd react if their skipper came into the shop. He found out that afternoon when he was there alone.

Carefully ducking his head under the low door, Daniel strode in and stood in the middle of the shop floor. 'Will you serve me?' he asked aggressively.

Matt felt his heart constrict. He came out from behind the counter, his hands clenched at his sides. He wanted to drag the other man out of his shop and toss him into the water. But what good would it do? Even if his aching need for justice lent him the strength to haul Daniel out of the shop and into the drink, the sweetness of revenge would last only a short time. Why risk spoiling the joy of opening his new venture? Hannah had the right attitude; he could never hold out an olive branch, but he might as well try to live under a truce, even if it was a bitter pill to take.

'Feel free to look around,' he said through gritted teeth and moved past Daniel to greet four of Porthellis's venerable pensioners.

The old gents had left their bench on the quay to indulge their curiosity. As they shuffled about, humming and hawing over the wares, asking the prices, remarking on the quality, Matt watched Daniel keenly. Eventually the old gents went on their way without one of them giving Daniel so much as a glance.

'How much you asking for this?' Daniel asked, testing the sharpness of a gutting knife on his thumb.

'One pound, two and six,' Matt replied tightly. He could almost feel Eric slashing his face. 'It's made by Forester's, stainless steel blade, solid wood handle. Guaranteed to last a lifetime,' he lowered his voice to an icy pitch, 'if you're lucky enough to be able to fish for a lifetime.'

'I haven't come to fall out, Matt.' Daniel stared at him while he took a handful of money out of his pocket. He counted the price out on the counter. 'Don't bother to wrap it. I'll take it as it is.'

'What's his game?' Matt murmured to himself, watching from the doorway as the arrogant red-haired fisherman made his way to his boat.

Over breakfast that morning, Greg carefully read a long, detailed letter from an old university friend. When he put it aside, he picked up *The Times*. He'd already read the headlines and used the paper as a cover to glance covertly at Leah. They would celebrate their first wedding anniversary in a week's time, his spy novels were selling well, his latest play was a success on the London stage. His life was idyllic, would be fulfilled when his child was born, be it a boy or a girl, but would things stay that way?

Rudolph Walenski was a scientist and a Jew and his family had been expelled from Poland last November. Thankfully they were now living in Kenya, having taken up Britain's offer of settling Jewish refugees in parts of the colonial empire, but his letter was full of disturbing accounts of the tightening grip of Nazi brutality. Buried away down here in Cornwall, Greg had thought little about Adolf Hitler and Nazi oppression.

British politicians who had visited Germany had, for the most part, claimed that Hitler was moderate, trustworthy and genuinely desired peace. Rudolph called them near-sighted prigs whose complacency was dangerous. There was an arrogant belief that Britain had won the Great War alone, that its powers were invincible, and while some forecast another terrifying war in Europe, most of the country was reassured by the politicians; when the Prime Minister, Neville Chamberlain had returned from Munich last year and claimed that the Anglo-German agreement with Hitler brought peace with honour, most people had believed him. Rudolph did not. He warned Greg to brace himself for war.

Greg pondered the situation deeply for the first time. For months now air raid shelters had been built in the big cities, sandbags had been filled and stacked against key buildings, there were compulsory gas mask drills in the schools. Greg had viewed these measures as no more than political manoeuvrings to silence government critics; now he began to wonder how Roscarrock could be fortified.

'What's the matter, Greg?' Leah had hauled herself up off her chair and was wobbling towards him. 'Was there bad news in the letter?'

Yes, there was, he thought, but he did not want to worry his heavily pregnant wife; they had so much to look forward to. 'No, darling,' he said. 'I was just debating whether we should go down to the village for the opening of the chandlery.' He gave a broad smile that fooled Leah entirely. 'I know the baby's due in three weeks' time and you're feeling cumbersome but you'll be fine if I look after you. Would you like to go?'

'No,' she replied, keeping the tartness out of her voice and winding her arms round his neck. He moved his chair so she could ease herself down on to his lap. 'I'm a bit tired. I think it's better that I rest. My ankles swelled up again last night and I'm not taking any risks with this baby.'

He kissed her cheek. 'You're right to be sensible. Grandmother says she might take a look at the chandlery next week. I'll go then.' He caressed her bulk, feeling their child moving about inside her. 'Want me to help you upstairs?'

'Yes, please.' She nuzzled his neck. 'To the nursery.'

'You spend all your time up there,' he chided her lightly. He had been put out at the refurbishment of the room after he'd said it must remain unaltered. 'Wouldn't it be better if you lie down on the sofa in our bedroom? The fire's lit. I'll tuck you up in a blanket. I've got some research to do. I'll come up and read it there, keep you company.'

'I want to go to the nursery, Greg,' she said in a voice that threatened to turn the request into a demand. She'd get her own way, too. Greg believed her pregnancy had made her highly emotional and he humoured her in everything. She was learning how to manipulate people, just like his grandmother did.

'Very well, as you wish.'

When they'd climbed the two flights of stairs, then the few steps that led up to the nursery, he settled her in the armchair at the fireside and placed her feet on the stool. He had kept out of the way while the room was redecorated and was impressed by the changes she had made. 'You've chosen well, darling. I can see why you like it up here.'

'I feel totally comfortable here,' she said proudly. 'Patrick likes it too. He sometimes pops in for a chat.'

'Well, I suppose I've got the study and you've got this little place of your own,' he said indulgently. 'But I don't want you making up the fire.'

'Don't worry. Mary does it regularly. Just think, Greg,' she pointed to the new rocking cradle, adorned with a white canopy, frills and ribbons, 'our baby will soon be lying in there.' She beckoned to him and he knelt at her side. Caressing his face, she whispered, 'I love you.'

'I love you too, my sweet darling.'

As Greg left, Mary entered. She bobbed a curtsy. Leah liked that. She also liked the under-housemaid calling her Mrs Opie or ma'am rather than Mrs Greg. 'Are you comfortable, ma'am?' she asked in her naturally quiet voice. Leah had thought she wouldn't like the new servant, so different in her ways to Lily, but Mary had a stillness about her which was soothing and Leah felt it would be good with a baby in the house. It was a pity she couldn't have Mary to help with the baby but she didn't have the background to provide the correct training that the heir to this grand house would need.

'Yes, thank you, Mary. I'm interviewing some more nursemaids later today. You can show them up here.'

'Yes, ma'am. I'll be back in a little while to see to the fire. Is there anything I can fetch you?'

'I left a magazine in the drawing room last night. You can bring that up.'

'Yes, ma'am,' and with a curtsy the mousy girl departed.

Respect at last, Leah thought smugly, closing her eyes to daydream. She thought back over Lily and Jowan's wedding. She had worn a new hat, smaller than the style she usually wore now that she was no longer concerned about concealing the thin scar on her face, and a fox stole draped round her shoulders. As she made her slow way up the aisle, Greg and her sister Naomi helping her along, her entrance had received nearly as much fuss as the bride's. Adela Skewes had set aside a sturdy chair for her so she wouldn't have to squeeze her size into a pew, and she had sat there, feeling full of importance throughout the ceremony.

She was careful not to giggle at Lily's exuberance during the reception held in the Rouses' cottage and smiled in the lofty way she was copying from Mrs Opie.

'Getting to be quite the lady,' Prim grinned proudly to Mrs Skewes over their teacups. 'It's going to be a big baby by the look of her.'

'A girl by the way she's carrying it all out in front,' Mrs Skewes had replied. 'I had three boys and carried them low and at the back.'

It's a boy, Leah scowled inwardly. She was going to provide a male heir for Roscarrock.

His name had now been agreed and, all being well, Edward Gregory Charles Opie would make his way into the world in about twenty-one days' time. He would love this little room as much as she did, with its pastel blue flock wallcovering, and cream and pale blue paintwork. Gone were the heavy, dark damask curtains, replaced with a gentle print in soft linen. The thick wool carpet was plain in Wedgwood blue, perfect for him to crawl on.

Her mind drifted back to the wedding. At the reception she had handed out pretty invitation cards to her sisters, mother, aunt, cousin Lizzie and the bride. It was to a tea party she would hostess herself. Mrs Opie had approved of the idea, declining her own invitation, saying her presence might intimidate her family. This was what Leah had wanted; she had also been glad that Hannah had said she couldn't come as she was too busy with the chandlery which was about to be opened.

Prim and Janet had not come either, but the other younger members, wearing their best hats and clothes, had filed into the drawing room where she sat like a queen giving audience. Lily, unaware that Leah wished to elevate herself, declared her formal attitude 'a scream', believing Leah was poking fun at Mrs Opie.

Leah played the piano, a passable version of 'The Blue Danube', with Miss Benson turning the pages of music for her. Her audience had clapped in delight, congratulating her accomplishment. She knew they would go home and enthuse about the afternoon. She told them not to wait to be invited again, to ring and ask if she was available. Hannah had paid a brief visit to Roscarrock a few days later. She hadn't seemed jealous, but after the novelty of opening her little shop had worn off, Leah hoped that the fact that she was establishing herself here would sink in and begin to rankle.

Feena had no such illusions. She had come to accept that Hannah would always be too occupied with the husband she adored to feel Leah was usurping her. She saw her sister's future as mistress of Roscarrock as right and proper. Hannah's place was with Matt, in the village, and there were plenty of people there to dance attendance on her. Feena also grudgingly recognized that all Matt's plans were cautious and sensible. He was unlikely to lose the shop and house; with his intelligence and thorough knowledge of the fishing industry, the business would probably be a resounding success. If only she could bribe a bank official . . . There was still the threat posed by Daniel Kittow, of course; sooner or later his actions were bound to make Hannah turn to Roscarrock, surely.

Pogo suddenly leapt off her lap and yapped at the door. Mary showed Jeff into the drawing room and withdrew to fetch Leah.

'Not bouncy like Jowan's maid but a nice little thing,' Jeff remarked, hurrying across the room to kiss Feena.

'Yes, I hope she doesn't fall foul of Daniel Kittow. I've heard he likes young, fresh girls like Mary.'

'Aw, he keeps his wanderings out of the village. I don't think we need worry about he any more. He's gone quiet.'

'What do you mean?' she asked sharply. 'He's only biding his time before he does something else despicable.'

'I don't think so. He's got responsibilities now and that often softens the wildest man. From what I've seen of it, he's good to his wife and seems to really care about that little maid of his. He seems eager for her to be part of the village.'

Feena made no reply because Mary had returned, but if Daniel Kittow had mended his ways because of his daughter, maybe it was time to look more closely at the little girl's origins.

'Mrs Opie is fast asleep, madam,' the maid said, standing straight, her small hands folded in front of her. 'I called to her but she didn't rouse. Shall I try again in a few minutes?'

'Oh, no,' Feena said; she had no desire for Leah's company. 'That would be cruel. She obviously needs her sleep. Mr Spargo has come with news about the opening of Mrs Penney's chandlery. I'll tell her all about it later.'

The moment Mary had bobbed and was gone, Jeff was back at the sofa. There hadn't been any opportunity to repeat their lovemaking and his body ached for Feena. 'Why don't you stay over somewhere for the night so we can be together? There's always someone in the house here.'

It made Feena feel good to be needed as a woman, but after the initial excitement of him reviving their old affair, she had come to realize the depth of her feelings for him were not as they had been before. He was certainly not worth the risk of her losing all she had. 'I can't, Jeff. If I went away I'd have to take Miss Benson with me. I can't manage on my own with my arthritis and we wouldn't be alone.'

'Pity.' He ran a row of kisses along her neck. 'I've given up Maggie Curnow but I don't know how long I can manage without love altogether.'

'Then you must find someone else, Jeff.' She pushed him away from her. 'There can never be anything longstanding between us. I wanted us to go away together before Hannah was born, but not now. I've got too much to lose here now.' She sounded inflexible, aloof.

Jeff jumped up and stared down on her, his face full of shock. 'I don't mean very much to you, do I? It's just Hannah really. And Nathan, Greg and his child are in front of me as well, aren't they?'

'Yes, of course. What else did you expect? You fill only a small need in me. We can go on like this or we can finish now. You'd still be welcome to come here as a friend when you see Leah.'

Jeff shook his head. 'You're a cool bitch. I forgot that for a while.'

'Well?' She was getting impatient. 'Have you made a decision?'

He was already heading for the door, cursing himself for allowing a woman to make a fool of him, a new and unwelcome experience for him. 'We might as well call it a day. I'm not going to risk losing Hannah and my other children's respect for something that's not important to either of us.'

Feena didn't give him a second thought. She rang for Mary to fetch her stationery then wrote to a private investigator on the matter of Melanie Kittow.

Chapter 29

Hannah picked up a pile of letters lying on the passage floor. Most were long brown envelopes addressed to Matt, presumably about the chandlery. Before moving on to the kitchen, she opened a small white envelope with unfamiliar writing on it, then raised her brows at the contents. It was an invitation for Nathan to attend Melanie's fifth birthday party on Saturday. This put Hannah in a dilemma. She would never take her son over Daniel's threshold but she did not want Melanie to feel rejected or to hurt Grace's feelings. Since the chandlery had opened a couple of weeks ago, the two women had enjoyed a few friendly chats. She'd have to reply saying plans had been made to take Nathan somewhere else that day. Not wanting Matt to know about the invitation, she hid it in her apron pocket; she'd burn it when Mrs Penney wasn't about.

Sitting up in bed with her breakfast tray, Feena Opie was reading her mail. One of the letters was from the private investigator. He had located Melanie Kittow's mother, a 21-year-old woman called Janie Wicks, a prostitute living in St Austell. Records showed the child had been legally adopted by the Kittows. Feena frowned irritably. She had thought to pay the mother to reclaim the child, thereby depriving Kittow of her. Perhaps Janie Wicks could be bribed to cause trouble. Would it be worth it? Feena reluctantly thought not. Daniel Kittow was a hard man. He had the law on his side concerning his daughter and cruel and efficient ways of ridding himself of a nuisance. She'd have to think of something else to rouse Kittow to his former bad ways.

Later that morning Hannah caught the bus to Mevagissey to consult the doctor. The sombre waiting room was quiet and she was surprised and a little embarrassed when Grace entered. Now she'd have to lie to her face about the reason for Nathan not attending Melanie's birthday party.

As Grace sat down beside her, she was pink in the face too. 'I hope you're not poorly, Hannah,' she said, smoothing at her skirt and resting her handbag on her lap as Hannah had done. They were a picture of two attractive, smartly dressed young women, their chins slightly raised, shoulders back, to show they were in control of their lives.

'No. I'm fairly sure I'm expecting again and after what happened last time I thought I ought to consult the doctor straightaway.' Her voice was tinged with hope, sadness and, Grace felt, resentment too.

'You're very wise.' Grace gave a little disconcerted cough. 'When is it due?'

'I've only just missed, so it will be about December.'

'I hope everything works out all right.'

'Thank you.' Hannah paused a moment to think of something convincing to say about the party invitation but Grace spoke first, blushing furiously.

'Actually, I'm here for the same reason. I'm hoping that I've conceived but my cycle's always been erratic so it's hard to tell. I couldn't bear waiting and wondering any longer so I left Melanie with Mrs Penrose and came here. I drove over. You must let me give you a lift home.'

'Thank you.' Hannah's mind was in turmoil. Would Daniel be pleased to be a father again? She'd always thought she knew him better than anyone but she didn't have a clue about this. She felt a measure of guilt, sitting here next to Grace, friendly, casual, when not long ago she had told her that Daniel had said he was in love with her. 'I expect Melanie would love a little sister or brother.'

'Yes, I hope so,' Grace said vaguely. Melanie would probably find an addition to the family difficult. She was used to being the centre of attention and Daniel spoiled her shamelessly. A feeling of panic came over Grace; she gripped her handbag tightly and her tawny eyes became haunted. 'I'm scared, Hannah.'

'Scared? What of?'

'Everything. Of carrying a child, giving birth to it. It's something I've never really wanted. I adapted quickly to having Melanie, she was a ready-made daughter, but I'm not a maternal woman. I don't know how I'll cope.'

Smiling, Hannah patted her hand. 'Every woman feels the same way, even if she's desperate to have a baby. You'll be fine.'

'But I haven't got a family to support me like you have.' She envied Hannah's calm acceptance of her condition, and that was despite having lost a baby.

'You've got Mrs Penrose, and any of us in the village will be glad to help out.'

'Do you think so? Even though the baby will be Daniel's?'

'Of course,' Hannah said confidently in a rush of sisterly emotion for the other woman. She studied Grace's long face. 'Have you been sick, specially in the mornings?'

'Yes, and my breasts are heavy and I feel silly and weepy. I mentioned this to Mrs Penrose. She has three sons so I thought she ought to know, and she thinks I'm pregnant.'

'Might not be long before you find out for sure.'

'Or you.' Grace relaxed a little and smiled.

Hannah knew she must mention the party invitation now and she owed it to Grace to tell the truth. 'I got the invitation to Melanie's party today. It was kind of you to think of Nathan but I hope you won't be offended, I couldn't possibly come to your house. You know why.'

'I understand,' Grace replied sadly. 'I didn't expect you to accept but at the same time I didn't want you to feel I'd deliberately left Nathan out. Hopefully, in time, things will be different.'

Hannah couldn't see how and said nothing.

'The party was Daniel's idea. He won't be there, he says no one would allow their children to come if he was, but it's not really a man's thing anyway, is it? I hope some of the children will come.' Grace was looking worried again. 'We've invited all the children of suitable age in the village.'

'My cousin Lizzie will bring hers. She stays friendly with everyone. So you'll have five to start off with.'

'You've cheered me up, Hannah. Perhaps,' she ventured, 'Melanie could pop in with a slice of cake for Nathan.'

'You're both welcome at any time,' Hannah said.

Grace felt she could cope with a pregnancy now. Daniel hadn't shared his feelings or intentions with her, but his efforts to live the respectable life she had once exhorted him to might help lessen the hostility towards him. If she and Melanie were welcome in the Penneys' household, it would go a long way towards making living in the village comfortable. She couldn't bear to think of Melanie and her child being treated as outcasts all their lives.

The *Sunrise* was thirty miles south of the Dodman. It was the middle of the night, the weather was bitingly cold, wet with patches of fog, the sea

257

was restless as if it begrudged giving up its bounty. The crew were exhausted but they had only hauled in seventy-six stone of flatfish on the long line and a netful of pilchard bait. At least the ray and skate they had would make a good price. Every now and then, when the men paused to ease their straining backs, they caught sight of the other boats heading for home, their bows dipping despondently into the waves, as if to tell they had probably not even caught their next lot of bait.

The *Sunrise* had more bait than it needed but with the rest of the fleet gone, there was no point putting up a 'flambow', a flare to signal that the others were welcome to share the surplus. Rather than waste time shaking it out and throwing it away, Daniel ordered it to be taken into port and given away. As he scrubbed the accumulation of salt and fish scales from his rough hands, he told Colville to set a course that would take them further away from home.

'No, I won't do it,' Colville said firmly, bringing the lugger round to head for home.

'What?' Daniel bellowed, furious he was being disobeyed. 'I'm as anxious as you are to get back but I have a bit of business to do first. It's no skin off your nose. I've offered you and each of your boys a bonus before now, 'tis your bleddy hard luck if you're too damned pure to take it.'

'Would be immoral t'take it and I won't be a party to your crimes no more,' Colville asserted, fixing his skipper with a hard stare. 'And I won't go on letting my boys be involved. We could all end up in prison. If it's not to your liking, you'll just have t'get a new crew and me and the family will move out of Porthellis.'

'You sanctimonious bastard!' Daniel's hands reached out for Colville's neck. 'Turn the boat round or I'll throw you overboard.'

'That's all you're fit for,' the engineer ducked his head to escape the throttling, 'threats and violence if you don't get your own way. What sort of a man are you, Daniel Kittow? Are you afraid to make your living honestly?'

George and Colville Junior squeezed into the wheelhouse, their eyes flicking anxiously from their father to their skipper who was shaking with rage.

'Out with 'ee,' Colville ordered calmly. 'Me and Daniel's having a private conversation.'

'No, we're bloody not!' Daniel swore. Shoving himself between the two younger Penroses, he strode to the cabin. 'Get out!' he snarled at Andy, and the youngest Penrose, who was endeavouring to pull off his oilskins, scampered out like a nervous puppy.

There were mugs of steaming tea and food on the table and Daniel sent them hurling across the cabin with one sweep of his arm. He could have torn the boat apart. He wanted to hurt someone, make someone suffer.

'Bastard. Bible-thumping bigot. Pious prig,' he raged, his breathing ragged. 'I'm only trying to make a living for my family.' As he said it, he knew it wasn't true. He'd passed on stolen goods for excitement, as rebellion, because he loved flouting the law and thumbing his nose at convention. To show himself what sort of man he was? Like a sailing ship suddenly deprived of a powerful wind, he collapsed on the bunk behind him. As if a lid had been whipped off a chest of treasure, he saw the hoard inside as his inner self, not sparkling, desirable, precious, but tarnished, contaminated, rotten.

He had always thought himself a winner, but now he realised what it felt like to have no one care about him in the whole world. Grace loved him but didn't trust or respect him. Melanie would climb on to his lap if he beckoned to her, give him a shy peck when he gave her a present, but he doubted that she had acquired love and trust for anyone but Grace.

And Hannah loathed him; she didn't care what he did as long as he didn't harm her family. She wouldn't give a damn if he died.

The pain of his existence hit him full force. For the first time in his life he felt useless, having no future to live for except two people who could only offer him a flawed love. Burying his face in his hands, he wept.

Mary Grayson told Lily that the younger Mrs Opie was in the drawing room and was expecting her.

'Here, take these.' Lily held out her chubby hands which were clutching a huge posy of primroses. 'Put them in water for Miss Leah, will you, please? It'll cheer her up, she loves wild flowers. I'll show myself in.'

'She's down in the dumps today,' Mary whispered, taking the long-stemmed pale yellow flowers. 'She can't wait for her labour to start and get the birth over.'

'No wonder.' Lily made an effort to keep her voice down. 'Going around like a beached whale would drive me mad too. Do you like working here, Mary?'

'Oh, yes, it's the best position I've had so far. It's my afternoon off today. I haven't been down into Porthellis yet. I thought I'd walk there to see Mrs Penney's chandlery.'

'Be sure to call on me then. The cottages next to the quay, number seven.'

'Thank you, Mrs Rouse.'

'She's a good sort,' Lily said, referring to Mary when she was sitting opposite a very grumpy-looking Leah.

'She rubs my back for me, which is killing me at the moment, and is very gentle.' Leah screwed up her face as she tried to wriggle into a more comfortable position. She was half lying on the sofa, her feet up on cushions.

'Getting you down, is it?' Lily nodded at the almost grotesque rise of her stomach.

'Oh, Lily, you haven't got a clue what it's like. I can't put my stockings on by myself. I can't see my feet unless I've got them raised up like this and they ache all the time. I've got constant heartburn. I have to keep rushing to the lavatory for a wee. My bosoms have gone into a horrible shape and it feels as if a heavy lump of dough is pressing down on my whatsitsname and hanging down to my knees.' Tears filled her eyes and overflowed. 'I've been beastly to Greg. I snap at everything he says. He won't love me any more. I'm fat and ugly and I'll always stay like it.'

Lily hugged her, stroking her long hair. 'Come on, you silly. Of course Greg still loves you. The moment the baby's born things will return to normal. Dry your eyes now. If Mary tells anyone you've been crying there'll be a fuss. She'll be here in a minute with the tea and I've told her to pile on heaps of cake.'

Leah found her hanky, wiped her eyes and blew her nose. 'I'm so glad you phoned wanting to come today. The time's dragged like years since you were here with Lizzie and my sisters. Have you got your wedding photos yet? I'd like to have one.'

'Be a few more days before we get them.' Lily returned to her chair and chuckled, her eyes twinkling. 'I hope I don't get caught with a baby yet. Now Jowan's finally got the hang of it I'm enjoying all the practising.'

'I'll tease Jowan when I see—' A sharp pull inside her tummy silenced her.

Lily dashed across the room. 'What is it?'

After a moment Leah sighed. 'Oh, nothing. I've had these twinges for days but nothing comes of it. The midwife calls every day. She says something much stronger and longer lasting must happen before it signals the start of labour.'

Mary came in with the tea tray. 'Are you all right, Mrs Opie?'

'Only another false alarm, Mary,' Leah said, despondent again. 'Thanks for bringing the tea. What lovely primroses,' she added when Mary left. 'Did you pick them, Lily?'

'Yes, my dear. Specially for you. The hedges are bursting with them this year. You should go outside for a little while, the air's fresh and sweet today. Shall I pour the tea?'

'Yes, please. I don't think I could move to do it.'

'Actually, I've brought you something you could add to the hot water. Epsom salts. I was talking to my mother-in-law about childbirth last night and she says she took it each time to get things going as her two boys were overdue. It's harmless, it won't hurt you. The worst that can happen is you'll get the runs.'

'I don't know,' Leah said uncertainly. 'If it was that easy the midwife would have mentioned it. Besides, it's three more days till I'm overdue. I'll hide it away and think about it then.' She took a sip of tea and rested the cup and saucer on her bump. 'Did Lizzie, Sarah or Naomi say anything about having tea here last week?'

'What, you mean did they enjoy it? They thought it was wonderful, said so all the way home.' She offered a plate of fancy cakes to Leah, who declined. Lily munched her way through two cakes, then said, 'Hannah will be able to come here again soon, now things in the chandlery have settled down. She works there all morning then catches up on her housework. They must have taken some good money. People have come from all over to look round it.'

I don't want to hear about Hannah, Leah nearly snapped. Why can't people think only about me and my baby? Why does her wretched name have to come up all the time? Even Miss Benson has been down to the village to see her stupid shop and come back talking as if she and Matt had opened a chain of big stores.

'I've engaged a nursemaid at last,' she said pointedly.

'Oh, good. What's she like?' Lily gulped down her tea, refilled her cup and started on another fancy.

'She's twenty-eight and comes from Par. Her name's Elsie Baker, she's got good references and is very experienced with young babies. She's gone home with her family for a while because the people she used to work for are going abroad to live. She's on the telephone and we'll contact her when my labour begins.'

'I'm glad you've got that sorted out. You want someone older like that, more sensible and trustworthy than a young maid.'

'That's what I thought,' Leah said.

'Hannah went to the doctor's yesterday. She hasn't said why. Your Aunty Janet thinks she could be pregnant again.'

It was too much. Must she have Hannah rammed down her throat every minute of the day? 'For goodness sake!' Her sharp movements knocked over the cup and although the tea wasn't hot, she screamed shrilly.

Lily sprang up, going to the door. 'I'll get a cloth.'

'I don't want a bloody cloth!' Leah shrieked at the top of her voice. 'I want you and everyone else to stop talking about Hannah all the time!'

Mary was taking a parcel from the postman at the door and she turned a shocked face to Lily. Greg hurried out of the study.

'Anyone would think Hannah was the only one in the world who mattered,' Leah screamed. 'I'm about to produce the heir to Roscarrock but everyone cares more about her than me or my baby just because Mrs Opie's her real mother!'

Greg pushed past Lily and hurried over to Leah. 'Darling, what are you saying? You're getting hysterical. What's upset you like this?'

Leah was sobbing wretchedly and wouldn't allow Greg to comfort her. 'She's not more important than I am. She's not! I hate Hannah! I hate her! Oh, God,' she sobbed like a tormented child, 'I hate her.'

Chapter 30

It had been Prim's turn to look after Nathan and she was making her way with him to the chandlery to hand him back to Hannah. Josh was lolloping along at her side, tickling Nathan under the chin, making him chuckle.

'Give over, Josh,' Prim ordered him sternly. 'You're making him wriggle. I can't carry him like this, he's too heavy.'

Josh understood the gist of what his mother was saying and held out his arms for Nathan. When they'd crossed the bridge, Prim handed him over. 'Hold him tightly but don't squeeze him,' she said, fussing with Nathan's jumper as he was held in Josh's strong arms.

As they went on, Josh swung his little nephew from side to side and Nathan howled with laughter. Prim tut-tutted good-naturedly.

Daniel was working alone on the boat, carrying out a bucket of ashes from the stove, and stopped to study the fair-haired little boy with his brain-damaged uncle. He was sorry that Nathan wouldn't be attending Melanie's party this afternoon. When the boy was older, what reason would Hannah give him for not mixing with his children? He couldn't care less if Matt always hated him but he didn't want Nathan to look down on Melanie and his coming baby. After the party, Mrs Penrose was going to stay on with Melanie while he and Grace dined at a hotel in St Austell to celebrate her pregnancy. He was looking forward to watching his new child grow inside Grace, its birth and infancy. It gave him hope.

Prim noticed him staring and stood still with her hands on her fat hips. Daniel could almost feel her animosity stretching across the water. He put down the bucket of ashes and returned to the cabin.

Josh was spinning Nathan round and round in a circle.

'Walk with him properly, Josh,' Prim said crossly. 'He'll get so excited Hannah will have a hard job putting him down for his afternoon nap.

Josh slowed down but he couldn't walk straight. Dizzy and out of control, he lurched away from Prim towards a patch of scrubby grass in front of a stretch of rough wall that overlooked the beach, or the water if the tide was in, as it was today.

'Josh!' Prim screamed. 'For goodness sake, stop!'

A primitive sense telling him to cling on to Nathan, Josh tried desperately to regain his balance. Prim could hardly believe her eyes as the next moment he toppled over the wall into the sea with Nathan.

'Help! Help!' she shouted, dancing about on her short fat legs. The water was deep and they were both in danger of drowning. She couldn't swim, Josh did not have the coordination to swim and there was no hope of him saving Nathan.

Hearing Prim's hollers, Daniel came aft. Seeing her alone in a frenzy he guessed what had happened. The few people who were about were running to the scene of the accident but he slipped over the side of the *Sunrise* and swam towards Prim.

A man jumped into the water and made a grab for Josh who was howling, panicking, gulping mouthfuls of salt water, his arms flailing about dangerously. He was too strong for the man and he was soon in risk of being drowned himself. A youth who had jumped in to search for Nathan went to his aid.

Stopping to scan the churning waters, Daniel could see no sign of Nathan. A tight coldness was feeding his heart with dread. Remembering how Hannah had been after her miscarriage, he feared she would lose her mind altogether if she lost her beloved son.

'What's going on out there?' Hannah asked a customer in the chandlery after glancing at Matt. All three went to look out of the door. On seeing Prim several yards away, standing mutely with her hands clamped to her face and frantic activity in the water, they ran to her.

Hannah shook her. 'What's happened? Mum, where's Nathan?' Prim's wide-eyed stare down at the water told her. 'Oh, my God. No! My baby!'

Letting out a cry of anguish, Matt kicked off his shoes and joined in the rescue. More people had arrived and Roy Rouse stopped Hannah from jumping into the water too. 'Leave it to Matt, m'dear. You'd be more of a hindrance.'

Her hands clenched to her chest, heart torn with fear, Hannah watched as a red head broke the surface and she realised Daniel was trying to save her son. 'Oh, please God,' she prayed aloud. 'Please, please let one of them find him.'

Kicking and struggling against his rescuers, Josh was gradually dragged to the wall and more pairs of hands reached down to haul him up. He was coughing and spluttering from the sea water he'd swallowed and began to vomit. Hannah didn't look at her brother, keeping her eyes on the churning water. A voice said, 'He's brought it all up, I reckon. Still, the doctor should be called t'come and look at un.' He was carried back out of the way and was forgotten as the fight went on to find and save Nathan.

Time and time again Matt and Daniel and a few other hardy swimmers ducked under the water and came up for air. Hannah was now in her father's arms, more terrified with every passing second that she had lost her child. She tried not to worry about Matt over-exerting himself.

Not finding the little boy in the area where he'd plunged into the water, Daniel struck out and searched about under the nearest lugger. He saw what looked like a rag. He reached out and grabbed it and it floated towards him. It was Nathan's jumper. Pulling the boy into his body, he swam sideways to get out from under the boat then he straightened up to head for the surface. He had only moved a foot when his shirt sleeve caught on the hull of the boat and he was impaled, trapped. He struggled to rip himself free but the cloth wouldn't give. He felt no pain but knew the sharp wedge of wood had sliced into his shoulder.

His lungs were bursting for air but there was no knowing how long Nathan had been under the water. Working up all his strength, he thrust the boy upwards, praying his body would break the surface.

Hannah cried out as Nathan suddenly appeared above the water. Matt had come up for air and he swam the few yards to his child. Nathan was limp against him as he made for the wall. Hannah was on her knees and leaning over the edge. With Jeff's help, she gently lifted Nathan away from Matt into her arms.

'Nathan? Nathan?' She wiped a hand over his pale face. His head rolled. His eyes were closed. 'Can you hear Mummy?' she pleaded. 'Please, darling, open your eyes for me.' She was about to give him artificial respiration when Nathan took in a loud breath and his eyes snapped open. He coughed and struggled to sit upright and began to cry. Hannah cradled him into her body and cried too. Then Matt, who had to be helped out of the sea, was dripping beside her. He took them both into his arms.

'Good job Daniel went over there for un,' Roy said grimly as the other rescuers came ashore. 'I saw his hand under the boy.'

Hannah looked across to where the water was slapping against the lugger. There was no sign of Daniel.

Janet was there with a blanket and Hannah wrapped it round Nathan. Moments passed, then more.

'Why hasn't he come up?' she asked anxiously. Now that her son was safe, she realised the last thing she wanted was for Daniel to be dead and she yelled urgently, 'Where is he?' Then she saw the red stain floating on the choppy surface.

Letting go of his wife and son, Matt went back into the water and swam to the place where Nathan had emerged.

'Matt, be careful,' Hannah shouted after him.

He dived under, swimming towards the bottom of the boat, and saw Daniel struggling to free himself, blood fanning out around him.

Realising he was trapped, Matt touched him, feeling for the place that was keeping him prisoner. Frantic for air, light-headed, death imminent, Daniel's fight was causing the slice of wood to cut deeper and deeper into his wound. Sensing someone was trying to save him, he forced himself to be still and allow the newcomer to free him. Matt felt round the flesh and the wood, then he pushed Daniel's body down and then up and away from the snag, blood pouring from the injury. Daniel was too weak to make for the surface. Matt swam upwards, taking him with him, then he felt Daniel rising quickly as other rescuers came to his aid.

Daniel felt the cold air hit his face. The great rush of oxygen he gulped in seemed to shatter his chest and he lost consciousness.

'We ought to say something to him, Matt,' Hannah said quietly. They were gazing down on Nathan sleeping in his cot.

'I know,' Matt said, slipping his arm round her waist. 'He saved Nathan's life but it still doesn't come easy having to thank him for it.'

'He was badly hurt.'

'It doesn't cancel out what he got his men to do to me.'

'I know. And you saved his life and that doesn't cancel out him saving Nathan. Thank goodness Josh is all right. The accident wasn't really his fault, he's had a terrible fright but I shall insist he never goes near the water with Nathan again. I don't want to let Nathan out of my sight but the sooner we go to see Daniel the better.'

'All the way to the hospital? Now?'

'No, your mother told me he's home. He insisted Melanie's birthday party went ahead. It must be over by now. Let's ask Grace if we can see him.'

A few moments later they were standing outside Chynoweth's front door. 'I never thought I'd actually knock on his door and ask to see him, except to knock his block off,' Matt sighed under his breath.

'I doubt if Daniel will crow over us or be nasty,' Hannah said. After all, she knew how Daniel felt about her. 'Let's just be careful what we say. We are truly thankful he saved Nathan's life, aren't we?'

'Of course. I suppose I mustn't let pride and ill feeling get in the way of duty.' Matt knocked on the door.

They heard someone coming down the stairs and Grace opened the door. 'Oh, Hannah! Matt!' She was wary of them. 'How's Nathan?'

There was a feeling of acute awkwardness. 'The doctor looked him over and said he's none the worse for the experience. We've taken him swimming often and he wasn't afraid. We're keeping an eye on him in case he gets a cold or something. How's Daniel?' She glanced at Matt. 'We were wondering if we could see him, to thank him for saving Nathan's life.'

'Oh! Yes, yes, of course. Do come in.' When they were inside the hall and the door closed, Grace whispered, 'I'm afraid he's being a bit awkward. He should have stayed in hospital for a few days and I'm having a hard task getting him to stay in bed. He's a bit weak and disorientated.'

Melanie, who had been playing with her birthday presents in the sitting room, peeped cautiously into the hall. Recognising Hannah, she tentatively moved forward and held out the doll in her hands.

'Hello, Melanie.' Hannah approached her. 'Did you receive the doll for your birthday? It's very pretty. I've got a little present for you.' She handed over the wrapped parcel she had brought with her.

'Thank you,' Melanie smiled. Because her father had saved a life, many parents who had initially thought otherwise had sent their children along to the party. Melanie had enjoyed the feeling of importance, the attention of about twenty children playing games for her sake and eating a feast prepared specially for her.

She was wearing a green frilly dress, a matching hairband on top of her red hair. Matt had not really taken any notice of her before. Her features were strong yet tender and completely feminine; she was going to be a stunning beauty one day.

Suddenly Melanie said in a loud, rather aggressive voice, 'Daddy doesn't like him. Bad man!'

'I haven't come to quarrel with your father,' Matt said. Her fierce expression was one he'd seen often on Daniel's face. He hoped she wouldn't inherit all his characteristics. 'I've come to thank him for something, if that's all right with you and your mother.'

Grace smiled apologetically. 'Darling, why don't you ask Mrs Penrose if she'd cut a slice off your birthday cake for Nathan? Hannah can take it with her for him.'

Melanie's harsh blue eyes were clamped on Matt's face and for a moment he felt embarrassed and angry about his scars. He wanted to turn round and stamp out of Daniel Kittow's house. He looked away and she pattered off to the kitchen.

'I'll show you upstairs,' Grace said. She was as delighted as if royalty had come calling. This visit boded well for the future. She and Hannah were both going to have babies next year and with each other to turn to it could even be fun. On the landing, she said light-heartedly, 'I'm afraid he's been swearing so I'll apologise in advance if he disgraces himself. He hates being cooped up.'

She popped her head round the bedroom door. Daniel was lying against the pillows staring moodily up at the ceiling. 'You've got some visitors, darling.'

'Who?' he barked.

Grace opened the door wide so he could see Hannah and Matt standing behind her. 'Hannah and Matt would like a few words with you. I'll go downstairs and make some coffee.'

'Come in,' Daniel said, pulling the covers up over his bare chest with his good arm. They could see he was in a lot of pain. His badly swollen, slashed shoulder had been stitched and bandaged and his arm was in a sling.

His visitors stood stiffly at his bedside. He kept his eyes off Hannah, stared at Matt.

Matt said in a formal voice, 'Hannah and I want to express our gratitude to you for saving Nathan's life.'

'Yes, Daniel,' Hannah added in a humble voice. 'We'll always be thankful to you.'

'I would have gone in for anyone's kid,' he said impatiently.

'I know,' Hannah replied. 'But it was our son you saved, at a painful cost to yourself, and we wanted to thank you in person.'

'And I should thank you in turn for saving my life, Penney,' he said, his tone less aggressive. 'I didn't know who pulled me out but I was told it was you. If I hadn't saved your kid perhaps you'd have left me down there.'

Matt gave an ironic smile. 'I might have thought hard about it, but no, Kittow, I wouldn't have let you die.'

'We wouldn't have wanted that, Daniel,' Hannah said in a small voice. Not so long ago she had been trying to get him hanged.

He looked deeply at her for a moment, his eyes asking her if she meant it. She smiled at him with sincerity. He nodded. They understood each other and his heart filled with a strange joy. Rubbing his arm with a rueful expression, he said in a friendlier tone, 'I'm sorry if you find me grumpy. I don't make a good patient.'

'We'll go and let you get some rest,' Matt said.

'Sit down.' Daniel painfully manoeuvred himself to sit upright. 'Grace is bringing up coffee.'

'No, thank you. We didn't come to make friends, Kittow,' Matt said firmly, pushing Hannah towards the door.

Hannah had hoped to leave on a better note but she allowed Matt to propel her down the stairs.

Daniel listened to them saying goodbye to Grace at the door, explaining they must get back to Nathan – only half the truth – then he sank down in the bed, feeling very emotional. A few hours ago he had faced death but hadn't really been frightened. He had saved a life and that made him feel good. His action had given him back some standing in the village but it didn't matter much to him. It was having Hannah come into his house, thank him, smile so gloriously at him, be kind to him, that moved him, for the second time in his adult life, to tears.

Chapter 31

Hannah was upstairs dressing Nathan when she heard a lighter than usual tread on the stairs. She kissed Nathan's cheek. 'Wonder who that is, darling.'

'Mum, mum, mum,' he cooed, trying to clutch one of his toys on the chest of drawers. He always wriggled about while he was being attended to and it took a long time to get him dressed. Hannah gave him the rubber duck to distract him while she pulled on his trousers. She smiled as Miss Peters came into the room. 'Hello, Miss Peters. Have you come to see Nathan? He's right as rain now.'

'So I can see. Your mother-in-law said 'twas all right for me to come up.' Miss Peters closed the door. She was wearing a grave expression, her shrewish eyes unreadable.

Nathan slipped out of Hannah's grasp and ran up to the tiny old lady, showing her the rubber duck, jabbering away in baby talk. As she put out her hand to take it from him and admire it, he pulled a mischievous face and threw it down hard on the floor. 'Hee, hee,' she wheezed. 'You're getting to be a proper little spurticle.' She ruffled his silky fair hair then put her hand in her apron pocket and produced a square of homemade fudge wrapped in greaseproof paper. He was soon nibbling on the treat, endangering his clean clothes with sugary brown dribbles. 'I've left un a stick of liquorice downstairs. Young'uns need building up in the spring.'

Hannah didn't like Nathan being given sweets before breakfast but it wasn't like Miss Peters to call on anyone as early as this and her sober manner was disquieting. Hannah got up from the nursing chair, put a bib round Nathan's neck and waited uneasily.

'I've got something to tell 'ee, Hannah.' Miss Peters parked herself on the small bed in the room.

'I thought you had. I take it something is wrong.'

'Aye. You haven't been out and about for a couple of days looking after the boy so you wouldn't have heard the gossip, although what's being said probably wouldn't be said to your face yet anyway,' Miss Peters finished with a surge of disgust.

Hannah was alarmed. 'What is it? I can't think of anything that would upset me.'

'This will,' Miss Peters returned bluntly. 'It'll get to the ears of one of your family sooner or later but I thought 'twould be best to tell you now. 'Tis going round the village, my dear, that Mrs Opie is your real mother.'

'What? I . . .'

Miss Peters kept her inscrutable eyes on Hannah. 'People are believing it. 'Tis known your mother lost a baby soon after its birth backalong then a few days later went off for a bit and came back with you. Like everybody else, I speculated where you came from and 'twas assumed you were the child of an unmarried relative. Now people are putting two 'n' two together and are coming up with four. I admit I believe like them. Out of the blue you were offered a job at Roscarrock when no one had been employed up there for many years. You still go there regularly and 'tis obvious Mrs Opie has a great fondness for you. Most unusual is that she has come to your home many times since you got married. 'Tisn't likely for a lady like she, for she's not a particularly kindly woman, to take so much interest in you if there wasn't a strong connection.'

A hundred thoughts were rushing through Hannah's mind. How this would effect Mrs Opie was the most prominent one. It could ruin her. She ran a hand down over her face. 'There's no point in me denying it, is there? And even if I did, no one would believe me after what you've told me. Thank you for being honest with what you believe, Miss Peters. Are they saying who my father's supposed to be?'

'No, haven't heard nothing about that.'

'So, who started all this? Only the Opies, my mother, father, Leah, Aunty Janet, Uncle Roy, Matt and Mrs Penney know the truth and none of them would say anything.' Her face turned as black as thunder. 'And two other people. One of them is Lily. She's very chatty but I can't see her spreading this sort of gossip knowing full well it would cause untold trouble.'

'If she was, I'm sure your aunty would know about it and she would've been here before me. Must be the other person.'

'He promised he would never tell!' Hannah seethed, only just controlling her rage. 'I should have known he could never be trusted. I'll kill him!'

Leaving Nathan with Mrs Penney, Hannah stormed down the street. She had seen Grace leaving home with Melanie earlier and it suited her that Daniel would be alone. Without knocking on the door of the new house, she barged inside.

'Daniel! Daniel! I want to speak to you!'

'Hannah?' His curious voice came from upstairs. 'I'm up here. Just a minute.'

She didn't wait for him to come down and was up the stairs in an instant. He was in the bedroom, wearing only his trousers, gingerly pulling on his shirt. She entered in such a force of furious energy he blinked and stared dumbly at her.

'You bastard! There can't be anyone lower or more evil on God's earth than you, Daniel Kittow!'

He looked totally bemused. 'What am I supposed to have done?'

'You know very well what you've done,' she screamed, clenching her hands into tight balls to stop herself from attacking him physically. 'You've told someone in the village that Mrs Opie is my real mother. Just about everybody knows and they believe it. There's no way it can be covered up now.'

'I promise you I did not,' he said in a serious, quiet tone. He was standing on the other side of the bed, his face pinched and unnaturally pale, as it had been the time he had accosted her on Hidden Beach roughly this time last year. The difference now was it was she who was in control. She was stronger than he was.

'I don't believe you.'

'I can't help that but I swear I'm telling you the truth, Hannah.' He kept calm but his eyes were imploring her to believe him. 'I meant it when I said I'd never cause trouble for you again. Why should I? I've settled down to family life and have another baby on the way, hopefully a son to take over the boat. Things aren't as bad as they were between us. I want us to be friends. Why should I risk that now?'

'You can't hide behind the fact that Matt and I came here after you saved Nathan. You obviously started off the rumours before then.'

He began to tremble and turned a sickly hue. She knew he was too ill to be out of bed, was in pain, but she didn't care. He deserved to suffer for what he'd done. His revengeful antics had shaken most of the people in Porthellis but except for the Joses, all had recovered. Not even his cruellest actions had succeeded in destroying Matt or her marriage. Roscarrock, however, would be knocked completely off its foundations.

'I don't know where the information came from but it wasn't me,' he repeated, his voice husky with discomfort. He put out a hand to steady himself on the bedpost.

'You lying swine. I could tear you limb from limb,' she hissed, making the operation with her hands.

'Go on then.' Still, he did not raise his voice. 'Do it, if it makes you feel any better.'

'It would only make you feel better,' she retorted. 'Actually, I couldn't bring myself to touch you.'

'Hannah, please—'

'Go to hell, Daniel.' She'd had enough of him, the sight of him, the sound of his voice, the powerful sense of masculinity he exuded even though he was weaker than she'd ever known him. 'You'll end up there anyway, so at the end of the day everything you've done will hurt you more than the rest of us. You don't worry me any more. There's nothing else you can do to me now, is there? You just sicken me. You're pathetic.'

He said nothing. He sat down on the bed, trembling, gulping as if he was trying to prevent a rise of nausea. She left him to his thoughts.

'I'll have to leave here! What else can I do?' Feena Opie exclaimed.

'I've been thinking about it as I walked here,' Hannah said, keeping up her pacing of Feena's sitting-room floor. She was too agitated to sit down. 'You should stay and we should take no notice of the gossip. You know what people are like. It'll be a seven-day wonder. And why care what people say anyway?'

'It's easier for you, Hannah,' Feena said pitiably. 'It's always been known Prim wasn't your real mother. After a while you'll be able to go on as though nothing much has happened. For me there are many things to consider. I shall never be able to show my face in Porthellis again, or further afield when the gossip spreads. I had no idea Lily knew. Her family may have been spreading the gossip for a long time so people outside Porthellis may know all about it already. People will ask why Prim took a child belonging to me. They'll chew over all the facts. They'll realise Jeff is your father. Why did I ignore you for twenty years? Why didn't I do something when Jeff threw you out after the boating tragedy? I may not mix much with society but the few friends I have will shun me for a heartless woman as well as a loose one. I couldn't bear that. Then Greg and his child will suffer too, people will always be whispering behind their backs.'

'Greg wouldn't care about that,' Hannah pointed out.

'If I go away, the gossip may stop in the fishing villages,' Feena went on as if Hannah had not spoken. 'It's the only thing to do.'

Hannah stilled herself and took her mother's hand. 'I know it's going to be hard for you but don't you think you're panicking?'

'No, I don't, Hannah,' Feena said vehemently. 'I don't really have you, do I? You'll never leave that common fisherman for me and Nathan will be his father's son. He'll never be as close to me as I hope. I don't really count in Greg and his child's future. All I really have is my reputation and I prize that above anything.'

Hannah turned and looked out of the window, at the graceful lawn and ancient oak tree, the magnificent gardens and peaceful wood, and the breathtaking view of the sea beyond it. Could Feena really leave this beautiful place? She was grief-stricken, sobbing. Hannah placed comforting hands on her shoulders. 'What will you do?'

'I'll move out of Cornwall, buy a property near the sea, like I planned to do with you three years ago.' She dried her eyes but continued to lean against Hannah. 'I'll take Miss Benson and Angie with me. Mary is loyal to Leah and I expect Patrick will want to stay here with his beloved gardens. It may not be a total disaster. You, Nathan and the new baby can come for holidays. Surely Matt wouldn't object to that. I'll be able to have you all to myself for a short while every year, which is more than I do now. I'll say I'm leaving so Greg and Leah can establish themselves here at Roscarrock, that it's been my intention for some time.' She ended faintly, 'It might not work out too badly for us, Hannah.'

'Don't do anything for a while,' Hannah begged. She loved her real mother, it was a heart-wrenching thought her going away. 'You may think differently in a few days.'

'No, I won't. From the moment you were born I thought about what I'd do if the truth ever came out.' She patted Hannah's hand. 'Well, there's no point in delaying the inevitable. Will you fetch Greg and Patrick for me, please? I'll tell them what's happened.'

In the bedroom she shared with Greg, Leah was dozing fitfully. She groaned as her baby kicked her. She opened her eyes and rang for Mary who promptly appeared. 'Would you mind passing me a drink of water,

Mary?' Leah motioned to the glass and jug on the bedside table. 'It's awkward for me to stretch across.'

'Certainly, Mrs Opie. You mustn't do anything that's strenuous for you. I don't mind how many times you ring for me.'

'You are kind,' Leah said, sipping from the glass. She had an idea that since her fit of hysterics Greg had ordered the under-housemaid to spend a lot of time with her and constantly report back to him, but she felt Mary had a genuine concern for her.

'Ma'am,' Mary said carefully as she put the glass back on the tray, 'your sister Mrs Penney is with the mistress at the moment. If she asks to see you, shall I say you're resting?'

'No,' Leah sighed. Greg wouldn't like it and he would again demand to be told why she resented Hannah so much. She'd just have to endure it. 'Will you help me to the sofa, please? I'd like to look tidy if she comes in here.'

When she was settled and Mary had gone, a wave of rebellion came over her. She couldn't bear to see Hannah. There had been such a fuss in the house when the news had come that Nathan had nearly drowned, and although Leah was as relieved as the others he was safe, she didn't want to hear about it again from her most favoured sister. Grunting with the effort, she got to her feet, couldn't slip her shoes on so left them, and waddled out of the room. She would go up to the nursery and hope Hannah wouldn't follow her.

As she got to the end of the corridor, she heard Hannah's voice at Mrs Opie's door. In so far as she could, Leah hastened to get away.

Hannah saw her disappearing round the corner. 'Leah. Wait a moment.' She had only seen her younger sister once since Lily's wedding, and although she expected a subdued reception she wanted to say hello before fetching Greg and Patrick.

Leah hurried up the first three steps to the nursery. Hannah called to her again and she quickly raised her foot for the next step. The sharp movement hurt her, an agonising pain searing her groin. Her hand wasn't firmly enough on the narrow banister and she lost her balance. She was falling. The shock of having nothing substantial underneath her, the gut-wrenching sensation of sinking rapidly and having no way of saving herself was replaced with terror of the harm that might be done to her baby. She screamed. Her hands instinctively clutching her distended middle, she landed like a block of wood on the corridor floor.

She was gripped with pain, crying and howling. Hannah ran to her and knelt down, feeling for broken bones. 'It's all right, Leah,' she said soothingly. 'I don't think you're hurt, just shaken up. I'll get someone to help you up.' She laid her hand over both of Leah's which were clenched together in a vice-like grip as a pain tore through her belly. Hannah recognized the way she arched her body. The fall had not injured Leah but it had brought on her labour. 'Greg! Mary! We need help. Quickly.'

Feena heard the commotion and after ringing her bell urgently came out of her suite in her wheelchair. 'What's happened? Did she fall?'

Hannah could feel a heavy contraction under her palm. 'Yes, down the nursery steps. She's in labour. She needs the doctor and midwife.'

Greg and Mary arrived together. Flinging himself down beside his wife, Greg lifted the top half of her body into his arms. Leah was hysterical, shrieking for her baby, trying to double herself up as the pain ripped and shuddered through her.

Hannah took her face between her hands. 'Leah! Listen to me,' she said loudly and precisely. 'You must calm yourself down. It's important we get you on to your bed for your sake and the baby's. Take a deep breath. Come on. The pain won't be so bad if you concentrate on being calm.'

Maternal instinct overrode her panic and pain; Leah knew she must obey Hannah's voice. 'Take a deep breath,' Hannah said again. Leah stopped screaming and breathed in. 'That's right, good girl,' Hannah said. 'Now blow out through your mouth.'

With Leah quieter and compliant, Mary, Hannah and Greg between them helped her to the bedroom.

Her own predicament forgotten, Feena had wheeled herself in front of them. She ripped the covers back on the bed then went to her rooms to use the telephone. She was back in under five minutes, after explaining first to Patrick, Miss Benson and Angie, who were grouped together outside the bedroom, what was happening and instructing them to wait downstairs until she gave fresh orders.

Greg and Mary were at the top of the bed; Leah was clinging to their hands. Leah was gripped with a fierce contraction and yelled like a wild animal. Hannah had pushed Leah's clothes up to her waist and told her to push.

'The labour can't possibly be that advanced!' Feena gasped.

'The baby's almost born,' Hannah said between gritted teeth. 'It can happen as fast as this occasionally. The fall helped to move things along. Take another deep breath, Leah, then push with all your might. It'll soon be over.'

She had spoken soothingly but she was racked with fear. The pain of labour could be intensified a hundredfold when the delivery came as quickly as this, the mother's body having no preparation for its most arduous task. With Leah writhing and thrashing, the risk of her haemorrhaging was greatly increased. Hannah prayed the baby wasn't very big and would pass easily out of Leah's body; if it didn't, the midwife might arrive too late to be of any use.

Feena couldn't bear to watch yet felt she shouldn't leave the room. She knew the next moments would be crucial. She wheeled herself to look out of the window. Rabbits were gambolling on the lawn. Would her great-grandchild and its mother come through safely and play there together?

Encouraged by Hannah's voice, which sounded as if it was coming from somewhere far away, Leah fought against her body's wilful attempts to curl up and clamp the baby inside her to prevent it being born. She pushed and pushed and pushed. Mary knelt up on the bed and steadied her legs.

'Push!' Hannah shouted.

Leah pushed. And screamed despairingly. And felt as if half her body had come away from her. The pain was indescribable. She was torn apart. Her strength had gone. She had no breath, no energy, nothing left to give. She fell back against Greg's body and thought she heard him crying.

Hannah worked swiftly, helping the baby's passage, her actions gentle and light. There wasn't a sound in the room except Leah's harsh breathing.

Deftly cutting the cord, aware of Greg and Mary's frightened stares, Hannah turned the baby upside down by the ankles and gently tapped its buttocks. Nothing. She smacked it. Nothing. No movement. Sobbing, she smacked the baby hard and gave it a little desperate shake.

It whimpered. A tiny cry. Then it bawled.

With tears streaming down her face, Hannah gently turned the baby in her hands and cradled it against her. It cried, a natural cry, a healthy sound, for its mother.

Leah came out of her stupor. 'Baby?'

Hannah carried the child to the head of the bed and laid the wet, naked little body on Leah's chest. 'Your son, Leah,' she wept with joy and emotion. 'Edward Gregory Charles Opie. The next heir to Roscarrock.'

* * *

Matt drew her into his arms. 'I've come to take you home, Hannah. Have you come down off the clouds yet?'

His touch made her cry again. They were alone in the drawing room. 'Oh, Matt, you should see them together. He's got a mop of hair as dark as Leah's and such a sweet little face. The doctor says they're fine. Leah's so happy.'

He caressed her hair away from her face, brushed her lips with his. 'And all due to you, darling. It must have been a frightening experience for you.'

'It was, for all of us. Matt, such a lot has happened today. Mrs Opie's determined to go away now the truth is out. I shall miss her terribly.'

'Of course you will, but it will probably be for the best. Hannah, I've got something to tell you.'

'Oh, Matt,' she clung to him. 'Not bad news.'

'No, not exactly. I wanted to get to the bottom of the gossip and I've been asking around the village. It seems Daniel wasn't responsible. It was the postman who started it off. He had delivered a parcel here and overheard Leah shouting in a tantrum that Mrs Opie was your real mother.'

'Leah?' She was astounded. 'But why should she do that?'

'I've also spoken to Lily. Leah was shouting she hated you. She was still jealous of you, darling, feeling left out, and things got out of hand. You may miss her, but it will be a blessing when Feena Opie goes away and leaves Leah and Greg to live alone here.'

Hannah rested against his chest, breathing in his wonderful familiarity, assured, feeling safe, cosseted. Eventually, she said, 'I said some terrible things to Daniel. I owe him an apology. Oh, dear God, Matt, I don't want there to be friction between us and him again. I couldn't bear that.'

'I don't think there will be,' Matt said, holding her tightly. 'I hate to admit it, but I've seen the way he looks at you. He loves you. And he's changed. He can never be trusted but I don't believe he'll try to hurt you again.'

After kissing the man she loved in an intimate, passionate embrace, she reluctantly let go of him. 'I must go up and see Leah before we go. Make sure everything will be all right between us in the future.'

Elsie Baker, the nursemaid, was in attendance. Hannah asked her for a few moments alone with the new mother. She took Leah's hand in hers and briefly told her what Matt had said. 'I'm sorry you've been so miserable, Leah. I was never any threat to you or your place here.' She smiled. 'I know I act a bit ladylike at times but I only want Matt and our children, our home down in Porthellis.'

'I'm sorry, Hannah,' Leah sniffed. She was drowsy from sedation, gloriously happy about her son, eager to put things right with Hannah. 'I feel so ashamed. I should have known you'd never do anything to make me feel small. I had no right to be jealous of you. If it wasn't for you, my baby and I might have died. Please say you forgive me.'

'There's nothing to forgive, my love. You only made yourself suffer. Now you can look forward to a happy future, just you and Greg. You can please yourselves what you do here and how you bring up little Edward. Go to sleep now. I'll come back to see you tomorrow. I want to spend some time with Mrs Opie before she goes away, then after that, just think, Mother will come here as often as you like.'

Chapter 32

Daniel was sleeping heavily, sprawled across the bed. In addition to his frayed breathing which filled the room, there was a strong smell of whisky. There were whisky stains on his sling. His hand hovered above an empty glass lying on the carpet. Hannah picked up the glass and put it out of harm's way.

She looked down at the closed eyes framed by long dark lashes, the tousled red hair, the superb features where such arrogance, cruelty and corruptness had played without mercy or decency. She was beginning to believe that somewhere inside him something remained of the adventurous, boastful, harmless boy she had once known; brought back to life by suffering, but only a little suffering compared to what he had inflicted upon others. He did not really deserve forgiveness for the terrible things he had done, yet she was relieved, uplifted, not to have a reason to hate him any more.

'Daniel.' He moaned, moving his head from side to side, but did not wake. Lowering her face close to his ear, she called softly, 'Danny.'

'Mmmm?' His eyes fluttered open, took an instant to focus on her. 'H-Hannah, didn't expect you,' he said groggily. ''Fraid after you left I got roaring drunk.' He did not stir but lay gazing up at her and she saw a gentleness, a new submissiveness filtering through the windows of his eyes.

'I've come back, Danny, to say I'm sorry for what I said to you earlier today.'

'You believe me now?'

'Matt found out the truth. He asked around the village. I know it wasn't you who started the gossip about Mrs Opie and me.'

'Guess I can't blame you for accusing me,' he said ruefully, wetting his dry lips. 'Does Matt know you're here?'

'He's downstairs talking to Grace and Melanie. He wanted to come up with me but I felt I should explain this to you alone. Grace is relieved that we're not on bad terms again. She's a good woman, Daniel. I hope you'll try to make your marriage work, make her happy.'

'I don't really deserve her, do I? Or you being here after me wreaking so much havoc in your life.' His expression was mixed with hope and uncertainty. 'Does this mean we can be friends? It's what I want more than anything.'

'I don't know. There's been so much hurt, I'm not sure if I'll ever want that. At least we don't hate each other any more and want to cause each other harm.'

Slowly, grimacing with pain, he sat up. 'I didn't really hate you, Hannah. I promise you on my children's lives that I will never, ever, do anything to hurt you again.' He wanted to say he loved her but she had told him never to mention it again; he would respect that, and anything else she wanted. She did not know if she wanted them to be friends, but she had called him Danny, as in the old days. Now there was the future to face, perhaps a time when their lives might depend on their drawing closer together. 'Do you read the papers, Hannah? Listen to the wireless?'

'Yes. Why? It's a strange question to ask.'

'No, it isn't. There's a real possibility that we're heading for another war. If such a terrible thing did happen, it would be good to think we'd be on the same side.'

'Matt thinks we might soon be plunged into war too. So many things have been happening close to home I haven't given it much thought.' She considered the new danger threatening her home, her family and the village; the sea and local beaches, the playground of her youth with Daniel. 'I suppose if war did break out it would be comforting to know who's on your side.'

'And when it's over,' he asked gently, 'to see the children, our children, playing happily side by side?'

'To hope that they would always stay friends . . . It's all I can say for now.'

There was a reflective silence. He gave her a brief smile. She left him and went downstairs to Matt.